FALLING ONTO COTTON

FALLING ONTO COTTON

MATTHEW E. WHEELER

Publisher's Cataloging-in-Publication Data

Names: Wheeler, Matthew E., author.
Title: Falling onto cotton / Matthew E. Wheeler.
Description: Bellevue, WA: M.D.R. Publishing, 2020.
Identifiers: LCCN: 2020907430 | ISBN: 978-1-7349138-0-4
(pbk.) | 978-1-7349138-1-1 (ebook)
Subjects: LCSH Organized crime--Wisconsin--Milwaukee--
Fiction. | Milwaukee (Wis.)--Fiction. | Restaurants--Fiction. |
Musicians--Fiction. | Crime--Fiction. | Family--Fiction. | BISAC
FICTION / Literary Classification: LCC PS3623 .H443 F35 2020
| DDC 813.6--dc23

In memory of Steve Kaufman, my first editor.

Dedicated to my mother, Lena May Negley.
She never got to read this,
but I think she would have loved Winnie.

CONTENTS

CHAPTER ONE

YOU CAN'T ALWAYS GET WHAT YOU WANT

SPRING 1990 – MILWAUKEE, WI

"I'm dying."

Chance thought it was the start of a joke. He studied the old man, saw the truth of it. The sheen of wealth and power his uncle wore like an armored suit had faded. His skin rusted from neglect, was a roadmap of broken capillaries across his nose and cheeks. Chance leaned back in his chair, breathed in slowly, paused, and exhaled with exaggerated drama.

"How?"

"Stage four lung cancer. Both lungs and there's nothing they can do except try to make me comfortable…at the end." Uncle Vinnie brought his oxygen mask to his face, and with every breath, particles of disease condensed into fog on the plastic, his wheezing audible from across the table. Two cigarette-stained, rheumy eyes watched Chance's reaction.

Chance ran through his choices like a grocery list, deciding on reserved empathy. "I'm sorry to hear that, uncle. Kinda thought you'd live forever." He picked up his wineglass and swirled the Sangiovese around the leaded crystal; its deep crimson shining in the candlelight reminded him of blood, passed down through generations, coming with obligations he didn't want.

Chance gazed around the private dining room of the hole-in-the-wall Italian joint his uncle frequented. He noticed a buildup of dust on one of the ceiling vents, which only reaffirmed his decision to never eat the food here. Giorgio, his uncle's muscle, nurse, and secretary rolled into one large package, stood at his usual post by the door.

"Well, who knows, probably would've had a couple-two-three years extra if I'd quit smoking. If I showed you my X-ray, you'd quit today." His uncle's Italian accent mixed with Wisconsin slang made even stupid phrases sound eloquent.

"I don't doubt it." Chance reached into his pocket for his pack of cigarettes, eyed the oxygen tank, and stayed his hand. "Is there anything I can do for you?"

"As a matter of fact, Charles, there is."

Chance bristled at the use of his given name.

"I want you to take over the family." Uncle Vinnie said it casually, like the thought had just occurred to him.

Chance flinched backward in his chair. Now he understood why Uncle Vinnie had moved up their monthly dinner by two weeks. This wasn't a confession or a lifetime of wrongs needing to be fixed. This was a recruitment.

Vampire-pale, with a dark suit that hung off his diminutive frame like gravity on old skin, Uncle Vinnie looked like an undertaker in an old Western. His slicked-back hair, plastered to his head with a Brylcreem shine, was an inch longer than normal. As if to compensate for impending death, he chose to let whatever could grow, grow.

"I'm not sure what to say. I've never even considered it and wouldn't know the first thing about running your...business."

"You've run a successful business for years. It's not that different."

Chance shook his head thinking about his own restaurant, Bella's. "Uncle, when a cook messes up on a meal, or a server gets a complaint, I don't have their legs broken. I'd say it's as different as different gets." He finished his wine in two gulps then grabbed the bottle and poured the rest into his glass, splashing some onto the checkered vinyl tablecloth.

"Yes, sometimes you have to use different methods to keep people in line. But not as often as you'd think."

Chance glared at Uncle Vinnie, knowing full well this was a lie.

"Charles, when a man comes to the end, he looks over what he's created, what he's sacrificed and built with blood, sweat, and tears."

"Don't forget murder."

"He doesn't want to let it go, give it to some stranger or someone who isn't family. Family is everything. Blood is everything."

"I wouldn't say Frank is a stranger. You've known him his entire life."

"Frank is old school. He's in love with the romance of violence. Every problem can be fixed with a gun. That won't work for much longer. The world is getting smaller." Uncle Vinnie took a sip of his water.

"Frank and his wife eat at my restaurant all the time. We usually avoid each other."

"Ahh, Sloan. A charming woman. Forty years too late for me, I'm afraid." His uncle started to pant into his mask, and the wine in Chance's stomach began to turn. After a few uncomfortable seconds, his uncle pulled the mask from his face, all traces of creepy old man lust gone.

"You're the only one left with my blood, Charles." The force of this statement brought about a coughing fit in which some of that prized DNA ended up in a linen napkin. Chance looked away.

"I'm not going to bullshit you. I promised your mother I'd keep you out of the business. I've honored that promise. But let's be honest. Someone's going to take over. Soon. I won't be here to protect you anymore. You have decades of animus with Frank. The only thing that's kept him in check is his fear of me."

Chance, considering the proposal, unconsciously shook his head. Moral issues notwithstanding, he never wanted that lifestyle.

"Yes, there will be sacrifices. But I'm the most powerful man in the state. There are benefits, as well." Uncle Vinnie shook his hand holding the oxygen mask to accentuate his point.

"Maybe the most powerful, but you also have the largest bull's-eye on your back," said Chance.

"Well, with great power comes all the little people who want to take it from you."

"Uncle, I don't want that. I've never wanted that. All I ever wanted to do was play music."

"Thankfully life taught you the foolishness of that dream."

Chance still felt the needle prick of a long-dead argument.

"It's simple. Either you take over the family before I'm dead, or Frank will have you killed before my body's cold." His uncle put his mask on the table, picked up his fork, and started in on his primavera.

Chance scowled, brought his fingers up to his temples and massaged. "I've always hated that term you use. Family. A collection of thieves and murderers. It's a dressed-up way of saying gang. And your top gang leader is a sociopath with a large chip on his shoulder." Chance saw by the expression on the old man's face he had pushed him right up to the line. Vinnie dropped his fork on the plate.

"You are the only person in the world who I allow speak to me that way. Be careful. Especially when you have no idea what you're talking about. I'm not going to debate with you the things I had to do to survive, or even thrive, in this country." He picked up the oxygen mask and took a couple of deep breaths. "Powerful men all use the Franks of this world to do what needs to be done. You think the government doesn't have a collection of Franks. You think the police don't?"

Chance closed his eyes. A string of bad memories flashed through his brain.

"Does he hate me that much, uncle? Really, it was twenty years ago."

"Yes. He does. You humiliated him, and he'll never forgive you."

Chance glanced around the private room of this shitty little cliché. Red and white checkered tablecloths, straw covered wine bottles, each with a candle coming out of the top.

An Americanized rendition of how Italians dined, straight out of *Lady and the Tramp*. He never understood why his uncle ate here. The emergency exit caught his eye, as if it would solve his problem.

"I don't want to be a mob boss."

His uncle put down his fork and wiped his blue-tinged lips with a napkin. "Charles, when did you ever get what you want?"

CHAPTER TWO

NIGHTS ON BROADWAY

As a lover's moon rose out of the depths of Lake Michigan, it cast its anemic light on one of America's many flyover cities. Not the established, high-achieving firstborn, like New York or Boston, nor the attention-seeking baby, like Seattle or Portland. Milwaukee was the neglected middle child. Even its "look at me" misbehavior was dwarfed by the antics of nearby cities like Detroit and Chicago. That being said, Chance loved this city. Loved the dirt under their nails, salt-of-the-earth people who resided here.

Chance shook his head. They were less salt of the earth and more salted, deep-fat-fried, marinated-in-beer and smothered-with-cheese kind of people. But they'd also give you the shirt off their back.

He looked away from the rising full moon and focused on the road as he navigated the massive '76 Lincoln convertible through traffic. Drivers honked to no avail as he meandered around, forcing everyone to get out of his way. Their Japanese matchbox cars stood no chance against his two tons of Detroit steel. Dean Martin crooned on the tape deck as Chance took a swig from a bottle wrapped in a brown paper bag.

After leaving his uncle at the restaurant, he drove through his old neighborhood, the roads lined with matching brownstones and tenements. Chance was reminded of what a cliché he was. Black leather jacket, Lincoln Continental from the 70's, and Rat Pack music. He thought about how hard he'd fought to get out of this place, only to end up back here. Faced with a choice he'd thought he'd left behind, and knee-deep in a Peyton Place affair with a mobster's wife. How many men over the years had ended up in oil drums for the same thing?

He took another swig of scotch and cursed himself. He had to end it. It was one thing to sleep with a married woman, but quite another to have an affair with Frank Bartallatas' wife.

Passing into the Third Ward, abandoned warehouses and breweries adorned the landscape. Lonely, silent brick buildings, cold and dark, windows broken. Thirty years ago, this was his childhood stomping ground, with a hybrid of Italian and English spoken in the collection of small shops. Butchers, bakers, and corner bars. Now progress stripped its identity. Fully integrated into the melting pot of America, the early arrivals of Irish, Italians, and Germans spread out and suburbanized themselves in neighborhoods no longer defined by ethnicity but by income and status. Going over the Milwaukee River, passing the Miller Brewing building, he chuckled, thinking of their TV commercials and how they reminded him of his affair with Sloan. "Tastes great, less filling! Tastes great…less *fulfilling*."

He pushed these thoughts away as he pulled up to the Knickerbocker Hotel, where his restaurant was located on the first floor. Bella's was one of Milwaukee's most celebrated establishments. The *Chicago Tribune* once wrote that if forced at gunpoint to eat in Milwaukee, it was the only acceptable choice.

He put the car in park, grabbed the brown paper bag, and slid out of his beloved pinnacle of American excess. Winnie, one of Bella's valets, stumbled over his two feet, his body still not used to its adultness, and extended his hand for the keys.

"O Captain, my Captain, how are you this evening?"

"Carpe diem, Winnie, but do you ever dance with the devil in the pale moonlight?"

Winnie smiled at the movie quote game they played. "Yippee Ki Yay...Mr. C. Great night as usual. The lot is full."

Chance examined Winnie. His light-blond hair needed a trim, as if to say his mother was no longer inclined to mother him. A few red marks were sprinkled around his face as a parting gift from puberty. He was gawkish, awkward in movement and seemed to be entirely uncomfortable in his own skin.

"You're not too stoned to drive Gracie, are you?" Chance gestured to the fifteen-foot black Lincoln with his thumb.

"No way, Mr. C. I wouldn't—"

"Relax, I'm kidding. But if you pull a Ferris Bueller and take her for a joy ride," he said as he put his hand on Winnie's shoulder and in his best Luca Brasi voice, "You'll sleep with the fishes."

Winnie laughed despite the poor impression. But the humor never reached his eyes.

"How is your mom doing?" Chance asked.

"Umm, you know...same." Winnie's shoulders slouched and he glanced at the ground.

"Yeah..." Chance gave Winnie's upper arm a squeeze. "I can appreciate what you're going through, Win. I've been there."

Chance looked around to discern if anyone was watching and lowered his voice. "Losing a parent is one of the hardest things. Especially one as cool as your dad. He was my friend but... you know for you."

Winnie regarded him with pale blue eyes for a second before his head fell back to his chest, small and deflated. He wanted to hug the kid.

"I've been meaning to stop by, see your mom. I haven't, I mean I promised your dad."

"Mr. C., can you not stop by? Most days she doesn't remember he's gone and seeing you..."

Chance stared at Winnie for a moment. "You can't do this alone Win."

"I'm not alone. I have Alex. And Hunter helps out a bit."

Chance nodded slowly. "I can't say it will ever hurt any less, but it will hurt less often."

Winnie peered up again. His mouth moved like he was going to say something, but instead nodded his head a couple of times the way a person acknowledges they've heard but don't necessarily agree.

Chance gave Winnie's shoulder another squeeze. "You ever need to talk; my door is always open."

"Mr. C., is it...? I mean, is it OK if we don't talk about it?"

Chance tilted his head and raised one eyebrow.

"I mean, I appreciate it, everyone, I appreciate everyone and how they think I need to talk. But I don't want to talk about it. I enjoy coming to work because I'm too busy to think."

"Of course." Chance considered him. "Listen, on the backseat is a first edition of *Batman: Arkham Asylum*. I'll be disappointed if it's still there next time I get into Gracie."

Winnie perked up. "That's the hardest comic to find right now."

"Consider it a tip for parking this boat of a car."

"Wow! Thanks, Mr. C. That's so rad."

Chance patted Winnie on the back. "Let's catch a movie this week."

"Yeah, cool. Have fun storming the castle."

Chance laughed as he turned and walked toward the entrance. He tucked the brown bag into his inside jacket pocket and glanced back at Winnie, reminded of his younger self: the best parts of his younger self. He also recognized the pain in the young man's eyes. Pain that created a mask, like the one he donned now as he was forced into smiles and handshakes, greeting guests entering the lobby of the hotel.

The Knickerbocker was eight stories of Neoclassical Revival. The reddish brick building, decorated with terracotta, also offered condos for sale. The elegant, seventy-year-old building's current owners were bipolar about what they wanted it to be. One night, drunk after work, with a female guest, Chance rented a suite. The next morning, he bought it as a condo—a built-in safety fallback for the many nights he left the restaurant three sheets to the wind.

He shook hands with a couple he recognized from many visits, greeting the man by name and complimenting the woman on her new hairstyle. She was all teeth and beamed at Chance, batting her eyelashes as if sending Morse code. He worked his way into the hotel, stopping to chat with the guests waiting in lobby in clusters of fours and sixes.

In one group stood the owner of the Milwaukee Brewers, chatting with Chance's high school friend Mitchell Genovese, an Assistant U.S. District Attorney back in Milwaukee who challenged the growing power of organized crime in the Midwest. A subject they consciously avoided every time they saw each other. Paranoia washed over Chance as he nodded to his friend. Could Mitchell see it? Was his uncle's offer written on his face?

Chance shook hands with a state senator he couldn't stand. A former Green Bay Packers quarterback was in an argument with the current Green Bay quarterback, probably about who had the bigger...throwing arm.

Chance worked his way through the usual collection of who's who and approached the city's current mayor and his wife, Stella, another old high school friend.

The mayor was all of the former fullback for the University of Wisconsin he'd been, and a little extra. His six-foot frame was still broad, but his belly showed evidence of three-martini lunches. The lobby's bright lights reflected glare from his ever-expanding forehead. The mayor shook Chance's hand with an exaggerated flourish.

"Great to see you again."

"Good to see you, Mr. Mayor. Did you get the check for your reelection campaign?" Chance tried to pull his hand back.

"Cashed it the same day, thanks," the mayor slurred. "But you're not at the maximum yet, and we need all the support we can get."

"Must have been an oversight, Mr. Mayor. I'll talk to Bernie about it. You know you can always count on me."

"That's what I was saying to Stella. You can always count on Chance McQueen."

Stella rolled her eyes. She must have heard this line 10,000 times this election. "Surely you can get us a table, Chance? I feel like we're cattle waiting out here in the lobby,"

Stella cooed as she took Chance's hand in both of hers, freeing him from the mayor's grip.

Chance grinned, admiring her form in the black cocktail dress. Her mahogany hair drifted down past her shoulders in long, curvy waves. Beautiful in a small-town girl sort of way, her melancholy eyes only enhanced her charm. Like a hint of perfume left on a pillow from the night before, he could smell the sadness of her unfulfilled dreams.

"I'm sorry, Stella, but we don't take reservations. It's first come, first serve, no matter how beautiful or important the guest is."

"It's so provincial. There are people here from the suburbs, for Christ's sake."

"Shut up, Stella. Everybody waits, you know that," said the mayor. "Besides, out here is where the action is."

Chance gave Stella an apologetic face, then forced his attention on her husband. "Mr. Mayor, how is the election going?"

"Those ungrateful sonsofbitches! I tell you what, Chance, stick to selling pasta. Politics is an ungrateful mistress." The mayor raised his empty martini glass to the hostess. "I've brought three years of prosperity to this city and how do they pay me back? Turner is within five points in the last *Journal* poll. Now I ask you, what does a man who inherited his daddy's real estate business know about running a city? I'll tell you: jack shit of nothing."

Chance raised an eyebrow to Stella. She rolled her eyes again and took a sip of her wine to cover a smile.

"To run a city, it takes..." The mayor paused; his face contorted as if he was fighting off gas. "What's the word I'm looking for?"

"Intelligence?" said Stella.

"Empathy for the people?" replied Chance.

The mayor shook his head in annoyance. "Balls. It takes huge brass balls to run a city. Honey, do I have brass balls?"

"Oh, the brassiest, dear," Stella deadpanned.

"That's right. And you need 'em for this job. The teachers want to strike, the Blacks are complaining about police brutality, and I've got this ADA from the Justice Department poking around on some witch hunt." The mayor nodded over to where Mitchell was standing.

"I'm sure somebody with your sizable anatomy can handle it…sir."

The mayor broke into a guffaw. "You always were funny. Even in college, I said that, didn't I, honey?"

"All the time, dear."

"My point is, we have potholes to fix, a downtown to revitalize, and taxes to cut. Turner wouldn't know shit about any of it."

The hostess handed the mayor a fresh martini glass, and he swallowed half of it in one gulp. His eyes drifted off toward the hotel entrance.

"Speaking of things to get done, Mr. Mayor, who should I call about getting the zoning change for the Milwaukee Women's Resource Center?"

"The what?"

"Remember, dear." Stella put her hand on the mayor's arm, steadying him. "You promised you'd get Ralph to change the zoning for the violence center on Dexter Ave."

"Right, right." The mayor pulled his eyes away from the regal blonde walking into the hotel. "Um, talk to Stella here. She's my point man on all things woman. Sounds fine to me, though. After all, gotta court the woman's vote." Chance pursed his lips and pushed down the sarcastic retort fighting to escape.

"Mr. Mayor, Stella, have a fantastic dinner. I recommend the marsala. I made the sauce, and it's one of my best. The MWRC appreciates your support and of course, dinner is on me."

"Oh, yeah? There's a nice bottle of '78 Barolo in your display case…and Chance, don't forget that check."

Chance winced at the thought of giving away the 200-dollar bottle of wine. "Of course, Mr. Mayor." Putting on his best Kurt-Russell-playing-Jack-Burton voice: "The check is in the mail."

The mayor hooted, "I love that movie," and staggered over to another crowd of prospective voters. Stella remained behind and again took Chance's hand in hers.

"You seem tired, Charlie. Are you getting any sleep?"

Chance smiled; nobody ever called him Charlie anymore. He reluctantly pulled his eyes away from the blonde standing in the lobby and considered Stella. "I haven't slept in years, but I pass out occasionally." Chance frowned as his gaze wandered back to the blonde, who was wearing an entire forest's worth of dead minks.

Stella noticed, and with her other hand reached up to touch Chance's cheek. "I worry about you. We aren't kids anymore. You don't look good."

"Were we ever kids? It's hard to remember that far back." He cupped her hand to his face. He glanced over to the mayor holding court and shook his head. "Why do you let him treat you like that? He wouldn't have been elected class president, much less mayor if it hadn't been for you."

Stella examined her husband and sighed. "Charlie, do

I need to remind you how stupid we were back then? Not an ounce of sense between us. Yet the choices we made, the mistakes we made…they last a lifetime, don't they?"

"Not all of us were stupid," he said in a hushed tone.

"No…you're right, but she's dead, we're not. Sometimes I wonder if she was the lucky one."

Chance winced.

"I'm sorry. That was…that was out of line."

He took a deep breath, slowly letting it out, his hand touching the bottle in his jacket. He pushed back on the wrong turns and previous life pains that always popped up when seeing old friends.

"Is that it, Stell? Have you given up on all your dreams?"

Stella stared at the floor, then looked up at Chance. "Charlie, you must know by now dreams are only God's way of hurting us." Tears threatened to flood down a time-intensive undertaking of powder and paint. She turned her head and wiped her eyes.

"What is it, Stell? What's wrong?"

Stella took a deep breath and faked a laugh to cover her embarrassment. "Do you ever wonder what would have happened if we'd gotten together instead?" She took a step closer. "How different our lives would be? We had an opportunity once…didn't we? Am I remembering that right?"

Chance nodded as he pulled up a long-dormant memory. "If I remember correctly, I went to pee in the woods and when I came back to the fire you were with the future mayor in his tent."

Her face lit up with a spontaneous laugh. "My god, what a hussy I was." She smiled up at him, but the brief spark faded from her eyes. "Just goes to show you nothing good ever comes out of casual sex," she said, laughing without warmth.

"I think on that point I have to disagree with you. Just because it ruined your life, my life, and several other people's lives, isn't necessarily a good reason to condemn it." He gave her hand a squeeze, the warmth and softness appealing to him. "We could'a been contenders, Stell."

She took a step closer to their shared illusion.

"But that was a long time ago."

She started to say something but turned her back and walked over to the mayor. Chance stood thinking about the bottle in his pocket. He turned around, and the blonde was now standing with her husband, Frank Bartallatas.

CHAPTER THREE

FORTUNATE SON

Chance pushed through the swinging doors into the kitchen. To a layman, it was complete chaos. Servers running around, barely missing each other with huge trays of steaming food. Cooks almost taking each other out with sharp knives and hot pans. The noise level reaching the decibels of the New York Stock Exchange. Shouts of "coming in, behind you, hot pan, order in" were all verses in the song of his kitchen. To him, it looked like a choreographed ballet. Each person understanding their role, moving with purpose. Air filled with steam and familiar smells; sounds of plates, glassware, and shouts in Spanish, English, and Vietnamese.

He called out to everyone passing, adding a personal touch. "Maggie, I love your hair up like that." Her focus melted and she flashed a wall of white ivory.

"Geoff, please tell me you didn't pick Miami last night?" Chance already knew the answer.

"Horseshit, Chance! Did you see that play? His hands were all over him." Geoff's soprano voice conveyed frustration as he effortlessly carried an overloaded tub of dirty dishes to the dish pit.

"Leah, how is the new boy toy?"

"Oh, he's wonderful, he took me to..."

Chance didn't catch the rest as she passed through the doors into the dining room. He walked deeper into the kitchen and called out "Hola" to Jose, his pantry cook, and Miguel on sauté. He smelled the air, thick with the aroma of a busy Tuesday night. Garlic was strongest, but a trained nose could detect hints of oregano, rosemary, coriander, and cinnamon. There was Italian sausage, fennel, boiling wine, mushrooms, and...cilantro? "Goddamnit, Chico," yelled Chance. "How many times do I have to tell you not to bring cilantro into this kitchen?"

Chico came from around the line, wiping his hands on his chef coat. "Jefe, Jefe, not to worry. It's experimental batch, not gringo batch. I have it this time, Jefe."

Chico was obsessed with creating an Italian-Mexican hybrid sauce. Despite many failed attempts, he hadn't given up. He strolled back behind the line and stirred Chance's award-winning red sauce, bastardized with bits of cilantro. Chico brought up a spoonful for Chance to taste. Chance blew on the sample and tried it. Vine-ripened tomatoes burst with a flourish, and the dance of flavors began. Oregano and thyme began to waltz. Black and white pepper started to do the Charleston, red wine and vinegar began to swing, and basil and garlic started a long, slow tango. Out of nowhere came the invasion of cilantro, screaming, "Ay ay ay," like the traditional Jarabe Tapatio dance. Chico peered up at Chance, eager for a verdict.

"Sorry, Chico, it still overpowers the dance," said Chance gently. Crestfallen, Chico sighed and seemed smaller. "Look at the bright side: if you ever do improve on my sauce, I'll have to steal the recipe from you and open up a chain of restaurants called 'Forget About It Tacos.' I'll be rich!"

The other cooks laughed, and Jose said something in rapid-fire Spanish. Chance eyed Chico, expecting a translation. "Jose says it would never work because Italian men would never take the toothpick out of their mouths long enough to eat a taco." All the cooks were laughing, and Chance mock-waved his finger at Jose. He broke into a grin and affectionately patted Chico on the back. Leaving them to their work, he walked past dry storage and out the back door into the alley, where staff used a collection of picnic tables for their breaks; nobody ever seemed to empty the plethora of overfilled ashtrays. The area was well lit and lined with birch and pine trees, but, like most alleys in America, held an edge of danger. Chance sat, lit a cigarette and pulled out the scotch from his bag. He took a sip, loving the familiar warmth. The air was cool, and crickets were rubbing their legs together.

"Jed, you can come out. It's me." From behind the dumpster, a disheveled middle-aged man stepped out wearing a green flak jacket and camo pants. Behind his straight, gray ZZ top beard, his face was clean. His alert eyes danced left and right as he approached, each step a decision on where to set his foot. After determining that they were indeed alone, Jed sat across from Chance with the eagerness of a child on Christmas morning, rubbing his hands together.

Chance took another pull from the bottle, then handed it to Jed, who wiped the opening, took a long swig, and let out a satisfied burp. They sat in silence and regarded each other. If his beard was trimmed and he dressed differently, he would resemble an eccentric schoolteacher with chalk dust on his fingers and clothes, and not a homeless vet with dirt under his nails and cigar ash on his chest.

The alcohol hit Jed's bloodstream, visibly releasing tension and causing a slight shudder. He took another swallow and offered the bottle back to Chance. "Thanks, but that's yours."

Jed grinned and nodded. "Your mob buddy is in the restaurant tonight," he stated in a deep baritone voice.

"He's not my buddy, but yeah, I saw him come in. He's here with his wife."

"That man is a killer. I recognize the look, but he never fought no war."

Chance nodded and took a drag off his cigarette.

"If I had a wife like that, I would be eating *her* for dinner." Jed smacked his lips together. "But I wouldn't talk to her after. She has more frost in her than a snowman. Or I guess snowwoman."

Chance frowned. "I'll have Jose bring out dinner in an hour." Jed would want to get a nice buzz before he dulled it with food. But Jed wasn't done speaking yet.

"That woman will warm your balls and chill your heart. Right before she eats both with a spoon."

"I can't argue with that." Chance wondered how much Jed knew. He smashed his cigarette down into the ashtray. "I have to get back inside." He headed to the door.

"Chance?"

He turned.

"Don't let Chico give me the sauce with the cilantro. It gives me gas." Jed patted his stomach.

Chance laughed. As he walked back in the door, his hostess came running in high heels. He reached out and caught her fall as she stopped abruptly in front of him.

"Whoa, there, easy does it. What's the rush?"

"Oh, gosh, thanks. Sorry." She took a breath as she straightened up. "Frank Bartallatas is here, with his wife." She adjusted her sweater, which had slipped off one shoulder.

"Relax, Julie. He's not the pope."

"He asked if you were here. Do you want to eat with them?"

Creases formed on Chance's forehead. He wondered if somehow Frank knew he'd just come from meeting his uncle. "Bring a bottle of red and tell him I'll be right there."

He watched Julie walk away. As she turned the corner, he looked back at Jed, who raised his eyebrow. Sloan, Frank, and the U.S. District Attorney, all here tonight. He let out a heavy sigh. "Guess I should go see what he wants."

CHAPTER FOUR

YOU'VE GOT A FRIEND

In the main dining room, Chance looked from table to table, radiating pride. Three wrought-iron chandeliers hung in the center of the room. They had to be lowered daily to replace the candles, but the ambiance was magical. The dancing flames cast shadows throughout the restaurant, giving it an old-world feel. Four white sandstone columns divided the room into nine separate areas. Three half-circle booths, each seating six in the booth with two chairs, lined the far wall; above them hung a thirty-by-ten-foot mirror which cost way more than he cared to remember.

The room smelled of melting wax, a tinge of vinegar from wine, garlic, and a dizzying array of competing perfumes. Experience told him what each table might need in the next few minutes, but he trusted his staff to recognize it as well. Table four was a group of suits in a heated discussion about sports, women, or stocks. They'd want another round in time to tell more lies.

The couple at table six hadn't talked to each other in twenty years. Their server, Maggie, would be tonight's entertainment, and they'd have her life story before dessert. The couple at table one looked exhausted. New baby for sure. They looked at each other and smiled, happy to be out of the house it seemed. He guessed the man with the constipated face at table two was going to propose to his girlfriend or break up with her.

Sloan sat in booth three with a glass of wine, her eyes scanning the dining room. Frank sat next to her, head down, shoveling a steak into his mouth as if afraid someone was about to take it away. Chance's Head Server Geoff approached the table and started to clear her plate away. Frank grabbed his hand and pointed his steak knife at Geoff, using it to emphasize whatever he was saying. Frank let go and Geoff beelined for the kitchen. *Shit*, thought Chance.

He told Leah to take a round of Grand Marnier shots to the suits while stopping at table six to give Maggie a break in order to get to her other tables. A woman's shriek pierced the restaurant, and everyone turned to watch table two. The woman covered her mouth with one hand, holding out a shaky left hand to the man on one knee. The restaurant applauded the newly engaged couple. Women in the restaurant smiled and tried to judge the size of the ring. Men craned their necks to judge if the woman was hot. Chance motioned to Geoff, who despite what Frank had done, still maintained an aura of a Black stiff-upper-lip British butler, even though he was from Chicago. Chance gave him the hand signal to bring out a bottle of champagne.

Leah walked up to him with a shot on her tray and pointed to the table of suits. He raised it in salute as they raised theirs, knocked it back, and waved. The Grand Marnier tasted sweet after the scotch.

He paused to talk with a couple who interrupted each other at every turn: a plumber and a schoolteacher from Brookfield. They had three kids, all moved away, and the plumber planned to retire soon. She was going to keep on working because she couldn't stand to be in the house with him all day. After two minutes of this, Chance was as bored with their relationship as they must have been.

He glanced at Sloan as Frank grabbed her arm and pulled her ear next to his mouth. She flinched as if she'd been hit. Chance felt his blood pressure rise, and he told the old couple to order the tiramisu, on the house. He made his way over to Sloan and Frank. As he arrived, Sloan glanced up at him and then over at Frank, her eyes sparkling, obviously enjoying the long-held animosity between the two men.

"Hello, Frank." Chance rested his hands on the back of a chair.

Frank was a large man with jet-black hair greased back and a ski-jump nose. His enormous hands could palm a basketball, and Chance knew for a fact that those massive fists had crushed more than one person's skull. His face was starting to go to fat, and he had the eyes of a villain. The kind that never reflected warmth, unless cruelty was the fire.

"Chance, I was telling Sloan I didn't think you were going to stop by our table. Now how rude would it be for the owner of our favorite diner to not stop by and visit with his oldest friend?" Sarcasm dripped from Frank's voice like the mushroom sauce he had spilled on the tablecloth.

Chance ignored him. "Good evening, Sloan, how are you?"

"I'm wonderful, thank you. I've had a pleasantly exhausting day," she replied with a massive display of white teeth.

The corners of Frank's mouth tightened. "Chance, I have to tell you, I was disappointed with the food tonight. The steak was tough, and the pasta overcooked." Frank sipped his sambuca and placed his giant hands on the table, palms down. "Plus, the service has gone down. That big queen was buzzing around the table like he was in a drag show or something. It's enough to give a man indigestion."

"First of all, *Frank*, I'm not surprised you would know what a drag show is. Second, the steak was part of the shipment you sold me. So, if you want better steak, then steal better steaks. Third, that 'queen,' as you call him, was in the Navy and served our country, so show a little respect. But I wouldn't want you to leave here with a bad taste in your mouth, so please let me buy the steak from you…again."

"I didn't think the Navy let queers in."

"Jesus, Frank," said Sloan. "Nobody says 'queers' anymore."

He gave her a hard glare, like he was going to respond. His eyes moved to Chance and he changed the subject. "I came in to talk a little business and try to get a good meal. I'd like to accomplish at least one of those goals." He opened his palms as if to call a truce.

"Gentlemen, I'm going to the ladies' room. Please don't kill each other before I get back."

Chance resisted the urge to watch her walk away.

"Christ, the mouth on her sometimes," said Frank. "Take my advice and never get married. It doesn't get easier the second time around."

Chance's fists tightened and he took a deep breath.

"Oh, sorry, I forgot you were engaged once." Frank tried to appear apologetic, but accomplished more of a sneer.

Chance slid down onto a chair across from Frank. Maggie delivered him a scotch and he nodded his thanks.

Frank surprised him with a change in direction. "You remember that time at St. Pat's when we drilled the hole in the ceiling of the girls' locker room and charged all the schmucks a quarter to take a peek?"

"I remember falling through the ten-foot ceiling and cracking my head on the bench. My dad called in every favor to make sure I didn't get kicked out, and every girl in school didn't talk to me for a year." Chance rubbed the scar over his left eye.

Frank bellowed a laugh, hitting his hand on the table, spilling water and wine. "Yeah, that was funny. I remember Reverend Mother thought you were a rapist."

"I remember it was your idea, and as I recall you kept all the money."

"You didn't rat me out, and you took your punishment like a man." Frank's face turned serious. "You knew the right thing to do, and you did it."

"What's your point, Frank?" The tension returned to the table like two gunfighters staring each other down on Main Street.

"My point is, knowing the right thing to do. Geno called me the other day and said you were canceling their contract. You realize your uncle gets a piece of that action, so why would you shit where you eat?" Frank drained the rest of the sambuca, careful not to swallow the three coffee beans in the anise-flavored liqueur.

"Funny, I just saw my uncle, and he didn't mention anything to me."

"He doesn't get involved in this petty bullshit. You know that."

"So, what you're saying is your cut has taken a hit, and how you pay my uncle every month has taken a hit." Chance's voice rose. "You come in here to my place, disrespect me, disrespect my staff, and lobby for a business that doesn't know how to pick up garbage every week or wash a towel correctly."

Frank held up his massive palms as if in surrender. "Chance, relax. We're just talking here. If you'd a' come to me and told me there were problems with Geno, I could'a fixed them. But instead, you buck the system and upset the apple cart. That's how apples fall to the ground and get bruised."

Chance, with the alcohol in his system clearly in charge, kicked the chair back, and wagged his finger at Frank. "Look, you Neanderthal piece of shit! I told you six months ago Geno was a drunk and an idiot. Nothing changed. I can't run a restaurant if the garbage stacks up for so long you can smell it halfway to Green Bay."

He noticed the glances from other patrons and lowered his voice to a razor-sharp hush, disappointing many of the diners. "I understand how the game is played, and even though Geno charged more, I went ahead with it. You're an idiot for putting him in charge. He shouldn't run a hotdog stand, much less a business I rely on every day. Your fault, Frank. It's on you."

Frank stood, his knees knocking the table and sending the wineglasses crashing over, their dark red liquid seeping into the white tablecloth like blood from a wound. "You listen to me. I don't give a shit who your uncle is; I'll pop you right now. Who the hell do you think you are to disrespect me? Your uncle's not going to be around forever. Who you think is gonna take over, huh?"

"You're such a cliché, Frank. A slumlord with a gun. Respect is—"

Geoff approached the table and in a low voice asked both men to calm down; Frank's shouting had reengaged the other diners, and he was panting like he'd run a mile.

Geoff continued in a measured tone, "Gentlemen, this is a conversation you don't want to have in public. I suggest you both sit down."

"Listen, you fucking peon, you don't tell me what to—" Frank yelped in pain as Geoff placed a hand on Frank's shoulder and whispered into his ear. Chance couldn't make out what was said, but after a couple of seconds Frank sat down, and Geoff eyeballed Chance with a "don't fuck with me" expression. Chance sank back into his chair, amazed Frank wasn't throwing Geoff across the restaurant. Geoff smiled at both men, walked over to another table, and began to clear empty plates. The guests at the table closed their open mouths and began to help him gather the remaining tableware.

· · ·

Whispers filled the dining room. Sloan picked this moment to walk back to the table.

Every man in the place broke his neck staring at her as she sauntered, and every woman sneered. Sloan noticed the one person not watching her with avid interest was Mitchell Genovese, his eyes locked on Frank and Chance.

She sensed the anger radiating off both men, yet they seemed resigned to sit in silence. Frank's black eyes were bloodshot with rage, and Chance was a sulking child.

She studied them. Frank was boorish and dumb, but violence was there under the surface. Seeing the fear in everyone's eyes as they entered a room sparked a fire in her chest. There wasn't a sensitive bone in his body, which suited her fine. Marrying him was the ticket to her ultimate goal.

Chance was different. Soulful, with more pepper than salt in his dark hair; his slight olive skin complemented his hazel eyes where green dominated brown.

Her two lovers were opposite sides of the same coin, and she was in control of which side would come up. Her breaths became shorter and more rapid as she contemplated taking one of them into the bathroom. It would be a huge risk to take Chance but knowing it could get her killed was part of the thrill.

Chance was thoughtful. A kind of masculine mama's boy, and in a different life, she might have liked that about him. More often, it annoyed her. She considered the two bulls again. Both were strong in their own way, yet Frank was easy to manipulate. Chance was smart but needed to be loved. It was almost too easy.

She sighed and wondered what they were thinking about, both coiled and ready to grab steak knives. She didn't have to see what happened to recognize her plan was working. She almost felt sorry for Chance. But empathy required a heart—something knocked out of her a long time ago.

Chance looked at Frank and sighed. "Frank, if you put someone else in charge, instead of Geno, I'll think about keeping the contract. Otherwise, take it up with my uncle." He rose without glancing at Sloan and made his way to the kitchen.

Sloan looked at her husband, his face blotchy, his body shaking with kinetic energy, glaring at Chance's back as if his eyes could shoot bullets. She was proud of his self-control, something not natural to him. She put her hand on his, and he jerked back.

"Breathe, darling. Just breathe," cooed Sloan.

"I'm gonna—"

"Do nothing." She pushed her nails into his hand. "After you meet with Chicago...well, then you can do whatever you want."

CHAPTER FIVE

OLD AND WISE

Jed sat at the picnic table and took a chug of scotch. "Don't just stand there in the dark, Little Cat. Come on over."

A young woman walked out of the shadows and sat down next to him. "One of these days I'm going to get you, old man." She pushed her retro cat-eye glasses up on her nose.

"Ha! Little Cat will have to be a dainty cat if she thinks she can sneak up on this Marine." He handed her the bottle, and without wiping the top she took a small measure, wincing at the fire down her throat. "What brings you around tonight?" he asked.

"I brought you more cigars." She reached into a bag with a monkey's head emerging from the top, little monkey legs coming out of the bottom, and pulled out a package of Swisher Sweets.

"Oh, the modern apparition of Venus is not only as beautiful as the Greek poets described, but as kind and generous as Saint Jude the Apostle."

"The patron saint of lost causes."

"Yes," he said, surprised.

"You're not a lost cause to me, old man." She took another pull from the bottle. "These are for you as well." Out of her monkey bag came a package of white tube socks.

"Little Cat, with your beautiful blue eyes. You don't owe me anything. You can share my hooch for free."

She put her hand on his. "I do owe you, old man...so much."

"You should be out dating young men right now, not sitting with this old man drinking from a bottle. What you're yearning for won't be in here." He took the bottle and shook it.

"Doesn't stop you from looking for it."

"Yes, but I had my roll of the dice, and decided I don't like the game."

"What game?"

"Never mind." He looked down at her. A halo of light radiated from her kind soul. But behind her eyes danced pain from a world that chewed up and spit out its youth. Scarring them, leaving them beaten and battered instead of light and free. "You should be out with your friends. You can't fix anything sitting here. Besides, you saved yourself."

"No! You saved me, old man." She put her arm around him and squeezed him tight.

"I did what anyone would have done, even that skinny boy you always hang out with." Jed sighed as the intoxicating smells of a woman floated around him.

"But he wasn't here. You were."

"You saved yourself. Now go and leave this old man alone with his bottle. I'm at a steamy part of my book, and I'd be embarrassed if you were around while I read it."

"You didn't... you didn't tell Chance, did you?"

"If Chance knew, that wannabe rapist would be in the

morgue, not in the hospital drinking his dinner through a straw. And your boss would be in jail."

A single tear descended down her cheek. She took off her glasses and wiped them away. "I wish he were dead. I wish you'd killed him."

"It's no small thing to kill a man. Something like that never leaves you." Jed hesitated, his upraised arm hanging in the air. Finally, his long-dormant instinct to provide comfort won out and he wrapped his arm around the young woman.

She wiped her cheek again, took another hit from the bottle, and reached into her bag. She pulled out a pack of gum and popped a piece in her mouth. She reached back in and pulled out a can of Right Guard deodorant. "I meant to give you this to, but I didn't want to—"

"Hurt my feelings?" he asked. "You don't like my perfume of the streets?" He smiled down at her. She wrinkled her button nose at him and he quietly chuckled.

"Tell me your real name, old man?" she asked, her voice strange from chewing and speaking at the same time.

"I told you, my name is St. Gertrude of Nivelles. I am the patron saint—"

"Of little cats. Yes, you are," she whispered. She got up and disappeared into the darkness.

He sat there awhile. Sometimes he was sure the girl was a figment of his imagination, conjured by his lonely mind out of a composite of girls from the road not traveled. Other times he was certain she was real, as his frequent hallucinations never had the lingering scent of Jean Paul Gaultier 'Classique'.

His thoughts drifted to Chance. Jed had wanted to say something to him, and it wasn't about the sauce. He grabbed his new bag of socks and deodorant and walked behind the dumpster, sitting down in his custom-built cardboard house, trying to remember what he wanted to say.

He took out a Swisher Sweet cigar and smelled the skinny, sugar-coated leaf. Out of one of the pockets on his flak jacket appeared a bronze Zippo. He read the engraving for the ten-thousandth time: *Am I my brother's keeper.* He had given Chance the exact same lighter as a thank you. He lit the Zippo and touched the flame to the cigar tip. With each puff, the fire blossomed at the end, and he inhaled the satisfying smoke deep into his lungs. Exhaling the pale blue fog, he remembered what he was going to say to Chance: *Evil is the man who kills his brother, and evil is the woman who kills his heart.* He nodded his head, not knowing if he made it up or read it somewhere. He would ask Isaac. Isaac would know.

No. Isaac is dead. Isaac didn't come back. He grunted and shook his head.

Grabbing his duffel bag, he opened it to inspect the day's catch. It had been a light but rewarding day. A white ceramic plate with only a small chip on the side. Perfectly usable. A Five Star college-ruled notebook with only half the pages used. He thumbed through grocery lists, doodles, and the beginnings of some bad poetry. He chuckled at the emotional angst it must have required to write *My blood drips into rivers that ~~goes~~ flow into deep oceans of pain and betrayal. I ~~dog paddle~~ swim out against the tide trying to ride the wave of my discontent.* He hoped whoever wrote this found some peace.

Lastly, he pulled out his prize of the day. A brand-new issue of *Cosmopolitan* magazine. Out of all the magazines in his extensive collection, *Cosmo* was by far his favorite, as they usually had the best perfume samples and interesting articles.

He was well-versed in *32 Ways to Drive Your Man Crazy*; *Six Places on Your Body He Should Pay More Attention To*. And *Hair on Fire! 10 Ways Your Curling Iron is Killing Your Hair*. He would save the new articles for his morning constitutional.

He flipped to the page offering the perfume samples and inspected the advertisement with trepidation. A young girl with a hat on. Confident that whoever Debbie Gibson was, she wasn't a fashion model. He wondered why she was selling perfume. *Electric Youth* was an oxymoron. He folded back the tape and held the page to his nose. He sneezed out the cotton candy on steroids. *Whoa!* Horrible compared to the Jean Paul his teenaged goddess had been wearing. He ripped that page out, crumpled it up, and threw it out of his makeshift window. Disappointed that his favorite part of the day was a bust.

He put the magazine on top of his collection and grabbed the bottle, holding it up to note how much was left. He smiled, satisfied the three-quarters remaining would be enough to lower the noise level in his head. He pulled out one of the many books in his bag and studied the cover: a shirtless man and a woman in a *Gone with the Wind*-worthy dress, embracing in a rainstorm, both soaked with passion and a "you know what happens next" expression. He turned to the last dog-eared page and lost himself in the heat of the words.

Hit singles like: "Joy to the World" by Three Dog Night, "(I've Had) The Time of My Life" by Bill Medley & Jennifer Warnes, and "Celebration" by Kool & the Gang.

This 16-cassette collection includes 160 of your favorite feel good tunes. Are you feeling Footloose? I know I am.

Operators are standing by, so have your credit card ready. This amazing collection, not available in stores, can be yours for 12 easy payments of only $24.95.

YOU DESERVE TO BE HAPPY, AND NOW YOU CAN BE. ORDER NOW!

TERMS AND CONDITIONS:
Si vos emere productum, nos mos persevero ad adiuro vos in reliqua vita tua. Vos conantur, ut aliquam sed inutiliter. Volumus etiam vendere notitia omni iure mailer in mundo. Retinemus ius vocare te ad cenam experiri et vendere plus effercio non opus est. Diam cavete.

CHAPTER SIX

ABOUT A GIRL

The twenty-four-hour diner was only a quarter full, and the elderly waitress standing at the counter appeared bored. The bar crowd was still an hour away, and she was smoking her fourth Lucky Strike in a row. Winnie sat in a booth drawing a comic book character, Chow Yun-fat, named for the Hong Kong action star, holding two smoking automatic pistols and scanning several dead bodies. Standing next to Chow, he had drawn a girl clutching a sawed-off shotgun. Inspired by his best friend Alex, over the last few years, as Alex had changed, so had Min-May.

Long, flowing, chestnut hair was whipped by a wind despite the scene being set inside a house. Her round eyes had long lashes sprinkled with glitter. Her petite frame was dressed in red leather, and oversized breasts spilled out of the corset. Her huge bee-stung lips, painted with bright red lipstick, were in a perpetual kissing pose.

The waitress put down her cigarette and approached Winnie with a pot of coffee. He covered the drawing and smiled at Mrs. White. She was older than his mother, but unlike Mom, she was always nice to him, and always sober.

"Still scribbling away, Winnie?" she asked. "When are you ever going to show anyone what you're working on?"

A warmth rose in his cheeks. "They're not scribbles. They're drawings. But they're not good enough to show."

"I don't know much about art, but the few peeks I've gotten over the years seem pretty good to me." She set the Bunn coffeepot on the table and lit up another Lucky Strike. A deep rumbling cough hit her, and her small frame convulsed.

"You OK, Mrs. White?

"I'm fine, I'm fine." She pulled out a handkerchief and spit into it. Winnie groaned under his breath.

"I got to quit these damn things." She took another drag off the filterless cigarette.

"Maybe you should at least switch to something with a filter."

"Then what would be the point?" Mrs. White jammed the cigarette down twice in the unused ashtray.

A group of Latter-Day Saints walked in, dressed in traditional short-sleeve white shirts and black ties. Mrs. White grunted and walked over to them, grabbing a few menus. They were all smiles and didn't try to convert anyone along the way.

Winnie relocated the still-smoldering ashtray to the far side of the table and picked up his pencil. The drawing was almost done. He studied Min-May and imagined, not for the first time, kissing her.

In his fantasy, he-as-Chow put his smoking pistols in their twin holsters and grabbed her. His Polo cologne mixed with her John or Gene Paul something in an intoxicating mesh of orange blossom, jasmine, and leather. Doves lifted off in flight around them as she gazed up at him with her huge blue-gray eyes, lashes fluttering, signaling him in code: yes, yes, yes!

He leaned down and pressed his lips into hers, feeling the slight moisture and pillow-like softness.

A low moan escaped from deep inside her and the world moved in slow motion. Wings flapped slowly as sunlight burst through a window, lighting them up on a stage, where no kiss had ever risen to this level of amazing.

He pulled back and she mouthed the word, "Amazing."

A bad guy on the floor moved toward a pistol. Not blinking or taking her stormy blue eyes off Winnie, she discharged her shotgun, sending hot lead into the gangster.

"Winnie," she whispered as she dropped the shotgun and reached up behind his neck, pulling him down once again toward her voluptuous lips.

"WINNIE!"

Winnie snapped out of the fantasy with a jerk. Alex stood across the table from him, leaning on the booth with an exasperated expression.

"What? Oh, sorry, Alex." Color flushed his cheeks as if she had caught him with porn.

"Where were you? I've been saying your name for an hour." Alex slid into the booth as Winnie grabbed his pad and closed it.

"Sorry, I was just thinking."

"Yeah, in what dimension?" She set her monkey backpack next to her, pushed up her glasses, and opened up the front panel. The monkey's head came out the top of the backpack as if he was stuck inside, with his legs extending from the bottom. His head, the starch long since defeated by gravity, hung to one side, the effect giving him a drunk demeanor.

"Umm, I was thinking about this new cartoon that came out called *The Simpsons*."

Alex took a cigarette roller from her backpack, placed it on the table, reached back in, rummaged around, and removed a pouch of tobacco with a Native American face on the label. "Is that the one on at night with all the weird yellow characters?" She rummaged around again inside Monkey's body. "Monkey, come on, give up the papers!"

"Yeah. It's pretty funny, actually."

Alex raised her hands as if scoring a touchdown. "Success!" She put the papers on the table and patted Monkey on his sad little head. "Thank you, Monkey." She pulled out long leafy brown strings from the tobacco bag and jammed them down into the roller with precision. "It'll never last. Who watches cartoons at night? Where's my lighter, Monkey?"

Winnie sat in silence, thought of a retort. He shook his head and let out a sigh.

Mrs. White walked up to the table and poured coffee into Alex's cup.

"Alex, need a light?"

"Hi Vera, yeah thanks. Monkey is being difficult." Mrs. White chuckled as she lit Alex's cigarette. She winked at Winnie and walked over to the host stand.

"So, do you have any new drawings?" Alex asked.

Winnie shifted in his seat. "Um, one."

"Well, come on, let me see."

He handed her the pad and studied her face as she analyzed herself in pencil. Her long brown hair had a touch of curl at the ends and framed her oval face in a way that sensualized her high cheekbones.

Alex took another drag, glancing at him and then back to the page. What had begun as an eighth-grade art class project had turned into a full graphic novel of Chow and Alex saving the world, one bullet at a time.

"I love how you controlled your line weight here; gives it a 3D effect." Her hand hovered over parts of the drawing, pointing out sections she approved of. She gave a heavy sigh and sat back in the booth, bringing one knee up to her chest.

"I wish I looked like this in the real world. It's funny, but you've turned my alter ego into my nemesis."

"Why do you say that?"

Alex looked thoughtful. "'Cause she is beautiful and fierce and you draw her with softness and grace. Not qualities anyone would accuse me of having."

"What? I accuse you; I totally accuse you." He paused and put his chin on his chest. "Wow, that sounds weird when I say it out loud." He was rewarded with a sly smile and pressed on.

"Alex, she is you. She is exactly you. I am not a fiction writer. I'm not saying you're totally badass with a gun, but without you there is no Min-May." He could feel heat radiating off his chest and he looked away from her piercing eyes. Softly, he added, "I didn't invent Min-May. I stole you and put you on a page."

He raised his head and was ensnared in her tractor-beam eyes. He tried to swallow but his arid tongue felt swollen and clumsy, his mouth full of words. Important words, life altering words, but with as little chance of being voiced by him as there was of there ever being more *Star Wars* movies.

She broke the spell by taking a drag off her cigarette and blowing the smoke in his face.

He waved his hand in the air and gave Alex a frown. "Seriously, Alex, secondhand smoke!"

"Seriously, Winnie, you smoke enough pot to be regulated by the EPA for carbon emissions."

Winnie rolled his eyes and took a sip of his coffee.

"Where are Prez and Hunter?" asked Alex.

"They said they would be here around one. Prez is working at his mom's shop, and Hunter's on a date."

"Which girl is it this time?"

"I think it's Eastside Catholic."

Alex grabbed another paper and started rolling a cigarette, shaking her head. "What? He already slept with everyone at Central. I don't understand what the girls see in him."

"I can't keep up with all of them, that's for sure. I'm not sure how Hunter keeps all their names straight. I'd think in the heat of the moment he'd call out some other girl's name."

"Gross... not a picture I want in my head." Alex made a puking motion. Winnie, not to be out done, made an even more dramatic puking motion, accompanied by sounds. Alex doubled down and pulled out her Chunk-from-*The-Goonies* impression of puking, dragging out the obnoxious sounds.

"You kids OK over there?" called out Mrs. White. Winnie waved to her, then held up his hands in surrender.

"You win. Can't believe you pulled out the Chunk."

"Whatever it takes, buddy." She brought up her thin arm, flexed and kissed her bicep. Then went back to making her cigarette. Winnie rolled his eyes and took a sip of coffee.

"I think Hunter has gotten worse since he got kicked out," said Alex.

"He's gotten worse since he bought that Camaro. I don't know what it is with you girls and cars, but you all seem to cream your panties whenever a dude has a great car."

"One, don't classify all of us women as the same. Two, don't be crass. Three, blame a society that teaches girls from age zero onward to not value or believe in themselves." Alex set the now perfectly rolled cigarette on the table. "Society teaches girls to have ridiculous views on body image. We need to be twigs with big breasts, consider all other women as threats, and if we open our legs, we're sluts, and if we don't, we're frigid." Alex began rummaging around in her backpack again, but didn't stop her monologue. "Blame the society with a million derogatory names for women, like 'bitch,' 'slut,' 'whore,' 'dyke,' and 'cunt,' that makes it perfectly OK to use them." Alex pulled out the silver Zippo in triumph. "Ha ha! Thank you, Monkey."

It was not lost on Winnie that Alex was a twig with big breasts. But he chose not to remind her. "Alex, are you watching Oprah again?"

"Shut up, nerf-herder. I'm serious. You don't understand what it's like to be ogled all day long no matter where you are. Men think they can say anything they want and it's perfectly acceptable. Just yesterday I was walking down the street and some asshole leaned out the window of his car and shouted, 'how much for head?' and took off with all of his asshole friends laughing. What about me walking down the street says it's OK to lean out of your car and scream something vulgar and demeaning?"

Winnie felt a tightening in his neck whenever he worried about Alex. She was Mona Lisa beautiful, no, Venus de Milo, no, like Kelly LeBrock in *Weird Science* beautiful. Yet played it down, wearing baggy sweatshirts and little-to-no makeup. "Are you OK?"

"Of course, I'm OK; that isn't the point. Ever since the seventh grade, everywhere I go men and boys stare at my chest and won't look me in the eye. All of you do it. Mr. Hinkle would stand behind me in class and try to peep down my shirt. My dentist, my father's friends, the pastor at our church. I'm wearing headlights on high beam and your perverted eyes can't seem to focus on anything else." Alex's cheeks became rosy, the way they always did when she was flustered or embarrassed.

"I look you in the eyes," Winnie said, his voice low.

"I know you do, but you don't count."

Winnie grimaced and felt a paper cut on his heart. Alex had been his best friend since the first grade, when she punched him in the stomach and took away the Etch-A-Sketch he was playing with. He'd cried, but for the rest of the day he followed her around. Alex's mom always liked to pull out a photo album of the two of them every Christmas. Pictures embarrassed Winnie, as he appeared sullen in every one. Alex's mom, Katiana, would always say in her thick Russian accent, "Vinston, you never smile. You are so handsome ven you smile. Alexandra, you must get Vinston to smile more." Only his mother and Mrs. Kopoff ever called him handsome.

"I'm sorry, Alex. I wish, I mean, I wish there was something I could do. Make it different somehow."

"Me too, Winnie. Me too."

Vera returned with more coffee. Alex pulled a Polaroid camera out of her bag.

"Vera, I want to get a picture of you and Winnie."

Alex had inherited her mother's love for photography, and she used a small vintage Nikon with black-and-white film.

Winnie gave her the Polaroid camera for her 18th birthday, and while she didn't use it often, his heart soared when she did.

Alex shook the camera in front of Winnie and burst into song. "Don't you," Winnie immediately joined in. "Forget about me. Don't, don't, don't, don't." They laughed together. Mrs. White shook her head.

"Sometimes you kids are just plain weird."

"Come on Vera, live a little," said Alex. She brought the camera up to her eyes, the viewfinder clicking against her cat-eye glasses.

"Oh, good heavens, Alex, I look frightful. I couldn't possibly take a photo with this handsome young man."

Winnie raised an eyebrow at another older woman saying he was handsome.

"No, Vera, you sit down right now next to Winnie. You are beautiful just as you are. Don't let society dictate your appearance."

Winnie rolled his eyes again.

Vera put the coffeepot on the table and sat next to Winnie. As she patted her beehive hairdo, he perceived a handsome older woman. Examining past the lines on her face, he imagined her full of youth and beauty. Hard living had etched deep fault lines under her eyes. A flash popped, and there was a familiar sound of the camera spitting out the instant photo.

"Hey, I wasn't even looking," said Winnie in protest.

Alex shook the photo with vigor. "Nope, this one is going to be perfect. Vera, thank you so much."

"I'll come back to see the results." She squeezed Winnie's shoulder, using it for balance as she got up from the booth. She grabbed her coffeepot and walked over to a table, the couple waving their hands in the air like they were at the arrival gate of an airport.

She handed the photo to Winnie. As the picture became clearer, he saw a new perspective. He was facing Mrs. White with a deep, almost melancholy, look. Mrs. White was staring at the camera but hadn't had time to put on her "camera face." The corners of her mouth were turned down, and even the cheap film was able to capture the air of resigned sadness. A woman that had accepted what her life was and knew her best days were behind her.

"Wow," said Winnie. "This... this is amazing."

"I know, right? The way you're studying her, I can't tell. What were you thinking about? No, wait, let me guess. That she used to be a beautiful woman?"

Winnie shifted in the booth, uncomfortable with how Alex could read him. "Yeah, I guess. Sometimes I watch her when she's standing at the counter smoking and she's so sad. She'll glance my way and put on a big smile, and I can tell it's only skin deep."

"How does that make you feel?"

"What are you, my shrink?"

"No, I'm curious. You had such a soulful expression." Alex shrugged. "I was wondering how you felt."

Winnie took a deep breath. "I guess... I guess she reminds me of Mom. She sits at the kitchen table smoking all day in her bathrobe. The only time she gets up is to go pop another pill she hides in her bedroom." Winnie picked up his drawing pencil, gripping it with both hands like an iron bar.

"She's still grieving."

"What about me? I'm still grieving, but I manage to go to work every day. I've become the parent. I love my mom."

Winnie paused and peered out the window. "But I am starting to hate her a little bit." The pencil snapped in Winnie's hands. "Crap."

"First of all, you shouldn't feel bad about your emotions." Alex reached across the table and rested a hand over Winnie's. "They're completely justified. Your mom is grieving in her way; you're grieving in yours."

Winnie was trying to find a way to change the subject when Vera returned. Alex pulled her hand back and Winnie instantly missed their soft warmth.

"Little darlings, it's going to get busy in a bit, so I brought you coffee in case I don't get back for a while. Do either of you want to get any food?"

Winnie waited for Alex to go first. "I'm OK, Vera, thanks."

"I'm fine, Mrs. White, thanks for asking. By the way, Alex took a beautiful photo." Winnie picked up the Polaroid photo and handed it to Vera.

She stared at it. "Well, it's not every day I get a picture of myself with such a charming young man. This is a sweet photo, Alex."

"Keep it. You're beautiful compared to the Neanderthal next to you," Alex said, not unkindly.

"Thank you. I know just where I'm going to put it." She carefully placed the photo inside her order book. "It's going to go right next to Isaac and Izzy on the mantel above the fireplace." Her eyes moistened, and she turned and walked back to the kitchen.

Winnie's own eyes filled with tears. He looked down and wiped them away as if he had dust in them.

"What was that about?" asked Alex.

Winnie didn't know how to respond. He delayed a few seconds, pouring more coffee into his cup. His hands shook as he tried to open the creamers. "Mrs. White had two sons, Isaac and Ishmael, and a husband named Abraham. They all died."

CHAPTER SEVEN

GOD BLESS THE U.S.A.

Chance stared out his office window at the birch trees across the alley, their white bark peeling away like dry skin. It didn't matter which season, their serenity always brought him comfort. He checked his watch. It was an hour after closing, and most of the staff would've headed out. Soon Geoff would come in with the night's till. His chin hit his chest as he replayed his actions tonight. He needed to end things with Sloan. He gazed into his scotch. *What you need is to slow down on the drinking.* He took a sip and let the amber liquid soothe away his worries. He would start tomorrow, turn over a new leaf, get back some of the respect he had lost tonight. A knock at the door pulled him out of his head.

"Are you all right?" Geoff sat, putting the till on the desk.

Chance eyed the money, trying to focus. "I'm sorry you had to do that. I should've never put you in that position. It was unprofessional." Chance struggled to maintain eye contact with Geoff and felt his face flush. He took another sip of his drink and grabbed the register tape. "But Frank isn't a guy you want to mess with."

"Don't worry. I've dealt with worse people. What's going on with you? You haven't seemed yourself lately." Geoff grabbed the scotch bottle and poured himself two fingers.

"I'm fine, really. I don't want to talk about it."

"OK, we don't have to talk about it, but I'm worried about—"

"It's just, have you ever been with a woman you know you shouldn't be with? That everything about her is all wrong?" Chance winced. "Sorry, I guess you haven't."

"Chance, I didn't know I was gay for most of my life. I was married to a woman for thirteen years." Geoff smiled. "So, I'd say at some point, yes, I was with a woman I knew I shouldn't have been with."

Chance closed one eye, trying to focus on Geoff, thinking he resembled Memnon, a character from *The Iliad*. Umber skin, with sun wrinkles around the eyes, his profile chiseled from granite. His high and tight black hair, never longer than a half inch, and his piercing tawny eyes gave him a wise, powerful air.

"How is it I keep forgetting you were married?"

Geoff tipped his glass toward Chance. "There might be a few conversations we've forgotten. But that isn't me. I'm not that person. I'm not sure I was ever that person." Geoff's eyes became unfocused. "I was acting out a role. God handed me a script and said, 'You get to play the Baptist Minister's son, prom king, college football star, Navy Seal, husband, father, oh, and to add a little drama, you're gay. But you won't know 'till the fourth act."

"So, you think God made you this way."

"Course God made me this way! You think I'd choose to be gay if it was a choice? I was married to what I thought was an ideal woman, with two beautiful children. I had a job I loved, was a deacon in my Church." Geoff took the rest of his scotch in one gulp. "I lost everything when I came out. Except my brothers. Everyone else lit their torches and grabbed their pitchforks." Geoff's voice lowered to just above a whisper. "They took my kids away, Chance. I only get to see them with supervised visits. Like I'm a monster or a child molester."

Chance, shocked into silence, took a breath, chose his words carefully. "I know. It's... well it's fucked, is what it is."

Geoff's face relaxed. "Don't get me wrong. I've accepted who I am. I'm proud to be me. But it wasn't easy."

"Your brothers still talk to you?" Chance poured three more fingers into Geoff's glass.

"Not my biological brothers. My Navy brothers."

"I still can't picture you in the military. I knew you were, but... I don't know, you don't seem... military." His eyes scrunched up.

"Jesus, how much have you had to drink?"

Chance shrugged, considered his glass, and put it on the desk.

"Yes, I was in the Navy for ten years. I was in the Seals for the last six. My brothers were great. When I came out, they said they had known for a long time." Tears formed, but there was warmth in Geoff's eyes.

"The Navy didn't kick you out?"

"Yeah, the Navy would've, if they had found out. My brothers didn't tell. I waited until my hitch was up and didn't reenlist. My CO knew what was going on, which is why he signed off on my paperwork quickly. They don't spend millions training to let you walk away." Geoff took another sip and set the glass down. "Unless, of course, you're Black and gay."

"Why haven't you told me this before? This is some badass shit."

Geoff's gaze went somewhere behind Chance. "Isn't something I talk about. Most people wouldn't understand, and so much of it I can't talk about."

Chance chewed on that for a while. "Why are you telling me now?"

"Well, we're best friends. And I guess it was feeling like a secret I was keeping from you."

A warmth beyond booze pulsed throughout Chance. After an awkward emotional silence, Chance stared out the window and sighed. "So, what did you say to Frank that got him to sit down?"

Geoff snorted. "I told him that the nerve I had a hold of wouldn't allow him to use his arms for a least another fifteen seconds. And if he didn't sit down and shut up, I'd kiss him passionately right there in front of everybody. The fact that he couldn't pull away would make everyone think he was kissing me back." A devilish grin spread across Geoff's face.

Chance's mouth dropped open for the third time in ten minutes. "Wow, yeah that would do it. Just be careful. Frank isn't a man you want to screw with."

"The day a thug like that can get the drop on me is the day I deserve whatever's coming. I actually think the guy is closet, but you never know." Geoff paused. "Is there something else bothering you?"

Chance's eyes widened. "Yeah. My uncle is dying."

"Uncle Vinnie?"

"Yep, the one and only." Chance ran his hands through his hair, letting out a deep breath.

"I'm sorry. I didn't realize you guys were close."

"There was a time when we were, but I was a kid. It was before I knew... you know... what he did." Chance grabbed his glass and knocked back the rest of the scotch. He poured another two fingers and held out the bottle to Geoff, whose eyes had softened into commiseration. Geoff inspected his glass and shook his head.

"There are a lot of reasons to hate the guy, for what he is, but he kept his promise to my mother and left me out of the business. He could've recruited me when I was young and stupid. But he didn't."

"And he helped you buy the restaurant."

"I paid him back, with interest."

Geoff raised both hands. "I know, buddy. I know. I'm just thinking your life could've been a lot different. It's one of the things I've always respected about you. You took a different path. Couldn't have been easy, with your family."

Chance closed his eyes, his knuckles turning white as he gripped the glass.

"What? Oh, shit! No. Tell me they're not pulling you in."

Chance replied almost in a whisper, "My uncle wants me to take over as head of the family."

Geoff sat there a second and then got up and picked up the bottle. He poured the remaining half into his glass and the rest into Chance's, splashing some onto the desk.

"Fuck me," Geoff said, almost under his breath.

"Yeah... fuck me," repeated Chance.

CHAPTER EIGHT

RUN TO YOU

Chance lay in his bed, smoking next to a sleepy Sloan. As the euphoria of orgasm faded, emptiness took its place. A nothingness stretched out over a sparse land, with a few trees and discarded bottles the only proof someone lived here. The type of land where echoes sat waiting for someone, anyone, to make a sound.

Afternoon sun beat through the windows, warming the room enough to keep the sweat on his body from evaporating. The sounds of construction hinted at breaking in, but they were good solid windows.

His head felt stuck in a vice. One side was criminal mastermind, which he wasn't, and the other was certain death at the hands of Frank. And that was before Frank would find out about him and Sloan. Maybe he should get out of town, sell the restaurant. He could ask Sloan to run away with him.

Did he want Sloan to run away with him? Was her marriage the only thing holding them back? Could they ever have more, or even be more? The image of Oliver Twist asking for another bowl of gruel popped into his head.

He smashed out the cigarette, nuzzled up to spoon her body, and ran his hand through her gold-spun hair. "Sloan, let's do something today. I'll take the day off. We could go to the zoo or," he paused, nothing coming to mind, "or something." Inspiration hit. "I can make a picnic. We'll go down to the shore, watch the cargo ships float by. Drink champagne, tell stories. I don't know anything about your childhood. You don't know about mine." He paused, unsure whether she was awake. "Let's take the weekend and drive to Door County. It's beautiful up there. The best part of Wisconsin. Beautiful forests, tiny little shops. There's a Swedish restaurant with real goats on the roof and quaint little cottages. We can light a fire and be naked."

He rested his hand on her shoulder. Her pale skin was slick as he ran his nails lightly up and down her arm. He loved the softness, the tiny, almost invisible hairs that perked up into goose bumps under his fingers. The deep sense of intimacy it gave him even though he knew with Sloan it was only an illusion.

"Stop doing that," mumbled Sloan.

"What, love?"

"I said stop it!" She threw the covers off and rolled out of bed. "You always do this. What do you think this is? You think we're going steady? You think we're boyfriend and girlfriend? You want to get matching promise rings?"

He pushed himself up and sat back against the headboard. He reached for his Marlboros as she searched for her underwear. "Why do you have to always be like this?" He lit a cigarette and slammed his Zippo on the nightstand. "Why do you always have to cheapen it?"

"Because it is cheap. We are having an affair. It's sex. It's just sex, God, why can't you be happy with that? Plenty of men would love to fuck me and not have to talk to me afterward. Why do you constantly need to turn this into something else?"

He took another drag and asked himself the same question. He swallowed his irritation and said in a measured voice, "Yes, when we started all I wanted was sex, too. But we've been there, done that. I want to have feelings for you. I want us to explore those feelings."

She rotated her bra around her body to cover her breasts. Pulling the shoulder strap up, it cracked like a whip against her skin. She softened her tone. "I am *married*. Frank would literally kill us if he ever found out. I knew what I was getting into with him. There is no leaving. It doesn't work that way."

"I can handle Frank if that's what you're worried about." He brightened at the thought of rescuing her.

"I don't need you to save me, and I don't want to be saved. I like you. You're different, but I'm not leaving Frank. It's not fear, and I'm not unhappy."

"I don't understand. What the fuck are you doing here if you're happy? Why are you cheating on your husband if everything is rosy in Bartallatas land?"

She pulled up her tan slacks and glared at him, the temperature in the room dropping precipitously. "I don't need to justify myself to you, or anyone. If you can't handle your role, that's fine. But I'll not stand here and fulfill this incessant need you have." She pulled on her turtleneck, adjusted her hair, and glanced at him again. He felt exposed with his flaccid penis lying there and pulled up the sheet.

"Chance, this is a lot of fun… Well, it's beginning to not be. I care about you. I like fucking you. You're an animal in bed—"

"Don't patronize me! I'm trying to have an honest conversation with you."

"Fine!" She found her purse and pulled out a hairbrush. She went over to the mirror, raking away at her long blonde hair.

He watched her in the mirror, trying to make eye contact, but she didn't respond. If he could get her to look at him, they could fix this. A whisper in his mind asked why he even wanted to. She focused on her hair and avoided his eyes. Satisfied with the result, she walked back to her purse, put the brush back and stood there considering the floor. She turned to him, but he couldn't read her expression.

"I wasn't patronizing you. But I think you need to figure out if you want to continue this relationship the way it is. I'm not Ellie, and won't ever be."

She still stood at the foot of the bed, but it was as if she'd reached out and slapped him. The room spun off center. Paralyzed, he couldn't speak, even if he'd known what to say. The name was enough to unleash a torrent of images.

"Frank told me about Ellie. I'm sorry. But I've been honest about the boundaries. If you want to continue, great. I'd love that. But don't expect anything more from me. I don't want to hurt you. But I will."

She left the room without a backward glance.

He sat there. After a while, he rolled into a fetal position, arms clutching a pillow. The echoes hanging out in his heart replayed the memory of sounds. Tires screeching, guns firing, and screams reverberating across the barren land.

1979

"Promise you'll do that to me forever, Charlie," said a breathless Isabella.

"Gladly. I'll stay here in the bedroom, the kept man, waiting for when you have an itch you need scratched." He was running his fingers through Ellie's black hair, massaging her scalp.

"Don't be ridiculous. You're going to be a rock star and have hundreds of girls throwing their panties at you on stage," she said.

"The only panties I want thrown at me are yours, on the way to the laundry."

"Better be, mister."

Sunlight peeked through a gap in the curtains, highlighting their intertwined feet at the end of the bed. He analyzed the differences in their toes, hers demure and pretty, his almost like hairy fingers. A rumbling in his stomach reminded him that breakfast wasn't going to make itself. He sighed, not wanting their lazy Sunday morning to end.

"You know what I love about us?" she asked.

"Humm?"

"I love how much we respect each other."

"Hmm."

"You know what else I love about us?"

"What's that, baby?"

"I love the safety I have with you. I don't just mean physically. It's safe to be myself." She lifted her head off his shoulder, propped herself up on her elbows, and gazed at him.

He smiled, loving the mole above her lip, the bushiness of her eyebrows, the etched marks of sleep from the pillow on her cheek.

"I know, babe. I'm with you."

"Expand," she said. It was a game she played when he would sometimes revert to his masculine forebears and grunt or give short answers.

"OK, I love how you know my soft underbelly. It's safe to show it to you. I can be exactly who I am when I'm with you. I don't have to pretend, or fake it." He reached out and tucked some hair behind her ear. "Whatever I do, I know you'll be standing there with me, supportive. I love I'll get to call you Doctor Wife. We're going to have the perfect life, and have lots and lots of babies."

"How many babies?"

"Eight, or maybe ten."

Her eyes widened. "Only if half of them come out of your uterus."

"Sure."

"What else? Tell me more."

"Well, I enjoy when we're alone and naked, you turn into a naughty French whore."

"What?" she yelled. "*Levati dalle palle* for calling me French." She hit him in the stomach and laughed. "You like that I'm a physician in the world, and your sex slave in this bedroom!" Her fingers found some of that soft underbelly.

"OK, OK, OK! You know I do." He squirmed around the bed; his feet tangled up in sheets. She jumped on top of him, holding his hands down. Her chest grazed his in a way she knew drove him crazy.

"You love that I'm smart and sexy. Say it."

"I love that you're smart and that Debbie from Dallas has nothing on you."

"Ohh," she yelped and tickled him again. He grabbed her right arm, then her left, and effortlessly held them together with one hand. He rolled her over and put her arms above her head. She briefly struggled. He bent to kiss her, and she snapped her teeth at his face.

"Ahhh, no… be good." He tried to kiss her again, and she did the same. He brought his free hand up in front of her face.

"I can do a lot of things with this hand, love. Be good, and I'll tell you a secret. Be bad and… well, you'll find out what bad gets you."

She thought about it for a second and a devilish grin appeared on her face. He leaned in for a kiss, their lips just touching when she bit down on his lower lip. Not hard, but enough for him to get the point.

"Owww." He pulled his head back. "That's it!" He let go of her arms and laid on top of her. She gave a start and wrapped her legs around him.

"Charlie," she yelled, breathless. "Tell me the secret."

CHAPTER NINE

TURNING JAPANESE

PRESENT

Hunter and Winnie played their current obsession, *Gauntlet*, at Loose Change Arcade. Winnie was the Elf, preferring speed, Hunter the Warrior, preferring power. They'd made a pretty good team so far; only twelve tokens had gone into the machine. The electronic symphony of game noise and flashing lights soothed Winnie. Bryan Adams sang about the summer of '69, and kids ran from game to game in a schizophrenic orgy.

"Warrior needs food badly," voiced the game.

"I need food," said Hunter.

"Over there," said Winnie, lost in the game.

"Shit! I shot the food."

"Don't shoot the food," said the ominous ghost in the machine. With his peripheral vision, Winnie saw Warrior turn into a pile of bones.

"Crap!" Hunter fed the machine another token. Warrior became alive again, as if nothing had happened.

"I've found the exit," said Winnie. They went through the exit, and the game paused to load the next level.

"So, what about Jennie over there? She's pretty cute."

Winnie craned his neck past Hunter to spy the tall blonde girl playing *Rampage*. She had been two years ahead of him in school. She was as tall as Winnie, taller actually, if you counted her hair. Kind eyes, and Winnie had always liked freckles.

"She has way too much Aqua Net in her hair. You can see it clump up in the front, and it's about to drip off or something."

Hunter snickered. "Yeah, but so what? She's easy."

"I'm not getting your sloppy seconds. Hey, don't shoot the potion!"

"Red Warrior shot the potion," voiced the video game.

"Sorry. But sitting around obsessing over Alex isn't healthy. You need to date someone. These are the days you're supposed to sleep with everyone you possibly can."

"That's you, Hunter, not me. I'm not obsessing over Alex." Winnie peeked at Jennie again and caught her inspecting him.

"Well, you should at least talk to Jennie. Her dad owns this place. How do you think I got so many free tokens?"

"I don't want to know." Winnie didn't want to date Jennie. Or any girl except Alex. Hunter knew it, and, in fact, everyone except Alex knew it.

A shadow appeared over the game. "Hey, Oscar Meyer." Winnie glanced up. Only one person ever called him that. Jake "The Tower" Webber. Biggest thing to come out of St. Andrews High School, maybe ever. Jake had won every wrestling title ever invented. His senior year at State, he tore some ligaments in his knee and still managed to win the match. Lost his full-ride scholarship, but not his place among the gods. It had gone from Winnie to Weenie to Oscar Meyer, in the span of one study hall.

"Hey Jake."

"Is Alex around?"

"Hi Jake," said Hunter.

"No, I think she's at home or something."

"Hi Jake," repeated Hunter.

Jake had this intimidating habit of not speaking for long periods of time. He would look at you. Like he was trying to decide if you were food or not.

"Tell her I'm looking for her, and have her call me," he finally said.

"Ah, sure Jake," said Winnie.

"She's not your girlfriend or anything, is she?" asked Jake.

"No, she is absolutely not Winnie's girlfriend," said Hunter.

Winnie turned and gave Hunter the death look.

"OK. Well, good to see you, Weenie. You're about to die," said Jake.

Sweat instantly formed under Winnie's arm pits. "What?"

Jake pointed at the game, then thundered off.

"Bye Jake," called out Hunter. "I think he's starting to like me."

They both put tokens into the game. But Winnie wasn't paying attention. What the heck could Jake want with Alex?

"So, as I was saying, it isn't healthy. Alex is great; I love her to death, but sometimes she isn't even nice to you."

"What?" said Winnie. "Alex is nice."

"No, I know, man, but sometimes she treats you like a little brother."

Winnie thought about this as his alter ego launched a magic attack against a horde of goblins. "I think you don't understand our relationship. The deepest conversation you have with a girl is, 'When do your parents get home?'"

Hunter became a bobblehead. "What else is there to say?"

Winnie closed his eyes. Hunter, a violin prodigy since he was eight, shocked everyone when he didn't get in to Juilliard. It was supposed to be a lock. Hunter's father beat him in a rage and disowned him. Since then, Hunter lived with Winnie and his mom. Once when they were both stoned watching *Escape From New York*, Winnie asked him about the audition. Hunter told him he'd thrown the audition on purpose. "Everyone has a sound to me," he'd explained. "My mother is a flute, my sister an oboe. Father was always the violin. So, I grew to hate the sound." Winnie never asked what his sound was.

"Hey, pay attention, your life force is going down," said Hunter.

"Blue Elf is about to die," agreed the game.

"Shit!" Winnie watched his elf turn into a pile of bones. He stuck another token into the slot. "I think I upset Alex the other day, but for the life of me I can't figure out why."

"Get used to it, man. She's pretty cool for a girl, but trying to understand what they're thinking is like trying to dance between rain drops without getting wet."

"Yeah, I guess."

"Besides, being perfectly honest, I don't want you and Alex to hook up."

Winnie stopped playing for a second and focused on Hunter. He could easily be a Hong Kong action hero if he weighed more than a cardboard paper cut out. Brooding good looks, sure, but a hundred pounds soaking wet.

"Hey, man, help me out here."

Winnie reengaged in the game, taking out a massive horde with a magic burst. "So, are you going to expand, or just leave it out there?"

"Look, man, I love Alex, I lo— um, you're great, and I appreciate how much you like her. But if you two get together, you'll be a couple. It won't be the four of us anymore. It'll be the two of you, with me and Prez flapping in the wind. I've seen it happen, man. When a girl gets hooks in you, all rational thought goes right out the window. Plus, I think Alex is frigid."

"What?" Winnie gripped the controller. He took a measured breath, let it out, and tried to calm himself before responding. The voice in his head told him to say, *You motherfucker, don't you ever talk about Alex that way! You get me? I will fucking mess you up, you violin-playing pansy.*

"I don't think Alex is frigid," came out instead, almost as a plea.

"Sorry, man. I don't want to see you get hurt. Girls are, well, different. You've never dated anybody. You gotta trust me on this. I know. Besides... I think the Tower might be moving in."

Winnie's shoulders sagged as the images on the screen blurred. Alex dating Jake? No... no way. Hunter was being a prick.

Winnie ignored the knife in his back. "So, what you're trying to say is, if I ever dated Alex it would change the nature of our friendship?"

Now it was Hunter's turn to stop playing and regard Winnie. "I guess that's exactly what I'm saying. I know you love her, man, but Alex isn't right for you. If it was going to happen, it would've already happened." Hunter went back to playing the game.

Winnie glanced over at Jennie again. She stared right at him. "Yeah, maybe you're right."

His thoughts went back to Alex, the pressure to tell her building in a coal-fed boiler on a speeding locomotive. For the thousandth time, a voice screamed, *tell her*! But fear of rejection was right there, standing next to him like the Grim Reaper, scythe poised to chop his stupid, useless head off.

"Blue Elf is about to die," remarked the video game. Winnie snorted at the truth of that statement.

CHAPTER TEN

GIRL YOU KNOW IT'S TRUE

It was a solid night in the restaurant, with the wait for tables stretching into an hour at one point, even though it was a weeknight. Chance checked the valet station where Alex was locking up the signs. Even though he'd bought her shirt in the kids' section, she was still lost in the white button-down, and he made a mental note to order polo shirts for the summer.

"Hey, Chance. Good night, huh?" Alex asked.

"Yeah, how did you guys do?"

"Prez is adding up the spoils right now. Are you headed over to Chan's?"

"How do you know about Chan's? You're not twenty-one yet." He raised an eyebrow.

"The staff talks about it. Isn't that where Leah met her new boyfriend?"

Chance chuckled. "I imagine that's where she might have met the last five."

Prez, whose real name was George Washington Lincoln, came jogging out of the hotel, his tuxedo vest bursting at the seams.

Definitely need to rethink the uniform policy.

"Hi, Mr. C. You going to Chan's tonight?"

"What is it with you guys? You want to apply for the job of being my mother?"

"No… that would be weird. Just sounds like a fun place. Wish I was twenty-one."

"It's not nearly as cool as you'd think. Don't you guys have a place you hang out?"

Prez glanced at Alex before responding, "Country Kitchen."

"The diner?"

"Yeah."

Chance smirked. "Yeah, I guess that is kinda lame."

"Here you go." Prez handed Alex a wad of cash. "All the signs are locked up, Mr. C. I got to take off if I'm going to make my bus. Milwaukee Metro, travel in style." Prez raised his Walkman headphones up from his neck to his ears. He clicked the play button and started bopping his head to the music.

"Night, Prez, thanks."

"Bye, Prez," said Alex.

Prez waved and started walking down the street, singing. Chance and Alex laughed.

"Violent Femmes?" asked Chance.

"Yeah, he's kinda obsessed."

"Strange."

"Yeah."

"Do you have a way home, Miss Alexandra Kopoff?"

"I'm walking. It's not too far."

"Nonsense, I can give you a ride. I imagine they won't run out of scotch at Chan's before I get there."

"You sure? I don't mind walking."

"No way. Come on, Gracie can get you home in real style." Chance noted a level of tension dissipating from Alex's shoulders. They got to the battleship of a car, and Chance opened the door for Alex.

"Wow, the inside of this car is amazing. You could fit both of my parents' cars in here." Alex set her backpack beside her and ran her hand against the plush seating.

"Yeah, I love this car. It was pretty extravagant when I bought it." Chance pulled out of the parking lot and turned left on Juneau Ave.

Alex didn't respond.

"You OK over there?"

"Chance, are you a gangster?"

Chance started choking on the spit he'd been swallowing. "No," he wheezed. "Why do you ask?"

"Well, you dress like a gangster, you drive a gangster car, I know gangsters come into the restaurant. You seem friendly with them all. We were just wondering. I've read *The Godfather*."

"Pretty shrewd for a teenage girl." Alex frowned. "Sorry, young woman. I'm not a gangster. I'm a restauranteur. But let's say for the sake of argument that I have some family members a little bit to the left of law and order." They drove in silence for a minute. "So, is this what my valets talk about?"

"Well... we've speculated about it. You can spot these guys a mile away, and they do seem to come in a lot. Most of them tip pretty well, except the one guy with the blonde wife. He's kind of a jerk." Alex covered her mouth. "Shit! Am I going to get whacked for saying that?" she asked in mock seriousness.

Chance laughed again. "You watch too many movies. I know who you're talking about and, you're right, he's a jerk."

"At the next light, take a left."

The neighborhood was filled with two story colonial homes. Built for large working-class families by the brewery barons, back when Milwaukee had them.

"So, can I ask you something?"

"Of course."

"What's with the monkey backpack? It seems a little…"

"Pubescent?"

"I was going to say childish, but that sounds better."

Alex stared out the window. "Winnie's dad gave it to me for my birthday a while back."

"Oh… OK, I understand." Chance drove in silence for a minute. "I miss him."

"He was the best. Best dad, and a great teacher at school. He was like a grownup ally, who hadn't forgotten what it was like to be a teen."

Chance smiled at the truth of it. He turned on his blinker and made a right on Warren Ave. "Did I ever tell you I liked your glasses? Retro cool."

"Yeah I found them on the rack at Woolworths. Had probably been there since the 50's." She pushed them up her nose.

"How is Win holding up?"

Alex paused before answering, "I don't know. Winnie's always been quiet. Never talks about how he feels much. I… I'm trying to give him space, but sometimes I want to shake him."

"He's had a traumatic experience."

"But it's happened to all of us. We all loved him. It feels like it's hit a pause button on our lives. Win, Hunter, Prez, me… we all seem to be treading water. Not sure what to do or how to... start life, I guess. We're all nineteen. Things are supposed to start happening."

"I can understand that. You all have to process this in your own way. Just remember, it isn't a race. It can be about the little moments in between the big ones."

He could spy out of the corner of his eye Alex studying his face. Alarm bells started to go off in his head.

"Can I ask you another question?"

Chance gripped the steering wheel tighter. "Of course."

"You volunteer at the Milwaukee Women's Resource Center, right?"

Chance pushed out a breath he hadn't realized he'd been holding. "Yeah, I do some work for them. Not as an advocate, but I help with emergency moves and raising money and stuff. Why?"

"What's it like? For the women who go there?"

Chance glanced over; she was staring out the window again. "Well, it's hard to put into words. Most women only come there after something horrible happened to them. But in a way there's something astonishing about the place. A woman comes in, many times in the middle of the night, after the most godawful experience of her life, and there are people, other women who have all been there, waiting to just grab on and hold, protect and comfort. And for the first time since whatever happened to them, they can feel safe." He glanced at her again. "Why, has something happened?"

"No! I was only wondering. Thought I might volunteer or something."

"That would be fantastic. We could use all the support we can get, especially from a fierce young woman such as yourself."

They rode the last few blocks in silence. Her hands were clenched, and the corners of his mouth turned downward. He turned onto her street.

"Thanks, Chance. For an old guy you're pretty cool." Alex smiled.

"Old guy, huh? Older, not necessarily wiser. Which house?"

"Next one on the left."

He pulled into the driveway and put the car into park. "All right, here you go, young lady. Would you like me to walk you to your door?"

She peered out the car window at the sidewalk, shook her head, and opened the door. "No thanks, Chance. Thanks for the ride," she said as she got out.

"No sweat. Have a good night."

She slammed the car door and ran up to the house. He waited until she got inside and pulled out of the driveway. The way she'd asked about the MWRC touched off a silent alarm in his head. He made a mental note to ask some questions.

. . .

He was hit by a wave of cigarette smoke in Chan's Chinese Emporium, where he spotted some of his staff through the crowd. Pitchers of beer, overflowing ashtrays, the jukebox belting out a Journey song—a typical night after work. He waved at Robb, the DJ who hosted karaoke. He was packing up his stuff, so thankfully Chance had missed the murder of classic songs.

Chan's served Chinese-American food right up 'till bar time. On many mornings, Chance woke up to white boxes of Chan's food, some not even touched, on his coffee table. One of everything always seemed like a good idea at two in the morning.

He smiled to his staff and walked over to Geoff, bellied up to the bar. "Is this seat taken, sailor?"

"It is now, you Scottish-Italian hunk," said Geoff.

Chance took a barstool next to Geoff's and waved two fingers at Chan.

"How business tonight, Mr. Chance?" Chan poured a generous amount of scotch. "You busy, busy?" He was five-three and maybe a hundred and ten pounds. He wore his long black hair braided, wearing traditional dress with a dragon stitched on the back.

"Chan, knock it off. Save it for the tourists."

"Come on, you know I gotta play the part," said Chan in a Wisconsin accent. Chan was fourth-generation American, and claimed his ancestors helped build the Trans-American railway.

"What took you so long?" asked Geoff. "I was about to invite that dreamboat over there to come sit down."

Chance looked over at the frat boy playing pool, his hat on backward, wearing a UWM sweatshirt and sporadic facial hair. "Seriously? He looks like a child."

"If he's in here, he's old enough." Geoff sipped his drink. "I'm kidding. I gave up on frat boys a long time ago. They are either so closeted they freak out after they come, or they are so queeny, drama doesn't even come close to describing them."

"Speaking of not old enough, I gave Alex a ride home." Chance peered into his amber drink.

Geoff glared at him. "And?"

"And nothing. I just... have you noticed anything different about her? Or have you heard anything lately?"

"What do you mean, 'different?'"

"I don't know. I gave her a ride home and she asked me about the MWRC."

"And you think..." Geoff's expression hardened.

"It could be nothing. But sometimes you get a sense about these things."

"Yeah... I do. I haven't heard anything, and she always seems like herself to me. She's been moody, but what teenager isn't?"

"I didn't realize you two knew each other that well."

"We have common interests."

"What's that? Young frat boys?"

Geoff laughed. "Somehow I don't ever predict Alex dating a frat boy. She's way too smart. No, we both love art. She's a sharp woman." Geoff paused and took a sip of his scotch. "Winnie's completely in love with her."

"I know. That kid has puppy love all over his face." Chance lit up a cigarette and peered around the bar. There were servers from several restaurants, including his. This was a bar for those in the industry. Stiff drinks, cheap prices, great food, open late.

"Yep. On the opposite side of the coin, were you aware Maggie's ex-husband trashed her apartment and stole $500 from her?"

"What? Why didn't she tell me?"

Geoff considered him for a long second. "I'm going to tell you something, Chance. Please take it in the spirit it's intended. You ignore the fact that your house is on fire because your neighbor lost their cat."

"I don't even know what that means."

"I think you do," said Geoff.

Chance closed his eyes. "Girl You Know It's True" by Milli Vanilli came on the jukebox. "I hate this fucking song," he said under his breath.

"Don't take it so hard. It's something for you to think about."

"Did Maggie call the cops?" Chance concentrated on something he could fix.

"She doesn't want to get Tom into trouble."

Chance frowned.

"So, what are you going to do about your uncle's offer?"

Chance's head swirled at the quick change in conversation. But that was Geoff.

"I honestly don't know. If it's not me, then it'll be Frank. If he takes over, you can count the number of minutes I'll have before someone takes a shot at me."

"Yeah, it isn't like the bad blood between you two isn't well known."

"Right. But this is the part I keep coming back to."

"What's that?"

"I don't want to be a fucking mob boss!" Chance realized he'd shouted and scanned the bar: nobody was paying any attention. "Besides the moral issues, which are considerable, I don't want to look over my shoulder all the time."

"I've been around, and fought against all kinds of tyrants and dictators in my life, and it takes a certain type of person to want that. That ain't you, buddy." Geoff smacked Chance on the back, causing him to spill scotch on the bar.

Chance glared at Geoff and raised his hand to Chan. "Chan, my friend, fill these up and leave the bottle close.

Geoff and I have to figure out world peace tonight. Kind of a homework assignment."

Chan poured a healthy two fingers in each glass. "Should I get another case from the back?"

Chance and Geoff both laughed as Chan went to help another customer. They both spun around on their barstools and scanned the crowd.

"What about that guy there?" Geoff indicated with a head nod. The guy in question was wearing an untucked plaid shirt, resting his hand against the wall, and was leaning in on a cute brunette.

"Nope. No way he scores. See the way she's holding her drink, with both hands in front of her? She's holding him at bay."

Geoff nodded at the assessment.

"What about that one?" asked Chance.

"Not a chance. That's crazy King Kevin. He only sings Elvis songs, and I'm pretty sure he's doing an impression for her right now. She looks like she's falling asleep."

They both laughed and sipped their drinks.

"OK, here we go. See the girl in the teal? She's looking at him," Chance indicated a guy in a Pabst Blue Ribbon hat. "He, on the other hand, is looking at Sheena Easton over there, and Sheena is looking right at you."

Geoff laughed. "Oh honey. So sad." Geoff waved at the girl and turned around his barstool. "I'm like Prince. I'm too sexy for both genders."

Chance spun around back to the bar, shaking his head. They sat for a bit, just enjoying their scotch.

"Maybe you should test it out. You know, practice on me," said Geoff.

"Practice what?"

"Practice acting like a mob boss. Give me some good mob-boss lines."

Chance had consumed enough scotch that this seemed like a perfectly reasonable idea. He cleared his throat.

"'I'm gonna make him an offer he can't refuse.'"

Geoff held out his hand flat and made the so-so movement. "Try another one."

"OK, let me think. 'Say hello to my little friend.'"

Geoff spit out the scotch he'd been drinking. He wiped his mouth on his sleeve. "OK, first, your accent is terrible. Second, no guy wants to refer to his thing as little."

"OK, OK, how 'bout this: 'I want him dead! I want his family dead! I want his house burned to the ground!'"

Geoff cleared his throat. "'Isn't that just like a dirty wop? Brings a knife to a gun fight. Get outta here, ya dago bastard.'"

Chance shook his head. "That's a pretty good Sean Connery."

"Yeah," said Geoff. "You'd better stick to selling pasta." Geoff put his arm around Chance and leaned in. "Look, man. You'll make the right decision. But understand, no matter what, I got your back."

CHAPTER ELEVEN

YOU SHOOK ME ALL NIGHT LONG

Chance, naked, lay on his back, sheets kicked down, snoring as the remnants of last night's poisons made their way through his system. His liver, used to being overwhelmed, fought on despite the assault, pledging to hold to the last man.

The room reeked of exhaled alcohol, stale cigarettes, and a hint of perfume. Next to Chance a woman lay on her stomach, a blanket covering her from the waist down. One arm was perched above her head, and her soft breathing was slow and measured.

As the midmorning sun beamed through the windows, the temperature in the room began to climb. Chance's body began to sweat out the alcohol. The woman stirred and rolled onto her back, her breasts bobbing, her left arm landing on Chance's stomach with a thump.

The phone in the other room began to ring, and unconsciousness loosened its grip on the chemical-induced coma. It rang fourteen times and stopped. Nothing happened for a minute, except Chance's snoring was now joined by the woman's softer version. The phone began to ring again.

As he became aware, he did a self-check, trying to piece together where he was before he opened his eyes. Nothing was coming to him, so he opened one eye a crack, then the other one. He was home in bed. *Good so far.* He lay there a few seconds and realized his morning erection was a point of discomfort, the pressure in his bladder telling him to get up. He became aware of an arm on his stomach, and he tilted his head to follow it back to its owner.

The shock was a bucket of ice water, followed by the pounding of a hammer in his head. *Holy shit!* His eyes tracked to a pair of sizable, pale, striking breasts. As his eyes continued up, they took in beautiful mahogany hair and a face that was lovely and well known to him. He was inspecting the very naked wife of the mayor.

Holy shit, holy shit, holy shit! Chance leaped from the bed. The hammer in his head almost sent him crashing down to the floor. His body protested, making his movements jerky and unstable. He scanned the room. Two empty bottles of wine were on the vanity, and a half-finished bottle of scotch was on the floor. He fumbled through the fog, wondering what the hell happened. The last semi-clear memory was of talking to Geoff at Chan's. *Oh shit oh shit oh shit!* He was frozen, half bent over, trying to make the pain in his head lessen.

"So, are you going to come back here and do something with that thing?" asked a sleepy Stella. She was now leaning up on one arm, the blanket pulled to her waist.

"Fuck, Stella!" Chance reached for his pants. He put one foot through his pants leg and attempted balance for the second. He hit the floor with a thud, both hands still clutching the pants. "Ow!" he yelled, the pain in his head momentarily forgotten as his side smacked the floor.

Stella giggled. "Charlie, come back to bed."

Chance managed to roll onto his back and pull the second leg of his pants up. "Stella, what the hell are you doing here?"

"Baby, you don't remember?" She looked wounded.

Chance stopped struggling with his pants and lay on the floor.

"Come back to bed, and I'll tell you all about it," she said with mischief in her voice. The phone in the other room started to ring again, the noise even more grating to Chance than Stella's playful tones. He got up from the floor, trying not to glance at Stella lying in the bed naked, but still peeking at Stella all naked in the bed. He grabbed the phone.

"What!" he barked.

"Jefe?" asked an accented voice on the other end.

"What?"

"Jefe, it's Chico. I've been calling you. You need to get down here. The truck is here but the meat no good."

"Chico, this isn't a good time. What truck?"

"Jefe, the truck... the special truck. It's here, but it's no good. We shouldn't take it, Jefe. You need to get down here." Chico's voice dripped with desperation.

Finally, the meaning of Chico's words dawned on him. "Shit... I'll be right there. Chico, don't accept anything. Tell them I'm on the way." Chance hung up the phone, not waiting for a response. "Shit!" *This is starting to be a banner day.*

As Chance ran around the room getting dressed, Stella relayed the previous night's events. She was lying against the headboard with the blanket pulled up to her neck.

"So, I told him I was going to my sister's and he said he didn't care. I drove around for a little while and decided I wanted a drink. I came here but you were already closed, so I went over to Chan's. You don't remember any of this?"

"It's starting to come back to me. We talked about high school and looked at yearbooks?" He didn't remember but saw two open yearbooks on the floor and made an educated guess.

"Yes!" she said, perky again. "And you said I was the most beautiful girl in school and had you known I'd grow up to be so beautiful you would have kicked his ass senior year."

He stopped rushing around the room and glanced at her. Pity mixed with guilt landed in his stomach. "Stella, it's an election year," he said gently.

"I don't give a shit if he was running for President of the United States. That prick has cheated on me for the last time."

Chance held up both hands, palms facing her. "Stella—"

"I already know what you're going to say."

"What am I going to say?"

"You're going to say last night was a mistake, and I shouldn't have come. That I should go back to my husband." Her voice was small, and her body seemed to shrink.

"That is not what I was going to say, entirely." Geoff's words from the night before about houses on fire and missing cats came into his head. He cleared his throat. "Honestly, I don't remember if we made a mistake last night, and if you don't want to go back to your husband, I will help you in any way I can. But, no, you can't stay here," he said, resignation in his voice.

Stella erupted into more of a bark than a laugh. "Don't worry. Nothing happened last night. You were way too drunk to be of any use to me. A forklift wouldn't have gotten you up. You were passed out before you could even get my bra off."

The venom stung and he closed his eyes. She was reacting to rejection, not to him. He sat there for a few moments trying to work that out.

Stella put her hand to her mouth, eyes wide. She reached out and grabbed his hand. "I'm so sorry. I don't know why I said that. Charlie, look at me, please look at me."

Chance took a second, opened his eyes, and focused on Stella.

"I'm sorry. You were so kind to me last night and sweet. I didn't mean it, I promise. I am so messed up right now." Tears formed in her eyes. Chance knew she was a first-rate actress, but could tell this was genuine.

"It's OK. I'm a little more than fucked up myself right now. I can't save you, Stell. I'm knee-deep in something I shouldn't be, and I need to extricate myself from it. It's horrible, self-destructive, and more than a little dangerous." He grit his teeth as if the words were hot coals dancing on his tongue. "I can't be the one you think will rescue you."

"That sounds more than a little delicious. Dangerous sounds fun," said Stella, tears forgotten.

"Knock it off. I'm serious. I'm not in a good position right now. I can't add the mayor's office and the entire police force to the people that want me dead if they found out you stayed here last night."

"I'm sorry. Maybe if you talk about it, I can help you," said Stella in the first voice that was her own.

"That's sweet, Stell, but I have to go deal with a thing. If you need a place to stay or something I can make a couple of calls, but—"

"I can't stay here. All right, I'll be gone by the time you get back."

He pushed down a twinge of guilt. He gave her a tight smile and started to turn around.

"But Charlie…"

He turned around and she had let the sheets drop.

"You have no idea what you just passed up."

His eyes took everything in, and he swallowed hard. "Ah fuck, Stella." He quickly walked out. As he passed the piano, he grabbed his keys, and the corners of his mouth turned upward. For the first time in a long time he'd made the hard but, hopefully, right decision.

. . .

Chance walked into the kitchen, where every cook gripped a knife in a way that had nothing to do with cooking. He raised an eyebrow at Miguel, who shrugged and pointed toward the back hallway. Chance cautiously walked past the line, where Chico sat against the wall, holding a rag to his head.

"Chico, what the hell happened?"

"Jefe, those men tried to drop off bad meat. It's spoiled, and I said no, then they do this." Chico took the rag from his head to reveal a gash that was still dripping blood.

"Shit! Miguel, take Chico to the hospital. Chico, put the rag back up, there, like that." Chance held the rag firmly.

"I can't miss work, Jefe."

"Don't worry, if this turns out like I think, you'll be getting a bonus. Tell the hospital it's under Bella's insurance. Have them call me if they have any questions. Can you stand?" Chance lifted Chico off the ground.

"Miguel, help him," barked Chance. "And when I say the hospital, I mean the *hospital*, not one of those clinics in South Milwaukee. Stay with him until he's released, or I get there."

Miguel helped Chico out the double doors. Chance's fists clenched, but he knew he needed a clear head. He took a deep breath and walked out the back doors. Two men were unloading white boxes from a delivery truck parked in the alley. About 200 steaks were stacked at the bottom of the truck's ramp. The wholesale value for that much unspoiled meat was about two grand. Since the meat was stolen, he would have paid about $500, and he would have cleared about four large. The refrigeration unit on the truck wasn't running.

Chance recognized one of the men from his younger days, and knew he wasn't the one responsible for Chico's head wound. Gary Locke was a small-time hustler that'd run trucks when nobody else was available. He didn't have the physique or moxie to be violent. Chance didn't recognize the second guy. He was as big as Chance and carried himself like a street fighter, which was why he was here. This wasn't about steaks.

Chance moved next to the two stacks of boxes. At the top of the ramp with another load on a dolly, Gary said, "Hi, Chance."

"Gary." Chance didn't take his eyes off the other guy standing near Gary. "Who's your friend?"

"He's not my friend."

"Shut up, Gary," said the second guy. Gary lowered his head.

"OK, let's do this another way. Who the fuck are you, and why did you assault one of my employees?"

The guy sneered and started down the ramp. "I didn't assault him. I was giving him some persuasion." He wore running pants and a T-shirt, with a half-zipped jacket a size too small for his large frame, under which something bulged on his left side. He stopped at the end of the ramp, within three feet of Chance.

Second mistake. The first mistake was bringing Gary as his backup.

"So, you're Chance, I got that part, but what's the problem here? We're just trying to do a delivery." The man unzipped his jacket, revealing the butt of a semi-automatic pistol hanging loose in his waistband. The guy obviously thought he could cross draw with his right hand before Chance could do anything about it. He was big, but Chance could tell he was slow. A street fighter, more brute than brains. If he had any real experience, he would've drawn the gun on the way down the ramp, but, instead, he thought the sight of the gun and tough talk would intimidate Chance. *Third mistake.* Bad guys always wanted to talk first.

"So, we got a problem, Chance?" Before he could finish the inflection in his question Chance took one step closer, grabbed the gun with his left hand, and brought his right elbow crashing into the guy's face. It wasn't enough to put him down, but it was enough to shatter his nose. With the couple of seconds, it bought him, Chance smashed the side of the gun against the man's head. The man crumpled to the ground, out cold.

Chance popped out the magazine from the gun and checked the slide. The guy didn't even have a bullet in the chamber. *Amateur.* He tossed the magazine into the dumpster and chucked the gun into the back of the truck, barely missing Gary.

"Whoa, Chance. I didn't have anything to do with the cook. That was Ralph," whined Gary.

"Gary, get down here."

"You ain't gonna hit me, are you?"

"If you make me come up there, I'm going to do a lot more than hit you."

Gary's shoulders slumped, and he walked down the ramp like he was going to his execution. Within four feet of Chance, he stopped and glanced down at Ralph's body. Ralph was still breathing, and Chance paid him no attention.

"I know what this is about, even if you don't. So, this is what I want you to do. Get these boxes back into the truck. Pick up this piece of shit, go back to Frank, and tell him I don't need any steaks right now. You think you can do that, Gary?"

"How am I going to get him back into the truck? He's gotta weigh 240, at least."

Chance considered popping Gary upside the head, but it wasn't Gary's fault, it was Frank's. "I'll send out a couple of guys to help you get beefcake back into the truck. But you're loading the fucking boxes. I don't want to catch sight of you for a while. Do I make myself clear?"

"Yeah, OK, no problem. You can count on me," said Gary, upbeat now that he wasn't going to get smacked.

Without another word, Chance turned and walked back into the restaurant to prepare for the lunch shift.

CHAPTER TWELVE

GANGSTA'S PARADISE

Frank Bartallatas sat at his Army surplus metal desk with the coldest gaze and the blackest eyes Gary had ever seen. Gary, a small fish in a big pond, was used to being scared. The sensation of impending doom never quite left him. He was always jittery, a caffeine high of fear. His blood pressure was off the charts, and a heart attack would kill him before he was fifty if some big fish didn't first.

As frightened as he was of Chance, no way did it compare to his terror now. Whatever was going on was way above his paygrade. Chance was untouchable. Nobody stole from Chance or tried to shake him down. Being the Don's nephew meant if Chance was walking down the sidewalk, you crossed to the other side of the street. So why was Mr. Bartallatas, the Don's main capo, messing with the Don's nephew? He couldn't figure it out, but whatever was going on, he was right in the middle of it.

Frank Bartallatas was pure evil in a massive frame. More than one little fish had disappeared after swimming too close to Mr. Bartallatas. Gary's voice wavered as he related the story. Two guys Gary knew of stood behind him, adding to his certainty that he was a dead man standing.

"So, let me get this straight. Chance told you he didn't want the steaks, Ralph is unconscious in the van, and you brought the van back here? The stolen van with stolen steaks. Have I got that right?" Frank's tone could have cut diamonds.

"I... I... I... wasn't sure wh... what to do, Mr. Bartallatas." The shakes started to take over Gary's body, and no matter how much swallowing he did, he couldn't get the arid dryness out of his mouth. His mind raced so fast it was just noise in his head.

"Jimmy, you and Bobby go and bring Ralph in here. Then dump the van and get back here." They were in the back office of Geno's Subs on Jackson Street. The frontage was a small shop on a street of small shops, all of which Frank owned in one way or another. "Gary, relax. I'm not going to hurt you today. Maybe tomorrow, maybe next week, but not today." Gary didn't relax, and if anything started to shake more.

"This goes in the book. Everything is in the book. You make additions and subtractions. It's simple accounting when you get down to it. Right now, you have a subtraction. Too many subtractions and not enough additions and, well..." Frank let the thought hang in the air. "You do understand what happens...?"

Gary stood there trying to come up with a right answer. He was thinking about math and books and his face wrinkled with concentration.

Frank sighed. "Gary, if you fuck up again, I'll beat you to death. You got that?"

At that point, Gary did get it. He nodded his head up and down like it was on a spring.

Jimmy and Bobby carried the still unconscious Ralph in and dropped him to the floor—a fish on a wharf, his head coated in blood.

"Hey, easy, you morons. That's Geno's cousin." The two guys shrugged like they were twins, gave the appearance of contrition, and left.

"Jesus, what a mess. Gary, run across the street to the clinic and get the doc. I don't care if he's with some patient. Tell him 'head wound' and to get over here now."

Gary turned around and almost took himself out with the side of the open door. Only his skinny frame gave him the grace to miss it head on, still smacking his arm hard.

Frank considered the unconscious Ralph. Part of him wanted to continue the beating Chance had started. To use his fists until there was nothing recognizable. But that would be a waste. And besides, it wasn't Ralph he wanted to beat to death.

He picked up the phone and dialed the number he knew by heart. It rang twice, and a familiar voice answered, "Yeah?"

"It's Frank. There's a problem with one of the soda machines, and I need to talk to the sales manager. It's costing me money. It's leaking all over the place."

"What do you mean leaking? Like leaking, leaking?" asked the deep voice.

"No, not that kind of leaking. It's not pouring right and it's costing me money."

"You sure you want to talk to the sales rep about that? He's the one who sold it to you, but shouldn't you try to work this out on your own? You know how attached to the soda machine he is."

"Giorgio, just let me talk to the sales rep!"

"OK, one hour." The line went dead.

Frank knocked on the front door of the large North Milwaukee house. It was in a Tudor style, not that Frank knew what that meant, just something he'd heard once. He adjusted his suit, having been frisked three separate times since the front gate. The door was answered by a middle-aged man wearing a dark suit. Giorgio was overweight and had heavy jowls from too much food and wine. But his eyes were clear as he assessed Frank. He opened the door all the way and let Frank pass into the foyer of dark wood. A grand chandelier hung from three stories up. The soft lighting gave the furnishings an antique glow and gave the impression that everything in there was old. Too old. *Except for this little tart,* thought Frank.

A freckled, red-haired girl of no more than sixteen stood waiting, wearing a black-and-white uniform. Frank didn't recognize her from the last time he was there. She took his coat without meeting his eyes and scurried down the hallway without a sound.

Frank glanced at Giorgio. "A new one?"

Giorgio frowned and motioned to the double doors on the left. Frank silently cursed himself for speaking first and stepped over to the dark mahogany doors. The dual door handles glowed in the soft light. It wouldn't have surprised Frank if they were solid gold.

"Frank," said Giorgio from behind him, "if you ever use my name on the telephone again..." He left the implied threat hanging in the air.

Frank turned, inspecting Giorgio. He took his measure and found it wanting. *Like everything else in this fucking castle.*

Frank's face softened a hint. "I'm sorry, Giorgio, you're right, that was a stupid mistake. It won't happen again." He only marginally kept the scorn out of his voice. He turned and opened the double doors to another room filled with old things.

Old things should be in a museum. The large grandfather clock was always a minute or two behind. The collection of antique pistols hanging on the wall would jam if you tried to fire them. Everything in this room was past its prime. Including the old thing behind the desk staring at him.

Vinnie Carmelo—Uncle Vinnie—was not what you would expect from a mob boss. His frame appeared emaciated, his skin almost translucent, as if he'd never seen the sun. A body on display at a funeral home, his black hair long and dull; his lips had a blueish tinge and his cheeks were too red, like the mortician had over-applied rouge. Frank wondered where the oxygen tank he'd heard about was.

Uncle Vinnie might have been handsome back in the day, but now he was just a creepy old man who liked young girls and a lot of old junk.

But you don't get to be where Uncle Vinnie was without knowing how to kick ass and chew gum. He wasn't a fool, and more than a few people, exactly where Frank was now, found out this fact a second or two before the lights went out.

Frank knew to be careful. He approached the desk and nodded. It wasn't the movies, where you would go around the desk, get on one knee, and kiss the ring. That was a Hollywood thing. Uncle Vinnie wasn't a bishop or the pope. Catholics take religion—in theory, if not in practice—seriously. The real sign of respect was standing until invited to sit and not speaking until asked to.

Uncle Vinnie glanced up from some papers he was reading. He peered past Frank to Giorgio and nodded. Frank tensed but forced himself not to show any reaction. *Just a test,* he thought. Odds were he wasn't about to be whacked. But in this life, it was always a possibility. He heard a drawer open and close, and it took every ounce of control not to glance behind him. The brush of Giorgio's feet on the oriental carpet made his spine tingle, and his muscles contract. He almost jumped when Giorgio pushed an envelope against his chest.

"That's the info on a county clerk in West Allis who needs an adjustment. She's said no once. Make sure it's not twice," said Giorgio in hushed tones.

Uncle Vinnie nodded again and Giorgio, as quiet as his 300 pounds could manage, left the room. As the door closed, Uncle Vinnie considered Frank.

"Frances, please, where are my manners? Sit, sit," said Uncle Vinnie in a voice much stronger than his frame suggested.

These are the games people play, thought Frank. As much as he thought he'd be different when he was in charge, he knew he already wasn't. It was like a teenager swearing they would be different from their parents. How they'd be so much better. Then they have kids and wake up one day and find out they're the same.

It was all about power. In this lifestyle, you used violence to get power. Once in power, you used fear to keep people in line, information to know when they were out of line, and violence to resolve any problem. That's how the system worked. Frank was no historian, but he knew this was how it'd been done since the first monkey picked up a rock and killed another monkey.

"Frances, I need to apologize to you. I understand there have been some difficulties in your crew, and I haven't been as helpful to you as I could have been." Uncle Vinnie put his hand over his heart as if he was in pain.

Frank knew what was coming and could do nothing to stop it. It was the wrong move to come here. He should have asked Sloan before making the call. *Stupid, stupid, stupid!*

"I have been remiss, and I apologize to you. I know dealing with my nephew can sometimes be difficult. I know you two have a history, some past run-ins. I understand how having one toe in the big pool and one toe in the children's pool can be frustrating. Honestly, there was a time I wanted him to swim over to our side." Uncle Vinnie's eyes peered up to the ceiling.

"But I promised his mother, God rest her soul, that I would keep him out, and I intend to keep that promise." His eyes bore straight into Frank's. "He is a civilian. He doesn't understand everything the way you and I do."

Uncle Vinnie picked up a framed picture of Chance's mother and handed it to Frank. It was a black-and-white photo of a beautiful young girl in a 1940's-era summer dress, squinting into the sun and holding a string of grapes up toward the camera.

"That was the summer before I left for America. It was not a good time to be a young boy in Italia. The fascists were in power and the devil Mussolini was systematically killing everyone that had belonged to the Italian Socialist Party. My father was a farmer, but an ardent supporter of the PSI. He, in his wisdom, knew it was only a matter of time. He got me out and to America. That picture was how I remembered her. It would be twenty years before I saw her again. She showed up in Milwaukee, married to an alcoholic Scot. But you know that already."

Frank studied the photo and noticed the characteristics Chance had inherited from his mother. Back when they'd been friends, his first crush had been on Chance's mother. He handed the photo back to Uncle Vinnie and sat back in the chair.

"You're wondering why I showed you that photo. It's simple, really. Family is everything. It's why we do what we do. Why we toil so hard for so long. To protect and care for our families. You have a son." Uncle Vinnie held up his hand as if to stop Frank from protesting. "An estranged son, I understand, but family, nonetheless. Now in a different way you are part of my family. I haven't protected you. I haven't cared for you as I should. That's why I have you in my home. To show you how important family is. So, you understand what a man has to and will do to honor his family." Uncle Vinnie leaned back in his chair, brought his hands together, almost in prayer.

"Frank, you've been a good earner. Good for the family. I won't be around forever. Don't make me choose between the future and family. Make peace with Charles." Uncle Vinnie's eyes bore into Frank.

With some unseen signal, the door behind him opened, and Giorgio stepped back into the room. Frank knew enough to not say anything. He nodded and walked toward the door with the envelope.

"Frances..."

Frank stopped and turned.

"Knowing why there is a question before you ask the question is more important than knowing what the answer is before you get the answer. You cannot truly have the last until you have the first."

Whatever that fucking means, thought Frank as he stepped out of the room.

Frank threw the envelope on the passenger seat and slammed the car door. The violence within him erupted, and he beat the steering wheel. Panting and sweating, he knew he'd made a big mistake. Understanding brought forth another burst of rage. What he needed was a face to smash in, not his own car. He could get a couple of rounds in at the gym. But the texture of hitting a man with gloves on wasn't going to give him the release he needed. There was another place, an underground club out in the burbs where nobody would know him, in the basement of an abandoned bottling plant. This time of day there would be a few guys sitting around waiting for a fight.

He parked at the nearest gas station and went into the phone booth, inserting quarters and dialing a number he knew by heart.

"Ya."

"Junior. That little bird you told me about working for you. The one close to the pepperoni cannoli." "Pepperoni cannoli" was code for Chance. One summer when they were teens, after Chance's father had died, to help make ends meet, Chance would sell them outside of pubs near the breweries. Frank could never get the nickname to stick, despite how much he'd tried.

"Ya."

"Squeeze him a bit. I need info on how to meet the man at a time he might not expect. Got that?"

"Ya."

"We're almost there, son. Have your guys ready." He hung up and checked the coin return, just in case.

Frank returned to his car and sat thinking about what his meeting with Vinnie had cost him. First off, it had cost him this extra bullshit intimidation job on some bitch clerk. Something for a soldier to handle, but he couldn't farm this out. That insult would normally be enough for him to break someone in half, but it was only the surface damage. Far more expensive was the ruling that he'd been at fault for putting Geno in charge of what should have been an easy and lucrative business. He wasn't running things correctly. But, even worse, he wasn't gonna get tapped to take over for Uncle Vinnie. Sloan was right. His lips tightened, as his meeting with Chicago was no longer exploratory. No matter what the price, it was a go.

CHAPTER THIRTEEN

I FOUGHT THE LAW

Mitchell Genovese sat at his desk, eyes closed, headphones covering his ears. Another lawyer on his team sat directly across from him, tapping his pencil on a notepad to the beat of "I Shot the Sheriff." As the Assistant U.S. District Attorney for the Great Lakes District, it was Mitchell's happy task to bring down the Carmelo crime family. Genovese had successfully prosecuted three top underbosses from the Porrello crime family in Cleveland. His bosses had then moved his talents to Milwaukee, where organized crime reached deep into the MPD, high-ranking city and state officials, hundreds of local businesses, and, if the rumors were true, into this very office. That was one of the reasons all the blinds were down as he listened to the newest batch of recordings. They were slightly muffled, but the voices were clear enough.

"Yeah?"

"It's Frank. There's a problem with one of the soda machines, and I need to talk to the sales manager. It's costing me money. It's leaking all over the place."

"What do you mean leaking? Like leaking, leaking?"

"No, not that kind of leaking. It's not pouring right and it's costing me money."

"You sure you want to talk to the sales rep about that? He's the one that sold it to you, but shouldn't you try to work this out on your own? You know how attached to the soda machine he is."

"Giorgio, just let me talk to the sales rep!"

"OK, one hour."

Mitchell took off the headphones and laid them on the desk. He rubbed his eyes. He eyed his assistant and nodded. "It will never cease to amaze me how fucking stupid these guys are."

His assistant offered no opinion, but got his pencil ready.

"So, this confirms what I saw the other night. It can only be Chance he's talking about."

His assistant checked his notes. "It certainly confirms what the informant said. And now that we have Giorgio confirmed on the recording, we can go back and cross reference every mention of the sales rep to being Uncle Vinnie as well."

"Yeah. More important, this proves the informant is legit, and not all is well in Frank's world. I think he's going to move up his timetable. We need to get somebody on Chance. If this goes down the way I think it will..." Mitchell paused to consider his options. "I want him protected at all times." Chance wasn't the only one whose family was in organized crime. Mitchell had been dealing with the gossip, frosty looks, and mistrust throughout his entire professional career.

His assistant's face curdled like he had tasted something bitter.

Mitchell held up his hand. "I know he isn't squeaky clean, but I know he isn't 'in' either. Until I ascertain any evidence that says otherwise, he's a civilian."

"Yes sir. I know he's your friend. But sir... we're stretched wafer thin as it is, and the overtime alone is going to crush our budget."

"Yes, but this is going to break. I can feel it. The protection doesn't have to start today. Beginning of next week should be fine. Pull a couple of agents out of Cleveland. They aren't doing anything there now, anyway."

"Yes, sir."

"How long until we get the info on the print we lifted off the informant's package?"

Bob checked his notes. "If there's a hit in the database, should be any day."

"Thanks, Bob. This is good. Nice work."

"Thank you, sir." Bob got up and left.

Mitchell sat back in his chair and let out a deep breath. Their informant was a possible godsend. Despite what he had said, these people were not stupid. Frank's mistake on the phone was the exception. These guys were disciplined, tightly held from the top all the way down to the soldiers and even dealers. In the year Mitchell had been trying to build a case, they had exactly shit. They had only managed to turn one low-level soldier early on, and they still were finding parts of his body throughout the city.

Out of nowhere, an informant had contacted him. The informant seemed well placed, which made Mitchell suspicious. People didn't suddenly turn on everyone they knew, offering to hand a violent criminal organization up on a silver platter. In his experience, they had to be threatened, coerced, or bribed.

The fact that the informant didn't want anything—not witness protection, money, or fame—made Mitchell take what they said with a bucket of salt. He could only speculate on their motives, but whatever they were, Christmas had come early for Mitchell and his investigation.

The thought of Christmas made Mitchell glance at the black-and-white photograph he kept on his desk. A typical American family: his parents, sister and a young scowling version of himself. On Christmas morning that year, he had come downstairs, giddy with a child's excitement at what Santa had brought for him.

What he found instead of a Red Ryder BB gun was the body of his father: piano wire wrapped around his neck, one eyeball dislocated from its socket. A jaded crime beat reporter from the *Milwaukee Sentinel* had dubbed it "The Stocking Stuffer Murder." Another unsolved mob murder. After a week, nobody cared.

Mitchell and Frank shared one thing. They both wanted to talk to the "sales manager." But Mitchell didn't want to talk about soda machines. He wanted to talk about pianos.

CHAPTER FOURTEEN

WHEN DOVES CRY

Winnie and Chance exited the Lakeside Cinema into the chilly spring air. Chance lit a cigarette, the smoke rising between the marquee's hundreds of lightbulbs.

"What did you think?" asked Chance as they walked to his car.

"That movie was so totally rad! That was exactly why I love movies. Totally forget for a couple of hours. Sean Connery was amazing."

"'Totally rad,' huh? You mean it was groovy."

Winnie smiled back at Chance. "No, I mean it was choice."

Chance waved his hand in a half circle. "Yeah, it was far out."

"Like totally tubular."

"Primo."

"Gnarly."

"Yeah, but can you dig it?"

"To the max."

Chance waved both hands in the air. "All right, kid, I concede." Chance unlocked his car's passenger door. "Don't get any ideas that just because I opened your door, you're getting a second date."

Winnie chuckled and climbed in. Chance walked around the car, took one more drag, tossed his cigarette butt into the street, and climbed in. "That scene when the sub flew out of the water was so cool."

Winnie put his seatbelt on. "Yeah, that was great. The last two movies I've seen were with Alex. We saw *Pretty Woman* and *Pretty Woman*, so this was awesome."

"You want to grab a butter burger at Culver's?"

"That'd be cool, Mr. C. I love Culver's."

They drove for a couple of minutes in reflective silence. Winnie spoke up first.

"I thought they did a good job of adapting the book," Winnie said. "Normally when they make a movie out of a book I like, they screw it up."

"You read a lot?"

"Two or three books a week, I guess. Don't sleep well, so I read instead."

Chance turned on the heater and the smell of cigarettes blew from the vents. "So, Win, I've been meaning to ask you. Are you and Alex dating? Tell me to mind my own business if you want."

"No, I mean, yes, it's fine, and no, we're not dating," Winnie said in a small voice.

"But you want to."

Winnie stared out the window. Chance thought he might have pushed it too far, too fast.

"Can I ask you a question?" Winnie didn't wait for a response. "How do you know if, when you love someone, have loved them for years, what your feeling is? You know, romantic love and not just friendship love?"

"Easy. Do you get butterflies when you first see them each day?"

"Like crazy butterflies."

"Then it's romantic love."

Winnie seemed to chew on that for a minute. "Alex can be hard to read. Like really hot and cold. But lately she's been distant. At first, I thought it was because of my dad. But now I'm not so sure."

"Friendships are like any other relationships. Sometimes they hit a rough patch. Usually communication is in the mix somewhere." Chance pulled into the Culver's parking lot and parked next to the blue-and-white sign.

"Like the other day I got done telling her Mrs. White's story—"

"Mrs. White?"

"She's a waitress at Country Kitchen, and she lost both her sons in Vietnam. Anyway, I told Alex the story and she started to cry. Afterward she barely said two words to me the rest of the night."

"Sounds like a haunting story. How were you feeling?"

Winnie thought about it. "I wanted to take care of Alex. I wanted to hold her and protect her."

"And did you?"

"Well, no, we both sat there. Alex doesn't, you know, hug and stuff."

"Is it possible a hug is exactly what she might have wanted?"

"I don't know. I usually know what Alex is thinking. Lately I seem to always get it wrong."

"Winnie, sometimes people don't know what they want or what they need, but they definitely know when they aren't getting it."

"Are you saying she wanted me to hold her?" He shifted in the seat.

"I don't know. I wasn't there, and I'm not Alex. But after an extremely emotional story, in which Alex was engaged, hence the crying, she was sitting with her best friend in all the world. But when she didn't get what she needed she became cold and distant. What would you want in a situation like that?"

"I would have wanted to be held." Winnie playfully smacked himself in the forehead.

Chance laughed. "Come on, I'm hungry. Let's go get a butter burger."

CHAPTER FIFTEEN

FAITHFULLY

Alex stood in front of the blank canvas awaiting inspiration. On a good day, the brush had a mind of its own, and she was its instrument. But now, she had nothing. She'd been on a dry spell for weeks... her mind always drifting back to that place and time.

In her head she referred to it as "the Event." She could unlock it, take it out and examine it, without having to experience it. Events happened every day, to people all over the world. Some good, some bad. Things just happened.

Most of the time in the light of day she could detach and examine the choices that put her in the car. Her flawed judgement and need for acceptance had her saying "yes" to parking in the alley *even though she knew* what he was expecting. The fact that she didn't even like him made her second guess all her choices.

She threw the brush down in frustration and sat in the middle of the room. When she was twelve, her papa had converted the attic into a half studio-half family room with a TV and VCR for her and her friends. She grabbed Monkey and took out her cigarette roller. After lighting her cigarette, she reached back inside Monkey and pulled out a small bottle of cheap vodka. She took a swig, scanned the room, and took a second one. She put the cap back on and shoved the bottle back into Monkey.

In high school she had been parking a few times. She would kiss, which sometimes was nice, sometimes not. She would allow for touching over the clothes, and once under the clothes. They would beg but she'd say "no." They'd whine, she'd say "no," and eventually they'd take her home. She didn't love them, and despite what they said in the moment, she knew they didn't love her. But somehow, somewhere, the rules had changed, and nobody had warned her.

After the Event, she started having a recurring dream of being buried alive. The earth was dark and moist, permeated with the smell of mushrooms and alive with creepy crawlies tap-dancing over her flesh. She couldn't breathe or open her eyes. She'd always wake up panting, nauseous, her pajamas soaked with sweat.

During the Event she'd kicked and punched, scratched and screamed, for all the good it did. But she wondered if Jed was right. Had she saved herself? Jed had been the one to pull the boy off her. Beating the shit out of him as she scrambled to fix her clothes.

She took a deep breath and realized she was standing; in her right hand was the brush and in her left the palette. An electric shock went through her body as she peered at the canvas. She stepped back. The canvas resembled a picture of the earth's layered crust, like she might see in science class. The top layer was on fire. Swaths of crimson, ruby, peach, rust, and carmine. Each layer under it grew darker and darker until at the bottom, surrounded by black, was a naked, pale-skinned woman. Legs spread, arms together above her head, which was turned in an unnatural position, her neck clearly broken.

Alex half sat, half fell to the floor, legs tucked beneath her. She brought her hands to her face and cried.

CHAPTER SIXTEEN

HOLDING OUT FOR A HERO

Back at the restaurant, Chance called and confirmed that Chico was going to be fine. He opened one of the filing cabinets and took out the file on Maggie Edwards. He picked up the phone and dialed the number. After three rings, a little girl's voice answered.

"Hello, Edwards residence, Cassie speaking."

"Hello, Cassie, this is Chance speaking."

"Chance!" Then, not speaking into the phone, "Mommy, it's Uncle Chance!" Then back into the phone, "Chance, when are you going to take me to the zoo?"

"The zoo, honey? Why the zoo?"

"'Cause Melody's uncle took her to the zoo last weekend, and she got a stuffed giraffe named Fido, and Uncle Geoff said he couldn't take me 'cause you work him too much, but you could take me."

"Humm, Uncle Geoff said that, did he?"

"Ahun, he said you would buy me a gorilla since you re... re... late to them."

Chance chortled. "Well, he's probably right. Cassie, is your mom around?"

"OK," she said, her voice getting quiet.

"Honey, what's wrong?"

In a hushed whisper: "Daddy's here. He's mad again."

The sound of her fear broke his heart. "Sweet girl, I promise I'll take you to the zoo soon, since mean Uncle Geoff won't do it, but it's important right now that I talk to your mommy."

"Promise," she said in a whisper.

"We'll go and see the monkeys, tigers, lions, giraffes, and hippos. And if you're good I'll feed you all the ice cream you can eat."

"Oh, Uncle Chance, they don't make enough ice cream for how good I can be."

He laughed again and a dial tone told him she'd hung up the phone. He redialed the number and pulled on the cord to untangle it as he started to pace around his office. He heard muffled voices and Maggie's exasperated voice.

"Chance, this isn't a good time right now."

"Maggie, I want you to answer yes or no. Is he there?"

There was a pause at the other end. "Yes."

"Do you want him there?"

"No," she breathed.

"Are you sure? 'Cause if you want him to never come back, I can make it happen. But you have to know for sure." After a second, he realized it wasn't a yes or no question.

"No."

"No, you are not sure, or, no, you don't want him there?" Chance was frustrated with his own stupid code of questions.

"Yes."

"OK, hold on, do you want him gone?"

"Yes!"

"OK, this is what you're going to do. You're going to tell him you have to take Cassie to the babysitter's, and you have to go to work. There's a big reservation that asked for you, and it means a $300 tip. Put on your uniform and bring Cassie here to the restaurant. Geoff will be here, and I don't want you to leave 'till I get back here. Do you understand?"

"Yes… that's fine, boss. If they requested me, I guess I'll have to do it."

"I'll see you here."

In the parking lot, Chance had backed Gracie in, not an easy thing to do in this size of a lot. It was one of those rare spring days in Milwaukee when it would reach sixty degrees after weeks of near-freezing temperatures. Everyone would be in shorts and T-shirts, even though it wasn't yet warm out.

He thought about Maggie. She'd worked for him for a couple of years and was one of his best employees. If you could make allowances for unexpected kid issues, single mothers were hands-down the best hires. They were driven, had the best guest-check averages, and usually didn't participate in the extracurricular activities that caused missed shifts and emotional drama.

She was waifish but lovely, and her maternal instincts were appealing to him. But he'd never gone there. Maggie was the type of woman you married, not messed around with. Plus, he had a rule to never date staff. Again.

He stopped at Liquor Lyle's to pick up a six-pack of Miller High Life bottles, but on second thought grabbed cans instead.

Driving past the historic Third Ward made him think of his childhood. He'd run with a bunch of toughs in his early teens, among them Frank Bartallatas. They ran numbers, did small-time hustles, and hosted dice games, nothing major. Kid stuff. Chance was so bad at hosting dice games; all the other kids knew they had a chance if you played with his dice—hence his nickname.

He pulled up to Maggie's apartment complex. Shady Trees Apartments had about ten trees. The paint, old and chipping, was a flat mustard color, and the cars under the covered parking were at least ten years old; he doubted many of them ran. He parked in a spot marked "Future Tenants." Grabbing the six-pack, he found building B, avoiding the randomly placed Big Wheels and kids' bikes, and walked up three flights. At the top, he bent over and took a second to catch his breath. It would be bad to get to the door out of breath when trying to intimidate someone.

The door was shit brown, but had a doormat with sunflowers on it, reading, "Welcome Friends." He took a deep breath and knocked. He heard what sounded like a soap opera from the TV inside. He knocked again louder.

"Hold on, goddammit!"

He knocked a third time, even louder.

A disheveled man in shorts but no shirt opened the door. He was unshaven, scrawny, and eyes were bloodshot. "What the fuck do you want?"

"For you." Chance threw the six-pack at Tom.

Tom let go of the door to catch the six-pack with both hands right as Chance kicked him square in the balls. Tom doubled over, his head smacking the doorframe. The six-pack

landed underneath him, one of the cans exploding white foam.
Tom lay prostrate in a puddle of beer.

Chance checked Tom's pulse, glanced about for witnesses,
and pulled Tom's unconscious body inside, closing the door
behind them. The living room and kitchen were connected in
the small apartment. A giant fake wood 1970's entertainment
center held a TV and record player; it must have weighed
500 pounds, and Chance wondered how Maggie had gotten
it up three flights of stairs. An overflowing ashtray and eight
or nine empty beer cans littered the coffee table, which
matched the secondhand couch. The tan carpet was worn in
high-traffic areas. The living room walls were white but at
an arbitrary point turned rust brown going into the kitchen.
Except for Tom's mess, the dump of a place was clean, neat,
and uncluttered.

Chance picked Tom up easily and laid him on the
couch. He walked down the small hallway and peeked into
the bathroom, tastefully decorated, with a small oil painting
of sunflowers. The shower curtain was see-through, and he
couldn't help but imagine Maggie in the shower, an outline
of peach through clear plastic. The thought left as fast as
it came.

He expected the wave of pink in Cassie's neat room:
pink walls, pink bedspreads, pink pillows, pink and white
stuffed animals. On the pink dresser were a few pictures: one
of a younger Maggie, wearing a college sweatshirt, standing
in front of the UWWI sign. A classic first day of college
picture, probably taken by a proud mom or dad. Maggie's hair
was teased up in the front like many 80's girls managed with
unlimited supplies of Aqua Net. Chance had hated it. The

hairspray formed droplets in their hair, crunchy to the touch. When he kissed a girl's ear, he tasted hairspray. Her brown eyes were squinting in the sun. She had a fresh, farm girl glow.

A second picture surprised him. Maggie wore a cute yellow summer dress, Geoff on her left in his classic military haircut, Cassie in front, younger than she was now, her eyes not tracking the camera but gazing off. And Chance was on the right, his arm around Maggie, his other hand on Cassie's shoulder. He covered Geoff with a hand, transforming it into a picture of the perfect family.

This must have been taken at last summer's employee barbecue party, but Chance didn't remember the photo. Not too surprising, considering how drunk he got. His shoulders slumped. Everyone talked about the great party and how much fun it was. But most of it was a blur to him.

In Maggie's room, there was a four-poster bed and a few more oil paintings of Van Gogh-style flowers. The bed was made but on the right-side Chance found what he was searching for: an open gym bag with men's clothes stuffed inside. In the bathroom, he grabbed the toiletries off the sink and stuffed them into the bag.

Back in the living room, he cleaned up the spilled beer and put four of the remaining cans in the refrigerator. He tapped the last can over the sink before opening it; only a small amount of foam leaked out, and he swallowed half the can in three gulps.

He didn't know much about Tom except that he'd married Maggie after she already had Cassie. Tom wasn't Cassie's father, so Chance wondered what Maggie had ever seen in the degenerate gambler and alcoholic. He finished the beer and

116 I MATTHEW E. WHEELER

put the can in the garbage under the sink. He grabbed another beer and returned to the living room.

He propped Tom up and shook him, then slapped him a couple of times.

"Tom, wake up." A bruise on Tom's forehead had started to form. It was going to be an ugly knot for a while. Tom stirred, consciousness slowly returning. He groaned and curled into a fetal position. "What the fuck," he mumbled, groaning.

"Come on, buddy, get up. You had a nasty fall, but stop whining." Chance propped Tom back up.

"What... what happened?" Tom's eyes popped open and he glanced around wildly, as if not sure where the hell he was.

"I need you to focus. I don't have a lot of time to waste here, so get it together. Here's a beer." Tom focused at the distinct sound of the beer can opening in front of him. He sat up and reached out, missing the can the first two times.

Chance grabbed Tom's hand and put the can in it. "Drink this."

Tom took a long pull on the beer, belched, and focused on Chance. "Who the fuck are you, and what the hell are you doing in my house?"

"It's your ex-wife's apartment, and I'm her boss. You may not remember, but we've met."

Recognition appeared in Tom's eyes. And he started turning green.

Shit! Chance ran to the kitchen for the garbage can and made it back in time to shove Tom's head in the bag as he threw up.

"Shit, Tom, really?"

Tom lifted his head out of the garbage can.

"You all right now? You're not going to puke again, are you?"

Tom wiped his mouth with his hand. "I'm OK."

Chance removed the bag from the can, tied it up, and set it outside the front door. An old woman from across the hall was standing in her doorway. She had curlers in her hair, and for some reason a sheet of plastic over her head. She wore a baby blue bathrobe and matching slippers.

"Are you going to kill him?"

"Thinking about it."

"Good. Man ain't no good." She picked up the cat rubbing her leg and shut the door.

He cleared a spot on the coffee table, sat down and stared at Tom; Tom looked everywhere except at Chance.

"Tom, look at me. Do you know who I am now? I'm not going to ask you again."

Tom peeked at Chance, then turned away.

Chance gave him an open-handed smack across the face.

Tom cried out and covered his face with his hands.

"Tom, you're a bully of women. You're a drunk and a complete loser. And I'm going to keep smacking you until you tell me if you know who I am." Chance stood.

"I know, I know, all right! Fuck! You didn't have to hit me."

"Please, I barely smacked you. Listen up. You know who I am, and you know who my family is. You get one opportunity to do the right thing. One chance only. Are you listening?"

"I'm listening, I'm listening." Tom's voice shook.

"There are some things I need you to do for me." Chance walked into the kitchen and returned with a large knife. Tom's eyes became as big as walnuts.

"I... I... I... won't touch her again. I promise, I promise. I'm sorry. God I'm so sorry." He started to cry.

Chance examined both sides of the knife as if he'd never seen one before. "Stop crying. I need you to help me out."

Tom perked, snot running out of his nose. "Anything. I can do it."

"I don't want you around anymore. I don't want you in Milwaukee. I don't want to have to think about you ever again. I don't want Maggie to ever see or hear from you again. I'm going to give you a chance to start over somewhere else. Do you understand what I'm saying to you?"

"Umm, no?" squeaked Tom.

Chance sighed. "Tom, pay attention. What's a city you've never been to in the United States that you've always wanted to discover? It's not a trick question."

Tom thought. "Umm, Florida?"

"Florida is a state, not a city, but close enough. You're leaving for Florida today. You're taking a permanent vacation to The Sunshine State. Lucky you. If you think about it in the right way, you've won The Showcase Showdown."

Tom sat there, confused. Chance stood and reached into his pocket, pulling out a roll of cash and counting out five hundred-dollar bills. He extended them to Tom, who sat staring at the money.

"I need your monkey-sized brain to come to terms with this faster. Leave for Florida today with this money. If you come back, this knife will be the last thing you ever see. 'Cause I'll cut off your balls right before I cut your throat. Understand?"

Tom nodded.

"Say you understand, Tom."

"I understand, Tom."

Chance smacked him again, harder. "Are you fucking stupid, or are you getting cute with me?"

"I... I'm sorry, I swear I wasn't. I understand I will leave town and never come back. Sunshine State, tonight. I promise, Chance. Please, don't hit me again."

"Good. Go wash your face and put a shirt and shoes on. We're leaving. Everything you're taking with you is in this bag. Don't grab anything else. And hurry up."

At the Greyhound station, Chance watched Tom buy a one-way ticket to Daytona Beach. A shithole if Chance ever knew one. Perfect for a shithead.

Tom showed his ticket to Chance, proud of himself like he'd just peed standing up for the first time. "I got it, Chance!"

"Great." Chance rolled his eyes. "Listen, I have a couple of friends who are going to watch you when you get off the bus in Daytona. They'll keep an eye on you. If you leave Florida for any reason, a week, a month, or years from now... Pop!"

Tom jumped. But Chance could see that the fear Tom had earlier was already dissipating. Chance thought about the other night with Geoff. He dropped his voice an octave. "I've done you this favor, Tom. Perhaps, some day I will need a favor from you. This is an offer you cannot refuse."

Tom's eyes narrowed. "Wait a second. Wasn't that from *The Godfather*?"

Chance grabbed Tom by the neck. "Get on the fucking bus, Tom. Get out of my sight."

"OK. OK. I'm going."

Tom boarded the bus, and Chance watched it pull away. The stink of diesel fuel and cigarettes filled the air.

He would never have followed up on his threats. He would have beat the shit out of Tom, but Chance knew it wouldn't have done any good. You don't make a bad dog better by kicking the shit out of them. They just get meaner.

He stood there a moment, enjoying the power. It was more than doing something good for someone he cared about. He took a cigarette out and brought it up to his mouth. He grabbed his lighter, but paused in thought. Tom, a lowlife, was afraid. Fear Chance had given him. That his family name brought on. There was something attractive about it. Power. He shook his head. He walked over to the payphone, dropped a quarter and dialed.

"Ya," said Giorgio.

"Hey Gio—" Chance stopped himself, remembering his uncle's warning about phones.

"It's," he looked around and rolled his eyes. "Pepperoni Cannoli."

"Who?"

"Fuck off fat man. You know who." Chance heard laughing on the line.

"Yeah, I just wanted to make you say it again. What do ya need?"

Chance took a breath. Looked around the station. He covered the mouthpiece with both hands, extending his arms. He moved it back and stopped for a second. Then put the receiver back to his ear.

"Hello?" asked Giorgio.

"I want to see. I want to see what we are talking about here. What goes on," said Chance.

He could hear muffled voices as if Giorgio had covered the phone.

"Yeah, OK. Meet me at Olive's in an hour. I'll give ya a tour."

"OK," Chance started to reply but he was met with a dial tone. He hung up and lit up a cigarette.

"I can't believe I'm even considering this," he said to nobody.

CHAPTER SEVENTEEN

TAKE THE MONEY AND RUN

Giorgio pulled up to the liquor store and turned off the car.

"To be honest, I haven't had to do this in years, but you wanted to see some of the stuff your uncle is into. No bullshit, right?"

Chance turned his glance from the store to Giorgio. "Yeah. I wanna know what I'd be getting myself into. I need to understand this."

They'd left Chances car at Olive's Italian restaurant. His uncle's favorite place to eat. This was their third stop on the tour.

"Fine. So, the first two places were easy. Regular customers for years. This one is new."

Chance got out of the car and watched as Giorgio struggled to get himself out, the car visibly rising in relief as the heavy burden exited. Giorgio got to the curb and buttoned his suit coat. He took a handkerchief out of his pocket and wiped his face. Chance wondered if he'd have to perform CPR at some point during this excursion.

"When we get in there, just like before, stand behind me and don't speak. There is a moment in their eyes when they want to say no. The job of a good collector is to make them pass over that moment so quick they don't even realize they thought it." Giorgio stuffed the handkerchief back in his pocket. "You don't want doubt. You don't want trouble. You want this as easy as paying the electric bill. You ask them if they've had any trouble, real caring like. Remind them it's a service. There's value here." He put his girthy hand on Chance's back. "Also, if they got paying customers, we wait our turn. Respect them. They'll respect you."

"So, it's not like in the movies, where you walk in with a baseball bat?" asked Chance.

"If it gets to that point, you've not done your job right. They already know what the stick is. You've got to remind them of the carrot." Giorgio looked down the street. He held up his arm and pointed down the block.

"What do you see here?" he asked.

Chance looked where Giorgio was pointing.

"Or better yet, what don't you? No bums on the street with their shopping carts. No derelict cars. No groups of hoodlums crowding out street corners. No busted-out windows or graffiti along the buildings. Now you tell me anywhere else in the city you see that. That's your uncle, and that's what he does for these businesses. That's why they pay every week."

Giorgio gestured to the storefront and Chance opened the door. Rows and rows of bottles lined the shelves. Browns with browns, clear liquor with clear. Various neon beer signs lit up the walls. An old Asian woman stood behind the counter with a clipboard in her hand. She was using a pencil to count packs of cigarettes. A boy, ten or eleven, stood behind the register. As recognition came in the boy's eyes, something flashed across his face, but disappeared just as quickly. The boy's hand reached over and pulled on the flower print dress. The woman yanked the dress back visibly irritated. Then she noticed Giorgio, and a hint of tension rose up her back. Chance stood behind Giorgio as he walked up to the counter. The woman put the clipboard down and dropped her hands to her sides. Her head bowed to the point where her chin was on her chest.

"Good morning, Mrs. Lee. How's business?"

The woman looked at the kid, who Chance assumed was the translator. The kid spoke rapidly, and the woman nodded. She responded to Giorgio, still staring at the ground. Firing off, she animatedly pointed at the window and shook her head repeatedly. Her eyes never coming off the floor.

"My grandma says greetings, sir. Business is good, but somebody smashed all of our windows on Sunday night."

"You don't say," said Giorgio.

The boy hung his head as he finished. Chance watched him. There was a quiver in his voice. Something mechanical or scripted, yet nervous.

Giorgio leaned forward with his arm braced on the edge of the counter. "Ask your grandmother if she called to report it?"

"I did sir. I called the police and reported it. But they still haven't come."

Giorgio stood up straight and looked back at Chance. His lips were tight, and his eyes were bunched in either annoyance or anger. He looked back at the grandma.

"That's because the cops don't care about you boat people. Now I told you to call us if there was a problem. You didn't call us, and you still have a problem. Two problems actually."

The woman finally looked at the boy as he translated. She nodded to the ground. Everybody just stood there. The boy and old woman, hands together, head bowed. Giorgio with his arms crossed. After thirty seconds the old woman shook her head a few times. A look flashed on the kid's face. Fear, but fear mixed with outrage.

Giorgio took a step towards the counter and both the old woman and boy visibly flinched, taking a step back. "You don't need to pay this week. Talk to your neighbors. Talk to the other business owners. I'll give ya a few days. But the next time you got a promise you call us." He pointed at the large window.

"Like we told you. These are the kinda problems we care about. You running a successful business. Cops don't care about that. But we do." As the kid translated, Giorgio grabbed a Snickers bar from the display. He ripped off the wrapper and took half of it in his mouth. Looking back a Chance while he was chewing, he reached into his pocket and dropped a ten-dollar bill on the counter.

"Keep it," he said in a muffled voice.

As Giorgio turned to walk out, the kid looked up, tears welling in his eyes. He grabbed and hugged his grandma. Chance took a step for the door, turned and looked back at the kid. Wet-faced rage looked back at him. Chance wondered if that was the carrot, what was the stick? He walked out of the store, and as Giorgio got in the car, the frame visibly lowered onto the tires. Chance decided he could completely relate to the car.

Chance came out of the disgusting bathroom, again thankful he was only drinking and not eating here. It was early for dinner, but Giorgio wasn't one to miss a meal. Chance sat back down at the table. He poured from a bottle of 1980 Sassicaia Super Tuscan, into his glass. At least they managed to have good wine. He looked at Giorgio, a napkin was tucked into his shirt like a bib. Using a chunk of bread, he was mopping up any remaining red sauce left in the oversized bowl.

Giorgio, for as long as Chance had known him, always claimed he was on a diet, even when his actions and immense girth showed otherwise. Beads of perspiration pooled on his forehead and ran down his jaw, which were grinding away at anything not nailed to the table.

Chance sat, picked up the glass, and brought it to his nose. "Giorgio, what is it with this place and my uncle? I'm starting to take it personally."

"Your place is great, but your uncle thinks it too expensive."

"Seriously? He's worth millions and my place is too expensive?"

Giorgio pointed the chuck of bread with red sauce falling off it at Chance.

"That's exactly why he's a millionaire. Besides the owner of this place saved your uncle's life once. It's about loyalty. No offense but you're only his nephew. And kind of a pain in the butt."

Giorgio raised his own glass and swallowed about forty dollars' worth of wine in one gulp. He smacked his lips together, then scanned the table as if to confirm there was nothing else edible. "We need a decision, Charlie. I'm here to guide you and help you make it."

"Are you threatening me?"

Giorgio raised his hands in protest. "I'm here to help. I don't threaten, I support. But your uncle doesn't have long."

Giorgio glanced up to the ceiling and crossed himself. He focused back on Chance and his eyes narrowed. "I've known you and Frank your whole lives. I'll be honest with you, Charlie, you're the future, Frank's the past. With your history and heart, you could take the family in a new direction. Your uncle knows how I feel, so I can tell you this. I don't like some of the things the family has gotten into the last few years. Things Frank has brought into the family. Bad things."

"You're not really selling it here, Giorgio."

"Look, I know you. I know you got moral qualms with the family. But it ain't all breaking arms and tough guy stuff. You saw today. Nobody got hurt. You remember Russo's store?"

"Of course. Old man Russo caught me stealing a Hershey's Bar when I was eight and beat my ass bloody."

"Taught you a lesson about stealing, didn't it?"

Chance smirked at the irony.

"Russo's store has been in the family for three generations. Now how fair would it be if Piggly Wiggly wanted to open a huge store across the street? Undercutting prices and driving Russo's out of business? We make sure they don't get a permit. Nobody gets hurt, and we protect the neighborhood."

"As fascinating as this economics lesson is, I got things to do."

"My point is, that's the way you would handle it, but Frank would shoot the CEO of Piggly Wiggly. If Frank takes over, he'll have you killed. I'll be out or dead, and that bitch wife of his will pull the strings. Your uncle is the only reason you two have coexisted in this town for this long. When he goes, so does your protection. But I gotta tell you, we need a decision this week. Or it will be made for you."

"Giorgio, if what you're saying is true... if I took over, I'd have to have Frank killed."

"Charles, if you tell me you're taking over, the decision will have already been made."

CHAPTER EIGHTEEN

SMOOTH OPERATOR

Winnie and Alex waited for the next car to pull up outside the Knickerbocker. Alex hadn't said more than five words to Winnie since they'd started their shift three hours ago. She hadn't really talked to him since they had been at Country Kitchen a couple of nights ago.

The driver of a Jaguar hesitated in handing the keys over to Prez.

"Don't worry, sir, Jaguar is my favorite cat. I'll take good care of her." The man finally handed Prez the keys. Over time, Prez had developed a manner that put people at ease. He had a short waves hairstyle, a little extra weight, and a huge shiny smile. Winnie again wondered what it must be like to be instantly distrusted because of your skin color.

Alex stood by the podium where tickets were kept, focused on a paperback about Mars. It was a slow night for the restaurant; Winnie figured the nice weather had people dusting off their barbecues.

Prez jogged back from the lot. "Man, did you see the way that honky eyeballed me when I asked to take his keys?"

"Yeah, his face was pretty funny. Like you'd asked to take his daughter out."

"Shit, like I would ever roll with a country club debutante."

"Prez, you would roll with whatever girl blinked at you twice."

Prez flashed a five-years-of-braces smile at Winnie. "Yeah, true."

A white Mercedes Benz pulled up to the stand.

"Alex, it's your turn," said Prez. Alex put down her book, grabbed a ticket, and opened the passenger door. A long, slender leg appeared, followed by a second. When Winnie and Prez thought there was nothing covering where the legs met, a purple skirt appeared. A tall, emaciated blonde in a white mink coat rose from the car. Alex went around the car and opened the driver's side. The woman was on the short side of twenty-five. The man, balding, with an eight-months-pregnant pot belly, was on the plus side of fifty. Prez sighed, and Winnie could hear his thoughts: *Another beautiful young thing and another rich, white asshole.*

The man grabbed the woman's arm, not a partner but a possession. Alex pulled away in the white Benz.

Prez shook his head. "Did you see what a dork that guy was?"

"Yeah, but he's got money. That's all you need in this world to get women like that."

"So, what's going on with Alex and you? You two having a fight?"

Winnie stuffed both of his hands in his pockets and moved his shoulders up and down.

"Well, whatever you did, you should just say you're sorry. It's a warm night, but it's positively frosty out here.

Whenever my mama gets mad, I say, *sorry*. Seems to work pretty good."

"That's just it. I have no idea what I'd be apologizing for. Everything seemed fine until it wasn't."

"Man, you two crack me up. You should kiss her and get it over with."

"Knock it off."

"You know you've wanted to for years. I don't know why you don't get it over with."

"I don't know, either."

Chance's boat pulled up. Winnie straightened his back and coughed at Prez. Prez followed his gaze and straightened his back as well. Chance pulled into the only open spot big enough for his behemoth. Winnie stepped toward Gracie, but Chance was already getting out.

"Don't worry about it, Winnie." Chance stepped onto the curb under the hotel's alcove.

Prez and Winnie gawked at Chance with a mixture of awe and nervousness.

"Looks like a slow night, hey, Prez?"

"Yes, Mr. C., a little slower than normal, sir." Prez inspected the ground.

"Probably the nice weather, right, Winnie?"

"Yes, sir, that's what we were saying, too."

Alex returned from the lot and hung a set of keys on the podium's rack.

"Good evening, Ms. Kopoff," said Chance with a honeyed voice.

"Good evening, Chance. Kind of a late start for you, isn't it?" asked Alex with a slight smirk.

"The great thing about being the boss is you get to write your own schedule."

"Ahh, yes, being the man must have certain advantages, I'm sure," cooed Alex with a mix of slight sarcasm and envy.

Chance put both hands up, palms out in front of him. "It doesn't suck." Alex, Prez, and Winnie all gave courtesy laughs in response.

"Winnie and I saw *The Hunt for Red October* the other day. You have to see it," said Chance.

"Oh, yeah," said Prez. "James Bond as a mad Russian with a nuclear submarine. What's not to love?" Prez brought up his forearm like he was adjusting his cufflink, and in a spot-on Sean Connery impersonation said, "'Oh, Miss Moneypenny. I am Bond, Black Bond.'" They all laughed as the roly-poly Black kid nailed the middle-aged British spy.

"Damn, Prez, that was sharp," said Chance. "Why can everyone but me do a Scottish accent?"

"You'd think it came with the name," said Alex.

"I know, right," replied Chance.

"If you enjoyed that one, you should catch his Captain Kirk. Come on Prez, do the Kirk," said Winnie.

"No, no, he doesn't want to hear that," said Prez with false modesty.

"Go ahead, Prez. I grew up watching *Star Trek*."

"OK, OK." Prez looked serious. Slowly speaking the first words and then rushing the last part with emphasis, Prez said, "'It seems... the alien life form... has taken over the ship. It wants... me to kiss... the only Black woman on television, or it will... destroy me and my entire crew!'"

They applauded Prez, and he took an exaggerated bow.

"That was amazing, Prez. Spot-on William Shatner. You should put an act together."

"That's what we've all been saying for years, Mr. C."

Chance pulled out a cigarette. Alex whipped out her Zippo and offered Chance a light. Winnie scowled at the ground.

"Thanks, Alex. So, where's the fourth Musketeer?" asked Chance.

"We phased Hunter early since it was so slow. So, I assume he's out on a date again," replied Alex.

"Kid sure seems to go on a lot of dates."

Winnie snorted, but it sounded like a half cough, half sneeze.

"He definitely is into more quantity than quality," said Prez.

Chance glanced at Alex and back to Winnie. "Winnie, it's the car. In your age group, a lot, not all, but a lot of women think a hot car is important."

"That's what I've been saying," said Winnie, triumph on his face as he glanced at Alex.

Now it was Alex's time to scowl. "I don't think classifying all women as shallow and materialistic is right, Chance—"

"I agree, Alex, and believe me I'm not. But at your age, people haven't figured out what's truly important yet in a relationship. You don't have enough experience yet—not you, per se, but your age group, in general, hasn't figured out that cars, money, good looks, are not the WMI of relationships."

"WMI?" asked Prez.

"'What's Most Important.' My point is, trust, honesty, respect, caring, tenderness, kindness, romance." Chance regarded

Prez. "Humor. It's a long race; sometimes it takes a bit of time to catch up." Chance winked at Winnie.

Winnie glanced at Alex and back to Chance. The corners of his mouth turning upward.

Chance put his cigarette out in the sand-filled ashtray. "All right, guys and dolls, I need to get inside. Prez, I know a few of the comedy club owners. If you put an act together, I can get you an audition, no problem." Not waiting for a response, Chance smiled at each of them and walked into the hotel.

A metallic blue Camaro pulled into the McDonald's lot and parked next to a sleek Corvette. Hunter got out with a bag. The Corvette's tinted window came down, and Hunter handed the bag to the young driver.

"It's all there," said Hunter.

The driver grunted, looked around, then opened the bag and inspected the wrapped bundles of cash. "This is more than I expected."

"Well, Frankie, I got a good introduction at Eastside Catholic."

Frankie frowned at Hunter, giving the impression of someone playacting Robert DeNiro. "What's the age cap?"

"Fifteen. I ain't selling to anyone younger."

"And why is that?"

Hunter looked around the parking lot. He hated standing there for any length of time. "'Cause fifteen-year-olds smoke pot and twelve-year-olds get caught."

"That's right. Just checking." Frankie handed Hunter a brown paper bag. Hunter stuffed it into his coat and started to walk away.

"Get back here. I ain't done with you yet."

Hunter's shoulders dropped and he walked back to the car.

"I need some information. This is important, and could mean a promotion for you. A lot more cash with less risk."

Hunter glanced at his Camaro. He loved this easy money. He could earn in a week what it took him a month to earn as a valet. But the stress and anxiety were killing him.

"I need to know about your boss, Chance."

Hunter stepped back and shook his head. "Mr. McQueen?"

"Yeah. You may have heard about an issue with a delivery. I need to talk with him and work that out, but I can't very well come into the restaurant. So, I need to know when he usually gets there or leaves."

"Why don't you call him?"

Frankie's eyes bore into Hunter. "Kid, are you fucking stupid or something? How many times have I told you we don't talk on phones?"

"Right, yeah, um… well, he doesn't have like a set schedule or anything. He pretty much comes and goes when he wants."

"Look, some of my people fucked up on a delivery of his. I got an envelope of cash I need to get to him to set it right, and I can't hand it to him in the middle of a restaurant crowd, see?"

"Right. Well he's usually there 'till close most nights. You know, he usually brings food or something to a homeless guy in the back alley. I don't know if he does it every night, but I see him while I run back from the lot."

"Yeah, that could work." Frankie's lips moved, but Hunter wasn't sure if he was trying to sneer or if he had back pain. "Kid, this could work out great." Frankie looked serious again.

"You don't talk about this with anyone. I mean anyone, Hunter. Not even Chance."

"But—"

"No! Understand this: you breathe a word of this to anyone, I will fucking firebomb your car with you in it. You got that?"

Hunter held up his hands. "OK, OK, Frankie, no problem."

This time Frankie managed a recognizable smile. "How many times have I told you to call me Junior? All my friends call me Junior."

Hunter considered the question. Frankie had never asked him to call him Junior.

CHAPTER NINETEEN

BRIDGE OVER TROUBLED WATER

Chance did his usual gladhanding as he walked through the half-full dining room. Thankfully it was a slow night, since the kitchen was understaffed without Chico, who was still nursing his wounds. Chance went through the same checklist he always did: temperature good, lighting right, music appropriate. The staff knew their jobs, and the guests were taken care of. A measure of pride pushed through the guilt about Chico. He had a great team.

Geoff gave him a look from one of the tables and nodded toward the office. Chance maneuvered through the dining room, nodding to guests along the way.

Maggie stood next to the desk, looking down at Cassie, who sat in Chance's chair, coloring. Chance smiled and shut the door behind him.

Maggie glanced up, fear in her eyes changing when she saw it was Chance. Cassie beamed with joy. "Uncle Chance!" She jumped off the chair and ran to him. Like an Olympic pole vaulter, she leaped into the air, trusting Chance to catch her. He pulled her up, wrapping his arms around her tiny body.

"Hello, Miss Cass." Cassie buried her head into Chance's chest, and all was right in the world. Maggie observed with a smile that didn't touch her eyes.

After a few seconds, Cassie straightened, arched her back, and rubbed her hands on Chance's cheeks. "Sandpaper," she said. "Uncle Chance, you didn't shave today."

"Well, I've had a busy day, little one. Did you draw me a picture?"

Cassie squealed and wiggled out of Chance's arms. He set her down and she ran to the desk, retrieving the picture. It always amazed Chance that kids ran everywhere, even if only a few feet. Too much energy, or excitement for a world that seemed new. She ran back to Chance and held out the picture, pride on her sweet face.

"Do you see what it is?"

"A gray lion."

"That isn't a lion. Guess again."

"A gray whale that swims in the Arctic."

"No, silly! Guess again." Cassie's Muppet voice climbed higher in delight.

"It's your Uncle Geoff."

Cassie squealed again and giggled. "Uncle Geoff said you would say that. He told me to draw you as a gorilla! See, here are the eyes, hazel just like yours, and here's your big ears." Her cheeks rose with a mischievous smile.

"Big ears? Big ears!" exclaimed Chance in mock outrage. He grabbed Cassie, tickling her, but like a Greco-Roman wrestler, she wiggled free. She screamed in delight and climbed underneath the desk. Chance's warmth faded as he glanced at Maggie, stress visible on her face, the lines around her eyes pronounced.

"He's gone," said Chance.

Maggie brought her shaking hand up to her mouth. "Is he dead?"

"What? No, I put him on a bus myself." He wasn't pleased that Maggie thought him capable of that. "I guarantee he won't be coming back."

"Are you sure? He's left before." Her voice vibrated with fear.

"Trust me, he's not coming back here. You'll never have to worry about him again."

Maggie let out a deep moan and, like her daughter, ran into Chance's arms, tears streaming down her face, sobs wracking her small frame. Chance held her tight.

Maggie's sobs abated. She put her arms around Chance's neck and pulled his head down close to hers. She kissed his left eye in a tender fashion, then his right. Chance was amazed at the sensation, not remembering anyone ever doing that before. She kissed his lips. Not quite in a romantic way, but longer than a peck.

Cassie started to sing, "I saw mommy kissing a gorilla," to the melody of "I Saw Mommy Kissing Santa Claus." Maggie and Chance laughed, thankful for the interruption. Cassie squealed again, something little girls do a lot, noted Chance, and she ran to them both, hugging both their legs. A tender moment not lost on him. He let his guard down and let himself fall into it. But after a few deep breaths a small warning light blinked in his mind. The back of his mind, but still there, blinking, blinking, blinking.

· · ·

As closing time approached, Chance grabbed a bottle of Johnnie Walker Blue from his desk, put it in his coat pocket, and left his office. He whistled "Luck Be a Lady Tonight" as he closed the door behind him. Something Giorgio said popped into his head, and the whistling stopped abruptly on a C#. If he said yes, somebody, not him, would kill Frank. Wouldn't that still be the same as pulling the trigger himself? Was he capable of that? Cold-blooded murder. He closed his eyes tightly, massaging his temples, and took a deep calming breath. He didn't want to think about it. None of it. Thankfully he'd have something to distract him tonight.

Chance had invited his entire crew, kitchen team and all, down to Cent Anni's, a swanky new piano bar. Maggie had left to take Cassie to her sister's, but promised to meet everyone there. In the kitchen, he told the team to hurry up and close so they could do more drinking on his dime. The few workers remaining cheered and redoubled their efforts.

Chance walked out the back door into the alley and sat at the picnic table. He took the bottle of scotch out of his coat and set it on the table, lit a cigarette, and waited. It was a clear night, and even in the city the stars were visible, shining away. He made no move toward the scotch, but instead whistled the song again.

Jed appeared from behind the dumpster and carefully approached the table. "Who the hell is strangling cats out here?"

"Your friendly neighborhood bartender."

Jed scouted the area. Satisfied, he sat across from Chance.

"I can't stay long, Jed. I'm taking the team out for a celebration drink. But I did bring you a treat."

"Is it underwear? 'Cause I could use some underwear."

Chance laughed. "No, but I'd think Goodwill would have underwear."

"Would you want to wear secondhand underwear?"

"Well, no. Point taken. I'll make sure to pick some up for you. Do you have a preference? Silk, perhaps?"

Jed chuckled. "That would be a hoot." He pointed to the bottle, licking his lips. "Is that a present?"

"Jed, never in your life have you had hooch better than this. It's sixty-year-old scotch."

"Does it have alcohol in it after sixty years?"

"Of course."

"That's all that matters to me." Jed reached for the bottle. He removed the corked cap and sniffed. "Smells pretty good." He knocked back a swig. He put the bottle down, examining the label. "This reminds me of the first taste of scotch I had after being up-country for sixty-three days. We got back to Da Nang, and Tito, Isaac, and I were sitting on the patio of this bar. Tito waved a bunch of greenbacks at the mama-san and asked for her best hooch. This is what it tasted like."

Chance knew better than to ask any questions.

"No, not Tito. Tito was dead; it was Jed and Isaac."

Jed handed the bottle to Chance, and Chance wavered a moment before knocking back a slug. "Oh, that is good." Hoping to draw Jed out further, Chance brought up Geoff. "Jed, I just found out Geoff was a Navy Seal! Can you believe that?"

"Pity the man with eyes that see all but understand nothing."

"You telling me you knew?"

"Of course, I knew. How could you not? I knew the minute I met him. You could spot those guys from a mile away. They all walk with the same swagger. As a Marine, I'll talk shit about a squid, but not those guys. They saved my bacon a couple of times. Speaking of bacon, it tastes better over here than over there. Tastes funny over there."

"Over in 'Nam?"

Jed rolled his eyes like Chance was a child at the blackboard with the wrong answer. "Over at the Egg and I on Broadway. The bacon tastes funny. I think it's because they're Indian and they don't have bacon in India. Or is it steak? Anyway, their bacon tastes funny."

Jed continued, "Isaac doesn't like the bacon over here; he says it's too Americanized. He likes it better over there." He grabbed the bottle and took another hit. "No, that isn't right. Isaac is dead, Isaac didn't come home. I keep forgetting. What's the celebration for?"

Chance had heard about Isaac before, but never that he hadn't come back. Chance always assumed Isaac was one of Jed's homeless friends. His upbeat mood deflated a bit. "I don't know. Thought I'd take the crew out. We're going to Cent Anni's." Chance rose.

Jed started to laugh and smacked his leg with his hand. "Oh, brother, you do enjoy trouble."

"What do you mean?"

"'What do you mean'?" parroted Jed. "Nobody ever notices me. That's how I know you probably kicked the shit out of a villain today. Overheard Maggie and Geoff talking about what her ex did and why she was here on her day off. Doesn't take a math teacher to put two-and-two together. Now you're going out and, let me guess, Maggie will be there. Oh, brother, you live by the sword, and the rain will rust it, 'cause you kept it out during the storm."

"I don't know what the hell you're talking about. I'm just taking my team out for a drink."

"Oh… safety in numbers, huh? Let me tell you something I've learned reading the definitive guide to women and their feelings."

"The Gloria Steinem book?"

"No! *Cosmo*. Listen up. All women love a knight in shining armor. No matter how much feminisms they got, deep down they all respond to someone that helps them. It's in their biology. Can't help it."

"Please don't take this the wrong way, but when was the last time you dated a woman?"

"Listen, you pasta-eatin' guido, I happen to be loved by many of the fairer sex. Maria over at St. John's shelter thinks I walk on water. Which, by the way, I can."

Chance stood there, his mouth slightly open in surprise. "How do you do it?"

"Do what? You're not asking for particulars, are ya? Gentleman never tells."

"No, how do you always know how to hit the nail on the head?"

"Son, it's pretty easy when all your friends are blockheads." Jed cackled and took another swig.

It was all he was going to get from Jed, so Chance started for the door. "Enjoy the scotch."

"Chance!"

Not sure he wanted to hear anything further, Chance turned around.

"Evil is the man that kills his brother, evil is the woman that breaks his heart. Brother, how many wars do you want to be in?"

"I honestly don't know."

"You should figure it out, 'cause once they start, you never come home alive, even if you come home alive."

Chance stared at Jed for a minute, turned, and walked back into his restaurant.

Hit singles like: "Rainy Days and Mondays" by The Carpenters, "Fire and Rain" by James Taylor, and a crowd favorite, "Blue Bayou" by Linda Ronstadt.

This 16-cassette collection includes 160 of your favorite feel-sad tunes. Do you think Love Hurts? I know I do.

Operators are standing by, so have your credit card ready. This amazing collection, not available in stores, can be yours for 14 easy payments of only $26.95.

**IT'S 2AM AND YOU ARE ALONE. BUT NOT ANYMORE.
160 OF MY FRIENDS AND I ARE COMING OVER. ORDER NOW!**

TERMS AND CONDITIONS:
Necesse est nos monere, ut tapes non erit circa multo amplius. Si hoc speramus vos emere, ita nos can adepto rid of our backstock. Nos devolvunt novum musica traditio ratio dicitur C. D. s anno altero. Hoc efficit, erit tibi emere idem musica collectis iterum. Diam Cavete.

CHAPTER TWENTY

BABA O'RILEY

They were sitting in the same booth, drinking the same coffee, talking about the same things. Alex wasn't sure how many more nights she could spend at Country Kitchen without going crazy. Prez and Hunter were rehashing the racial and cultural differences of *Star Trek* and *Star Wars*. Without listening, she could recite the arguments verbatim. *Star Trek*, filmed in the 60's, had Asians and Blacks in the lead roles, as well as the first Black-on-white kiss in television history. *Star Wars* was "white bread" until the second movie introduced a lead Black character.

"Unless you count Darth Vader, who was a Black dude," said Hunter.

"He was a Black voice, but a white dude in the suit," countered Prez.

"Point, counterpoint," said Hunter. "If you look at all the aliens in *Star Wars*, they're symbols of all the different ethnic groups coming to America in the 60's and 70's. I read somewhere that's what George Lucas meant by all the aliens. Supposed to represent the melting pot of America after the 60's, with all the boat people during Vietnam."

"I think I remember reading that," said Prez in a sarcastic tone. "You remember the cantina scene when the bounty hunter sits down with Han?"

Hunter took the bait. "Yeah, the greenish guy with the funny hair."

"Remember how the guy talked?"

"Yeah."

"According to George, he took a bunch of slant-eyed languages, mixed them together, and that's what it sounded like." Prez started laughing and then whined after Hunter punched him in the arm.

"Would you two grow up, please?" said Alex, frustrated. Winnie sat next to her, but hadn't joined the conversation. Alex sensed him stealing looks at her. She felt a bit sorry for how she was treating him. "Why don't you guys ever talk about anything important?"

"Like what?" asked Hunter.

"I don't know, maybe about how Nelson Mandela was released from prison, or how George Bush is planning on going to war for oil?"

"Who's Nelson Mandela?"

"Whoa, you did not just say that, Hunter," exclaimed Prez.

"Yes, I did. Who is he?"

"The man singlehandedly responsible for bringing down apartheid!"

"Oh, yeah, that guy, yeah, I knew who you were talking about; I forgot his name."

Prez rolled his eyes and glanced at Alex. "Kids," he said, shrugging his shoulders.

"Screw you, Prez, you spend your days up to your elbows in cock rings and dildos."

Prez's mom owned several adult novelty stores in the greater Milwaukee area. The kids in high school had called her the Queen of Cocks. Not to her face, though, as she was a force of nature. Considering the wealth of slurs available to the average teen, Prez was fortunate to have the nickname he did. Alex had never had the courage to go into one of the stores.

Prez giggled. "You know what we got into the store?" He waited a second. "Edible underwear." Everyone blinked at him. Even Winnie glanced up at Prez.

"Seriously, guys, hand to God. It's underwear you put on and eat!"

"That's disgusting!" said Alex.

"Why would anyone want to eat their own underwear?" asked Winnie.

"You dope. It's for your partner," said Prez.

"Oh... oh!" said Winnie, blushing along with Alex. The only one not blushing was Hunter.

"What are they like?" asked Hunter.

"Kind of like Fruit Roll-Ups."

"Can you get me some?"

Prez glared at Hunter. "Dude, you are seriously too much."

"What? I enjoy Fruit Roll-Ups." They let out a collective groan.

Alex rolled another cigarette—her fourth in the last hour. "Seriously, guys, don't you feel bored? Don't you want to do something different? We do the same things all the time."

"Hey Alex."

Alex looked up and up and up. Standing there smiling down at her was Jake Webber. They'd been study buddies in chemistry class Junior year, but hadn't talked much since then. Well, actually not since an awkward parking experience that had left both of them embarrassed.

"Hi Jake," she replied.

"Hi Jake," said Hunter.

"Um… you going to the bonfire Saturday?" asked Jake.

Alex looked at Winnie, then back to Jake. "I don't know. Maybe."

Jake stood there, staring at her. She started to imagine herself as a slab of beef.

"Yeah. Cool. I'll shotgun a beer with you. We can talk or something," said Jake.

"That'll be riveting," said Prez under his breath. Alex kicked him.

"Sure Jake. Just make sure it's warm beer. Can't shotgun cold ones," said Alex.

Jake was a statue. "OK." Finally, he walked towards the other side of the restaurant.

"Bye Jake," called out Hunter.

"Hunter, he is going to pound you into next week if you keep that up," said Prez.

"Yeah, and he'll use your bones as toothpicks," said Winnie.

"Shut up. He's sweet. And he's the only upper that ever stuck up for you, Winnie Morris," said Alex. Winnie's shoulders sagged.

"Your right. That was mean."

"Anyway, this is exactly what I'm talking about. Another bonfire, another night at Country Kitchen. Aren't you guys bored to death of this?" asked Alex.

"Is that it, Alex? You're bored?" asked Winnie, coming alive.

She considered Winnie, Hunter, and Prez. Winnie looked like he'd decoded a secret message. His light blond hair was hanging over his eyes. Hunter, with one side of his head shaved, the other long and gelled to the side, had a classic skate punk style. He had piercing eyes, but not much going on behind them, she thought. Prez sat there with his classic puppy dog face. He wanted to be petted and told what a good boy he was. She felt guilty for thinking such shallow thoughts about her friends. She was crabby.

"Yes, I'm bored. We should be experiencing something other than the movies every Friday night, or this week's party in the woods with the same people and the same stories. Talking about how fucked up they were the week before." She noticed the hurt on all three faces and softened her tone.

"Don't get me wrong, guys, I like hanging out, but because we didn't go off to school, we're missing out on so many things."

She had hit a nerve with all of them. Something they didn't ever discuss.

"I know it's a sore subject, but, seriously, we need to do something or I'm going to go crazy!"

"Like what?" asked Winnie.

"I don't know. Let's take a trip or something. Let's go somewhere, see something, meet new people."

"Where would we go?" asked Hunter.

"We could go to Chicago, or we could take a long weekend up in Door County. Hell, we could fly somewhere, anywhere." The guys all glanced at each other as if she was asking to go to the moon.

"All I know is I can't keep doing the same things every week. I feel trapped. Like I can't breathe." She lit her cigarette.

Prez, eager to please, spoke up first.

"We haven't been to Great America in a couple of years."

Hunter spoke up next. "Door County is fun. I went up there last summer, and they have this restaurant that's got goats on the roof."

"OK, guys, that's the spirit. I know we all have money saved up. Let's think of something fun to do." She eyeballed Hunter. "Just the four of us."

"What? Why you looking at me?"

"I don't know, 'cause maybe you always have to bring some pixie along," said Prez.

"When have I ever—"

"Camping two summers ago at the Dells: Tricia, or Alyssa or something," said Prez.

"The Michael Jackson concert two summers ago: Michelle," said Alex.

"The campus tour for UW last year, the girl, what was her name, the one already in school at Marquette: Mandi or Bambi," said Winnie.

"OK, OK, OK," said Hunter.

"My birthday party last year, the horrible hippie chick that didn't shave her armpits and wouldn't eat hot dogs, what was her name?" asked Prez.

"Daisy," said Alex.

"No, it was Rose," said Winnie.

"Violet," said Alex. All of them were laughing now.

"Poppy," said Hunter.

"Chrysanthemum!" said Prez.

"Poppy!" yelled Hunter without heat. "All right? Her name was Poppy."

"Damn, I knew it was a flower," laughed Prez.

"I'm shocked you remember her name," said Alex.

"You guys suck. All right, only the four of us. Doesn't mean I won't meet someone when we get there."

"What about you, Winnie? Where do you want to go?" asked Prez.

Winnie thought for a few seconds. "San Diego."

Prez tilted his head like a dog.

"Kinda far, don't you think?" asked Hunter.

"Two words for you... Comic-Con." Winnie grinned wide.

Hunter pounded the table. "Wicked!"

"That'd be awesome!" exclaimed Prez.

The corners of Alex's mouth moved upward.

Winnie's face changed from glee to disgust to fear. Alex tracked his eyes. Kim Novell had walked in with Billy "Bully" Buddy. Her stomach dropped and she had trouble breathing.

Kim was the most annoying girl in the world, and Billy was Winnie's archnemesis from school. That's who he was to Winnie, who was sinking lower in the booth. But to her, Billy was the Event.

CHAPTER TWENTY-ONE

COWARD OF THE COUNTY

Kim ran up to their table, full of pubescent energy.

"Hello! I've missed you all so much." She leaned into Prez first, giving him a hug and kissing his forehead. Prez appeared annoyed, but as Kim leaned over Prez to give Hunter a hug, her breasts pressed into Prez's face. She didn't seem to notice, but Prez most certainly did. She straightened and went over to Winnie, giving him a hug and kissing his forehead with a loud *smack*. He glanced at Alex, and she was as white as a sheet. Her hands were clenched into fists and she was staring straight ahead.

"Prez, I love you. You are such a cute teddy bear," said Kim. Five-four and feather light, she had short hair, dyed almost the same color of red as Mrs. White's. She was dressed as a hippie—no bra, a tie-dyed shirt, rose-colored glasses. "I mean it. I miss our study hall together. That's when I got to know the true you, the beautiful you."

"Um, thanks?"

"No, truly. I love you all. I'm so glad to run into you. I was saying to Billy how much I miss all those great times we had at school."

Billy had slowly walked over to the table and was standing behind Kim. Billy was six-foot-one, 190 pounds of muscle. His hair had always been short cropped, as if he had gone to boot camp instead of college on a football scholarship. But now it was long in the front like a surfer from California, instead of Johnny B. Good at Michigan. Winnie wouldn't have been surprised if Billy had been out searching for gays or Mexicans to crush under his goose-stepping bootheel tonight. But someone had done a number on Billy's face, his eye blackened and nose broken. Sloth from *The Goonies* popped into Winnie's mind. Billy's sheepish glance was the last thing Winnie would expect from his nightmare of the school hallways and gym class.

"What great times were those, Kim?" asked Alex.

Kim, oblivious to sarcasm, plunged right in. "Oh, my gosh, so many great times. All the parties, the field trip to the EAA flight museum, Mrs. Larsen's class. Prez, scoot over." She sat next to him without waiting for him to move.

"You all remember Billy, right?" asked Kim. The response was a collective groan.

"Ah, guys, he's not like that anymore. He's changed!" Kim scowled, like they had told her they didn't like her new puppy.

"No, it's OK, Kim. I deserve it. I deserve a lot more, actually," said Billy through clenched teeth. "Winston, I mean Winnie, I was a jerk to you, and I can't apologize enough. I was mean, cruel, and a bully. I know I made your school experience hellish, and I've been wanting to apologize to you." He glanced at the rest of the group, but focused on Alex. "To all of you, really."

Winnie and Prez regarded each other. *Billy Bully apologizing?*

Billy eyed each of them. He did have an apologetic, messed-up face. But it didn't match what they'd known about him.

"College and certain events have opened up my eyes."

Kim coughed in an exaggerated fashion.

"And Kim, of course. She's shown me how I don't have to hold on to my insecurities, but channel them into good by facing them head-on."

Kim held herself as the proud teacher of a student who had recited back the lecture correctly.

Billy held out his alien claw toward Winnie. "Really, Winnie, I am sorry. No hard feelings?"

Winnie's first response was to reach out to shake it, but Alex put her hand on his shoulder.

"No, Billy, I don't think Winnie is going to shake your hand today. You can't come in here, give a half-assed apology, and think all's forgiven."

Prez's eyes went wide at the tone in her voice.

Billy glanced at Kim, unsure of what to say, his hand still extended but slowly lowering.

Kim said, "Jeez, Alex, lighten up, Billy's trying to make amen—"

"Fuck you, Kim," Alex interrupted. "I don't think I will lighten up. I don't care if the two of you have gone and had a Shangri-La moment while drinking beers and smoking pot. Or if a humanities class made you realize how much of an asshole he was. We're not going to sit here all kumbaya where all is forgiven. You know how many people Billy told that you were a slut after he got into your pants at Megan Riley's homecoming party? Do you remember not coming out of the girl's bathroom for half a day that next Monday?"

Kim looked down at the table.

"I've apologized to Kim. I was a different person then."

"'Then'? Really. How long ago was that, Billy?" She said his name as if it tasted of battery acid.

Winnie, Hunter, and Prez sat there, their mouths hanging open.

"Do you remember the time you put the bag of cow shit in Winnie's locker?"

Billy winced, his eyes darting to Winnie before settling on the floor. "Yeah. I feel horrible about that," he said quietly.

"Nothing good comes from bringing up the past," said Kim.

Like a spear, Alex's finger jabbed toward Kim's chest. "Shut the fuck up." It moved toward Billy. "Cow shit day was the day Winnie found out his dad was going to be dead in a month. You fucking piece of shit. What gave you the right? You repeatedly tortured and humiliated a kind, generous, tender, and beautiful boy, for what? To make yourself feel better? Because you're insecure that you have a little penis?" Alex wiggled her pinky finger. "And now you come in here to our place and think an apology and a handshake will absolve you of all evil. Get the fuck out of here, Billy, go back over to Perkins and hang out with all your Nazi friends, you fucking date rapist."

"I didn't... it wasn't like that," yelled Billy.

The horror on his face was plain, and he turned around and hurried out the door.

"Christ, Alex, you didn't have to do that! You've really changed, and not for the better," cried Kim, getting up from the table.

"Kim, one day you're going to wake up and realize that piece of shit isn't any different. He's the same mean, small person he always was. On *that* day, I'll feel sorry for you."

Kim took a deep breath and glared at Alex. "I still have love in my heart for you, but right now I don't like you very much." Kim twirled around and chased after Billy.

The four of them sat there in silence, stunned.

Winnie considered Alex. "Date rapist?"

Crimson exploded on her cheeks and down her neck. Her hands were shaking as she reached for her roller. "Just something I heard."

Prez raised his hand like he was in school. "So, let me get this straight, Alex. You think Winnie's a beautiful boy?"

CHAPTER TWENTY-TWO

I WANNA BE SEDATED

Chance pulled up outside Cent Anni's Piano Bar with Chico. Tossing the keys to a pimple-faced kid in a black vest, he pulled out his roll and peeled off a twenty. "Take good care of her, kid. She's the love of my life."

"Yes, sir, Mr. McQueen, thank you," croaked the kid, his voice still changing.

Chance put his arm around Chico.

Behind a velvet rope a line of thirty to forty people waited, all dressed in their best. Women in their all-over print silk shirts from Versace, doorknocker earrings, or miniskirts. Guys in power suits or tied-over-the-neck sweaters. Most people were smoking.

Chance walked up to the entrance and the doorman unchained the rope. He palmed a twenty into the guy's hand and overheard a woman say to her date, "Who is that?" He loved it, though he knew it didn't mean anything.

His friend Anthony had been a visionary, opening an upscale club in Milwaukee's former meatpacking district. The factories had closed years ago, and this part of town was considered D.O.A. Much like in New York, Anthony predicted old warehouse districts were going to be the next hip place to live. Urban life had become an interesting alternative to the slow death of living in the suburbs, with their strip malls of tanning salons, dry cleaners, Chinese restaurants and Blockbuster Videos.

The VIP area was marked off and reserved for Bella's. The area was raised up three steps, and Chance made a note to self not to trip later. Long sheer silk curtains hung from the rafters, discretely separating the occupants from the cattle in the bar.

"Chico, I'll go into the VIP room, say a few words, announce you, and you come in, comprende?"

"Si, Jefe." Despite a bandage taped to his forehead, he seemed no worse for wear.

Chance got a rousing ovation from his staff, over two dozen of them, all with a drink in their hands, standing or seated around huge circular couches behind the silk curtains. He held up his hands for the group to settle down and stop cheering.

"Well, I can see by that reaction you're all drunk," said Chance to a chorus of laughs and catcalls.

"We love you, Chancie," called out Geoff.

"Geoff, I don't care how much I drink tonight, I am not going home with you."

After the laughter faded, Chance made eye contact with each one of them. "Seriously, I have a few things to say, and then we'll get this party started. I've been in this business a long time. Like a lot of you, I started washing dishes, but took the time to learn other skills. I didn't work my way *up*, because every position in a restaurant is just as important as the other. I worked my way *around*. When each person on the team does their job correctly and to the best of their abilities, you have a place that flows, and the ambience is magical.

"One of the most rewarding parts of our jobs is we help provide great memories for our guests. We are the centerpiece of families' and friends' best times together. To do it effectively, we need to be a family as well. And that is what you all are to me. Family. I love each of you for who you are, your hard work, your dedication. And I don't say this enough, but I thank you. From the bottom of my heart, I thank you. Someone give me a drink!"

Maggie grabbed a bottle of scotch off the island bar, poured two fingers, and brought it to Chance. She handed him the glass with a wink and sat back down.

"I know this was last minute, so thank you all for coming. But before we get to the drinking and dancing, there's one member of our team not here with us. A man whose dedication and devotion to making the best quality product is unparalleled. A man who protects our business with his face if necessary." A few people laughed.

"I would like to raise our glasses. Oh, wait, Maggie can you grab me a Corona?" asked Chance. Maggie did so.

"Everyone raise your glass... to the man, the myth, the legend. Chico Hernández!"

Chico whooshed through the silk, and out came a roar of hoots and cheers. Chance handed Chico the Corona.

"To familia!" said Chance, raising his glass.

"To familia!" they replied in unison.

. . .

Junior sat at a high-top table where he could watch the VIP area out of the corner of his eye. Ray sat across from him with a clear line of sight on Chance and his group. Two untouched drinks sat on the table in front of them. The buzz of music and crowd noise made conversations almost impossible. Not that Junior had anything to talk about with Ray. Ray was not the smartest guy in his crew, but he was smart enough to be a lookout at short notice.

After the call had come in from Hunter, Junior had to scramble to get there. He hadn't even had time to contact his dad. Dad... it was weird to think in those terms again. For so long they'd had to pretend to be estranged. For one, so he could be protected from his father's enemies. And two, so his father could be protected from Junior's activities. Selling drugs was a death sentence if you were part of the Carmelo family.

But the money. There was so much money. His dad's crew couldn't steal enough trucks in a month to make up for what Junior made in a day.

Junior casually glanced over to the VIP area and saw Chance walk over to the self-serve bar and pour himself a drink. He'd only met Chance once when he was a kid. But his father's hatred of the man had been passed down.

"Boss, when are you gonna do it?" yelled Ray. Junior almost reached across the table and smacked him in the face.

"Shut the fuck up and keep watch."

Ray reached for the drink in front of him and Junior gave him a hard stare. Ray's hand dropped to the table and he hung his head.

"Pick your fucking head back up and watch for Chance." Junior regretted bringing this moron with him. Not that it would matter much after. Ray was not long for this world. Junior shifted in his seat with nervous energy. It was starting to happen. His dad's plan was coming together. Soon Frank would be the Don, and Junior would be his right-hand man.

Junior's thoughts drifted to Uncle Vinnie. What a fucking hypocrite. Junior knew of at least four other crews that were all selling drugs. He'd never understand the old guard. These old men with their red wine and pretend traditions. Like there were degrees of being a criminal. You pimped, robbed, and murdered. You sold what people were buying. Sure, you could steal a truck full of VCRs, but people were selling their VCRs to buy his drugs. That was the market. He could practically guarantee that half the people in this bar had drugs on them.

Junior glanced at Chance. The guy looked like a total hoser. He wasn't sure why Frank wanted him ended, but it was made a top priority. He just needed Chance to go and take a piss.

. . .

"So, I told the lady, I'm sorry if you feel Tito is staring at you funny, but he has a lazy eye, he looks at everyone that way," said Geoff, laughing at his own story the loudest.

Chance sat on the couch, Maggie on his left and Geoff

on his right. They watched Tito trying but failing miserably to hook up with Leah. One of the most amusing aspects of the business was seeing who ended up with who, and who struck out. Chance was fortunate with the relatively low drama between his staff. Most hookups didn't turn into anything other than a couple of nights, and only a few times were there hurt feelings. As long as things didn't affect the business, Chance knew there was no upside to trying to police romance.

"Chance, did you get a glimpse of Geoff's artwork while you were at my place today?" asked Maggie.

Speaking of hookups, thought Chance. But he dismissed it. Yes, it might be available for the taking, as Maggie was gazing at him like he had a halo around his head. But taking advantage of it would cheapen what he'd done.

"That was your art, Geoff? The flowers?"

"Yes. It's what I do when I'm not slaving away for you, oh wise master."

"Wow, I'm impressed. I thought they were reproductions of somebody famous. Like Van Gogh or someone."

"Thanks, Chance, that's a nice compliment. I mostly just dabble. You know who the real artist on our team is?"

"Who?"

"Alex. She's amazing. The girl has extreme talent. Blow-me-out-of-the-water kind of talent."

"Geoff, don't cut yourself short. I think you're amazing too," cooed Maggie. Chance peeked down at her slim, smooth legs. He jerked his head back and tried not to think about her short skirt.

"Thanks, Maggie, but seriously, Alex is hands down the best artist for her age I've ever seen. And I've been to a lot of countries and seen a lot of art. Did you know she's already had two showings here in town?"

"Really?" said Chance. "I didn't know that."

"Don't tell anyone, but she got a full ride to Chicago School of Art and Design last year."

Chance considered this. "Why didn't she go? What the hell is she still doing here working for me?"

"Shit! I promised I wouldn't say anything. Crap, I've had too much to drink." Geoff took another swig of his drink. "Seriously, you two, forget I said anything. And for god's sake don't go and ask her."

"Oh, no, Geoff, the cat's out of the bag. Spill it now. Maggie and I won't say anything, right, Maggie?" Chance glanced again at Maggie's beautiful face.

"You know we would never..." Maggie said to Geoff, staring at Chance.

Geoff gazed at them, then, and decision made, plunged in. "I ran into her at her first show, having no idea she was the artist. I was shocked. Our little Alex. Standing up there in a woman's black cocktail dress. She was spectacular. But her art was even more spectacular. Not the little girl that parks cars, I can tell you." Geoff paused as if he had left the here and now.

Chance followed Geoff's gaze. The silk around the VIP room had been pulled back at Chance's request. No sense paying the VIP price if the staff couldn't get the ego boost of having everyone notice them. Partying like rock stars is great, but being seen to party like a rock star is even better.

"Alex didn't go off to school because of Winnie," said Geoff.

"What?" said Chance, sitting up on the couch.

Geoff looked at them both. His eyes went to the ceiling and he let out a deep breath. "After Winnie's dad passed, Winnie was understandably a mess. I mean it happened so fast; I think they were all in a state of shock. I'm not sure if she even understands her decision, but she didn't want to leave Winnie alone."

Chance used the seriousness of the conversation to slam his drink. The ice cube bumped his nose as he knocked back the shot of scotch. He got up, wiped his nose on his sleeve, went over to the bottle service bar, and poured himself another double. Said a silent prayer for his friend Eugene Morris and took a gulp of scotch.

Maggie looked at Chance and then back to Geoff. "Those poor kids." Her hand tightened on her own glass. "Just starting out, and then life sucker-punches you."

"Well the real problem is Winnie's mom. She's completely checked out. Winnie has to take care of her because apparently she's drugged out twenty-four-seven," said Geoff.

Chance set down his glass on the table and rubbed his hands against his face. "What is it about this world?" he said almost to himself. "I'm going to go use the restroom. Will you both be OK?"

"We'll be fine," said Maggie.

He waved over at a small huddle of his staff, all laughing and having a great time. He smiled. It was almost an answer to his question, seeing the people he cared the most about having fun. He remembered the stairs out of the VIP area at the last second and managed not to make an ass out of himself. He took a right and walked deeper into the bar area. Hung on the walls were black-and-white pictures of the Rat Pack. All the boys laughing with drinks in their hands, smoking and having a grand old time. He stared up at Sinatra. Chance thought—not for the first time—that he had been born in the wrong era.

He passed several high-top tables along the wall. Deeper into the club, the room expanded. Seven or eight half-moon booths were on the right side, with the long mahogany bar running down the left. The place was packed to capacity. Being a big guy, it was easy to get people to move out of the way. Past the booths was the small stage, and Chance felt a tinge of envy mixed with regret. On the grand piano, a bald guy was banging out Elton John's "Saturday Night's All Right for Fighting" and in front of the stage various twenty- and thirty-somethings danced, their sweat shining under the lights. The smells of smoke, layers of vanilla, and flowers competed with musk and spice.

Anthony, behind the bar, motioned for Chance to belly up. It was a game they always played. When visiting each other's establishments, the owner would pour their most expensive liquor. Two shots each. They would shoot the first one and bullshit over the second, remarking on the quantities of their mortgage payments they'd swallowed. Chance was in the lead, having poured four shots of Louie XIII cognac. At $3,800 a bottle, Chance didn't think Anthony could beat him.

Anthony's olive complexion, slicked hair, and good Roman nose came with an easy smile. "Chance, you fucking goombah, you ventured out of the VIP room to hang with us little people," yelled Anthony over the music. The drip in the suit next to Chance guffawed, and Anthony gave him a hard stare. The guy almost choked on his drink and turned away from Chance.

Chance smirked. "What kind of king would I be if I didn't let my loyal subjects behold this most regal of men?"

"I think I've got you this time, you pathetic wannabe gangsta. Where did you get that leather jacket, Mobs-R-Us?" Anthony laughed.

"At least I have style. No self-respecting Italian would be caught dead dressed like a J. Crew cover model." Chance fluttered his eyelashes and said in a high voice, "Excuse me, sir, is that Bugle Boy you're wearing? Why yes… yes, it is."

Anthony laughed even louder. Anthony was in the same boat as Chance. They'd grown up together, danced around the fringe of petty criminal enterprises, got lucky, went to college, came back and became legitimate business owners barely on the fringe of the Milwaukee mob. Not in, but not exactly out.

"I think I've got you this time, Chance. Hundred-and-fifty-year Grand Marnier. I haven't tried it yet, but I bet this will be as smooth as butter." He lined up four shot glasses and poured the amber liquor into each, careful not to spill a drop. They both picked up the shots and said, "*Salute.*" They tapped the shots on the bar and knocked them back.

The warm liquor coated Chance's throat, sickly sweet after drinking scotch all night. It was as smooth as butter, with a distinct orange flavor. Only a slight burn on the back end.

"Damn it," said Anthony. "Not even close." His shoulders sagged.

The piano player launched into Billy Joel's "Only the Good Die Young," and more drunk patrons sang along. Chance scanned the crowd, eyes occasionally pausing on a lovely, spirited, or devilish woman. He made eye contact with several, smiled briefly, as if to acknowledge the mutual appreciation of their good looks, and moved on.

As Anthony started to talk about something, Chance noticed Stella holding court at one of the booths. She didn't see him, and Chance examined her. His breath caught in his throat, not sure if it wanted to go out or in. Her hair was in long, slow curls, flowing over her shoulders. Eyes sparkling, she was loving the fact that she was queen, holding court over the cream of Milwaukee society. Chance recognized several of the women, their husbands being the movers and shakers of the city. He'd even slept with one of the wives last year. Janise something or other.

"Hey, are you even listening to me?"

Chance glanced at Anthony. "Yes, you were saying you suck, and I am king."

"Fuck off, Charlie!" Anthony said, smiling. "That's a table of some beautiful trouble."

Chance's gaze wandered back to Stella.

"What I would give to be in the middle of that group," said Anthony. Chance nodded at his bluster. He'd married his college sweetheart, and Chance knew he was still in love. He would talk a great game, but Anthony was hitched for life. *With his soulmate.* Envy churned in his stomach.

"Mary would have your balls for breakfast, and you know it."

"Are you kidding me? She doesn't let me leave the house with them. She keeps them in a jar on her vanity." They both chuckled.

Mary was one of Chance's favorite people. One of the few beautiful married women Chance had zero inclination to sleep with. A sister to Chance, and a woman he could be honest with, having no need to impress or charm. She also called him on his bullshit, which he loved.

"How's Mary doing?"

"Still pregnant, and big as a house. But don't you fucking tell her I said that. She's more beautiful now than I've ever seen her. She doesn't believe me when I tell her, though. She'll walk into a room and say, 'Look out, beached whale coming through!' She's doing good, though. Everything is checking out fine."

Chance glanced back over at Stella, who was staring right at him, a slight smile on her lush lips. As they made eye contact, her smile widened, as if to say *Hi*.

"Stella turned out to be a pretty choice, huh?" said Anthony. "If I had known in the eighth grade she was going to turn out this hot I'd 'a never dumped her for Melissa Brunsback."

"You only dated Melissa 'cause she would let you feel her up behind the roller rink."

"This is true. I'm still proud of the fact that I was the first one in our class to touch boobs."

Chance turned back to the bar. "I got to go to the head," said Chance. "Give Mary my love." He slammed the second shot, smirked at Anthony, and started to push his way toward the bathroom.

CHAPTER TWENTY-THREE

I WANT YOU TO WANT ME

Maggie stared into her vodka tonic as if it contained tea leaves telling her future.

Geoff, next to her, sipped his scotch, comfortable in the haze but troubled over his current romantic status. "It's not as if I didn't know what was going on. I knew what it was, and I knew how it was going to end. I just couldn't help myself."

"I know what you mean," said Maggie. "Part of me wants to down this drink and jump off the cliff. But that's exactly what I'd be doing. Jumping off a cliff with no parachute, wondering if I'm going to hit water or rock."

"It's not as if he hid the fact that he was married. He was at least honest."

"I know he's involved with that married woman. I know he only gets involved with married women, as a way to stay emotionally unattached. All of the single women he's ever gone out with have lasted exactly three dates."

"I could go over there right now and kiss him, right in front of his wife."

"I'm so scared to tell him how I feel. He's my boss. I don't want it to get awkward at work."

"I could do it. I could march right up to him and plant one on him. I bet he would be so shocked he wouldn't know what to do."

"He is so great with Cassie. And she adores him."

Geoff downed the rest of his scotch in a single swallow. "I'm going to do it." He stood. "Fuck it!"

"Wait, Geoff, what are you going to do?"

"I'm going to walk right up to him and kiss him right in front of the waif."

"No, you're not, don't be ridiculous. Sit back down here, Geoff... now!" Maggie pulled at his arm.

Geoff sighed and sat back down. He reached over to the half-full scotch bottle and poured another two fingers. "You're right. I couldn't do that to him. It's his life. If he wants to be miserable pretending to be straight, what's it to me?"

"He doesn't deserve you, sweetie. Look at you. You're an African god. You're buff, totally beautiful, smart, sexy, talented."

"Keep going, sister."

"Funny, kind, charming. Any man would be damn lucky to have you."

"You forgot amazing in bed."

"Well, I wouldn't know. I can only imagine it to be true."

"Plus, I'm hung like a horse."

"Ouch! Keep that thing away from me."

They both giggled and hugged each other. Geoff spilled his drink, but neither of them noticed.

Maggie let go and regarded Geoff. Sadness was turning down the corners of her mouth. The piano guy started singing "Beth" by Kiss.

"God, I hate this song," said Geoff. "My ex-wife's name is Beth."

"I never would have thought you'd like this song, anyway."

"Maggie, dear, they don't take away your Black card 'cause you like a white band."

She smiled but glanced away, uncomfortable. He sighed.

"So, what should I do?" asked Maggie.

Geoff inspected her: beautiful, fragile, single mom, carrying too many bricks on her shoulders. He clasped her delicate hands within his, squeezing gently. "Honey, you're a beautiful woman. Strong, fierce, passionate, and kind. You're an amazing mother and have a most precious child. But, sister, you've got horrible taste in men. As do I, I know, pot calling kettle. You look for a man to rescue you. You watched *Snow White* and *Cinderella* one too many times as a little girl. There's no man like that. Don't get me wrong. Chance can be Prince Charming. I love him to death. But he's as broken, if not more, as you are."

"But that's just it. We can fix each other. I'd be good for him. He'd be so good for me. For Cassie."

"The best."

"He gave me five hundred dollars today. Said there was a mistake on my last paycheck, and he was really sorry."

"Did he now?"

"Don't you think that's a bit odd?"

"It's unusual for Bernie to have an accounting error. But I'm glad they caught it."

Maggie playfully hit Geoff in the arm. "Stop right now. You know what it was. The exact amount Tom stole from me."

"Was it?" Geoff raised an eyebrow.

Maggie hit him again, harder. Geoff smirked. She hit him again.

"OK, OK, jeez. Stop beating me, woman."

"You told him."

"OK, maybe I did. We were drunk the other night. I probably said a lot of things."

"That's my point. Who does things like that? Nobody, or at least very few people in my experience. Plus, he got Tom out of town." Maggie brushed a stray lock of hair from her face. "He's such a good man, the way he takes care of all of us." Tears formed in her eyes.

"Maggie, Chance is my best friend. He's a wonderful but flawed man. There's a lot of pain, and he doesn't deal with it. He fixes everyone else's lives and drinks to hide from his own. Is that the environment you think is healthy for a relationship? Is that the kind of environment you want Cassie to grow up in?"

Maggie reached out and touched Geoff's arm. "You know what it's like out there. Men are either Tom, a fucking sadistic asshole, or you, a hunk, but gay as the day is long."

Geoff laughed and wiped away Maggie's tear before it reached her chin. He cupped her face with his massive hand.

Maggie pushed her face against his hand, a kitten snuggling for warmth. "Everyone has baggage, Geoff. We all do. But Chance is the kindest man I've ever known. I know he'd never hit me. Or Cassie. I know he's sweet, thoughtful, giving. He's successful and isn't going to rip me off—"

"You forgot devastatingly handsome."

Maggie giggled. "No, I most definitely didn't forget."

"All right out there," said the piano player into his mic. "This one goes out by request. If you've ever danced to this song at your high school prom, grab a partner and get out on the dance floor." He started singing "The Air That I Breathe" by The Hollies.

"Oh, I love this song so much. I wish I were dancing with Chance right now."

Geoff got up and carried their empty glasses to the self-serve bar. He poured a double count of Grey Goose, squeezed a lemon, and poured in the tonic water. He stirred it with his finger and put his finger in his mouth.

"Actually, that tastes pretty good," he said. He made the same for himself and carried the drinks back over to Maggie. Most of the staff had left the VIP room to dance in the bar.

"Honey, I don't know what you want me to say. Is Chance a great guy? Yes. Will he break your heart? Probably. Will it crush him if he does? Most certainly. Not to mention the fact that his family isn't exactly the Cleavers. I know he cares for you and Cassie. But he doesn't make good decisions when it comes to women. In that regard, he's as fucked up as we both are. He picks out the ones that will hurt him, because of his guilt. Or he picks out the ones he thinks he can save—"

"What happened, Geoff? You've known him the longest. What does he feel so guilty about?"

"I don't know much. He was engaged, and she died. He won't ever talk about it."

Maggie sipped her drink. Blinked rapidly and took a bigger sip. Geoff followed suit. The piano guy started playing "Love Shack" by The B-52's.

"Enough of this. Let's go dance, honey. Let's shake our butts and get happy." He stood, holding out his hand to Maggie.

Maggie stopped as they headed toward the dance floor. "Oh, shit!" She nodded toward a stunning blonde walking past the entrance to the VIP area.

Sloan Bartallatas, and she was alone.

CHAPTER TWENTY-FOUR

SHOULD I STAY OR SHOULD I GO

Chance stared at the man gazing back from the bathroom mirror. The eyes, more green than brown, were overpowered by dilated pupils. The shots were hitting his bloodstream, but he was energized and not yet in a sad, slow, slobbering drunkenness.

Don't do this, Chance. Do not do this. When his thoughts didn't have the desired effect, he said it out loud. "Don't do this, Chance. Do not do this. She's an employee. You're already involved with a married woman. You don't need this. You need to make a good decision here, buddy."

His reflection swayed, and he put his hands on the sink to steady himself. He regarded the eyes of the man looking at him. "She's beautiful... and just because you can, doesn't mean you should. Right?" His reflection shrugged his shoulders at him.

"You know you care about her. You know you love Cassie. It could be perfect." The yearning in his voice was clear. "With everything going on in your life right now, Charles Dougal McQueen. Really."

He looked down, ashamed at even considering it.

"Listen," he said to the mirror, "you're going to go out there. Say hi to Stella and her friends, make excuses, go back to the VIP room, hang out with your staff, and go home alone."

He slapped himself in the face. "And you're going to call Sloan and end things. That's seriously fucked up. You're an asshole. It needs to end. OK, you're gonna be strong." He took a deep breath and pushed it out fast. Took another one, trying to clear his head. "You're gonna make the right decision here. I'll kick your ass if you make the wrong decision."

He stared deep into his own eyes. Yup, he was talking to himself in a mirror. He laughed. The reflection laughed back at him.

"OK, you're not drunk yet. Let's go do this."

He smiled at himself. A toilet flushed and a guy walked out of a stall and started washing his hands. Chance started to wash his hands as well. The two men glanced at each other in the mirror.

After thirty agonizing seconds, the other man turned off the water and looked directly at Chance. "Buddy, don't worry about it. I do it all the time." He grinned at Chance, grabbed some paper towels, and walked to the bathroom door. "Good luck," he said as he left.

Chance snickered and peered underneath the stalls to make sure nobody else was in there. Went back to the sink to grab some paper towels. The music got louder, and the bathroom door opened, and Chance watched through the mirror a dude stumble in.

. . .

Winnie stared at the boy gazing back from the bathroom mirror at the Lakeside Theater. His dishwater-blond hair hung over his left eye, and he decided for the twentieth time to get a haircut. He turned on the tap and splashed lukewarm water on his face, which didn't revive him as he'd hoped. He gripped both sides of the sink, hanging his head to avoid the accusatory eyes glaring back at him.

"Don't even think about it. You love Alex, so put it out of your mind." The surprisingly high ceilings gave a slight echo to his words; he absently thought Lionel Richie would sound great in here.

After Prez and Hunter had bailed on them, Alex suggested they catch a movie. Winnie vetoed a third viewing of *Pretty Woman,* and they compromised on *The Handmaid's Tale,* which Winnie might have liked had he been able to concentrate on the story. But he could only focus on one thing.

His mind had run the gamut: it didn't happen, it couldn't have happened, he was assuming, he'd misunderstood. But no matter how many times he went over it in his head during the movie, he kept coming back to the same thing. A girl, woman, female, had offered him sex.

For the 400th time he replayed the conversation. He and Alex had been standing in an excessively long line waiting to get popcorn. *Cry-Baby* with Johnny Depp had just come out and Winnie was surrounded by an army of pubescent girls, all shrieking at decibels that could shatter glass. Even Alex, who always defended anyone with two X chromosomes, looked visibly annoyed.

"Why don't you grab our seats and I'll wait here to get your Laffy Taffy?" he suggested, to her obvious relief. He watched her go and looked over the sea of Jordache jeans, ESPRIT sweatshirts, and whale-spout ponytails. He imagined Chow running in with his dual pistols blazing, protecting hordes of Valley Girl wannabees from the evil clutches of Hans Gruber. A tap on his shoulder pulled him out of the fantasy and he turned around. Jennie, whose parents owned the arcade and who was good at certain things, according to Hunter, stood there smiling at him. She had slightly crooked front teeth and he wondered if they ever caught on anything she put in her mouth. He shuddered and pushed it from his mind.

"Hey, Winnie. I wanted to tell you I was sorry to hear about your dad."

Winnie stared at the ground and repeated his canned statement. "Thanks. Yeah, everybody liked him."

"I had him my senior year, and he was by far my favorite. I never thought history could be interesting, but he made it entertaining."

She clasped her hands behind her back and he immediately looked at her chest. As blood rushed to his cheeks, he thought of Alex admonishing him. He turned around and focused on the mullet in front of him. It curled at the ends and was dyed bleach blond. Not really a good look. He felt a tap on his shoulder again.

"So, I saw you at Loose Change the other day. I was hoping you'd say hi, but you seemed really into your game."

Winnie's eyebrows furrowed. She was a couple of years older than he was, and he was pretty sure they'd never spoken before, so he wasn't sure why she expected him to say hi. "Um, yeah, sorry."

"Are you going to Billy's party tomorrow?"

Now Winnie was sure she had him confused with somebody else. "Um, I don't think so."

The corners of her mouth inverted, and she did the thing with her hands behind her back again. "I got a new car." She straightened her shoulders and grew an inch. "It's a blue Rambler. It's kinda rusty, but totally cool."

"That's great," he replied without enthusiasm.

"I was thinking maybe we should hang out sometime."

No girl had ever asked him out, but he was pretty sure that's what happened. Her eyes were bloodshot and now he noticed the faint smell of pot mixed with the easily recognizable scent of Aussie hairspray.

His lips moved like he was speaking, but no sounds came out. He brought his fist to his mouth and coughed once. "Really?"

She showed her crooked front teeth again. "Yeah, maybe? We could um... go to a party, or the movies." She looked around as if realizing she was at the movies. "Come back to the movies." Her laugh was insecure and appealing. She looked right at him. "Or we could just go and park somewhere. You know, in my new car."

"Park?"

"Yeah, you know, park. Somewhere private."

"Um, I'd have to ask my mom."

There was more of that insecure and appealing laugh. "You're funny. I like that you're funny." She reached up and moved his hair from his left eye.

"Hey, kid, you gonna order, or what?" The lady behind Jennie pointed to the counter, and to Winnie's surprise he'd finally made it to the front of the line. He stammered something close to words and Jennie giggled again.

"I'm in the book, so call me sometime."

As he stood in the bathroom recalling what had happened, he got a chill, and his body shook as if someone had just walked over his grave. His cheeks flushed with embarrassment.

"You have to ask your mom? What the hell was that?" He spoke out loud. "You are such an idiot."

He'd been so flustered he had forgotten Alex's Laffy Taffy. It was putting it mildly to say she'd not been pleased. Guilt hovered above him like a cloud of cigarette smoke. Not about candy, but about cheating. He finally brought his eyes up to meet the ladies' man in the mirror.

"You're gonna walk Alex home and you are gonna tell her how you feel. It's as simple as that. And you're not gonna think about phone books or parked cars or anything else."

A voice echoed from one of the stalls. "Dude, are you seriously having an argument with yourself in the mirror?" The echoes faded into the sound of a toilet-paper roll being used.

"Um, bye," was all he could think to say as he ran out of the bathroom.

. . .

Junior watched as Chance left the bar and walked towards the hallway where the bathrooms were located. He pushed his lips together in anticipation. His hand went into the inside pocket of his jacket and his fingers brushed up against the semi-automatic handgun. He looked around and saw nobody paying attention. He leaned over so his body was blocked by the table. Took the gun out under the table and reached into his other pocket. Grabbing the silencer, he screwed it on expertly, having practiced hundreds of times. Putting the gun into the outside pocket of his trench coat, he stood up and looked at Ray. Ray looked Junior up and down and gave him a nod. Nothing showing.

Junior turned around and started to make his way through the sea of bodies. The singer had finished "Only the Good Die Young," and had started up "Brown Eyed Girl." All the drunken idiots were singing along, the level of noise just short of deafening. Junior made his way past the bar, careful not to make eye contact with Anthony. He didn't think Anthony would remember him from years ago, but with what was about to happen, he didn't want to take any chances. He laughed out loud as his brain processed the inside joke.

He would walk in, nod if Chance turned to him from the urinal, and make like he was going into the stalls. After he confirmed nobody else was there, he would do Chance from behind. Right in the back of the head. Drop a few baggies of coke to make it look like a drug deal, turn around and book it out the back door. Ray would be back there with the car, and they would go to a quiet stretch of lakefront and get rid of the gun. Well, get rid of Ray, and then get rid of the gun. Bad luck if anybody else was in there to, but it would be a game-time decision. He didn't want a massacre, and multiple bodies only added to the number of cops that would be investigating.

He got to the door of the bathroom and paused. He took a deep breath. He put his hand into his jacket pocket and around the butt of the gun.

"Junior!"

He spun around, almost bringing the gun out, but stopped short. "What the fuck, Ray? You're supposed to be out the fucking back." Ray ran up to him with his hand still up in the stop position. He leaned in and half-yelled over the noise.

"I know. But your mom… I mean your stepmom, is here."

"What the fuck are you talking about?"

"Look." Ray turned and indicated back towards the bar. Junior leaned past Ray and sure enough, there was Frank's wife, Sloan. Standing at the bar, paying for a glass of wine.

"What the fuck? What's she doing here?"

She turned away from the bar and started walking back towards where Ray and he had been sitting.

A drunk woman stumbled down the hall towards them.

"Is the little boy's room all full?" she asked, falling into Ray. "Now you know what us girls have to deal with all the time." She giggled, pushed herself off Ray, and stumbled into the ladies' room.

"Fuck," Junior mumbled. The door to the men's room opened. They both froze. A man that wasn't Chance walked out. "Excuse me," he said as they stepped back giving him a path. Junior brought his fingers to his temples and rubbed them. He couldn't go out the front. Couldn't just stand here either.

"Chance can't see me here." He grabbed Ray and pushed him into the door of the men's room.

"What the," Ray yelled as he fell against the door, pushing it open. Junior turned around and looked at the back door. *Alarm will sound if opened.* He took out a Swiss Army knife and jammed the blade between the door and the handle box. It easily popped off. He found the wire he hoped powered the alarm. Pulling out the wire cutter tool he took a deep breath and said a silent prayer. He snipped the wire and pushed open the door. No shrieks or flashing lights. He walked out to the alley, softly closing the door behind him. He finally exhaled. The quiet background of traffic noise a welcome respite to the thumps of bass from behind the door. Chance wasn't the only one that got lucky tonight.

CHAPTER TWENTY-FIVE

LIMELIGHT

As the song ended, Chance said a silent *thank you* to the music gods for letting him escape the dance floor, and he pushed his way to the bar, trying to catch his wind. Maggie and Geoff joined him on either side. Stella's crew was still on the dance floor, fueled by sugar and alcohol.

"Damn, Chance. You are the whitest white-man dancer," said Geoff.

"What? I thought he was good," Maggie breathed out.

"No," said Chance in between gulps of air. "You two put me to shame. I am an old white geezer next to you two."

Anthony put a scotch in front of Chance. "Who would have thought a goombah like Chance would bust a move? This one's on me for giving me the privilege of seeing that. Can't wait to tell Mary that Chance had a vertical seizure. She's going to pee her pants when I try to act that out for her. Of course, she is seven months pregnant, so the bar's set pretty low in the urination department. I wish I'd had my camcorder," said Anthony, laughing. "Geoff, Maggie, what can I get for the only two people who didn't look as ridiculous as Al Pacino over here?"

"Two double vodka tonics with lemon. I think I danced away a perfectly good buzz," said Geoff.

Chance grabbed his drink and turned around from the bar. He glanced at Stella, dancing with a guy having a fit. Chance turned back to the bar and lit a cigarette.

"How can you smoke when you're still out of breath?" asked Maggie.

"That's why I'm smoking. All this dancing is giving me too much oxygen. Guys, this has been a great night. I'm so glad you both came. It wouldn't have been the same without you."

"What? The night's not over yet. We're just getting started, Chancie."

"Yeah, this has turned out to be a marvelous day," said Maggie, staring into Chance's eyes.

"No, I know, but I wanted to tell you both how much I love you. And don't call me Chancie," said Chance, smiling.

"OK, Chuck," said Geoff, laughing.

"God, even worse!"

"Did you see Tito dancing with Leah?" asked Maggie.

"Oh my god, I know!" said Geoff. "I would never have thought that would happen. Talk about a United Nations meeting. El Salvador and Vietnam. I wonder what their kids would be like."

Maggie punched Geoff in the arm. "Stop it. I think it's beautiful."

"Ouch, Maggie. Why do you keep hitting me?"

"Oh, poor big bad Navy Seal. Jesus, you big wimp! How did you make it through Hell Week if you can't take a punch from a hundred-pound girl?" asked Chance.

Maggie punched Chance in the arm hard and turned to Geoff. "What's a Navy Seal?"

"Never mind, Mags," said Geoff.

"Jeez, Maggie, have you been working out or something?" Chance rubbed his arm.

Geoff and Maggie laughed.

The music stopped and the piano guy stood up. "OK, I'm going to take ten. Don't nobody go nowhere."

The house music came on: Frank Sinatra's "Fly Me to the Moon." Stella and her crew returned to their booth. She eyed Chance as she sat, her expression unreadable.

"How about we all go back to the VIP area?" asked Geoff.

"Just a minute." Chance glanced at Stella. She was laughing at something her friend had said. Stella responded, and all four women scrutinized him. He smirked and pushed himself off the bar. He approached the piano guy at the end of the bar. The piano guy shook his head. Chance put his hand on the guy's shoulder. The piano guy shook his head again. Chance reached into his pocket and handed the guy something. The piano guy nodded, and Chance walked back over to Maggie and Geoff.

"What was that all about?" asked Maggie.

"You'll see. Anthony, can you kill the house music?"

"Crap, Chance, really? You're going to piss off Joe."

"Who's Joe?"

"The piano guy. When you did this to the last guy, he wouldn't go back onstage."

"Are you going to sing?" asked Maggie.

"Hey, it's not my fault the guy sucked," said Chance.

Maggie asked Geoff, "Is he going to embarrass himself?"

Geoff shook his head.

Anthony pointed at Chance. "You apologized to the crowd that he sucked, right before you started to play. He tried to go up there after you stopped, and the crowd booed him. I had him booked for four more nights."

"This guy isn't as bad, besides... he has a drum machine." Chance grabbed his drink and walked onstage.

"I don't understand," said Maggie. "What's the big deal?"

"When he gets in a mood like this, it can either end up very good, or very bad," said Geoff. "Before he was a restaurant owner, Chance was a musician. A damn good one, in fact. I've heard a couple of tapes. He was in the studio recording his first album with Columbia Records when Ellie was killed. They were billing him as the next Frank Sinatra."

"How come I never heard this before?"

"He never finished the album. I didn't know him then, but Bernie the accountant told me about it. So now if he ever sings it's because he's drunk, and he'll either be amazing and happy, or he'll get completely depressed and it'll be a shitshow."

"I did know him back then," said Anthony. "He was amazing. It was truly sad when Ellie died. All of the music in him died, too."

CHAPTER TWENTY-SIX

PIANO MAN

Chance finished "It Had to Be You" to a standing ovation. The bar was going crazy. He got up from the piano, gave his customary shy smile and half wave. Before he even got off the stage, two scotches were handed to him by the cocktail server. She tried to point out the two different women that had bought them. Chance knocked back one and set it on the piano. He raised his other to the crowd. He glanced at Anthony, who was in a passionate discussion with Joe, the piano guy.

Maggie and Geoff pushed through the crowd surrounding him.

"That was amazing!" yelled Maggie.

"Yeah, man, unbelievable!" said Geoff. "Way better than my cousin's wedding."

"Thank you. It was fun," said Chance with false humility.

Strangers were patting him on the back. The house music came back on: Dean Martin crooning "Return to Me."

Stella and her friends made their way up to him, all squawking at the same time.

Chance considered them and Maggie and Geoff. "Hey, let's all go back to the VIP area and get some drinks. I need to sit down."

Maggie glanced at Geoff, a bit deflated. He said, "Don't worry, Mags. You got this."

As they made their way to the VIP room, patrons repeatedly stopped Chance. Several cocktail napkins with phone numbers were thrust into his hands. One woman grabbed him by the neck and pulled him down for a kiss. He laughed and gently pushed her back. He stopped dead in his tracks. Sitting at a high-top table was Sloan. Hands wrapped around a white wine, looking at him with a soft, low sadness.

Chance pulled on Geoff's arm. "I'll be right there."

Geoff raised an eyebrow. "You sure?"

"Don't worry. I'll be right there."

Maggie glanced back, made eye contact with Chance. He flashed her a smile. She turned and kept walking.

Chance stopped in front of Sloan's table. "Hi."

"That was impressive," said Sloan sweetly.

Her tone caught Chance off guard. "What are you doing here?"

"Frank's out of town, so I came to check out Anthony's place. I called you at the restaurant, but you must not have gotten the message."

Chance tilted his head at her soft and caring tone.

"I noticed you've taken out your staff, so I don't want to keep you. But I have some things I want to talk to you about. About how I've treated you." She hung her head and folded some hair behind her ear. "About how I feel."

"You do?"

"Yes, I do. I have a lot of emotions running around, and I want to talk about them with you. Can we meet for lunch tomorrow? Frank doesn't get back for a couple of days." She flashed a wolf's grin.

"I don't think that's a good idea. I've been doing a lot of thinking, too. I don't—"

She held up her hand. "Please, let's not do this here. I know you have a lot of things to say. I want to express myself before you say them."

What the fuck? he thought. *Are those tears in her eyes?*

"Please, Chance... let's meet for lunch. If you feel the same way after we talk, I'll understand. I haven't exactly been my best lately."

Chance stood there, unsure of what to do. A minute ago, she was in his rear-view mirror. The affair, all but over.

"OK, we can meet for lunch." *Why deal with an emotional problem today when you can put it off until tomorrow?*

"There's a little place over by UW-Milwaukee. Harry's Bar and Grill. It's quiet; we can talk there." She reached out to grab his hand and gave it a short squeeze. "One o'clock?"

"Um, sure, that's fine." He pulled his hand away.

"OK, 'till tomorrow." She winked, got up from the table, and walked out. Chance couldn't help but gaze at her perfect ass as she sashayed down the hallway. She peeked back and caught him. He looked away quickly.

You are an idiot, he thought. Not for the first time that night, and not for the last.

· · ·

On one side of the couch, Maggie seemed to be deep in thought. On the other, Stella was telling Geoff a story about junior high, when Chance had given Nichelle Anders a pair of cubic zirconia earrings at a dance, even though she didn't have her ears pierced. He ignored the laughter at his expense and sat down on the couch, closer to Maggie. She glanced up and smiled at him.

"Have you had a good time tonight, Chance?"

"The best. Have you?"

"So far." They held their gaze briefly until she blushed and looked away.

Chance had consumed enough alcohol that any worries about what was going to happen next was a whisper at a rock concert. He could tell that Maggie was in the exact same spot. The anticipation of what might be was pure joy and excruciating tension. Chance was extremely good at putting things he didn't want to think about in a box. And right now, Sloan was not something he wanted bouncing around in his head.

Maggie was exactly the type of person your mother always hoped you'd marry. Beautiful, but not hot. Sweet, but not a wallflower. She had motherhood written all over her, but in many ways, to Chance, it only made her more enticing. She was someone you could laugh with, confide in, show weakness without worrying about her judging you. She'd be your best friend, champion, support system, the foundation of a life Chance had so far found elusive.

Maggie was not a plaything. Not someone you took lightly. She was something serious. A white picket fence, PTA, mow-the-lawn-on-Saturday kind of girl. It hit every fear Chance had. A dream he had given up on years ago. Somewhere in his mind, he knew alcohol was dulling and enhancing each sensation. Rational thoughts, responsibility to the feelings of others, desire, hope, and bone-crushing fear.

Stella leaned over, put her hand on his knee, and whispered into his ear. "Charlie... I'm going to fuck you tonight."

Maggie was conversing with Geoff and Janise, one of Stella's friends.

"I'm gonna do things to you that have never been done to you before."

"Stella, you're drunk. I think you should relax."

"Charlie, you can have me any way you want tonight... any way."

CHAPTER TWENTY-SEVEN

PARENTS JUST DON'T UNDERSTAND

Alex sat at the kitchen table while her mother moved about doing busywork. Alex sipped Kazakh tea, letting the fennel seeds and sweet honey roll around on her tongue. This taste more than any other reminded her of childhood. It was loving in its heat and sweetness.

She had returned from the movies with Winnie and had had a surprisingly awkward goodbye on the porch. Not able to sleep, she'd wandered into the kitchen. Happily, she found her mother also suffering from insomnia. A late-night session with her mother was just what she needed to soothe a cauldron of conflicting emotions swirling in her stomach with the tea.

Alex's mom was a small woman who'd maintained her ballerina body. She had rich black hair showing the earliest signs of silver. Her high cheekbones and oval face were classic Slavic features. The pale blue eyes Alex had inherited could be sharp and piercing. But for the lines under her mother's, they could be mistaken for sisters.

"So, I don't know what to do. Sometimes I want to hit him over the head and say wake up, and yet at the same time the thought of changing anything scares me to total death."

"You and Vinston have never even kissed?"

"Gosh, no, Mama, haven't you been listening?"

"But at times you vant to?" Her mother turned to face her daughter.

"Yes... no... I don't know, Mama. That's what I'm talking about. Sometimes I want him to so bad it makes me crazy. Other times I don't even want to look at his face."

"Vhen you feel like you don't vant to look at his face, is it shortly after vhen you vanted him to so bad?" Most of the time Alex never even noticed her mother's thick accent. But four V's for W's in one sentence, stood out.

Alex nodded. "Well, yes, I guess so. We've been friends since forever, and I can spend all day with him and feel great. He understands me on so many levels. And I miss him when he isn't around. I can't imagine what I'd do if I didn't have him in my life."

"Alexandra, I vant you to really think about this. You are young and beautiful. You are full of so much life, and you remind me of me when I was your age. I have seldom seen a friendship like the one you and Vinston have. I used to vorry you vere spending so much time with this boy. I would tell Papa it wasn't natural. But he was so devoted to you, and followed you around. He would always share his toys with you, or give you his portion of dessert. He always let you pick which game you vould play, or vhich television show you would vatch. I liked him around you. I figured when the two of you hit your teenage years you would drift apart. But you both held on strong and stayed the best of friends. I knew a day vould come vhen you would have to decide which way you would be as adults."

Alex shifted uncomfortably. Her mama made her sound selfish, and the part of her that agreed was kicking her in the chest.

"Alexandra, you and Vinston have been the best of friends since you vere six years old. If you go down this path, take a chance and change your relationship with Vinston, you will never get back your friendship if it doesn't vork out. Right now, you have the heat and fire in your heart. Your body has become a beautiful shrine to vomanhood. Your hormones are buzzing around you, and of course, you look at Vinston and because he knows you and because he loves you, you vant to do things vith him."

Alex didn't bat an eye. She and her mama had a long history of frank discussions. Partly it may have been due to how early Alex's body began to change. But Katiana had always treated Alex like a younger sister.

"Heat and fire can lead you down a dangerous path, vhich isn't real. It can cloud your judgment and make you a different person from your true self. The love you have for Vinston is real. Your friendship is real. I am not saying you two can't or von't make it vork. But at your age, vith so much to experience and learn, it would be one in a million. Are you villing to take the chance of not having him in your life for a few moments of physical joy?"

Alex let the words sink in. They spoke to her deepest fears about Winnie and her. He was as much a part of her life as breathing. She couldn't imagine how she could live her life without him.

"Truly, Mama, I don't know what to do."

"Don't know vhat to do about vhat?" asked Alex's papa, walking into the room, rubbing the sleep from his eyes.

Papa is showing his years more than Mama is, thought Alex. Everything about him now was mostly gray. His once-black hair, his once-blue eyes. His skin, once perfect, dotted with broken capillaries.

Her papa spent most nights sitting in his study drinking vodka, smoking his homemade rolled cigarettes, and listening to records of Rimsky-Korsakov, Mussorgsky, Balakirev, Borodin, and of course Tchaikovsky. He had been the choreographer for the premier St. Petersburg Ballet Company, and, after they immigrated to America, he became the Director of the Milwaukee Ballet and Opera House. He was a kind and gentle man. She could remember sitting at his feet for hours, listening to the music and craving his gentle hand rubbing her head or stroking her hair.

He always had an aura of sadness about him, and when she was younger she thought for sure it was because of her. But she didn't know anything of their life before coming here. They never spoke of it, of what happened.

But sometimes he could be so funny, and she'd catch joy in his eyes, in such stark contrast as it blazed across his face.

"Alexandra is thinking about kissing Vinston, Andre."

Alex's papa snorted. "So, we have come to dis. Katiana, vhere is my vodka! The day every father dreads has come upon us. Lord, take me now, for I am not ready for this day. I cannot face my little daughter kissing the squeaky-voiced boy from down the street," said Andre with great dramatic flourish.

"Papa, stop being so silly," Alex said in a serious voice, but with a smiling face.

Andre held up his hands in mock surrender. "So, vhat is the problem Sasha? You vant to kiss the squeaky-voiced boy, then kiss him."

"Papa, stop pretending you don't like Winnie. And his voice hasn't squeaked in years."

"Not true, not true, Sasha. I vas talking to him last week and his voice vas like choking cats in heat. Besides, vhat kind of parents name their child after an imaginary bear that eats too much honey? Vinnie is such a silly name. How you could kiss someone vith such a silly name, I vill never know." He grinned at his daughter and wife. Alex smiled back at this repeat of a conversation they'd had about Winnie's name many times over the years.

"Andre, I was explaining to our daughter how she vould be risking their friendship if they vere to take a chance and change their relationship." Her mother gave Andre a warning shot.

As usual, Andre missed, or chose to ignore it. "Vhat is the problem? If you love the boy, you should kiss him. Vhat is gained by not taking the chance on love? I would prefer you took the vows and became a nun. But it is not my life to live. If you must kiss a boy, I would much prefer it was the Pooh bear than some stupid Neanderthal football player who doesn't know a French overture from a minuet."

One of the reasons her father loved Winnie so much was because Winnie loved classical music. More times than not, it would be Winnie and her sitting next to her papa's feet on the floor.

"But, Papa, what if I try with Winnie and it doesn't work? I'll lose him as my friend."

"Sasha, nothing in this vorld is gained by worrying about vhat might happen. If you vant to live your life without risk, vithout chance, vithout love, then maybe you really should go and become a nun. Everything in life vorth anything is vorth taking a risk. Consider your mama. If I'd not taken a risk, then I vould have never known the most beautiful voman in the world. Yet she is even so beautiful vhen she is standing there staring at me with the look of death. Love often comes with great pain. But it is through great pain ve can know great love."

His face softened as he gazed at her mama.

"You have known the Pooh bear your vhole life. He is vho he is. If you love this boy, then you should explore that love. Ha, now beautiful sirens in my kitchen. How many papas love and respect their daughters so much they vould say such things?"

Both women smirked at the familiar form of peacock this father and husband could take on. If he fixed a leaky sink, he was the world's greatest plumber, even if it started to leak the next week. If he changed the oil in the car, he was the world's greatest mechanic, even if it took him six hours and a box of Band-Aids to do it.

She viewed her parents. So different in the way they saw the world. Her papa's words had brought heat to her chest like Kazakh chai and vodka mixed together. Maybe she should kiss Winnie and get it over with. They might not even like it. Then again...

CHAPTER TWENTY-EIGHT

CAN'T FIGHT THIS FEELING

Chance blinked repeatedly and realized he was on his living room couch. Maggie was next to him. He tried to figure out how he had gotten there. He remembered getting into the cab with Maggie and Geoff. And then nothing. Maggie was talking about something. He squinted one eye to observe her more clearly. There were candles lit, and he had a glass of red wine in his hand. Soft music played, and it took another few seconds to realize it was Kenny G. *Seriously? Kenny G?*

He absorbed Maggie's beauty in the warm haze of the candlelight. He slowly realized he had been in a walking blackout. For some reason, he had come out of it. He examined the coffee table and saw a half-eaten pizza from Pizza Shuttle.

"So, after I told him I was pregnant he dropped me. Wouldn't take my calls, avoided me at school. I heard the next semester he transferred to UW-Stout. He isn't a part of our lives at all, and, frankly, I'm happy about it. It's hard sometimes being a single mom, but I don't have to share Cassie with him."

"Do your parents help out at all?" asked Chance, jumping into the conversation.

"They try to, but the farm isn't doing well since my brother died. It's just the two of them, and they're getting old. I keep telling them to sell, but my dad is stubborn."

Chance locked in on Maggie's face. "Cassie's great."

"Yes, she is. It's funny. I think back to when I first found out I was pregnant, and I seriously considered getting an abortion. I was nineteen, a child myself. I couldn't even think about raising a child. And after his parents actually slammed the door in my face, I knew I'd be alone. There was no way I was going to move back home. Now, though, I can't even imagine what my life would be like without her. She *is* my life. She's my best friend."

"Cassie's great."

She laughed. "Chance, you're drunk!"

"No, I'm not, err, well, yes, I guess I'm pretty drunk since I can't remember anything after the cab." Chance hung his head.

She grabbed his glass of wine. He let go with no protest. She put it on the coffee table and gazed at him. They stared at each other. He pointed to the stereo with his thumb.

"Who put this on?"

"I did. I love Kenny G."

"Oh, OK, good. I'd have to beat myself up if I had."

"Hey, you own it," said Maggie, smiling.

The part of his brain that analyzed decisions, determining what a good decision was and what constituted a bad decision, was awash in scotch and wine. It was trying to send out a message, but like a drunk driver, it was getting lost on the way home.

He leaned over, cupped his hand against her face. "So beautiful." He kissed her.

This was quite a different kiss from the one in the office. Soft and tender, but full of passion. He brought his other hand up and cupped her other cheek. Her lips tasted of wine and fit perfectly with his. He took her bottom lip between his teeth and pulled back slightly. After letting go, he heard her take in a breath. He plunged back in, his tongue reaching out for hers. Having found its target, it would dart back home, only to venture out a bit later. For what could have been hours, days, or weeks, they kissed in the candlelight. Sometimes soft and gently, other times passionate and firm. He wasn't thinking about anything other than the kiss. His focus was on giving and receiving pleasure. He controlled the tempo.

Maggie's head was swimming. Not from the alcohol, but from the kiss. Never in her life had she been kissed like this. She didn't even know it was possible. It was as if he knew exactly what she wanted before she did. He was showing her how she wanted to be kissed. She pushed these thoughts away and surrendered to the warmth. Wanting to hold on to this most perfect kiss forever. Her body was tingling. Blood rushed to her lips, which felt fat and vibrating. The butterflies in her stomach spontaneously combusted, heating her whole chest. She wanted to be inside his skin, in his blood, in his heart and lungs. She needed his body against hers.

Not stopping the kiss, she pushed him back and climbed on top. She felt a firmness and heat radiating between them. She pushed in, grinding herself against him. His arms were wrapped around her, engulfing her small frame. There were no thoughts, only sensations as she thrust her hips against his crotch. He took one of his arms from around her, and she felt herself being lifted off the couch. She wrapped her legs around his back, and he carried her effortlessly. He lowered her down gently on the bed.

Her eyes were shut tight as she felt part of his weight on her. Moments later she realized she was naked, as the coolness of the air hit her exposed skin. She felt his hot flesh pressing on top of her. His lips went away. Jolts of electricity shot between her breasts. His lips sucking, his tongue caressing, teeth gently biting. It seemed to be happening everywhere at once. Her stomach, her wrist, the bottom of her breast, her throat, her earlobe.

She heard the nightstand drawer opening and then a crinkle of plastic being shoved under the pillow and wondered how much practice it'd take to be that smooth at grabbing a condom.

His weight shifted, and his hand moved down, pressed in and held her tight, and slowly the pressure pushed down and spread her apart. She was on fire as he kept his hand there, applying pressure but otherwise not moving. She clamped her hand over her mouth as she came, her body shaking a few times. He hadn't even entered her, and each part of her body was exploding.

She kept her eyes shut. The rush, like nothing she'd ever felt. She had no muscle memory for what her body was experiencing. It was quick. Just as she had control, his fingers traced the edge of her lips. Her body was slick, but his movements were measured. Slowly around, tracing the outside, and then the inner part of her. He seemed to purposely avoid the spot, fingers moving in a circular fashion.

The currents were building again, and she was already three-quarters of the way there. Right when she wanted him to do something else, his finger grazed the spot. It was like she had stuck her finger in a light socket. But infinitely more pleasurable. Distracted by sensations, she didn't notice his weight moving away from the side of her body.

He spread her legs, and it wasn't until she felt his tongue taking over the movements of his fingers that she realized what he was doing. For half a second, she thought of how she didn't enjoy it when men did this. But it only lasted half a second as he massaged her. His tongue plunging inside of her, and around her. Sucking her into his mouth. She arched her back as she let go of everything but physical pleasure. Then as his tongue pressed down her body convulsed into mini orgasms.

She wasn't conscious of anything outside of this bubble. Her body being wracked with tremors. As his tongue made circular motions, the feelings built and built... each time she thought it was the crest, it paused and then rose higher.

He sucked her into his mouth and held it inside. All of his movements stopped, and she exploded.

She wriggled and convulsed, her hips bucking like a wild horse. She no longer had a body. Not arms or legs, not skin, or teeth, or a face. She was soaring into the stratosphere and plunging off a rollercoaster at the same time.

Lights danced behind her eyes, reds, greens, yellows, a star going supernova. Sounds not human escaped from her lips as she screamed, unconscious of the noise. If she had hands, they would be pounding onto the bed, but she didn't. She was above anything as mundane as a body. It kept going and going. There was no thought, no consciousness. Only unimaginable joy. She was within light itself. Flying into infinity.

Chance lay on the bed, his head squeezed between Maggie's legs. As their iron grip loosened, he felt small tremors still hitting her body. Nothing like what had happened three or four minutes ago. The warmth of the pure intimacy was better to him than any orgasm he could experience. Euphoria coated his body like sweat. He blew air lightly on her lips, and he felt another small tremor hit her body.

She was still panting, and her body was slick. Her skin glistened like glitter in the candlelight. To his annoyance, Kenny G was still blaring away in the background. He used the sheet to wipe off his face, and, careful not to disturb her post orgasmic joy, lay down next to her. He pushed his elbow into the pillow and rested his head onto his wrist. He stared down at her, her eyes still shut. Her eye makeup was streaked, and eyeliner made a trail away from her eyes like she'd been crying, yet she looked amazing, the glow coming from her like a streetlight burning through fog.

Her skin was smooth and blemish free. Her small breasts were perky, and he absently wondered if she had breastfed Cassie. Her dark nipples added an exotic spice to her appeal. He noticed her belly wasn't perfect, but he decided he preferred it exactly the way it was. It was a Cassie mark, and it made her all the more feminine. Her dark bush was trimmed in a way he had never seen before. A pyramid with the top pointed down as if to say, *it's here, hello?* He smiled at this thought and reached over and started to graze his fingernails through it. He knew this was a pleasing sensation, like someone giving you a back scratch or a head massage, only certainly more sexual.

She was still lying there, and if not for the movement of her chest he'd start to worry. He thought about whether he wanted to continue. He was perfectly content right now. He glanced back at Maggie, and for the first time since they had started, he saw she was looking at him. A look of awe, and it only made the experience better. He beamed at her. She rolled into him, grabbing him and hugging him fiercely. Her head was resting on his, her tears like spring raindrops moisturizing his skin. He caressed her back.

He wasn't surprised by this reaction. But he was touched.

"I know, baby. It's OK, there, there," he said softly. He ran his hand up and down her back. She held on even tighter, putting his neck into a death grip.

"Ow, OK... OK, it's all right."

"I'm so incredibly sad," she said into his ear.

"I know, baby, I... what?" His neck snapped back as if the air had punched him. She didn't respond, but cried harder.

He wondered if this had brought up some buried trauma. After a few minutes of her crying, and him lying there concerned but patient, her nose made a noise that was definitely not sexy. Her grip around his neck receded, and she moved back so she could look at him. He tried to wipe the tears from her face, but only succeeded in smearing the mascara even more. He pulled his hands away as if her face were on fire.

"It's, OK, baby, you're safe here." His mouth bunched up over the mess he'd made.

"Oh my god, I must look horrible."

"Well, you looked better ten minutes ago, but you're still beautiful."

She chuckled, which sounded pretty funny with a plugged nose. He reached out behind him to the nightstand and grabbed a handful of tissues.

"Thank wu," she said. She sat up and blew her nose. "I'm sorry."

"Whatever it is, you can tell me."

"I know. That's not what I'm upset about." She blew her nose again.

"OK," said Chance, even more confused. He waited for her to expand. She put the used tissue down on the bed, pulled her knees up to her chest, and wrapped her arms around herself, as if suddenly conscious of her nakedness.

He lay there, looking at her back. He brought his hand up to rub it again.

"I was lying there so incredibly happy. I have never, never, felt like that before." She turned to him and put her hand on his thigh. "I can't even begin to describe how amazing it was. Then I got sad. Like a wave, it rolled over me. I was thinking about you, and how unbelievably amazing you are, and then I thought about Ellie."

"What?"

She gripped his thigh tighter. "You have so much pain, and yet are so wonderful, and I don't know what happened, but I felt so sad. For her, for you."

He pushed himself against the backboard.

"I'm sorry, I'm sorry," she said in a rush, laying her head on his stomach. He sat there in shock, staring off at nothing. She was crying again, but he barely noticed. The reversal was a kick to the balls.

"Please, I didn't mean... I just... it just hit me."

He sat there; the ambiance of euphoria sucked out of the room by the vacuum of space. After a few minutes, he looked down at her. He took a breath and let it out. He could almost hear cigarettes and alcohol talking from the next room.

"It's OK," he said in a measured tone. "Why don't you go to the bathroom and freshen up? As beautiful as you truly are, Maggie, you look a little bit like a demonic clown," he said, trying to lighten the mood.

She cringed, and even in the low light he could see her face flush. She got up from the bed and walked on shaky legs to the bathroom. He got up and went to the small bar. He poured himself a measure of scotch and knocked it back in one gulp.

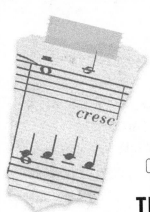

CHAPTER TWENTY-NINE

THE WAY WE WERE

She stood at the sink glaring into the mirror at the mess looking back. Her face was red, rubbed raw from crying, and Chance's facial hair. She turned on the hot water and searched for a face towel. Surprisingly, there was a full closet full of towels. Hand towels, face towels, bath towels. There was also rubbing alcohol, Vaseline, cotton balls, Q-tips, packaged toothbrushes, two unused hairbrushes, and men's and women's disposable razors. She couldn't tell if she was amused by the obvious nesting, or annoyed by the frequency of overnight guests. She put the towel under the steaming hot water and proceeded to clean her face.

"Stupid, stupid, stupid," she kept saying as she scrubbed. Going from a level of bliss never dreamed of to a weepy emotional mess. Her reflection gave no clue as to her actions. She braced herself against the sink, her body, not quite in tune with the rest of her, still tingling and shaky.

"It's no wonder he can't get over it, when stupid bitches like you bring it up. Real smart, Mags." The steam from the sink coated the mirror, and she was glad for the respite from accusing eyes. She gripped the sink, her knuckles white as she pushed down the sob. Her thighs were sticky, angry from chafing, and it hurt when she wiped herself off.

"Stupid crazy bitch has sex and starts blabbing about his dead fiancée. Real smart, Mags." Cold rage coursed through her. Not at Chance, or even herself. She was pissed at dead Ellie. It didn't make sense, but she didn't care. It was like Ellie's jealous ghost had invaded her body as punishment. Almost as soon as the rush of anger hit her, it left as fast and pity filled its wake. She wet another washcloth and finished wiping her face. It was the best she could hope for. Her eyes were still puffy, but the makeup streaks were gone. She took one of the hairbrushes from the closet and pulled it through her rat's nest.

She'd go out there and not bring it up unless he did. She'd try to pretend it didn't happen and ascertain how much damage was done. Maybe she could bring him around again. She could go down on him. It wasn't something she liked much; Tom having expected it all the time. He would push her head down until she gagged. God, she hated that, one of a long list. This thought brought her back to Chance, and what he'd done for her today. Tears formed again and she took several deep breaths. She nodded to her reflection as if to say, *you can do this.* She took a deep breath and opened the bathroom door.

She turned off the light and peered into the bedroom. It took a second for her eyes to adjust. The room reeked of cigarette smoke, and soft piano music that didn't sound like it was coming from a stereo. She found him at the baby grand, playing a sweet but unfamiliar melody. He'd put on sweatpants and a sweatshirt. She searched for her bra and panties. He didn't say anything, but the music stopped. Finally locating her underclothes, she turned away from Chance and started to put them on.

"I put out a pair of sweats and a T-shirt for you."

She found them folded neatly on the bed. *This concludes the romance portion of the evening,* she thought.

The pants were charcoal and fit her rather well. Definitely not his pants. She pulled on the T-shirt, which was only slightly too big, and adjusted the sweats.

She tentatively walked toward the piano. He didn't say anything, took a drag from his cigarette, and started to play again. The butterflies were back, and she sat down on the bench next to him.

"Would you like a drink?" he asked quietly.

"No, but if you have some water?"

He got up and went into the kitchen. She heard the water running, and he came back out with a glass, handed it to her.

"I'm going to have a drink." It smelled and sounded like he had already had one while she was in the bathroom. He walked back over to the bar, poured a drink, came back to the bench, and sat down with a heavy sigh. They sat there for a few seconds. He tapped his cigarette over the ashtray and took another sip from a rocks glass. Finally, he glanced at her. A chiseled face etched in grief, and it broke her heart.

"I don't want you to feel bad."

She broke his gaze as she crossed her arms and hugged herself.

"I've been thinking about it, where it came from." He paused. Took another drag off his cigarette, exhaling away from her. His hands went back to the keys and started back on the melody she'd heard earlier. "I understand, and I guess in a way I should apologize to you."

"Apologize to me?"

He sat there playing, not saying anything. She could tell he was searching for the words he wanted to use. But she had no idea what he wanted to say.

"Maggie, you are the perfect woman. I think you're special, and Cassie's amazing. Part of me wants a future, wants to reach out and… and be with someone in a healthy, honest way. But part of me is completely trapped in the past."

Her heart sank. It was going to be a *this was a mistake* kind of conversation. He reached up and stubbed out his cigarette. Took a sip of his drink and glanced at her again. His eyes were glassy and a little unfocused.

"Maggie, I shouldn't have—"

"Before you say it, talk to me. Tell me what happened. Open up to me." She took his hand in hers. "You told me I was safe here. I know that. You're safe here, too. It's all right to talk to me about her. About what happened."

He pulled his hand away and crossed his arms. She moved closer and grabbed his hand again.

"Talk to me. Let it out."

He sat there for a long minute not saying anything. She wasn't sure if she was making the same damn mistake again.

"I tell you what. I'll play you a song I wrote. I'm better at music than words." He stared at her, but didn't start playing. "Um, sorry, you're gonna have to get up from the bench."

"Oh, oh! Sorry, right." She jumped up.

"You can pull up a barstool, or better yet, get naked again and climb on the piano."

The surprise laugh leaped out of her and she covered her mouth as it echoed off the walls. She dragged the stool over to the piano.

"I gotta warn you, the song is a little bit sad, but I think it will help fill in some blanks."

He started to play a slow and mournful melody, which sounded like a 60's folksong. As he sang, his rich voice filled the room.

"Catch me if you can, I'm the Gingerbread Man
I know how to run away from love
Catch me if you can, I'm the Gingerbread Man
For me there is no peace, no God above

It started with his mom, who did not want this child
And a dad that was mad and never knew to smile—"

"Oh, god, forget this rubbish. I'm sorry, but that's absolute shit," he said, cringing.

"Chance, that is hands down the most depressing start to a song I've ever heard."

His laugh boomed throughout the room like a bass note on the piano and she relaxed, having gotten it right.

"Yeah, it's a bit of a wrist-slasher, isn't it?"

"Well, I'm far too depressed for sex now." This time they laughed together. Some of the tension dissipated from the room. She gave him a couple of seconds and spoke softly. "Chance, what happened?"

The smile faded and his lips went neutral. He let out a long sigh.

CHAPTER THIRTY

SHE'S GONE

1979

The procession of mourners formed an orderly line, umbrellas overlapping like armor plating on a black beetle. His memory stealing directly from an old movie about a red balloon, the color of the world was muted blues, blacks and grays, with the exception of red roses in the hands of relatives, coworkers, and friends lined up to pay their last respects. Some passed the grave and simply tossed the flower in, while others, seemingly aware of the flowers' fragility, leaned down to lessen the distance, as if the flowers' frailty was a metaphor: life was precious, happiness fleeting, and security brittle.

Chance stood in mute disbelief as he accepted condolences, hugs, and empty words of sympathy. He had no idea what to do next. All the understanding and knowledge he'd accumulated over the last twenty-plus years had evaporated to the point that the simple act of breathing required forethought.

Despite his efforts to comfort and reassure, Ellie had died afraid and in pain. Eyes wide, filled with tears as she choked to death on her own blood. Taking their baby with her. No amount of pain in life before this gave even a whispered breath of what was to come.

His uncle was the last to approach, and three letters formed in Chance's mind, clear through the fog of images and torments rattling around his head. He grabbed onto them, clutching them tightly: "Why?"

His uncle stared at him for a long moment and put his hand on the shoulder not in a sling.

"Charles, even if I tell you what I know, there will never be any understanding. You'll never fully get an answer to that question. Thousands of things had to have happened exactly as they did for us to be here standing together right now."

Chance became alive enough to feel a flicker of anger. "Uncle, don't tell me any of your philosophical bullshit. Was this because of you?" Chance glared down at him. To his uncle's credit, he didn't flinch away, but brought his hand up to Chance's cheek.

"In a way. The shooter was from Kansas City, payback for something your father did years before." He dropped his hand.

"My father? He was a drunk and a bully of women and kids. But he was just a bookkeeper. Don't fucking lie to me."

"Charles, your father was an excellent accountant and a horrible husband and father. And he was always frustrated that he never went further in life. Against my better judgement, one time I let him handle something..." His uncle paused and glanced around. "...heavy. He fucked it up, of course. It was years ago, but Sicilians have long memories, and the Civella family never forgets." He stepped back. "So, yes, in a way I am responsible."

Chance tried to tap into the rage he knew was there, somewhere. Giorgio stood fifteen feet behind his uncle. But he was so fucking tired. There was a feebleness to his bones, and he wanted to crawl away and sleep forever.

The moment passed and he turned away from his uncle and approached the grave.

Chance didn't know how long he'd been standing there before he looked up and saw Frank Bartallatas standing at the other side of the grave. A white rose in his hand, he stared down into the grave, a strange look on his face. Frank and he had been friends once, and oddly it was Ellie who had destroyed that friendship. They had seen each other periodically at family get-togethers, but had always given each other a wide berth.

Frank said something Chance couldn't hear, perhaps a prayer, crossed himself, and dropped the rose into the grave. He looked up at Chance, and pure unadulterated hatred crossed his face, quickly replaced with something Chance took for contrived empathy.

Frank circled the grave, approaching Chance the way a dog catcher might approach a rabid dog, both hands up to convey peaceful intent. "Chance, I'm supposed to take you to the reception. But before that, I have something to show you." He put his hands down and indicated the parking lot.

Chance didn't respond. Frank put his hand on Chance's shoulder, nudging him forward.

"Come on. I have a bottle of scotch in the car; it'll help."

In the car, Chance took a swig from the bottle Frank passed him. It tasted like gasoline mixed with dirt, but the warmth it brought to his stomach was something. A sensation that held comfort like a hug. He took another sip.

They drove in silence, Chance staring but not seeing out the window. He clutched the bottle. Frank glanced his way a few times, but otherwise ignored him. After a while, Chance came out of his stupor enough to realize they weren't headed toward his uncle's house. The large brick buildings and factories were in the Third Ward.

"Where are we going?"

"I've got something for you. A present, you could say. We'll be there in a minute."

Chance lay his head against the window. He could feel the vibrations of the road and suddenly he couldn't breathe, the smell of old cigarettes and rotting leather choking him. He rolled down the window and stuck his head out, letting the rain coat his face.

"Hey, fucking roll up the window, it's raining."

Chance ignored him until he felt the rain had numbed his face. He leaned back in and rolled up the window.

Frank pulled into an old Schlitz bottling plant, closed down a few years before. He stopped the car and turned to Chance. "You know, if you hadn't sucker-punched me in school, Ellie would probably be alive today."

"What? What the fuck are you talking about?"

Frank's presence, more than his size, seemed to fill the entire car.

"If you hadn't sucker—"

"That was years ago. What the fuck, you're still mad about that? You were harassing her!"

"We were just talking," Frank yelled back. He repeated, more quietly, "We were talking."

"That's not what it looked like to me, nor did she feel like you were just talking."

"Whatever." Frank opened his door. "Get out. I've got something to show you."

The young Black man was gagged and tied to a chair, his hands behind him and his feet wrapped in duct tape. Someone, probably Frank, had put a beating on the kid, his lips cracked, his bleeding nose clearly shattered. He mumbled something as they entered. The kid's eyes were wide, nostrils flaring for air through dried blood and snot.

"What the fuck is this, Frank?"

Frank stared at the kid like a lion gazed at its prey.

A few wooden crates were against the far wall, but otherwise the cinderblock room was empty. It had a musty beer smell, like an old bar that had never been cleaned. The kid was now screaming into his gag. He looked more angry than scared.

"Frank?"

"This is one of the guys. One of the guys who killed Ellie," Frank waved his hand dismissively, "and shot you. He claims he was only the driver." Frank walked up to the kid and backhanded him. His head snapped back, and the chair went up on two legs from the force.

Chance bent over and puked. The only thing in his stomach was scotch, and it wasn't nearly as comforting coming up as it had been going down.

"What the fuck, Chance?"

The smell of the puke mixed with the yeast made him dry heave a few more times. Then he wiped his mouth and stepped toward the kid. Then he ran, grabbing the kid by the shoulder, pushing the chair backward. It fell and took Chance with it, the kid cracking his head on the cement. Chance landed on top of him and screamed into the kid's face, spit mixing into the kid's blood.

"Why!" he screamed, shaking the kid by his shoulders. He screamed the word again for as long as his breath held. Finally, he stopped and rested his forehead against the kid's cheek. The kid was mumbling something, and Chance reached to remove the gag. But Frank pulled him up to his feet and spun Chance around like a rag doll to face him.

"Chance, just fucking do it. You don't need to listen to his bullshit. He's gonna lie to you and tell you bullshit about your uncle." Frank turned toward the kid. "But we know this was some gangbanger stuff. Wanted to shoot some white people, didn't we?"

Frank pulled out a switchblade, clicked the slide. The knife sprung up about five inches. He held it out to Chance, handle first.

"Here's your chance to get some payback. Cut him up slow or cut him up fast; don't bother me none."

The kid eyed the knife and started yelling again.

Chance looked at the knife, then raised his eyes to Frank. The excitement radiating from Frank made his stomach flip again. Frank grabbed Chance's hand and put the knife in it. But Chance dropped it immediately, as if it was white hot.

"What the fuck, Chance? This is about Ellie. Be a fucking man. Do him."

It was like the smell of blood had turned Frank into an animal. His eyes were buggy, his movements jerking wildly.

Chance backed up. "I don't want this. I don't; this isn't me. This isn't what Ellie and I were about." He kept backing up, and Frank tilted his head like a dog would.

Chance turned and started to run out of the room.

"She was too fucking good for you! You hear me? You fucking pussy! You fucking caused this," yelled Frank as Chance ran.

Chance ran outside, into the rain. Wind tried pushing him back toward the door. He didn't stop. Blood from the kid mixed with rain got into his eyes and he didn't stop. Ellie's killer was in a storage room in an abandoned factory and he didn't stop. Ellie and his unborn child were still dead, and he never stopped.

CHAPTER THIRTY-ONE

BREAKING UP (IS HARD TO DO)

PRESENT

Chance passed out on Maggie's lap. She guessed he'd never shared the story before, the pain in his slurred voice a Ginsu knife. She stroked his salted hair as he snored, his two-day stubble tickling her thigh.

He was beautiful. Sometimes he would stare at her across the dining room, and her knees would become weak. It wasn't just a cliché. He was kind, sweet, giving, and amazing with his fingers and mouth. She felt heat rush back to her cheeks and chest. He was successful, and amazing with Cassie. But he was a high-functioning alcoholic, and she had enough experience with low-functioning alcoholics to know they were all unpredictable.

He'd always be in love with Ellie, and right or wrong, she would stay the perfect woman in his head and heart forever. *How does a girl compete with that?*

Plus, she wasn't sure she could ever trust him. He couldn't help but flirt; it was how he communicated with all women. He charmed little girls, old women, and, of course, the beautiful married ones. And women were always flirting back. If he put his mind to it, he could make the most pious nun forsake her vows.

She traced the scar on his shoulder with her finger, the skin white and raised—an ugly scar, representing a horrible act. How could he shower each day and not think about Ellie? How could he ever truly make room in his heart for someone else?

She was pretty sure she was in love with him. Dreamed of a life with him. White picket fence in the suburbs. Perfectly manicured lawns, a dog, maybe a little brother for Cassie. She pictured Chance in a golf shirt, clean-shaven, holding his son. Then Chance as he was, standing on the lawn holding a hose. Leather jacket, cigarette hanging from his lips. Bloodshot eyes and two-day growth. She laughed out loud.

It made the first fantasy so unrealistic. Truth was, the selfish part of her liked him dangerous. Enjoyed the fire behind his eyes. His unpredictable nature. It was supremely sexy. The mom in her sighed. She needed a guy that fit on the manicured lawns. A man who made a good living and didn't drink much. A man who would throw the ball around with Cassie on the weekends, who would teach her how to drive and change a tire. A man who carried a briefcase and not a gun, or a bottle, or a needle. Who wouldn't hit her or Cassie, who came home at night not smelling like cigarettes, booze, and whatever woman he'd been with.

When Tom turned out to be a complete loser, she'd promised herself and Cassie she'd never make that type of choice again. How many nights had the two of them fallen asleep in the tub after locking themselves in the bathroom?

She cupped Chance's face with her hand. God, she wanted him. She wanted to experience his weight pressing down upon her. His hot breath on her neck. But he was broken. Not that she wasn't, but how could two broken people ever fix each other?

She woke with a start. Her head on his chest, back aching from her awkward position. Light came in through the windows and she glanced at her watch. 6:33. Cassie would be waking up soon. Chance was softly snoring.

Such a beautiful man.

She lifted herself off him, but he didn't move. In the bedroom, she considered her options. She didn't want to leave without saying goodbye, but she also didn't want to face the awkward morning. She found her clothes on the floor and dressed. After making herself as presentable as possible on such little sleep, she found a pen and paper in the kitchen.

She sat at the kitchen table, listening to the sounds of his breathing from the other room.

Dearest Charlie,

I think I've earned the right to call you Charlie, since we've seen each other naked. I can't thank you enough for what was a wonderful, amazing, and beautiful evening. Honestly the best group date I've ever been on. You're a kind, sweet, caring gentleman and the most unselfish person I've ever known. I'm truly touched deep in my soul with how much of yours you showed last night. It was a beautiful thing. I will treasure it always. In the time I've known you, I've come to love your humor, strength, beauty, and many, many talents! What you did for Cassie and me yesterday was truly life changing. Getting Tom out of our lives, for no other reason than you care, shows your true character and heart. I can never thank you enough.

Your soul is so beautiful and in so much pain. It broke my heart to see how much hurt you're carrying with you. I understand better now, about the married women, the booze, the distance in which you keep yourself. I think sharing it with me was a great first step to your freedom. But it was only a first step. One of the things I realized last night was you truly set me free. Free to make better choices, for Cassie and for myself. Free to be brave, to stand on my own. To choose to share my life with someone on my terms. My body and mind scream to try to heal your heart. That my love and Cassie's love would make you whole. But I've made that mistake too many times. It would be a slap in the face of the gift you gave me if I plunged back into something or someone I cannot really fix.

I fell asleep on your chest, and I would give up so much to be able to do it every night. But it wouldn't be fair to you, to Cassie, or myself. We cannot heal your heart. That is something you will have to do on your own. Know I could love you, easily for the rest of my life. Maybe someday we'll have the opportunity. Until then, please let us not speak of this beautiful night. If you don't want me to work for you, I understand. I'm sorry to leave all of this in a note, but I have to pick up Cassie, and I wanted you to be able to sleep.

Thank you for all the gifts you gave me yesterday. I will remember forever,

Maggie

CHAPTER THIRTY-TWO

SHE'S ACTING SINGLE (I'M DRINKING DOUBLES)

Chance walked into Harry's Bar and Grill fifteen minutes early, but she was already waiting for him. His hangover was in full force, and the note from Maggie only added a layer of shame.

A bored, college-aged bartender stood midway down the beautiful walnut bar polishing wineglasses, her tongue sticking out slightly in concentration. Behind her, a four-tier backbar was stocked with every kind of booze imaginable. She glanced up at him as he passed and gave him a warm smile. He indicated the blonde sitting in the dining room and winked back at her.

"Hello," said Sloan, smiling. "I wasn't sure if you were going to come."

"Sloan." He studied her and again was in awe of her physical beauty. At five-eight, she was tall for a woman; her hair, parted down the middle, fell to her shoulders. She had large blue eyes, which only sparkled when aroused or causing pain. Otherwise, they were cold and pale. She had a small button nose, high cheekbones, and a symmetrical face that sported little makeup. She wore a cream-colored wool sweater that accentuated her chest, and her long graceful fingers were wrapped around her wineglass.

"I'm glad you came down. Isn't this place cute? With all the brick, it would fit perfectly in Georgetown."

"I've never been to Georgetown, so I'll have to take your word on it." The way the dining room was set up, they weren't maximizing the amount of seating, but he had to admit it was an attractive place. A place where you would find a lot of lawyers drinking martinis at ten bucks a pop. A server in black pants and a white button-down shirt approached the table. A bistro apron hung down past her knees, giving her a stick-like appearance. Straight up and down, zero curves. She was lost in a man's shirt, her pulled-back hair severe. But she smiled as she reached the table and her femininty radiated from her perfect teeth and shining eyes.

"Good afternoon, y'all," she said in a thick Southern accent.

"You must be a local girl?"

"Yes, sir. Local by way of Austin, Texas." She gave him a glance as if to say, *buddy, don't be a pain in the ass*. Sloan assessed the server.

"Can I bring something from the bar, sir? Perhaps a cold beer, glass of wine," she paused for effect, "a shot of tequila?"

Chance laughed, liking the girl. "Well, Miss...?"

"Lauren."

"Well, Miss Lauren, I usually don't drink tequila before 1:30 in the afternoon, but now that you've planted the seed, I will take a shot of tequila, and a tall blonde."

Her eyebrows raised as she glanced at Sloan.

"A different tall blonde, Lauren," he said with a laugh. "A Miller High Life."

"Oh, right, I forget that's what y'all call beer. And Reposado, Silver, or Anejo, sir?"

The girl knew her tequila. "Anejo, of course, Lauren."

She pointed down at the menu. "The appetizers are on the first page, and I recommend the spinach and artichoke dip. It's great for sharing. I'll be right back with your drinks, sir," she said, emphasizing the plural on drinks.

Chance regarded Sloan, who at this point was not smiling. "What?"

"Do you seriously always have to flirt with every waitress you come across?"

"I wasn't flirting. This is my business. This is what I do when I go out. I'm always looking for fresh talent."

"Talented at what?" She dropped it by picking up her menu.

Content to let it drop as well, he picked up his, but it reminded him this wasn't a date. He was here to do a specific job. He needed to stay on point.

1988

He met Sloan for the first time at his uncle's house in North Milwaukee. Each summer his uncle hosted a barbecue for his "family" and all of their families. Chance, of course, was a guest, but also the caterer. Thirty to forty families, all with ties to organized crime, would come together on the banks of

Lake Michigan to celebrate what great citizens they were. It was like the scene in the movie *The Godfather* where Michael's sister was getting married. All the men in summer suits, all the women in dresses. All the kids good-looking and happy.

Those invited would be local and state politicians, cops, prosecutors, the clerks of courts and zoning, even a couple of judges. They'd all attend because this was when the dole was paid out. One by one they would file into his uncle's office. One by one they would all come out several thousand dollars richer. The amount depended upon how important they were to the organization. But always more than any bent person had a right to expect.

If you were a zoning clerk and expected to fast track a few things throughout the year, a few hundred bucks ought to do it. But with Uncle Vinnie you would walk away with a nice fat envelope in your breast pocket, to the tune of a couple grand. If you were a municipal judge for the State of Wisconsin-Milwaukee, you could expect five or ten times that amount.

As his uncle once explained it, it was smart to have them all together when the cookies were handed out. If they all knew who each other were, they would all look out to make sure everyone stayed on the program. If the feds tried to target a bent judge, somebody at the state or even federal level would get wind of it, and they could circle the wagons. Delay a subpoena here, find out about a wiretap there.

Chance had to admit: it was ingenious to have all the "straight" people policing themselves. All of them had their hands in the cookie jar, so all had a vested interest in everyone staying bent but not broken. Anything the feds could target on someone, to get them to flip, was dealt with way before the feds could hear about it. A judge who liked little boys, or a prosecutor with a gambling problem. These issues would be taken care of quickly and quietly.

If someone wasn't toeing the line, he or she might find all their funding for reelection dried up. Or the permits for the new addition to their house were never issued. Or their garbage never got picked up. There were endless ways to get to someone. People might get whacked. But, generally, civilians tended to be off limits; way too much heat.

It took Chance and his team three days to prep for the barbecue. There would, of course, be pasta, with all the sauces and meats to go with it. But also a full pig, roasting for hours with an apple stuck in its mouth. Every kind of seafood you could get overnighted from the coast to Chicago and driven up to Milwaukee. Sea bass stuffed with crab and Italian breadcrumbs. Lobster Florentine. Crab legs the size of a child's arm. Gulf shrimp that would melt in your mouth. Flounder, swordfish, smoked salmon.

The cheese table would make even the most pretentious Frenchman smile. Wines from all over the world: Super Tuscans, First Growth Bordeaux, and up and coming California Cabs. But the highlight of the year was the dessert table.

It would be set up in its own air-conditioned tent. Chance eventually added security guards so nobody could get a peek, especially the thirty or so kids running around. As soon as the sun went down, and right after the grand finale of the fireworks, his uncle would pull on a rope and the sides of the tent would come down.

Underneath the white twinkly lights was the most decadent display of sugar-inspired debauchery known to man

An assortment of truffles, macaroons, and summer tarts; classic Italian desserts—tiramisu, amaretto biscotti, panna cotta, a dizzying array of cannoli. Peach and goat cheese Napoleons, cobblers with every fruit possible, pies, chocolate gelato sandwiches, and chocolate pot de crème.

But the biggest draw of the night, which impressed even the toughest critics, being the children, was what they called the holy trinity: three fountains of molten sin, flowing with dark chocolate, white chocolate, and caramel. To dip in the river of dreams was an assortment of fruits to marshmallows, Oreos, Twinkies, graham crackers, gummy bears, brownie bites, cheesecake squares, and peanut butter balls.

Underneath the twinkly lights, surrounded by dozens of hoppers all high on sugar, Chance met Sloan. Sloan had an addict's need for all things sweet. Chance was pretty sure he'd seen her elbow a kid to get to the dark-chocolate fountain. He had laughed out loud as he stood there with his glass of wine. She flashed him a frown, but then smirked like they were both in on a conspiracy. Of course, he noticed her much earlier, but had been far too busy to talk to her.

"If I had known, Miss, that you were going to throw around elbows like Kareem Abdul-Jabbar, I would have snuck you past security earlier."

"Oh, no, taking down a few of these little bastards is part of the fun," replied Sloan, not missing a beat. Chance laughed again. She was wearing a simple, sleeveless, white cotton dress, but was wearing it in a way that said devil in disguise.

She exited the fray carrying a large cannoli that engulfed her slender hands. She walked not toward him but not away from him either, satisfaction on her breathtaking Norwegian face. The white twinkly lights made her natural blonde hair appear as strands of pure gold.

"I noticed you got the best one in there," said Chance as she passed him. She considered him, and whatever she saw was enough to cause a smile to pass her lips.

"Well, it is the biggest, and it helps to have sharp elbows and a longer reach than a 9-year-old. Sometimes the biggest doesn't always turn out to be the best, though," she said mischievously as she sat at a table.

Not missing the innuendo, Chance replied, "I happen to know that particular one is the best. It has dried cranberries dipped in dark chocolate, with a touch of sea salt mixed in the ricotta cheese. I almost saved that one for myself."

Sloan bit into the cannoli, making a surprised sound as part of the shell fell onto the table. Chance motioned to the empty chair. "Do you mind if I join you?"

She grunted, which he took as an affirmative response. A piece of shell stuck to her upper lip and Chance was taken by an urge to kiss it off.

"I'm not going to share with you," she said.

"I'm fine with my wine, thank you. I haven't seen you here before. Is this your first year?"

The little Mongolian hordes, now high on their sugar rush, were running in between tables, once-clean faces and clothes smeared with chocolate and powdered sugar; one even had a gummy bear stuck to her forehead. Chance noticed a lot of the adults, once with clean faces, now had sun burns and a purple tint to their lips from their own drug of choice.

Sloan scarfed down the last half of her cannoli. There was a large diamond on her finger, and he tried to picture who might have won this beauty. Not a cop, with the size of that rock. Maybe a judge. He heard Judge Connolly was married last month. As he watched her, he was fascinated. She licked each one of her fingers, paying no attention to him. He knew she was playing with him. He decided he enjoyed the game.

"I'm pretty sure I'd have remembered you here before, so I know this is your first time. What I can't figure out is who gave you that boulder on your finger."

She considered him for the first time since the start of her quest for sugar. "You're right. This is my first time here. And yes, I am newly married. Since you seem so interested, which one do you think is my husband?"

"I don't think I have enough information to make an informed decision. Clearly, you are beautiful enough to command any man's attention. East Coast WASP if your accent is real, so you're comfortable with money and power. You obviously have your appetites, and aren't ashamed of them. What about him?" Chance indicated a massive man with a triple chin and pants two inches too short.

She snorted. He warmed to her laugh; Chance could tell she was self-conscious about it.

"Well, fashion sense is rather attractive. I do like a man who doesn't care what anyone else thinks."

"And your admiration for sweets would be shared."

"Why not that one?" She pointed to a man who was past his best days by a couple of decades.

"Way too old. Couldn't keep up with you."

"Maybe I have daddy issues."

"Oh, not you, I can tell already you were always Daddy's little girl; you had him wrapped around your finger from birth. No, your issues would have been with Mommy."

With the slight frown tugging at the corners of her mouth, Chance thought he might have hit a little too close to home.

"What about that one there?" She indicated a large man commanding the attention of several other men and women.

"The power part would suit you, but I happen to know his wife. He's the mayor, and while I'm surprised he hasn't hit on you already, you'd find him boorish and rather simple."

She laughed again. "He did hit on me an hour ago, and you're right, he was boorish. You're pretty good at this."

"No, your husband would have to be big, strong, rich, and completely confident. Definitely not a sycophant, which rules out public service. But besides me, I don't see anyone here that matches the description. Except for the rich part."

"Ah, yes, the black sheep of the family. The restauranteur. It explains the cannoli. I've heard of you, prodigal nephew."

"Oh, this is so unfair. You know who I am, and I've no idea who you are."

"I don't know much. My husband has talked about you. He seems to be a big fan of your little café."

Chance snorted at the word café.

"I know you're not in the family business; I know you're the favorite nephew of Uncle Vinnie, who is a very... charming man. I know you were once a lounge singer, and you have something of a reputation with the married women in this city." She crossed her arms over her chest.

"Your husband told you all of this?"

She paused before speaking. "No, I asked about you earlier, when you looked like the caterer but were mingling with all the guests. I was curious. Where I'm from, the help doesn't get to drink wine during the event. They usually steal a few bottles for later. Your name is Chance McQueen, and I don't think my husband is going to like that I'm talking to you."

"Do you always do what your husband wants?"

"Clearly not," she replied, the corners of her lips turning upward.

"So, tell me how you and your husband met? Give me a clue."

"Is that how you'd care to spend this time, talking about my husband?"

"Good point. How are you finding Milwaukee?"

"Boorish and simple."

He was losing headway. He took a sip of wine. "Not all of Milwaukee is simple. There are some dangerous parts of this city."

"Ah, nice recovery, Mr. McQueen. Please do tell."

He grinned. "Well, there's the Milwaukee Zoo. A lot of wild and dangerous animals in there."

She snickered. "Oh, I'm sure, dairy cows and deer. Rather ferocious."

"Maybe what can make Milwaukee so dangerous isn't what you do, but whom you do it with."

"Knowing my husband, that would be dangerous indeed, Mr. McQueen."

"Hum… It's winter here for so long we have to become experts at indoor games, jigsaw puzzles, crocheting, stamp collecting…"

"Wow, those do sound riveting."

"So at least tell me your name—"

A man's voice spoke from behind him. "Her name is Sloan. Sloan Bartallatas. My wife." Chance turned to find Frank Bartallatas standing behind him.

"What's this about stamp collecting? I didn't know you collected stamps," said Frank.

PRESENT

"I was thinking of when we first met," said Sloan. Chance responded with a raised eyebrow. "It's interesting to think about your first impressions of someone, later on after you've gotten to know them. Did they turn out like you'd hoped, or were your first impressions all a projection of something you carried with you?"

"I can't do this anymore, Sloan. It isn't good for me," said Chance. "I'm not getting what I need out of this."

She stiffened her back. The slightest crack she'd allowed in her wall was immediately filled in. The small measure of need that had momentarily escaped was taken out back to the woodshed and beaten to death. Swirling her half-finished glass of wine, she absently wondered how long she'd have to sit here listening to him whine about his "needs." She glanced at her watch for the fifth time.

"It's not only that you're married to Frank. Or that you're emotionally unavailable. I think even if you weren't married, this wouldn't be able to go any further. I think this has gone as far as something like this can go."

Any rejection she might have felt had long since turned into something cold and reptilian. It had been the same since her father had left her to be raised by her pathetic, coke-snorting mother. Rejection was not something she ever allowed herself to suffer. She had known for weeks Chance had been trying to screw up the courage to do this. It made her wonder what she had liked about him in the first place.

She took a sip of her wine and analyzed him. He looked like shit. She could tell he'd had a long night. She had almost considered keeping him a while longer after hearing him sing last night. He'd been so sexy, with flashes of the man that got her excited in the beginning. Strong, supremely confident, every woman in the room wishing he was with her.

But his pathetic need for emotional reassurance was a game she never had the tolerance to play. It was one of the reasons she'd chosen Frank as her way in. Frank was the only man she'd known where what you saw was what you got. The only thing Frank ever needed reassurance about occasionally was his intelligence. But thankfully it wasn't often. Dumb people seldom realized they are dumb.

"It's important to me we part as friends. It's been great, and a part of my heart will always have love for you. If you ever need anything... ever, I'd be there for you."

For fuck's sake. "Chance, let me give you some free advice. You put me, you put all women, on a pedestal. You make us into something we're not. I'm not some goddess who needs to be worshiped and taken care of. You say you're a feminist, and yet you treat women like they are porcelain dolls. I'm not some tender flower. I poop, I pee, I blow my nose, I sometimes have mean thoughts, and I fuck."

Chance grimaced as if he'd swallowed a spoonful of vinegar.

"I'm not some perfect little creature who never does any of those things. I'm human, like every other woman out there.

You make us into something we will never be. In your head, you have memorialized Ellie into something she wasn't. Until you realize that, it won't matter who you're involved with. Not the skinny little tart from last night, not the mayor's wife, and most certainly not me."

He took a pull from his beer, pain visible on his face.

"I'm not saying this to hurt you. Well, honestly, that's neither here nor there. You have this pathetic need to get things from me I can't give you. Nobody can give you."

Finally, the moment she'd been waiting for, the reason she picked this restaurant, walked through the kitchen doors. She changed gears. She took a deep breath.

"Look, I don't want to part with us saying dreadful things to each other. We're grown-ups. This has been fun, but we don't have to hurt each other. I'm sorry. I'm not what you need or want. Let's just get up, hug, and part as friends."

Chance's eyes were unfocused. She got up and gathered her purse. She reached in to grab her wallet. Chance jumped up, putting his hand on her arm.

"No, no... I got it," he said, still looking shell-shocked. He reached into his pocket and pulled out a hundred-dollar bill. He threw it on the table and stood there looking at her. Because his back was to the bar, he hadn't seen Gary Locke walk in with a load of boxes on a dolly. But Sloan did. Waiting until she was sure Gary was looking in her direction, she saw the surprise flash across his face. She grabbed Chance and gave him a long hug. At first, he didn't respond. Slowly he raised his arms and put them around her.

"It'll be OK, Chance," she whispered. "This is a good thing. Really, it's for the best. I'm sure in a few days you'll truly understand why this had to happen." She leaned up on her toes and kissed him on the cheek. With that, she left a bewildered man standing there.

Out of the corner of her eye, she saw Gary drop his boxes and run a beeline for the kitchen. She was satisfied with herself. She wanted Frank to find out. Wanted him blind with rage. Chance was going to get exactly what he wanted. He would be reunited with Ellie. Sooner than he thought. The final piece of her plan was coming together.

CHAPTER THIRTY-THREE

DEATH ON TWO LEGS

Bob burst into Mitchell's office without knocking. "We got it! We got the fingerprint back."

Mitchell sat up in his chair. Bob didn't bother to sit down when he got to Mitchell's desk, riffling instead through the sheets of paper in his hands.

"OK, Sloan Bartallatas, born 1962, current age twenty-eight, spouse Frank Bartallatas. Her maiden name is Carter. Daughter of John Henry Carter—"

"Wait? The millionaire from New York, Carter?"

Bob's head bobbed up and down, a shit-eating grin on his normally stoic face.

"The same John Henry Carter who basically financed Reagan's election in '79?" asked Mitchell.

"Yeah, that one."

Mitchell sat back in his chair, the force of this revelation pushing on him like sideways gravity. "Sloan is his daughter? I don't understand—how does a blueblood end up here, married to the mob? And why does she suddenly decide to become an informant?"

Bob scanned the pages in his hand. "So, this is where it gets weird. I made some calls to our New York office. In 1974 she was registered at Horace Mann prep school in New York. She was twelve, but only attended classes for half the year. She was pulled out of the school. No reason listed. She doesn't appear in any system again until age seventeen in Chicago. 1979 she gets arrested for cocaine possession... oh, this is interesting. Molly has on here that she spoke with the arresting detective on the case. He still remembers it. A Detective Gordaski. Says Sloan was busted with six grams of cocaine."

"Six grams? What's a seventeen-year-old doing with six grams?"

"Apparently the detective wondered too. He said he was sure the girl was holding for the mother." Bob shuffled the papers in his hand. "Mother is Beth Ann Foster, formerly New York socialite, married John Henry Carter in 1961, and divorced 1966. Anyway, Detective Gordaski still remembers Sloan, because, quote, 'She was da most beautiful girl I'd evah seen—'"

"Bob, don't ever try to do a Chicago accent again. That was horrible."

Bob put up his hand in mock surrender. "I'm quoting Molly's brief here."

Mitchell's smile faded. "Right... get on with it."

Bob put his stoic face back on. "Detective Gordaski had Sloan in the interview room for five hours, trying to make her give the mother up. He said she ran rings around him and his partner. After five hours of being smacked around by a seventeen-year-old girl, a lawyer from Dewey, Dutch & Waterman showed up and got her released."

Mitchell raised an eyebrow. One of the best firms in Chicago.

"Gordaski said even though they had her dead to rights on possession with intent, the case was dropped, and she was never charged."

"OK, Mommy's or Daddy's people took care of it. Get to the part of how she ends up here, married to a mobster—"

"I'm getting to that part. There was a half-sister from Beth Ann, a Bethany Lynn Foster, born 1967, no father listed."

"Ahhh, the reason for the divorce. Not John Carter's child," said Mitchell to himself.

Bob's eyes scanned the paper. "OK, got it. Sloan is attending Loyola University, 1982... oh, fuck!"

"What?"

Bob blinked and took a deep breath. "Bethany Lynn was found here in Milwaukee in 1983. Sexually assaulted, strangled."

Mitchell, fitting pieces of the puzzle together, felt a slow burn in his stomach, radiating out to his chest, arms, and legs. He closed his eyes. "How?"

Bob didn't answer.

"How, Bob? How was she strangled?"

"Piano wire."

As she left the restaurant, Sloan's singleminded focus allowed her to push down any thoughts of Chance. Any emotions she may or may not have felt for him were irrelevant to her life's ambition. Revenge.

Frank had been her ticket into the Carmelo family. Chance was unknowingly going to help her bring it all crashing down. Playing the one off the other in order to get to Uncle

Vinnie was all that mattered to her. These wop motherfuckers were either going to end up dead or in prison for life.

She reached her convertible BMW and got in, the tan leather warm on her legs.

Out of nowhere, a sob erupted from her chest like a surprise burp.

What the fuck? Her muscles tightened as if she could prevent what was about to happen. Another sob wracked her small frame. She dug her nails into her thigh, hoping pain would allow some self-control. There was no way she could be crying over what had just transpired. She had done far worse to plenty of other men.

But was she being honest with herself? She thought back to the last time they were together. Chance had been grazing her skin with his fingers, and she was falling into it. Dreams of something more, of a life with more, were forming in her post-orgasmic haze. That's why she'd gotten so mad. Had been so cruel to him. He scared her. What she felt scared her.

When she felt she had a measure of control back, she imagined her sister. The reason for all her sacrifices.

Control, the core of her ability to navigate the massive lie which had become her life, disappeared like a bottle of booze left at an AA meeting. As tears poured down her face and the sounds of true, deeply repressed pain fought their way out of her heart past all her defenses, she succumbed to the long-buried loss that made up her entire life.

Discarded by her father for the sin of beginning puberty, she was sent to live with her drug-addicted mother. The only saving grace from her mother's beatings and the rapes by her mother's plethora of boyfriends was her younger sister.

Bethany was an old soul trapped in the body of a little girl. She had the heart of a giant, the wisdom of a sage, and the forgiveness of Christ himself. At eight, she took care of every stray animal in the neighborhood, cleaned and cared for their mother, and nursed Sloan after the many abuses. She gave Sloan unconditional love, and inspired those around her to try to do better, even though they would fail again and again.

When Sloan entered high school, she managed to get Bethany out of that wretched environment, and they went to live with a family friend. Both thrived in their new home, and for a minute Sloan thought maybe there was more to life than pain. When she left for college, she was happy to see Bethany hit puberty in a home safe and full of love. She came home on weekends to visit and took joy in the simple sisterly pleasures of long talks over nail polish and Yoo-hoo. They had impassioned debates over which musician was the hottest: Sloan preferred Prince and Bethany the soft and pretty boys from Wham!.

Sloan's many wounds hadn't healed, but she was beginning to feel things again. Slowly, time was doing what time always did. It took away the worst of the incomprehensible pain and left behind the sting or, during good times, a dull ache.

But Bethany wouldn't give up on their mother. Secretly, she would still visit. Clean up her condo, make simple meals, and administer kindness to all the animals she came across, human or otherwise. On one of those visits she simply disappeared.

One cut from a steak knife and the promise of more was all it took Sloan to motivate a junkie mother into admitting she had sold off her pubescent daughter. Her mother had spiraled down in her addictions until the monthly check from the family trust went to pay the interest on the drugs consumed two months' prior. The jewelry long since gone, any stocks and bonds sold, and her body well past the point of any trade-in value, her addiction was the only thing left.

Bethany was passed through the ranks untouched and was given to an aging mobster whose lust for young flesh was well-known in certain circles. Her old soul was trapped in a young girl's body. Her love for the world came from a love for herself. As she showed no fear in loving the world, she showed a ferocious heart in protecting herself, allowing nobody to violate that which was only hers to give. Yet in a world where men still use violence to get their way, Bethany never had a chance. Those were the findings of the Milwaukee coroner, who said he had never seen so many defensive wounds on a young girl. "She must have fought like a lion," was his haunted conclusion.

The sobs subsided, and absently Sloan wondered about Chance. Had he somehow dulled her finely crafted edge? She was so close to her goal, to achieving the only thing that had prevented her own suicide or, worse, commitment to a mental institution.

Revenge fueled her every breath, allowed her to sleep next to a pig of a man like Frank. Allowed her to spread her legs and take his rotten seed. Vengeance fueled her every smile and eyelash flutter at Uncle Vinnie. And indifference allowed her to use Chance for her own ends, a man whose own heart had been destroyed by violent loss. She pushed it all down again, into the deep well where the only sliver of a soul still resided.

Back in control, Sloan cleaned herself up and started the car. There were a lot of things to do while Frank was out of town. She had eight tapes of various Carmelo family associates discussing a multitude of felonies, including some with Uncle Vinnie. Dropping them into the mailbox for ADA Mitchell was only step two.

CHAPTER THIRTY-FOUR

I WON'T BACK DOWN

Chance parked in a spot reserved for volunteers at the Milwaukee Women's Resource Center. He put Gracie in park and slowly put his hands down into his lap. Of all the reactions he'd expected of Sloan, from rage to inconsolable crying, a hug and a "take care" wasn't even on the list.

His body felt weird. A combination of vibrating detachment, with a distinct humming, hanging over the edge of nausea. He tried to analyze it, and decided if you removed all the pleasurable sensations from being drunk, what you were left with was his current state. He took some long slow breaths, trying to shake it.

He pushed all thoughts of Sloan away. He could work it out later. Right now, he needed to get his mind in the game. He had two emergency moves to plan for Saturday. Two courageous women had decided enough was enough and were making a break from their abusive spouses.

Both men were getting out of jail Monday morning at the earliest, making these easier weekend jobs. The women would go through their respective houses with red masking tape, marking what needed to be removed. Chance and his volunteers, usually about twenty of them, would swarm into the house like locusts and load a truck in under a couple of hours. The woman and her children would be driven across the state line and set up in an undisclosed location.

He pulled a neon pink MWRC Volunteer nametag from the glovebox—Chance's idea after seeing fear in the eyes of some women when he entered the center. A man, a man they didn't know, in a place where they were supposed to be safe. The pink sign alleviated the victims' anxiety.

He scanned the center's parking lot, as he always did, checking for anything or anyone out of place. Over the years they'd had issues with men coming to the center, searching for their wives and kids. You had to be buzzed in through two secure doors before you could get into the building. He scrutinized each car and the park across the street. His eyes spotted a girl with a ballcap sitting on a bench at the bus stop, but nobody else seemed to be hanging around. He walked up to the entrance and looked up at the camera. A loud buzzing proceeded the clicking of the locks. He walked into the foyer, turned back to make sure the door closed, and waved at Mandy through the security glass. She nodded and buzzed him through the next door.

The massive turn-of-the-century mansion had been donated by a widow of a beer baron. The baron had terrorized his wife for thirty-two years before falling face first into his pea soup, of an apparent heart attack. Although there were rumors. The widow lived another twenty-two years but as a final fuck you, in 1972 had left the mansion to a fledgling organization trying to protect women.

Since then the MWRC had offered sanctuary for thousands of women and children, fleeing abusive men. And support for thousands of more survivors of sexual assault. There were eight drafty bedrooms that were used as a temporary refuge. Sadly, they were always full. Other rooms had been converted to office space, a rec room, and a nursery.

Chance walked into the mail room and grabbed his E-Move packets for Saturday. He walked up the grand staircase, smiling as he heard the echoes of children's laughter bouncing off the high ceilings. As he got to the top of the staircase an office door opened and Valerie the RC Director walked out, her arm draped over an old Asian woman.

His body reacted before his mind could catch up as he grabbed onto the railing, almost falling down the stairs. Physical pain shot out from his chest, blurring his vision. But not enough to hide Mrs. Lee. Her face awash in bruises and cuts. A butterfly bandage over her left eyebrow and her right cheek grotesquely swollen.

She looked at Chance. Raising her hand, her index figure pointed right at him and she screamed.

Chance sat in Valerie's office like a delinquent kid awaiting suspension. He was leaning over, his head in his hands. His stomach was inching its way to the back of his throat. Breathing came in short and rapid bursts, his brain screamed for the warm comfort of a cigarette, yet he knew that would push his stomach passed the final barricade.

Valerie walked into her office and sat behind her desk. At four-foot-eight, her feet barely touched the floor, her orange hair, normally kinky and wild, was pulled back in a severe bun, only adding to harsh disappointment written on her freckled face. She brought her fingers together as if in prayer, rested them on her lips. Her elbows on the desk. She leaned forward and tapped her index fingers together, like a praying mantis over a meal.

"I've never liked you Chance. Never fully trusted you. You swoop in here with your easy charm, and privileged arrogance, like some kinda white knight. But I tolerated you because your good at fundraising and your coordination of E-Moves has always been solid."

Chance found it hard to maintain eye contact with her. His white whale within these walls had always been her respect. She leaned back in her chair; her stature seemed smaller but her presence undiminished.

"You sat in that very chair five years ago and swore to me you had nothing to do with your family's criminality."

"I don't—" he started. She cut him off with her hand.

"I don't know what your relationship is to our client. Her English is as bad as my Mandarin. But I do know this." Valerie pointed her finger at Chance in the same way Mrs. Lee had just done.

"She's afraid of you. Not because you're a man, but of *you* specifically. The police brought her here because they didn't know what to do with her. Is there any light you can shine on how she got assaulted?"

"I don't, I mean I wasn't..." He looked at the floor. "I don't know." *LIAR*, his brain screamed.

"I can't have this. It's counter to everything we are doing here. You're done." She got up from her chair, came around the desk and stopped right in front of him. She reached out like she was going to put her arm on his shoulder. Instead she ripped his carefully constructed pink Volunteer sign, from around his neck.

"Lou Ann and Naomi will escort you out. Thank you for your years of service," she said flatly. She opened her office door and two women, Chance had worked with for years, were standing in the hallway, arms crossed, hatred in their eyes.

He got up from the chair and walked past Valerie. His hands at his sides, his head drooping low.

"Chance," said Valerie.

He stopped and turned around.

"Don't come back." With that she turned around and shut the door.

· · ·

Alex was sitting on a bench in front of the bus stop. She'd watched Chance walk in earlier and now watched as he stumbled out like he'd just been in a bar. He half-tripped down the steps and when he got to the sidewalk, he leaned his arm onto the side of the building. Maybe he was sick or something.

After a minute or two he stood up and zombie walked to his car. She waited until he pulled out of the parking lot. She stood up and adjusted her ball cap. She looked across the street at the building. Rocking back and forth on her feet. She knew she was not OK.

She sat back down and put her knees up to her chest, hugging them closer. She didn't know if she had the strength to go in there. Talking to the old man behind the restaurant was different. He'd been there. But she'd hadn't told anyone else. To admit it. To say it happened. Somehow that would make it real. Something she couldn't just ignore.

She couldn't tell Winnie. He worried too much as it was. Plus, it would break his heart. That she'd gone out with his worst enemy. She squeezed her legs tighter. Why? Why had she said yes? She pounded on her knees and tears ran down her face.

A woman walked out of the center and stood on the sidewalk looking in her direction. She turned her head both ways and started across the street. Alex quickly took off her glasses and wiped her face with her shirt. Her nose was stuffy, and she took Monkey off her shoulder. Opening the front, she reached in to find some tissues, her eyes never leaving the woman as she crossed the street and came to the bench.

"Hi," the woman said. Alex nodded and brought the tissue up to her nose. She turned her body away from the woman as she blew.

"Do you know if the number five has come by yet?" The woman asked.

Alex finished wiping her nose and shook her head.

"Do you mind if I sit down?"

Alex shook her head again.

"My name is Valerie. I thought since you've been sitting here for an hour, maybe we could talk."

CHAPTER THIRTY-FIVE

KISS THE GIRL

The four friends sat in their usual places in Alex's attic, which had been transformed years ago into her studio and the family room. Alex's canvases, covered with sheets, filled one end of the large room, almost the length of the house. On the other end was a TV, VCR, and an odd assortment of things to sit or lay on.

Prez held court on the plaid La-Z-Boy. Hunter lay on a sky-blue futon, his back supported by a huge teddy bear Alex had won at the state fair ten years earlier. Winnie and Alex sat next to each other on an oversized pink beanbag, knees touching.

They were watching the end of one of Alex's favorite movies, *The NeverEnding Story*. Winnie had bought the VHS tape two years earlier for Alex as a Christmas present. Having watched the movie at least twenty times now, he'd since decided to be more careful in his choice of presents. He couldn't be blamed, however, for the second feature, *The Little Mermaid*, which Alex had bought herself.

On the screen was the scene of a prepubescent girl, tears welling in her eyes, yelling to Atreyu to say her name.

Hunter mocked in a falsetto voice: "Winnie, SAY MY NAME!" Prez giggled, and Alex shushed Hunter. No matter how many times she watched the movie, she was transported into the drama of the story. Winnie's knee was on fire, and he didn't want to move.

The movie ended, and the credits scrolled. Prez indicated for the bong, and Hunter grunted as he strained against the harsh pull of gravity.

"Damn, Hunter, where did you get this shit?" asked Prez as he took in a double lungful of smoke and suppressed a cough. "This shit is good." He exhaled a long stream of blue smoke and held out the bong to Winnie. "You want to hit this, Winnie?"

"No, thanks, I'm cool right now."

"Alex, you sure you don't want to try it? This is the best shit I've ever had," said Prez.

"Considering how much it seems to lower your IQ, Prez, I don't think I'm interested. You know, 'Just Say No' and all that."

"It don't lower your IQ, Alex, it just lets you perceive things from a different perplexion," said Hunter. Winnie and Alex both cackled.

"Thank you for making my point for me, Hunter. I think you meant perspective."

"It frees your mind, Alex. Like you're up in the clouds, and you're looking down on all the people. Like you're in outer space, and you're looking down on all the people. 'Cause you're an alien species that has evolved in outer space, and you can look down and see all the people," said Prez.

"Christ, Prez, you sound like an idiot," said Alex.

"No, Alex, he's right," said Hunter. "You're in space, but you're alien, and you don't have any arms, 'cause you don't need them to float in space. And you're floating around, and you see this beautiful blue planet. And you're like 'Hi, blue planet,' and the blue planet is like 'Hi, space alien, come down and look at all my people.'"

"For the love of god, the two of you sound like morons. I'm going to stop inviting you over if you're going to get this stoned."

"You got any chips, Alex?" asked Prez, unphased by Alex's words. Alex made a noise of frustration and threw a bag of Cheetos at Prez's head. The bag hit Prez square in the forehead. About three seconds later Prez's arms made a catching motion.

Winnie, Alex, and Hunter all doubled over. "Is this what I sound like?" asked Winnie.

"Yep," replied Alex.

"Christ!" said Winnie. "Watching Prez is way better than 'Just Say No.' This is your brain, picture an egg in a frying pan. This is a brain on drugs, cut to Prez."

Alex snorted. Prez was still trying to get the Cheetos bag open.

"Yeah," said Hunter. "This is Prez on Cheetos. Don't eat Cheetos." Hunter started laughing uncontrollably. After a couple of seconds, it infected Alex and Winnie. The only one not laughing was Prez, still fighting with the Cheetos bag.

"Why would you make a bag of Cheetos you can't open?" asked Prez in all seriousness. This made them all laugh even harder.

After a minute Alex got up and opened the bag for Prez. "I don't want you to get an aneurysm." She popped the VHS cassette out, and static blared out of the one speaker. She quickly turned the volume down. Prez chewed on a Cheeto, enraptured by the snow on the TV. He was concentrating so hard, Winnie wondered if he was receiving coded messages.

"We should talk about our trip," said Alex. She pulled out a huge Rand McNally map book from a bookshelf and placed it on the floor between them, opening it to a full-sized United States map, with a highlighted route from Wisconsin to California.

"I've taken the liberty of mapping out our route. The highlights of our trip will be Rockport, Illinois; Lincoln, Nebraska; Denver, Colorado; Las Vegas, Nevada; and Los Angeles, California."

"Vegas sounds pretty cool." Hunter ran his finger down the map.

"If we all split the driving and stay on the road at least twelve to fourteen hours a day it should take us about four days to get there. This is contingent upon how many times we stop, and how much time we spend at the places we stop," s aid Alex.

"We have to stop in Vegas, and it would be cool to catch Hollywood," said Hunter.

"Remember, our goal is Comic-Con. Not cruising for hookers on Sunset Strip."

"I wanna spot Sammy Davis Jr. in Vegas," said Prez.

"Is Sammy Davis Jr. even still alive?" asked Winnie.

"I don't know, but my mama would kill me if I stopped in Vegas and didn't see him."

"We'll be in Nebraska forever," said Winnie.

"What's in Nebraska?" asked Prez.

"White people, and corn," said Hunter.

Prez's face got serious. "You think they got the clan in Nebraska?"

"It's Nebraska, not Alabama," said Alex.

"It's not like they haven't ever seen a Black person, Prez. They aren't gonna look at you like an alien or something. I mean they have TV," said Winnie.

"My mama says white people are white people. No matter if they from New York, Nebraska, or Alabama," said Prez.

"That's a terrible thing to—" Alex crossed her arms. She looked at Hunter, then back to Prez. After a moment she gave a short nod and looked down at the map.

"So, I've figured out the mileage, and budgeting for food and motels. I figure we can get there and back if we all kick in $500," said Alex.

Prez whistled. "Whoa, Alex, five hundred bucks? My mama would kill me if I spent five hundred dollars."

"Prez, when are you going to stop hiding behind your mama?" asked Alex in frustration.

"I don't know, when I'm fifty, or she dies," said Prez in all seriousness. "You met my mama; you know how she is."

Alex shrugged in agreement. All of them were scared to death of her. It was always "Yes ma'am, no ma'am." Even Hunter was respectful to the woman.

"I know I can swing it, but not much more," said Winnie. "I don't know, Prez, maybe we can chip in a little more, and you can do more of the driving or something."

"Oh, sure, you think I'm Morgan Freeman, you want me driving Miss Daisy," said Prez.

Everybody laughed, including Prez.

"I can cover it," said Hunter.

"What?" asked Alex.

"I'm saying not to worry about it, I got it covered."

"You sure?" asked Alex.

"Yeah, don't worry about it. But when Prez is driving, I get to sit in the back, and he has to wear a suit and a black hat. Oh, and he has to address me as Mr. Hunter."

Prez threw a handful of Cheetos in Hunter's general direction.

"Nice throw. Now you get to clean it up," said Alex.

Prez tried to get out of the chair, with no success.

"OK, now seriously, we still have to figure out the car thing," said Alex. "We can't take Hunter's Camaro across the country. Not with that tiny back seat."

She scanned each one of their faces, but they all seemed to be drawing a blank.

"Well, this is the issue we need to figure out. Otherwise, we aren't going anywhere," said Alex. "So maybe a little bit of Ariel will help us." She got up and put in the second VHS tape. A collection of groans went up, but secretly they all liked it.

Fifteen minutes into *The Little Mermaid*, Prez's soft snores could be heard over the delightful soundtrack. Hunter lasted a minute or two longer. Alex and Winnie's bodies were now fully touching as they sat side by side in the beanbag chair. Both were equally aware of the other, and drew comfort from the physical touch.

Normally Alex would be engrossed in the movie's heavy-handed lessons: exploring new worlds and not being trapped in a box. But her thoughts were fixed on the warmth of Winnie's body and the distance she felt between their two souls. She'd had an emotionally taxing day, yet the unspoken things between them felt like a canyon.

"Win?" she said softly, half expecting an echo.

"Yeah?"

"Are you doing OK?"

Winnie paused before answering, letting out a deep breath. "I'm doing OK, I guess."

She waited for more.

"I have a sense I've done something wrong, but I don't know what it is."

A blanket of guilt descended on her.

"You're far away from me. Even though you're right next to me. And I can't help but feel it's because of something I did."

She took a deep breath before speaking. "I'm sorry, Win. You haven't done anything wrong. I'm just... it's just..." Snapshots flashed through her mind: her mother, Billy Bully, the fantasy of holding Winnie's hand as they walked down a boardwalk, and even a flash of Chance's handsome face. "It's like the walls are closing in, or every room I'm in is filling with water. Like something is supposed to be happening right now, but nothing is."

Winnie nodded.

She continued, "There's something I'm trying to deal with. To figure out, which has nothing to do with you. Right now, it's affecting everything. I think my painting sucks, my self-confidence is gone, and with you—"

"Stop it, Alex. Seriously, you have amazing talent."

"Yeah, but you have to say that. You're my best friend," she replied, wanting more.

"It doesn't matter if I'm your best friend or not. You have more talent than any person I know. It's almost like your work is a living, breathing thing that changes based on how I'm feeling. If I'm happy, I notice happy themes; if I'm sad, I see sadness. I've never had an emotional reaction to a painting the way I have with yours."

It was what she needed to hear. A rush of love washed through her and her eyes welled up with tears. Thankfully, Winnie was staring at the TV.

"I understand what you mean by a room filling with water. I feel the same thing. Like I'm supposed to have a purpose. Or should be doing something, anything! But I'm not doing anything. But you have so much talent. You're incredibly smart. And really... you have to know how..." Winnie shifted in the beanbag. "I mean, you know you're beautiful... on the outside. On the inside too, of course. I mean you're so..."

Her cheeks were on fire, neck flushed. Even the tips of her ears felt hot. Another moment when she wanted him to kiss her. To touch her. She imagined she lived under the sea. He'd be able to receive sonar pings she was sending out in waves. Or a whale song traveling great distances through the ocean. She couldn't understand the power Winnie's words were having over her heart and her body.

In the background, Sebastian started singing "Kiss the Girl," and Alex almost laughed out loud.

"I know I'm your best friend," said Winnie. "So maybe I don't count as much. And I know we don't talk like this."

It was right there. She could sense the words about to come out. She took in a breath and held it.

"Alex... I..."

She wanted to hear the words at the edge of his tongue. Part of her was petrified he might actually say them.

Winnie let out a sound of frustration. He turned toward her, his hand rising slowly to her face. Her breath caught.

Prez let out a long fart. Grunted in his sleep and turned over. The tension of the moment burst like a balloon, as both Alex and Winnie giggled at the shock of it.

"Oh, Jesus," snickered Alex as she brought her sweatshirt over her nose up to her glasses.

"Christ, Prez!" snorted Winnie as he did the same with his shirt. They both giggled under their shirts. They settled down, and Alex grabbed Winnie's hand. She gave a quick squeeze, but kept her fingers interlocked with his. Safe for the time being. Watching Ariel walk on legs for the first time, she understood Ariel's unbalanced and shaky feeling. She felt exactly the same way. And it was exhilarating.

CHAPTER THIRTY-SIX

LET IT BE

Gary sat on his corner barstool, at his corner bar, as he did most nights when he had money. It was as dingy inside as Gary was on the outside. Balls set out on the old pool table in back, its felt faded green, would all roll to one side of the table. Most of the 70's records in the old jukebox were scratched and would skip once or twice a song. A collection of old neon beer signs tried to shine their anemic lights through the haze of smoke. A cigarette machine sold smokes without a federal tax stamp next to the two putrid bathrooms.

A decrepit bartender stood with a dirty towel in one hand and a cigarette hanging from his mouth. He appeared bored, or constipated, or maybe a bit of both. A collection of old timers sat in the same spots they always sat in, staring down into their beers or occasionally looking up at the black-and-white TV playing the Brewers game. For two bucks you could get a beer, a shot of something tasting like paint thinner, and an unfiltered cigarette. For the price of a beer, you could be mostly left alone. What you couldn't get for any price was a clean glass, anything resembling service, or advice bartenders are supposed to always have at ready supply. This one would grunt at you.

What Gary needed was advice. After two hours, he wasn't any closer to figuring out what he should do. This afternoon, the boss's wife was hugging the Don's nephew. Of all the shit he'd gotten himself into, this was by far the worst. The rising bubbles in his beer provided no answers.

If he kept his mouth shut and Mr. Bartallatas found out he'd known, he was dead meat for sure. And he was pretty sure Mrs. Bartallatas had seen him. But if he told Mr. Bartallatas, he might not even get past saying her name before he was dead meat. One time he'd gotten a backhand from Mr. Bartallatas for accidentally looking at Mrs. Bartallatas' chest.

On the other side, Chance wasn't someone he wanted to mess with either. Everyone knew that the Don protected Chance. In fact, Gary was surprised that Mr. Bartallatas had sent that shipment of bad meat.

He knocked back the rest of his Schlitz and signaled the bartender for another. The bartender finished his cigarette before moving at a snail's pace to refill Gary's beer. Gary wished he had someone he could talk to.

It occurred to him that if he told Mr. Bartallatas his wife was stepping out on him, and that Gary was only telling him 'cause he was a stand-up guy, it had to be worth a few additions into his "book." More than enough to wipe out any of his subtractions. It might even be a promotion.

But it could be worth more to Chance, who was a lot less likely to beat the shit out of him. It wouldn't be blackmail. He'd find a way to talk to Chance and let him know that he knew, and that his secret was safe with Gary. Maybe Chance could get him a job working directly for the Don. Which would be way better than working for a scoio... a scocio... a crazy person like Mr. Bartallatas.

Decision made, he felt much better. He drained the rest of his beer and held up the empty glass. The bartender, thoroughly engaged in cleaning his nails with a pocketknife, ignored him.

"Hey, a little service over here." Gary waved his glass like a torch. The bartender didn't look up.

"Hey, fuckface! Can I getta beer or what?"

"Fuck you, Gary. You got any money?"

"Do I got any money?" Gary said in a mocking voice as he pulled out a hundred-dollar bill. He waved it and slammed it on the bar.

"Well, I'll be." The bartender slowly walked over to Gary's greasy glass.

"And a shot of Jack—"

"Whoa, big spender tonight."

"And get one for yourself, for da great service," said Gary.

The bartender poured the pint of Schlitz, and also set two short glasses in front of Gary, pouring two double-sized shots of Jack Daniel's. Not waiting for Gary, the bartender knocked back the first shot and then grabbed the money.

"Hey! I want my change."

The bartender hit a few buttons on the register, and a drawer opened. He threw four twenties and a five back on the bar.

"You could at least say thank you for da shot," whined Gary.

"Fuck you, Gary."

"You're not going to want to talk to me like dat if you know what's good for you. I'm going places in dis world, and you're a fucking bartender." Gary knocked back his shot and felt a satisfying burn of high-end whiskey. Way better than the shit he normally drank.

"Gary, the only place you're going to is the floor after I knock you off that barstool."

Gary swayed a little, almost falling off on his own accord, the beers catching up with him.

"You can think that if you want to, but in a couple of days, you'll be sorry. I'm movin' up in da world. So, pour me another fucking shot," slurred Gary. "And fuck it, since you're such a pleasant person, pour yourselves one too, hell, pour all da guys a shot."

That got the bartender's attention. Gary, a notorious tight-ass, never bought anyone anything. The bartender rang a cowbell, and a few old-timers looked up. The bartender poured five shots of Jack and set them in front of the semi-awakened men.

"Gary bought a round. Mark it on your fucking calendars." A few of the guys peered down at Gary, trying to decide if they knew him. A couple of others raised their beers and grunted.

Gary raised his shot glass. "To me, motherfuckers! And working for da big guy."

The bartender took down his own shot. "I'm pretty sure Mr. Bartallatas wouldn't like you referring to him as 'the big guy.'"

"I'm not talking about him." Gary stood up on the first rung of his barstool. He raised his glass and knocked back his shot. "I'm talking about da big, big guy. Fuck Frank Bartallatas.

I'm going higher than him. I'm not gonna work for a guy who can't even control his own wife."

Gary tried to sit back down, but instead slid off the edge of his stool. He hit the ground and started laughing uncontrollably.

"Hey, Gary, get on up here, let me buy you another drink, on me. What are you talking about?"

Gary picked himself up off the floor. Gave the bartender a dirty look. "I ain't telling you shit."

"No, no of course not, but come on up here, and I'll buy you a drink anyway."

"Yeah, dat's more like it," he slurred. "I gotta hit da head first." As he stumbled toward the bathroom, the bartender went over to the phone.

Gary's head was on the bar. A rough hand smacked him on the shoulder, but Gary didn't budge.

"Gary, it seems you've had a few tonight. Let me give you a ride," said the large man. Boots, pants, shirt, and a leather trench coat were all in black. Pale bloodless skin and Bob Ross hair left an overall impression of a 1970's movie vampire. John Carbone lifted Gary by the back of the collar and smacked him in the face a couple of times. Gary mumbled something unintelligible.

All the old-timers were gone, and the only other person in the bar was the bartender. John smacked Gary again, but got only a few groans for his trouble. He set Gary's head back down and looked at the bartender.

"Give me a pitcher of water." With speed not seen in years, the bartender leaped to the pitcher and carried it over.

The man poured the pitcher of water over Gary's head. Gary tried to take in a breath, but got only more water for his trouble. He started coughing and jerked his head up off the bar.

"What da fuck," he coughed out.

"Come on, Gary, help me walk you out to the car."

Gary didn't open his eyes, but tried to rise to his feet. John put his beefy arm underneath Gary's. He glared at the bartender.

"He was never here tonight."

The bartender nodded. "Do you want his change?"

"Keep it. He won't need it." He half-led, half-carried Gary out of the bar.

. . .

John Carbone was six-five, two-fifty, and an unapologetic killer. Cold, precise, unfeeling. Frank Bartallatas' hired gun for over ten years. Except he never used a gun. Guns were messy, guns were loud. Guns put you in the can during a routine traffic stop. No, John Carbone's preferred way of dealing with problems was piano wire, which, as the owner of John and Sons' Piano Emporium, gave him a perfect excuse to carry death. He bought and sold, repaired and moved all manner of pianos. He also taught lessons; his large frame and cold dead eyes were enough to scare the kids into practicing their scales. He had talent, but sizable fingers kept him from becoming a virtuoso.

There were no sons in John and Sons, only daughters. Their mother died of breast cancer a few years earlier; the only thing that made John happy was watching the girls play.

The piece of shit lying on the boxcar floor was Gary. John had known Gary was going to end up this way. Sometimes you just looked at a person and knew they were going to meet with an untimely death. Gary was too stupid to be trusted with anything sensitive or important. But nonetheless, he'd found a way to become a nuisance. John lost track of the number of Gary's he'd killed over the years. It had been easy to get Gary to the freight area of the train station. Told him he'd earn $500 to help move some boxes. Gary being drunk readily agreed.

It hadn't taken any pressure to get Gary to spill everything: from a case of beer he stole and claimed broke in the back of the truck, to the ten cartons of cigarettes he swiped from the warehouse when no one was watching, to what he saw with Chance and Mrs. Bartallatas at Harry's Bar and Grill that afternoon. Then he rambled his master plan to blackmail Chance into getting him a job with Uncle Vinnie. *As if that was ever going to work.* On the surface, it wasn't much. Two people in a restaurant sharing a hug and maybe a kiss on the cheek. But John knew Chance's reputation, and also how much Frank and Chance hated each other.

This could get messy. While John worked hand in hand with Frank, nobody knew his real boss was Uncle Vinnie. His job was to keep an eye on Frank and keep the Don informed. Right now, Frank was on his way back from Chicago, where he'd been meeting with the Tesseo family. Frank wanted to be in charge. Chicago wanted more of a piece of Milwaukee. Frank didn't have the muscle to take over from Uncle Vinnie, yet. That's where Chicago came in.

If Frank found out Chance was sleeping with his wife, it would be all the excuse he needed to take Chance out. Not even Uncle Vinnie could prevent it from happening. But the loss of face Uncle Vinnie would suffer by letting his favorite nephew get whacked would force him to go to war. A war the Don didn't want, and was trying to prevent.

Damn it, Chance, why can't you keep your dick in your pants?

He unwound the piano wire from around Gary's neck. It wasn't like the movies where people went to sleep and died. Eyeballs tended to pop out, and they always pissed and shit themselves.

The boxcar door slid open, and John's heart froze. He took a breath only when he saw it was Frank, with a beaten-up Ralph. John realized Frank was supposed to be in Chicago, and there was no way he could have known John and Gary would be there unless he'd been followed.

"Well, John, what do we have here?" Frank climbed up into the boxcar, a pistol in his hand.

John thought about talking his way out. In about three seconds he realized it was useless. "How'd you know?" John dropped the piano wire to the floor. A tingle of fear went up his spine.

Ralph closed the boxcar door behind them and pulled out his own pistol.

"Know what, John? That my wife's been fucking around, or that you worked for Vinnie"

John sighed. He had to give Frank credit. He hadn't thought he was that smart.

"I've always known about my whore wife and Chance. You might say I even encouraged it. As for you, Judas, I've known for a couple of years. Ironically, Sloan figured it out."

John let out a heavy breath.

"So, you're making your move."

"Yes. I am." Frank pulled a six-inch-long silencer from his coat pocket. He screwed it into the end of the barrel. "In a couple of days, Vinnie, Chance, and my wife will all be a memory."

"My daughters?" asked John, resigned to his fate, his shoulders falling.

"Oh, don't worry about them, John. We'll take care of them. Right up to when they turn into teenagers. I'll have them turning tricks on the street in South Milwaukee, a lesson to those who betray me. Those big Black bucks will love a piece of white teenage—"

John screamed and rushed for Frank. Frank, caught off guard, stumbled back, and Ralph fired off three rounds of his unsilenced gun. The roar from the gun in the enclosed box car was ear shattering. One lucky round took off most of the top of John's head. He was dead as he fell, his massive hand reaching Frank's gun arm.

"Jesus Christ, you stupid fucker," yelled Frank, not able to hear his own voice, the ringing in his ears overpowering. "What the fuck did I tell you about the silencer?"

"Holy shit," yelled Ralph, not able to hear a word Frank was saying. "Did you see how fast he was? Christ, he was fast." He touched a hand to ear and looked at the blood on his fingers.

Frank opened and closed his jaws, trying to get the ringing to stop. If he didn't need Ralph for what was coming, he would have dropped him right then.

Frank looked at Ralph and shouted, "Pick up the fucking shell casings, you fucking moron."

Ralph winced as he put his hand back up to his ear. "Hey, we should pick up the shell casings!"

Frank's hearing was returning, and he rolled his eyes. He took a garbage bag out of his jacket and threw it toward Ralph. He made a sawing motion. "Go get the saw from the car."

"Yeah, I got a saw in the trunk of the car," yelled Ralph.

"I know there's a fucking saw. Go get the goddamn saw out of the car!"

"I'll be right back. I'm gonna go and get the saw out of the car."

Ralph opened the sliding door and stumbled out into the night.

"It's a shame, John," said Frank to John's lifeless body. "You see the fucking idiots you've left me with." It was going to be gruesome work. Cutting off the hands and heads. The bodies they would leave on the train, and with any luck they wouldn't be found until Nebraska.

Frank took in a deep breath. The sweet smell of blood mixed with other bodily fluids. The next couple of days were going to be extremely busy. Everything with Chicago was in place. Their guys would be up there in two days. His only regret was that he wasn't going to be able to watch the light go out in Chance's eyes. No, he had more important things to take care of. Uncle Vinnie and that fat fuck Giorgio. It was way too risky to leave to anyone else. Even the heavy hitters from Chicago. But afterward, he'd be able to take his time with his wife. Oh, she thought she was so smart, setting up Chance with Gary.

Yet there was a small worry about his wife. He wasn't quite sure what she'd thought she was going to get out of setting up Chance. She was slippery as a snake, and as cold as one too. But he pushed those thoughts out of his head and concentrated on the next step.

Ralph returned with a large saw. He looked at the bodies, and then at Frank.

"Don't just look at me, get to work. We have a lot of shit to do tonight."

When Ralph just stood there with a dumb look on his face, Frank sighed in frustration. He made a cutting motion with his hand across his throat and pointed down at the bodies.

Enlightenment flashed across Ralph's face.

"Boss, you got some blood on your face," yelled Ralph as he bent over to start the task at hand.

Christ, it's hard to get good help. Frank took out a handkerchief and wiped his face. The noise of saw on bone echoed inside the box car.

CHAPTER THIRTY-SEVEN

YOU'RE MY BEST FRIEND

In a booth at Country Kitchen, Chance drank coffee and smoked cigarettes. One after the other. Head down, deep in thought about Maggie, Ellie, and Mrs. Lee An uneaten plate of over easy eggs and burnt bacon was pushed aside. He wasn't hungry but had ordered them to be kind to the waitress. Nobody likes to wait on people who only order coffee.

"You want some more coffee, honey?"

Chance glanced up at the fifty-something waitress holding a coffeepot.

"Yes, ma'am, thank you."

"You didn't touch your food. Not hungry?"

"No, ma'am."

"Please, young man, call me Vera. I'm not old enough to be a ma'am to you," she said, smiling.

"No, ma'am, I mean Vera, you're certainly not." Chance flashed her a big smile. "In fact, Vera, when do you get off work?"

"Oh, listen to you, you charmer, I'm not old enough to be your mom, but damn close," Vera giggled. "What's your name, Mr. Charmer Pants?"

"I'm Chance, Vera, nice to meet you."

"Not *the* Chance?"

"That depends. Do I owe somebody money?" He lit another cigarette.

"The young man there talks about you quite a bit."

Chance turned around to where she was pointing with the coffee pot. Winston Morris sat in a booth, head down, but stealing glances at them.

"Ahh, Winston. Yes, I probably do owe him money, since he's my bookie."

"He is not!"

"You're right, Winston is actually the enforcer... you don't pay, and he breaks your leg."

Vera cackled again. "I can see why he likes you so much." She refreshed his coffee and took away his plate.

Chance caught Winnie's eye. Winnie tried to act surprised and gave a half-wave.

Chance sighed, stubbed out his cigarette, picked up his coffee, and headed over.

"Hey, sailor, you come here often?"

Winnie blushed. "Hey, Mr. C., I didn't know you hung out here."

"Are you kidding? This is like the nightlife hot spot. Everybody who's anybody hangs out at Country Kitchen." Chance slid into the booth.

In his best Brooklyn accent, Winnie replied, "'Applause, applause, applause.'"

"Winnie, I find it refreshing that two strong men," Chance indicated them both with his index finger, "feel confident enough to recite lines from *Pretty in Pink*. How you doing?"

"I'm cool, Mr. C., just hanging out." Winnie put away his sketchbook.

"Where's Alex? I thought the two of you were attached at the hip."

"She's on her way, I think."

"And the other two troublemakers?"

"Prez is on his way, too, and Hunter may stop by. I'm sure he's on a date or something."

"Man, that kid. I own a restaurant, and I don't get as many dates."

"Oh, you seem to do pretty well for yourself, Mr. C."

"What about you, young man? Any changes with you and Alex—"

"We're just friends."

"But—"

"But we're friends, Mr. C."

"OK, but if I were you, I wouldn't let her get away."

Winnie sat with something clearly on his mind. Chance looked around. Besides one old guy wearing a well-used hat that said *I'd Rather Be Fishing*, the restaurant was deserted. The carpet was old and stained, and some of the booths had tears in the fabric. The temperature was good, but the overhead music left something to be desired. Something you would overhear in an elevator, or at a dentist's office.

"Does it get any easier with girls, or women?" asked Winnie.

A genuine smile pushed back the folds of Chance's mouth. "Oh, man, I can say it most definitely doesn't get easier. At least for me, it hasn't. Sometimes the more you think you know, the less you really do. I wouldn't worry too much about it. You have a great heart, kid, I can see that. A lot of good in relationships comes from paying attention. Paying attention to your partner's needs. You're already good at it."

"I am? I haven't been in a real relationship."

"Do you remember last winter when we got all that snow dumped on us and we had to close for two days?"

"Yeah."

"The day we opened back up, it was Alex and you working outside. She was wearing a ridiculous wool hat, but didn't have any gloves."

Winnie's chin hit his chest. "I made her that hat in art class."

"Yeah? I guess it's the thought that counts. I'd say don't open a yarn store; it doesn't play to your strengths." They both chuckled. "Anyway, it was cold. And I saw you come into the restaurant a couple of times and make tea. It stood out to me because I've never seen you drink tea. So, I followed you out and saw you hand it to Alex, to warm her hands. That's what will make you great in a relationship."

Winnie grinned at the memory.

"A big heart is what's most important. The rest of it will come."

Vera arrived at their table to top off their coffee cups. "How you boys getting along?"

"Right as rain, Vera. Is it always this slow?"

"No, not usually, but the construction on Madison killed us all week."

"Oh, right. I came the other way. Vera, you look familiar. Have you served anywhere else?"

"Not unless you were in Fargo in the 50's."

"Ever been to Bella's?" He was sure he'd seen her before, but couldn't place it.

"Do I look like the type who can afford a swanky place like that?"

"We always allow a beautiful woman into our establishment, don't we, Winnie?"

"Of course." Winnie rolled his eyes as he put three creamers into his coffee.

"My gosh." Vera fanned herself. "Pay attention, Winnie. This is how you make an old woman blush."

"Yes, Mrs. White."

"White... White, I know that name from somewhere. This is going to bother me all night."

"Well, Chance, unless you go to St. Peter's Church on Jackson, I can't see how we've met before. And believe me, I would remember a handsome young man such as yourself."

"Mrs. White!"

"Oh, pooh you, Winnie. I'm older, but I'm not dead."

Chance was laughing the way a good-looking man, used to being flirted with, laughed. "It'll come to me."

Vera set down her coffeepot and put a filterless cigarette to her lips.

Chance lit his Zippo and touched the flame to its tip. "Why don't you have a seat for a minute and take a break? I don't think the fisherman over there is going anywhere."

"Well, OK, but only for a minute." She sat beside Chance. "It isn't proper for the staff to sit down with the guests."

"Mrs. White, you sit down with me all the time."

"Hush now, Winnie."

A strange warm glow spread throughout Chance's body. He was puzzled—until he realized he was enjoying himself. Sober.

"So, you two have known each other for a while?" asked Chance.

"Let's see here. Winnie's been coming in here for what, three, four years?"

"Five. I had started my freshman year."

"My word, five! Lord, where does the time go?"

"I don't know, Vera, but if I find out I'll grab some for both of us," said Chance.

The bell over the door clanged. Mrs. White got up. "Damn, a woman can't catch a break." She looked right at Winnie. "'I'll be back,'" she said with a terrible Bavarian accent. Chance and Winnie both snorted as she walked away.

"Wow, Win, she's pretty great."

"Mrs. White? Yeah, she's awesome. Kind of a second mom to me." Winnie glanced out the window, then back at Chance. "She's had a tough go of it. Lost both sons in Vietnam, and her husband died shortly after."

Chance watched Mrs. White pour coffee grounds into a massive percolator. "That's terrible."

"Yeah, sometimes when I get down or feeling sorry for myself, I remember how it could always be worse. Doesn't make me suffer less, but usually stops me from spiraling down the drain."

"Pretty smart. Other people's tragedy doesn't lessen our own pain, but does make us realize what we do have in our lives. You're wise beyond your years."

Winnie sipped his coffee. "I'd like to do something nice for her, but I'm not sure what. She came to dad's funeral, even though she'd never met him. She has such a kind heart."

"Maybe that's where I've seen her." He sat there a

moment. "I got an idea. What are you doing tomorrow night?"

Winnie shrugged. "Don't know, supposed to do something with Alex, but not sure yet. Maybe a movie or something."

"I think I have a way you can do something nice for Mrs. White and have a kind of date with Alex."

Winnie's eyes widened and his cheeks flushed. His back straightened, giving the illusion he'd grown two inches.

Alex walked into the restaurant, her stride determined. Her glasses were completely fogged up. She took them off and started to clean them with her sweatshirt. "What's up with the ridiculous construction? I almost killed myself getting over here. I had to climb over like fifteen different rock piles," she put her glasses back on. "What the... Hi, Chance." Concern flashed across Alex's face as she glanced at Chance and Winnie sitting together.

Chance smiled up at her.

"Alex, I'm so glad you're here. Winnie and I have been talking about Mrs. White and how important she is to him. I have a most excellent idea."

CHAPTER THIRTY-EIGHT

ONCE IN A LIFETIME

Alex and Winnie left, and Chance felt a small measure of pride at having outlasted two teenagers. Even if it was at a diner.

Mrs. White was bussing up the last table after an unruly crowd of drunks. A few balance-challenged patrons served as a cautionary tale of what Chance might become with his current level of alcohol consumption.

On a napkin, he drew two columns. In the left column, he wrote all the current issues in his life: His uncle and the proposition. Frank. Frank's wife, but he put *Sloan* in parentheses as possibly a problem no more. Maggie, Stella, loneliness, and his culpability over Mrs. Lee. Even though he'd written down her name, it was a box of pain he couldn't even begin to open up.

In the right column, he wrote *Alcohol*. Except for his uncle and Frank, he could trace all of his problems from the left column to the one item in the right column. Under *Alcohol* he wrote in big block letters, *Fear, Guilt*, then drew a line from each up to *Alcohol*. Under that he wrote: *Alcoholic???*

Looking down at the list, he asked himself for the first time if he could stop. Really stop.

He thought of the last ten years and the choices he'd made since Ellie. Alcohol was just a thing. It was what you did at night, or during the day at a ballgame, or in the morning at Sunday brunch. He could say it was the fast and loose restaurant industry, or a way of coping with sadness. It made him more social and fun. After a bad night or long binge, he could stop or would stop for a while. But those stops were getting shorter and shorter. Poor choices were becoming more frequent. All of his negatives were alcohol-related in one way or another. And they all stemmed from one night. His eyes glazed over as it came rushing back.

1979

Chance was leaning up against a light post where he'd been waiting for Isabella outside the recording studio. It had been a great session, with at least four of the songs done and ready to be mastered. Chance was high on life, and a joint or two.

He saw her pull up in his brand-new Lincoln. He smirked as he watched her turn a parallel park job into an almost endless dance of pulling forward and backing in. Finally, she put the car in park about four feet from the curb. He smiled as he climbed in.

"Ellie, my love," he said after a prolonged hello kiss. "That was... good job parking, baby."

"This beast? Piece of cake." She brushed imaginary lint off her shoulder. They both gave each other knowing smiles.

"We had a great day today," said Chance.

"Oh, I can't wait to hear all about it. I've had a great day as well. But you first. No, wait. Do you want to drive?"

"No, babe. Practice makes perfect. But I have to tell you this first. I talked to Bernie—"

"Slimeball." Ellie frowned.

"Well, he is a manager, honey. It's the way they're built."

"Ugh, hearing his name makes me feel like I need a shower."

Chance chuckled. "What if he cleared it with the studio that we can get married before I go on the road?"

"What?" she screamed. Her hands shook as she grabbed and hugged him, instant tears glistening in the street light.

It was one of the many things he loved about her. She was not ashamed to cry or laugh or dance or sing whenever the mood struck her.

She pushed him away, laughing. "Tell me! Expand, please."

"Well, I realized that I was scared of losing the contract. That what I've worked for, what we've worked for would be lost." He grabbed her hands, covering them with his. "But I don't want fear holding us back. And I don't want to do this without you." Chance leaned over and gently kissed her forehead. "We both know it's gonna be hard on the road." Chance brought her hands up and kissed her fingers. "I need to know you will be there when I come home."

"Of course, I'll be there."

"So, I talked to Bernie yesterday, and I basically told him it was going to happen one way or another. His job was to find a way to sell it to the studio. At first, he tried to talk me out of it."

"Of course, the toad."

"But then he went to the studio and said it was a dealbreaker, and that with my demographics, family man is a good thing. And they caved."

"Wow, they must really really want you."

"I guess." He grinned at her. Then his face became serious. "So, Isabella Joy Antonia, will you do me the honor of becoming my wife? To have and to hold from this day forward. In sickness and in health. For richer or poorer. I promise to honor and obey, especially the 'obey' part."

She snorted and hit him on the arm.

"In case you forgot, silly, you already asked, and I said yes."

"Yeah, well, that was to get into your pants. Now I mean it." She laughed again and hit him even harder.

He rubbed his arm and leaned over and pressed his lips upon hers. Seconds turned to minutes, minutes turned into hours, hours into lifetimes. Finally, after ten lifetimes they broke apart and came up for air. His lips were tingling, and as headlights lit up her face he could discern complete happiness sparkling in her eyes. He knew his were reflecting the same colors.

"So, what's your good news?" he asked as he waved at Bernie walking out of the studio.

She placed both hands on her stomach. "Well, it's ironic Bernie thought a family man—"

The sound of brakes slamming down on tires echoed in the night. Chance whipped his head around and peered past Ellie out the driver's side window. A car had screeched to a stop right next to them. Shock coursed through his body and he couldn't process what he was seeing. A man in a ski mask stared right at him. The lips coming out of a hole in the mask mouthed words. The world slowed to a crawl. Even though his brain reacted to the gun, his body couldn't move any faster. The driver's side window shattered inward, spraying glass shards. A pink mist exploded in the car, and for minutes afterward hung in the air.

PRESENT

Chance pulled himself out of the memory. Out of the dark place. He used the napkin to blow his nose.

Mrs. White approached with her coffeepot, and he crumpled the napkin and put it in his pocket.

"You know, young man, if you're waiting for me to get off work, I'd say your chances are fifty-fifty."

Chance laughed, glad for the release. "You're a feisty broad, aren't you, Vera?"

She refreshed his coffee. "And you look like you have the weight of the world on your shoulders. Thought you could use a good laugh."

"You're a lifesaver." Chance indicated the other side of the booth. "You got time for a smoke break?"

"Until the fishermen start coming in around four, I got time for whatever you have in mind, young man."

Chance laughed again as she sat, turned the other coffee cup right-side up, and poured herself some coffee.

"I suppose if I'm going on a date with you, I should probably get to know you a bit."

"A pseudo-date. I know you only said yes so we could get Winnie and Alex out for a romantic evening."

"Don't sell yourself so short. You're not too bad-lookin'. And you do have a charm." She winked at him and pulled out a cigarette from an alligator skin case. "But what about you, young man? What's your reason for going out with this old lady and a couple of kids?"

Chance immediately flicked open his Zippo, lit it by snapping his fingers, and extended it across the table. "Honestly, they remind me of myself and someone I cared for a long time ago. And with what's going on in my life right now, being around them is wonderfully distracting. Besides, I promised Winnie's dad I would look out for him."

"I didn't realize you knew him."

"Gene and I went way back. We used to be in a band together."

Cigarette in hand, she started to lean forward, but stopped and tilted her head to the left, focusing on the lighter. Her face visibly paled and her hand shook.

Chance sat there, his arm extended with his Zippo burning. "Are you OK, Vera?"

"It's just... where did you get that lighter?"

"A friend of mine gave it to me a couple of years ago." He flipped the Zippo closed and held it out to Vera. Her hand reached, shaking, but paused an inch away.

"What's wrong?"

"My sons both had a lighter like that... from their father, before they went to Vietnam." She leaned back in the booth and put the unlit cigarette down.

"I'm sorry. It gave me a start, that's all. It looked so familiar." She fumbled in her apron and grabbed her Bic lighter to light her own cigarette, hands still shaking.

"There are millions of Zippos out there."

She absently nodded. "For a second..." she paused. "Both my sons were MIA, lost in Vietnam. So... sorry... screwy way the mind can torture you. Does it have an inscription?"

He set it down and pushed it toward her. "Yeah. It says, 'Am I my brother's keeper'."

Vera brought her hand to her mouth and choked back a sob. Chance jumped up and slid into the booth next to her, putting his arm over her shoulder and pulling her close.

Vera's small frame convulsed with every breath. Chance held her tight, his nose pressed into her beehive hair, which smelled of strawberries and cigarettes.

After a minute or two her breathing relaxed, the sobs abated, and he became conscious of how close he was to her. He took his arm from around her and slowly slid out of the booth and returned to the other side.

"Vera, maybe it's one of the same lighters, and maybe it isn't. Maybe my friend knew your sons. But I wouldn't want to get your hopes up."

Vera lit another cigarette but used her own lighter. "I want to know what happened. I don't know... anything. I never have." Silent tears retraced paths down her cheeks, dripping into her lap.

Chance's mind was racing. Jed had the same lighter. It was a set of two, and he'd given one to Chance as a thank you. What were the odds?

"My friend lives behind my restaurant. Like in a cardboard box. I have to warn you; he isn't always clear in the head. He is a vet. I don't know what happened to him over there; he never talks about it with me. But maybe tomorrow night I could bring you to him after dinner and we could ask him together."

"He might have known my boys. He could be a friend. Maybe was with them."

"Or it could be something he found, or was left behind somewhere. There could be a million other reasons why he would have these lighters."

He cleared his throat. She seemed small and fragile. He didn't want to push, but now he was curious.

"Vera, can you tell me a little about your sons? If you can bear talking about it."

CHAPTER THIRTY-NINE

DAYBREAK

Chance sat at his kitchen table drinking his morning coffee and reading the paper—which a hangover usually prevented. He felt great. No massive headache, no horrible taste in his mouth, no trying to puzzle out what might have happened the night before. It was a refreshing change of pace. His brain was sharp. His mood elevated into a euphoric level, matched only by his unusual craving for sugar. Chance was not a sweets person, but was currently destroying a large custard-filled donut.

Part of the natural high he felt came from having made a decision. No matter what it took, he was going to bring his uncle, Frank, and Giorgio, to justice. He knew himself enough to know he couldn't do what they did. But after seeing Mrs. Lee, he couldn't live on the sidelines either. He had to do something. After calling and leaving a message for Mitchell, his shoulders were already straighter. This is what Ellie would want. What he wanted for himself.

In the shower, Jed was singing a collection of popular 60's rock songs, his voice surprisingly good. Every few days Jed would come up the back stairwell, knock on Chance's door, and head straight for the bathroom. He always knew when Chance was alone. Never once had he interrupted him with a lady friend. Chance had left out a new pack of Fruit of the Loom underwear, as well as Jed's only other outfit, which Chance had laundered since Jed's last visit.

The more Chance thought about his crazy idea, the more it felt like providence. Vera was a lonely middle-aged woman who had lost two sons in Vietnam. Jed was a lonely Vietnam vet with no known family, and had possibly known her sons in Vietnam. Maybe, just maybe they could help each other.

Jed walked into the kitchen wearing only two towels: one wrapped around his head like a woman, and one wrapped around his body. Jed pulled a can of Miller High Life from the fridge. He expertly popped the top and took a large swallow. He sat next to Chance and grabbed the comics section. An *Odd Couple* scene it truly was, Chance and Jed sitting at the kitchen table enjoying the morning paper.

Jed picked up his pack of Swisher Sweet cigars off the table, took one out, and lit it with his bronze Zippo that matched Chance's.

Chance pulled his out. "Jed, can I ask you something?"

Jed snickered at a *Calvin and Hobbes* comic. "That Hobbes is such a troublemaker."

"Why did you give me this lighter?"

Jed didn't look up from the comics. "Because it's hard to light your cigarettes with your finger."

Chance smiled. "True, but why this lighter? I treasure it, but why did you give me this lighter and not a random Bic? It seems like a family heirloom or something."

"No, it can't be an heirloom; that is the incorrect word. An heirloom is an item of personal property that is connected to a family estate. The owner, me, can give it away while I'm alive, but it can't be willed to someone if I die. It would stay with my estate." Jed paused. "Oh, I guess under that definition, it can be an heirloom."

"Whatever it is, it seems to be important to you. So why did you give it to me?"

Jed took another sip of his beer. "Chance, are you feeling insecure about our relationship? Are you in need of some words of affirmation?"

Chance chuckled. "No. I wondered if it had a story behind it?"

"Yes, there is."

Chance waited. Jed didn't say anything. Just kept reading the comics.

"OK, so will you tell me the story?"

Jed snorted and in an exaggerated fashion closed his paper. "Yes. It was given to Moses from Ramesses the Second, ten years before Moses brought the ten plagues into Egypt. It is quite historical. Probably worth some money if you want to pawn it." Jed picked up his paper and started reading again.

Chance knew he had run into a brick wall. He tried a different tactic. "Did someone else before me own this lighter?"

Without looking up, Jed replied, "Well, of course. Ramesses the Second obviously owned that lighter. Mine was Moses' lighter. Since I am a modern-day freedom fighter, and you are an evil tyrant oppressing the Mexican masses."

"Ouch. I don't think I oppress anyone."

"Chance, you need to relax. Am I my brother's keeper? You are my brother; you keep me fed and clothed. I am your keeper; I keep watch and keep you safe. Speaking of which, there are two men from Illinois parked outside the hotel. They're not the fuzz, but they aren't hotel guests either."

"Can I ask you a question about Vietnam?"

"Do you have any more beer?"

"A six-pack of Schlitz under the counter, so it's warm."

"Beggars can be choosers, but that is how they stay beggars," replied Jed in his usual fashion. He got up and found the six-pack, opened a can, and took a long swallow. "Ugh, almost better to be a beggar."

"Hey, don't drink all of that today. I have a special surprise for you tonight, and I don't want you so drunk that you pass out before your dinner."

"What kind of surprise?"

"A fantastic bottle of booze for your birthday. But first I wanted to ask you a question about Isaac. You've mentioned him before, and I was curious."

Jed looked thoughtful. "No, I don't think so."

"I don't understand."

"That's right, Chance. You don't." Jed picked up the newspaper again.

Chance sat there in uncomfortable silence.

After a couple of minutes, Jed raised his beer and took another large swallow.

"What are you going to do for the rest of the day?" asked Chance.

"Man my post, of course. I don't like those two guys outside. They have a shifty look about them. Greasy wops or something."

"Hey, you potato-eating paddy! I'm half-Italian," said Chance in mock indignation.

"Yes, and amazingly enough I still hang out with you. Whoever said political correctness has gone astray was correct."

Chance laughed. "All right, you hairless mick. Seriously, I've seen babies with better tans and more hair on their chests than you." Chance got up. "I have to get down to work. Leave the people in their car alone. For all you know they could be bird watchers. Plus, you know Mitchell has guys hang out in front to note who's coming and going."

"These aren't Mitchell's guys."

"OK, well, let yourself out when you're done. Seriously, don't raid my liquor cabinet. We have special shit for tonight." Chance rinsed his cup out and went into the hall. He put on his leather jacket and did the pat-down, making sure he had his smokes and keys.

He wondered again if he was making a colossal mistake. But he was in way too good of a mood to worry about it.

. . .

"I think you're making a colossal mistake," said Geoff, sitting in Chance's office. The lunch shift was about to start. "The story is fantastic, but what are the odds Jed knew this woman's long dead sons?"

"I know, I know, it's like something out of a movie. But think about what we know about Jed. He's a Vietnam vet, he sometimes mentions an Isaac. And the lighter. It has the same saying on it. What are the odds? How many Isaacs could there have been in Vietnam?"

"Um, hundreds? That war went on for over ten years. Millions of men served. Besides, we don't even know if it's his real name." Geoff peered out the window. "You could hurt someone here. You bring her out there, and she sees a guy in camouflage, about her son's age. But he doesn't know her sons, never did. You fill her full of false hope. Hope for closure she'll never have. Not to mention Jed, bless his heart, isn't exactly the most stable person."

"That's why I want you there with me. You're a vet. You can help me if things get out of control."

"Oh, no, you aren't going to involve me in this craziness." Geoff held up both hands.

"Think about it. There are so many things that add up."

"Add up? Or are you pushing a circle into a square because you want it to fit?"

Chance lowered his eyes.

"Look, I know how much you care about Jed. And it sounds like this woman made an impression on you. You want this to be true because you always want to help people." Geoff paused. "Chance, look at me. This is classic you. I'm not trying to be out of line here. But you can't go back and fix the past."

Chance felt his hands shaking. He glanced up, heat radiating off his face.

Chance ran his hands through his hair. Then he put them on his face and held them there. The rising and falling of his chest slowed, and the color behind his eyes faded. "You're right. I know you're right; it is too crazy. I don't know what I was thinking." His shoulders sunk and he lowered his head.

"You're thinking about Jed. You're thinking of this woman and how you might be able to take some of their pain away."

Chance raised his head, and there were tears in his eyes. He didn't wipe them away.

"Brother, do you want a hug?" said Geoff, smiling.

Chance snorted and thought about it. "You know what? A hug sounds good right about now, you bronze teddy bear."

They both stood and met around the desk. "Let's just make sure we don't cross the streams," said Chance. Geoff laughed and grabbed Chance, pulling him tight. Chance awkwardly smacked Geoff on the back, but Geoff held him.

"You're a great man, Chance. You have to forgive yourself," said Geoff quietly into Chance's ear. Chance's body stiffened and then slowly relaxed.

The door opened, and Maggie walked in. "Shit, Chance, please tell me I didn't turn you gay?"

"Maggie, you don't understand the power I wield," said Geoff, not taking his arms from around Chance. "Actually, beautiful, get on in here. Chance needs some *ménage à trois* loving right now."

Chance and Maggie both laughed. Maggie wiggled her way in between the two men.

"Umm," she breathed, "I could get used to this."

Chance hugged them both tighter.

"As interesting yet weird as this is," Geoff let go of the two of them, "I'm gonna sneak out and let you guys talk." Geoff backed away but shook his finger at both of them. "No office sex. We open in ten." He looked at Chance. "Oh right... that's probably enough time for you." He winked at Maggie and sashayed out of the office.

They both stood there a moment, then let go of each other and stepped back.

"Did you get my note?" asked Maggie.

"Yeah, um, about that."

CHAPTER FORTY

MAYBE I'M AMAZED

Winnie admired himself in the mirror over his dresser. His dad's vintage 70's suit looked fancy—way out of style, but he felt good wearing it. His skin was thankfully clear, his hair, full of mousse, would stay in place even in hurricane-force winds. God knew it had better, considering he'd spent at least ten minutes on it. He was excited, but also wanted to throw up, like his heart was exploding out of his chest like in his favorite alien movie.

He was going on a date with Alex. Yes, Chance and Mrs. White would be there. But they were getting dressed up and having a kind of date. He was even borrowing his mom's car to pick up Alex. He addressed his own reflection.

"You're going to tell Alex how you feel." It came out a bit squeaky, so he took a deep breath and said it again. "You are going to tell Alex how you feel." The reflection responded with a nervous laugh.

"You can do this! You're going to do this." The person in the mirror paused. "You're going to do this?" He vented out a frustrated sigh. He wasn't sure he could do this. What if she laughed? What if she slapped him? What if she got pissed and walked away from him? What if, as in every fantasy he'd ever had, she kissed him back?

He pointed a full bottle of Polo at his chest. A full squirt of cologne hit him in the face, and he coughed. It smelled good. Just didn't taste good.

On top of the dresser lay a sheet of paper with his one and only completed poem. If he found the courage to give it to Alex, there would be no hiding how he felt.

The days are short and the nights are long
Our time apart has come and gone
We embrace as old friends and lovers to be
A hunger in my eyes that only you can see
A battle of wills began tonight
Because of my desire I lost the fight
Your kiss would be that of magic, your lips oh so tender
The fantasy of this I will always remember
Love is like a fire that leaps inside me
Before you I was blind, but now I can foresee
Like the breath of night, or dawn's first light,
I wonder if what I am doing is perfectly right
To keep you for my own, not share with my fellow man
A beauty so unflawed,
I am not sure how I really can
For it would be like taking all the stars,
to hoard in my own little piles
And leave to the rest of the world
a darkness that goes for miles
But one thing I do know
my love for you is so strong

I want to spend forever with you,
is eternity too long?
So, take me if you want me
I will give you all my love
And our lives will be at peace
like that of a little white dove...

He sprayed the fancy Japanese paper—called *feather waltz snow*, which had cost him ten dollars for five sheets—with Polo. He rolled up the poem, tied it with a red ribbon, and tucked it inside his pocket. He loved the suitcoat's secret pockets. He inspected himself in the mirror again and for once liked what he saw. Off his dresser he picked up a mixtape he'd spent three weeks carefully crafting for Alex. Each song carried a ray of insight into his throbbing heart. He put the tape into a case and dropped it into his front jacket pocket.

It was like he was going to the prom, which both he and Alex had missed due to his dad's death. He opened his Velcro wallet to double-check on the five crisp new twenties behind the worn-out picture of him and Alex at his sixth-grade birthday party—when he'd figured out he loved Alex. He'd always loved Alex. Seven long years had gone by since that realization. Tucked inside a flap was the smashed condom his dad had given him on his sixteenth birthday. Winnie looked at the door to his room. A memory from several years earlier walked in. His dad, still strong and alive.

"Win, can I talk to you?" his dad had asked, uncharacteristically nervous as he walked into Winnie's room.

Winnie took his headphones off. "What did you say, Dad?"

"Can I talk to you for a minute?"

Winnie turned off "Glory of Love" by Peter Cetera. "Sure, Pop."

His father shut the door behind him. He stood for a second, as if unsure what to do next. Winnie sat up and rested his back against the bed's headboard, embarrassed because he'd been listening to the same song over and over again on his Walkman.

"Winnie, your mother told me about, um… well she told me she walked in on something yesterday…"

Winnie's face turned beet red. His dad sat at the end of the bed, his hands in his lap, his face as red as Winnie's.

"So, um, I, well, I wanted to come in here and ask. Well, you know, if you've got any questions or anything?"

"No," said Winnie quietly.

"I wanted to say it's perfectly natural. Um, what you were doing."

Winnie stared at the X-wing fighter on his bedspread as if he'd never seen it before.

"I mean at your age I was…" His father looked at the door like he was planning to make a break for it. "What I mean is, everybody does it."

Winnie's eyes lifted to his dad's. "They do?"

"Well, yes, when I was your age, I was going for some kind of record or something." His dad chuckled. "Win, it's a normal thing. There isn't something wrong with you. You're changing. You're becoming a man."

"Do girls do it?"

"Well, I certainly hope so." The smile faded and his dad took another deep breath. "I know you've had sex-ed in school. So, you know what the body parts look like. You know the basics of all that stuff, right?"

"I think so," said Winnie, already feeling better. "I know there is a lot of kissing, and the penis goes into—"

"Um, yeah," his dad interrupted. "You have the basics. I'm sorry, Win, I'm not good at this. My dad never had this talk with me, so I'm not sure how it's supposed to go. I know why you have the last three Sears catalogs under your bed. I know it's for the women's underwear section and not toys anymore. Even if your mother doesn't want to admit it. Well, until yesterday, that is. It's OK, and I didn't want you to feel ashamed or anything."

"So, Dad?"

"Yeah?"

"How do, how do you know when you are ready?"

His dad sat there for a minute, thinking. "Well, Win, your body is going to be ready long before your heart is. Your hormones will be screaming for it, as they probably already are. But it really is so much more. It's about sharing yourself with someone you love. It's about giving more love than receiving. Do you notice there's a central theme there?"

"It's about love," he said.

"Yes, yes, it is. Oh, it's about passion and friction. But the important thing is that you're with someone you love more than yourself. It isn't about getting off. That's what the Sears catalogs are for. You'll be ready when you know the person you're sharing it with loves you as much as you love her. It's all about being ready in your heart. It isn't a race. It has to be the right time. With someone like Alex. Someday… um, down the road," his dad said quietly. His father reached into the pocket of his Oxford shirt and held something out to Winnie. A Trojan condom. Winnie had seen them in sex-ed class and at school, with some boys already carrying them around.

"This part is important, Win. Use this when, well, when the time is right. Making love can be a marvelous thing. But it isn't always safe. And you don't want a little Winnie running around for at least ten years or so. Do you know how to use this?"

"Um, yeah, they showed us on a banana at school."

His father laughed again. "We should all be so lucky."

"What?"

"Nothing. Don't worry about what you have versus what anybody else has. I know teen talk is all about who has the biggest penis but, remember, those who talk the most usually have the least. It doesn't matter, anyway. Being a great, um, lover, well, it's not about size. It's about giving. Taking the time to learn about your partner, and opening yourself up to them as well."

As Winnie stood there gazing at the door, he tried to hold on to the memory. But it was fading, the image of his dad was fading. His eyes blurred. He was going to tell Alex. He better understood now what his dad had been saying. And every sign Alex had given him he'd missed. The long looks, the mood swings. God, he was such a fool!

CHAPTER FORTY-ONE

PSYCHO KILLER

"So, Frank, where's John? I thought he'd be with you tonight."
If Uncle Vinnie had any concern over John, it wasn't showing
on his face.

Frank wiped his lips with a cloth napkin and took a sip of
his wine. "I have him running some important errands for me."

They faced each other across a backroom booth at the
Bamboo Tree, a small family-owned Chinese restaurant, one
of many places in Frank's growing empire. He loved Chinese
restaurants, dry cleaners, and convenience stores. These people
were used to paying out protection money, and never gave him
any trouble.

The lieutenants for both men were sitting a couple of
booths down. Newly-promoted Ralph and Giorgio were
staring at each other, a couple of bulls fenced in the same yard.
Frank was still surprised Vinnie would meet him here. The
busboys, waiters, and even the bartender were all Frank's. This
was going to be easy as pie.

"And how is your lovely wife?" asked Vinnie. A small
ping bounced off Frank's radar. He stared at Vinnie, but saw
nothing behind the small black orbs.

"She's fine. You know Sloan, happiest when she's spending my money." He took another sip of wine, not liking the small smile that flashed across Vinnie's face.

"Yes, I do know Sloan… Frank," said Vinnie.

Frank put his fork down and frowned at Vinnie. It wasn't much of anything, the sound that followed. A small cough followed by two more small coughs. Frank knew. Small caliber, .22, but it wasn't time yet. He hadn't given the signal.

Frank turned his head toward the sound. There was Ralph. Blood soaking through his shirt. His mouth opened, trying to make a sound, but nothing came out. Giorgio caught Ralph's head before it hit the table. Frank glanced around the room. The four minions in the room, his pretend bussers, bartender, servers, stood there watching him. Nobody pulled a gun; nobody came to help him. He slowly turned back and eyed Vinnie. He let the air in his lungs out. Either his guys in the next room were dead already, or had been turned. Either way, it didn't matter. Frank had made his play and lost.

Vinnie picked up his wineglass, the blood tones in stark contrast to his pasty skin. He took a sip, eyes peering over the top of the glass at Frank. Those cold dead eyes.

"Frank, I don't blame you. I'm not even mad at you. But you have to understand you never had a chance at this. Those hitters you brought up from Chicago. Let's say they have been made to see the error of their ways. No, Frank, they're not dead. I don't need to get into a war with Chicago. The capo you were dealing with down there, on the other hand, is dead. He was a thorn in the side of Don Genovese, as you're a thorn in mine. So, you see, everything is the same. Business will go on with hardly a ripple."

"How? John?"

"Among others, Frank. Now, I want to be clear with you. This isn't about vengeance. Your ambition outmatched your intelligence. Can't really fault a man for that. It was always going to end this way, since you tried to take out Charles."

Frank raised an eyebrow. "You knew 'bout that? Why'd you let me live? Why waste all this time? Why didn't you take me out then?"

"Frank, it's like trying to explain to a small child why the moon circles the earth and the earth circles the sun. But I'll indulge you a little." He took another sip of wine. "For you it was personal. You acted out of ego. That's why you fucked it up, but I also knew from that moment I would always be able to predict what you would do. Ego is the worst way to make decisions. But also, in your favor, I needed your father's people. Kansas City was trying to control Vegas at the time. Your father, before he died, had ties to Genovese, and I needed Chicago on my side. Taking you out wouldn't have helped me, and would have made my life harder. The smartest thing you did was to not ever say a word and to take care of the driver yourself. And, yes, I know about that too." Uncle Vinnie pushed his plate forward.

"Had the fact that you tried to kill my nephew come out, of course I would've had to kill you publicly. But since you had enough sense to keep your mouth shut, I was able to use you in the way I needed to. I knew at some point I'd kill you for it. But you served a purpose. And now your purpose has concluded."

Frank reached for his wineglass, proud that his hands didn't shake. He took a big gulp, mind racing, trying to spot an angle.

"Originally I told Charles that Ellie died in revenge for the sins of his father. He bought it then, but I might tell

Charles who killed his fiancée. And how after I found out I immediately took care of you. But I may not. It's at my whim. He's going to take over for me, so he'll need to understand how these things work. It's called the long game."

"Speaking of a long game, where's your oxygen tank? I thought you had one foot in the grave."

"Oh, I'm not quite that far gone yet. Little misdirection for your enemies is the art of war. Charles will be the figurehead, as I miraculously manage to hold on awhile."

Frank saw his last card to play and smirked at Vinnie. He even managed to laugh. A frown crossed Vinnie's pale face.

"So, you don't know about John?" asked Frank.

"Yes, I do know about John. Right now, he's at Bella's. You see, John wasn't the only person keeping me apprised. Your lovely wife has also been confiding in me. So, yes, I do know about your second attempt on my nephew's life. And, no, the two hitters from Chicago won't get to him, Frank."

Frank snickered again. "Apparently, it's been a few days since you talked to John, 'cause John is dead, and right about now Chance is probably dead." Frank took another sip of wine. He knew he wasn't getting out of here alive, but damn if it didn't make him feel good to know Vinnie hadn't figured everything out.

Vinnie's eyes narrowed to slits. He raised his hand and snapped his finger. Giorgio came over, still holding the small gun.

"Take two guys. Get over to Bella's immediately. I don't care how, but get Charles to my house. Hit him over the head if you have to, just get him away from that restaurant."

"What about him?" asked Giorgio.

"Leave the rest of the guys here. Don't worry about him."

Giorgio looked disappointed.

"Hey, Giorgio, go fuck yourself," said Frank.

Giorgio took a step toward Frank, but Vinnie held out his hand. "Frank, let's not get crass here." Vinnie dismissed Giorgio with a wave of his hand. Giorgio moved as fast as his 300-pound body was able. Frank chuckled again.

"That is disappointing about John, if it is true."

"Oh, it's true. I knew he worked for you. Keep your friends close and all that. But I didn't know about Sloan. It was a mistake to let her live," said Frank.

"A mistake I'll not be making with you, Frank." Vinnie threw his napkin on the table and motioned for his guys. Four of them came to the table, all with pistols in their hands.

"This wasn't going to be personal. But I think since I like Sloan so much, this got a lot more painful for you." Vinnie glared at the men. "Take him out back and beat him to death. Leave his body."

Frank considered his options. Taking a bullet here in this booth sounded a whole hell of a lot better than being beaten to death. But then again, maybe he'd have a fighting chance. He snorted out loud when he thought of the word *Chance*.

"Something on your mind, Frank?" asked Vinnie as he got up from the booth.

"Actually, I was thinking of your nephew," said Frank, also starting to slide out of the booth. No use prolonging the inevitable.

Vinnie raised his eyebrow to indicate Frank should continue.

"But for a brief second in time, we probably would have been best friends forever. It's funny how one split second can change your whole life." Frank let the air out of his lungs in a resigned awareness. Or maybe even a thankful admission that he wasn't entirely sad to see it all end. The bricks of pain and despair, from childhood on, were crumbling in the final moments. His slouching shoulders were starting to lift; the weight that had been pressing down was lifting.

Vinnie noticed the shift, said nothing, turned, and left.

"Come on, Frank. Let's go nice and easy here," said minion number one.

Frank was crying now. Not from fear, or sadness, but from the sensation of freedom. Maybe for the first time ever. A look of surprise passed between the four men as if to say *what a wimp*. Frank didn't care. He wasn't afraid. A hyper-awareness washed over him. From colors of the walls to exotic smells in the air, mixed with kitchen noises as they passed through the swinging doors. This was what he wanted. Since childhood there had been nothing but pain, with a few bumps of pleasure along the way.

A strange language shouted back and forth by foreign people. The sounds harsh and biting. Not eloquent like Italian, or even French. Frank felt steam in the air, the water droplets grazing his skin, floating into his lungs. Time had slowed down, so the last minutes of his life stretched into hours. What would've been flashes in real time were visions of the few pleasant memories that spanned his life: The Red Ryder BB gun he got for Christmas; scoring the winning touchdown at Regionals; his wedding night with his first wife; the birth of his son five months later; the first time Sloan smiled at him. He absently wondered if he would recognize her in hell. God knows they both deserved to go there.

Because he was hyper-aware, he was the first to spy the tray full of dirty dishes slip from a waiter's hands. He was the first to react, as the sounds of crashing distracted everyone else. All pleasant memories and thoughts of contrition vanished in a single overwhelming need to survive. As they turned toward the noise, Frank was in motion. A six-level wire rack was on his left, filled with pots and pans and utensils. As he passed it, Frank already had both hands on the rack, and he pulled it crashing down on three of the men. Two of them didn't even see it coming, and the third didn't have time to put up his hands. The fourth man, who was ahead of Frank, was starting to swing his attention from the dish pit to the noise behind him. The man never had a chance to register what happened before Frank snapped his neck, a twig under the paw of a grizzly bear.

As the shouts in whatever gibberish language filled the air, Frank calmly picked up a pistol off the ground. Two of the men were struggling to get out from under the pots and pans and the heavy rack on top of them. Frank shot them twice without thinking. The third wasn't moving at all, but Frank shot him for good measure.

One cook was screaming at the waiter. Another was slapping the kid in the face. As Frank walked through the kitchen and out into the night, he knew he had to get out of Milwaukee. If he could get to Kansas City, he'd be safe. He needed to see his wife one more time.

This 16-cassette collection includes 160 of your high school dance favorites. Do you think Girls Just Wanna Have Fun? Me too!

Operators are standing by, so have your credit card ready. This amazing collection, not available in stores, can be yours for 16 easy payments of only $28.95.

Go back and relive the place you couldn't wait to get out of. Order now!

CHAPTER FORTY-TWO

IN THE AIR TONIGHT

The door opened, and Mrs. Kopoff was standing there wiping her hands on an apron. "My, my, Vinston, you look so handsome!"

From somewhere in the house, Alex's father, Andre, called out, "Is that the Pooh bear?"

Winnie blushed and frowned.

"Come in, Vinston, come in, you vill catch your death standing out there." It was a warm spring evening, but Mrs. Kopoff was always saying open doors would invite the Grim Reaper.

Winnie stepped inside the cozy house. Mrs. Kopoff eyed Winnie appreciatively. "Such a handsome suit, Vinnie. The flowers are beautiful. Here, I must put them in vater." Mrs. Kopoff clapped her hands and reached out to grab the bouquet of flowers Winnie had picked up on the way over. "And you're taking our Sasha out to a fancy dinner. Alexandra is putting on a dress. You have made an old woman so happy. I never thought I would live to see the day my beautiful daughter would vear a dress. You remember, she stopped vearing them when she was eight."

Winnie didn't remember Alex ever wearing dresses, but nodded anyway. Mr. Kopoff entered the kitchen with his usual glass of vodka in hand.

"Who is dis man in my kitchen?" he said. "Dis cannot be the Pooh bear."

"Andre, stop it," Mrs. Kopoff said playfully.

"Who vould have thought the Pooh bear has grown up to be a man. Vinston, you look very nice tonight. Katiana is so happy you're taking Sasha out tonight to fancy restaurant. They have been fussing around the house all day." He held out his hand to Winnie. Winnie shook it the way his dad had taught him. Firm grip and four to five shakes up and down.

"Vinston, I'm glad you're here. I've picked up newest version of Borodin: *Symphonies Nos. 1 & 2* from the Philharmonic. Come into the study and I will put it on, yes?"

"Nyet, husband. They must go to restaurant," said Mrs. Kopoff, her back to them as she stood at the sink filling a large green vase with water.

"Thanks, Mr. Kopoff. Maybe tomorrow night? We need to get going soon."

Mr. Kopoff reached back and grabbed his wallet. "Do you need money, Vinston?"

Winnie held out his palms and waved no. "Thanks, Mr. Kopoff, I'm fine, I have money."

Mr. Kopoff beamed at Winnie. He put his arm over Winnie's shoulder and lowered his voice. "Vinston, I'm happy. Should you experience the urge to kiss my daughter, as her father I'm saying you have my permission."

"PAPA!" said Alex, arriving on the scene. "Winnie and I are just friends. Stop teasing him."

Winnie didn't even catch what Alex said, so floored was he over her arrival. He sucked in his breath, or lost it, or didn't need it. His eyes widened as he took in all of her. His childhood friend had become a woman before his very eyes. Her hair was curled and up in a style he'd only seen in magazines. She was wearing a strapless pink dress, which flowed out to her knees. The contrast of color to her rich dark hair was... pink carnations dipped in semi-bitter chocolate. The dress revealed more of her skin than he'd ever seen before. She had a small freckle over her right breast, both of which were pushed up high, and Winnie quickly moved his eyes to her shoes. They matched her dress, and even more shocking than the color was their high heels. Her handbag also matched in color. The first thought that came into Winnie's head was *ballerina*.

Alex's father took his arm off Winnie's shoulder. "Sasha."

Mrs. Kopoff took in her breath sharply behind him. Mr. Kopoff wiped away a tear.

"Stop it, you guys. It's just me!" said Alex, her cheeks flush.

"Sasha, you're the image of your mother. You take my breath away," said Mr. Kopoff, still crying.

"It's a dress," said Alex, clearly relieved at the reaction she was getting. Winnie stood there, his mouth hanging open. A sharp jab in his ribcage shook him out of his stupor.

"Well, Vinston, what do you think of my daughter? Too beautiful for you, no?" said Mr. Kopoff.

"Um, wow. Alex you, you... I mean, I... I, you..." stammered Winnie.

Mr. Kopoff laughed. "Well said, Pooh bear."

"Alex, I don't know what to say. You look so good."

A frown formed on Alex's face.

"I mean great! No, more than great, so... so perfect."
Winnie blushed again. "I've never seen anything so perfect,"
he said quietly, almost to himself.

Alex's smile perked up.

"Much better, Pooh bear," said Mr. Kopoff.

"Oh, Mama, why are you crying?" Alex rushed over to
her mother and grabbed her hand. Physical touch was not
something Winnie had seen between the two women. But Mrs.
Kopoff grabbed her daughter and hugged her tight.

"You look so beautiful. Oh, don't cry, Alexandra, you
don't vant to smear your makeup," said Mrs. Kopoff.

"All right ladies, we must get picture of the two lovebirds."
Alex wiped the tears from her eyes. "Papa, stop it!"

Winnie stood beside Alex, and they awkwardly put their
arms around each other. Winnie could feel the heat of her skin.
He almost forgot to look at the camera.

"OK, say 'borscht'!" Mr. Kopoff tried to snap the picture.
Nothing happened.

"Husband, give me the camera." Mrs. Kopoff held her
hand out. Mr. Kopoff said what sounded like a swear word in
any language. He pointed the camera at himself and it went off,
the flash blinding him. He said a couple stronger words. Alex
and Winnie both giggled. Mrs. Kopoff shook her head sadly.

She took the camera away from the now blind Mr.
Kopoff. "Vorld's greatest photographer." Winnie wasn't upset
with the extra time he had to hold Alex, although his arm was
starting to tingle.

Mrs. Kopoff adjusted the camera and pointed it at the
still-smiling Winnie and Alex.

"Say 'cheese,'" she said. "OK, one more, in case. You both
look vonderful."

"Alex, we should get going." Winnie glanced at his watch. "Yes, let's."

Alex hugged her papa and mama one more time. Mr. Kopoff gave Winnie an exaggerated handshake. "Keep my Sasha safe, Vinston."

"Yes, sir."

They walked outside, and Winnie hurried to get to Alex's side of the car first. He opened the door for her, and she gave him a brief curtsy. As he closed the door and walked around the car, he got a thumbs-up from Mr. Kopoff. Mrs. Kopoff grabbed her husband and held him tight. Mr. Kopoff gave Winnie another thumbs-up and appeared to grab Mrs. Kopoff's behind, judging by the way she jumped.

Winnie smiled to himself as he got into the car.

"Get me the hell out of here... Pooh bear," said Alex.

They both laughed as Winnie put the car in gear. He let out the clutch, and the car jerked once, twice, tossing Alex's head forward. He put the clutch back in.

"Jesus, Winnie, remind me to never rob a bank with you. You're a valet, for god's sake, how can you not drive a stick?"

"Sorry! Sorry, nervous I guess."

Winnie revved the engine and slowly let out the clutch. One little jerk and they were off.

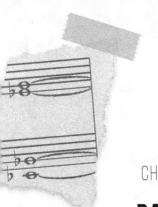

CHAPTER FORTY-THREE

BAD MOON RISING

The two men had been sitting in the Lincoln Town Car parked across the street from the Knickerbocker Hotel all day with nothing to do but talk and wait for night. They'd discussed the Cubs, White Sox and Brewers. About the Bears' dismal 6-10 season, and the Packers' heartbreaking 10-6 record.

They both became animated over how fake the movie *Goodfellas* was. Junior, in the driver's seat, was convinced you couldn't believe any story written from the viewpoint of a rat. Mickey, who was borrowed muscle from Chicago, swore he'd met the infamous Henry Hill, in Florida back in '78.

"I swear, dat little fucker had beady eyes. Had I known den what I know now, I woulda taken him out den."

Junior was impressed with the breadth of the man's experience. He had stories going back decades. New York, L.A., and most recently all the glitz and glamour of Vegas.

"Kid, I gotta tell ya, it ain't like what it used to be like. We used to be kings. I'll tell ya something that little Scorsese fuck got right. We'd walk into a show or a restaurant without tickets or reservations and they would make a table for us.

People knew who you were, and didn't fuck with ya." Mickey looked out the passenger window. He grabbed a cigarette out of his pack on the dash.

"Crack a window, will ya?" complained Junior. Mickey pushed the button and the window went all the way down. He pulled up and the window went all the way up. Up, down, up down, until finally the window was open a crack.

The leather from Junior's gloves made a stretching noise as he tightened his fists.

Mickey sighed. "I didn't choose this life. It chose me." He took a drag and attempted to blow the smoke out the cracked window. Junior waved his hand as the car filled with smoke anyway.

"Kid, I'm gonna die in prison, or from a bullet. What I ain't gonna die from is freedom in my old age, in some nursing home. You're young... you should—"

"Yeah, but what you don't understand is, I like it. I like the money. I like the fear I see when I walk into a room. And I like smacking people around. You don't understand. I like it," said Junior.

Mickey slowly shook his head. "I understand, kid."

Junior peered out the driver's side window at the hotel. Cars were starting to pull up to the valet spot. A skinny Asian kid and a Black kid ran around the cars, opening the doors for rich white folk. *As it should be,* he thought. "You ever eat here?" asked Junior.

"Nah, I hate Milwaukee."

Junior let that slide. Truth be told, he didn't much care for the city either. It was hard to hide his appetites in a city this small.

"He makes good sauce," said Junior.

"Well, how long did this guy think he was going to live, being Uncle Vinnie's nephew?"

"Chance ain't ever really been in the family. But he is in the way, so." Junior stuck his chest out, stretching his back. They'd been sitting there for hours. "I think I'm gonna scout the alley again. Stretch my legs a bit."

Mickey put his hand on Junior's arm. "Hey, relax. We're too close to split up now."

Junior glared at the older hitman. While technically he was in charge, he'd be a fool not to follow the other guy's lead. He rubbed his gloved hands together. Somehow, they were both cold, clammy, and sweaty all at the same time.

Junior glanced at the entrance to the hotel and saw Chance standing at the valet stand. "Hey, that's our guy."

"Yeah, that's him all right."

"What are we waiting for? He's thirty feet away from us."

"That's not the plan. The plan is to hit him in the alley between ten and eleven."

"Come on, Mickey, he's right there. We can be out of the car and do it in twenty seconds. Dead is dead. Why does it matter if it's the alley or right out front?"

Mickey sat there thinking. "What about collateral damage?" he asked.

"Just not a bloodbath. That was the only instruction. He's talking to those two kids that are going to, I don't know, prom or something. Come on, Mickey, I could hit him from here."

Mickey took the Beretta nine-millimeter out of his coat pocket, popped the clip out, slammed it back in, and chambered a round.

Junior felt a charge flash through him. He pulled out his gun and did the same thing.

"All right. I want to be within ten feet before we start shooting. Two in the chest and two in the head. After he's down, shoot out a couple of car windows. That'll keep everybody's head down. Remember to drop the guns in the street. They're clean. No fuckups, Junior. We get back to the car and hit the interstate in two minutes."

"Yeah, OK, no fuckups," said Junior, the adrenaline coursing through his body.

"With any luck, Vinnie is already dead. This is clean up." They put their guns back in their coat pockets, gave each other a "let's do this" look, and got out of the car.

. . .

A car was ahead of Winnie and Alex as they pulled into the restaurant's valet area. Chance was waiting for them in the valet spot. Prez, behind him, rocked back and forth on his feet. Chance opened the passenger door to a Porsche while Hunter ran around to the driver's side.

Winnie grinned at Alex. "Royal treatment."

"Yeah, this is so exciting. I feel like Cinderella."

Hunter sped off in the Porsche, and it was Winnie's turn. He put the car in first and let out the clutch. To his horror, the scene at Alex's parents' house repeated itself. Jerk, jerk, stall. He could see Prez barely holding it together as Winnie clenched his teeth. He somewhat successfully pulled into the spot, jammed the parking brake on, and put the car in neutral. Alex shook her head at Winnie as Chance opened her door. She accepted Chance's outstretched hand and got out. Winnie was out before Prez could come around and reach his side.

"Christ, Win, remind me to never rob a bank with you." Prez handed Winnie a ticket. Winnie frowned at his friend, but reached into his back pocket to grab his wallet.

"You can't be serious, man. Shake it off. She looks amazing; have a great time." Prez patted Winnie on the shoulder. Winnie went around the back of the car as Chance, still holding onto Alex's arm, spun her around in a complete circle.

"Absolutely breathtaking, Alex. You are the vision of Venus reborn. I'm completely speechless, as your beauty drives all coherent thoughts from my head," said Chance.

Not really speechless, thought Winnie sourly. Winnie was shocked when Alex, holding on to Chance's hand like he was Prince Charming, curtsied like she was born to do it.

"Thank you, Chance, I must admit I feel rather pink," she replied.

"Ahh, but pink, my dear, as in 'pretty in,' is the best of colors."

Winnie scowled and jammed his hands into his pockets, only to have to awkwardly pull one back out when Chance ripped his focus from Alex and reached out his hand to him.

"And you, young man, are you not the image of Prince Charming himself? I must admit I'm quite jealous of how great you wear that suit." Chance was wearing a black suit and a stylish skinny black tie.

"Thanks for inviting us, Mr. C.," stammered Winnie, trying and failing to match the grip on his hand.

"Winnie, how many times do I need to tell you to call me Chance? I'm not your boss tonight, I'm your friend." Chance let go of Winnie's hand and extended his toward the hotel lobby. "Now we're just waiting for my date. But you both don't need to stand in the cold. Go on in; Maggie has us set up in the private room."

"I'm excited, Chance. Thanks so much for inviting us," said Alex.

"I'm the one who's excited. Don't be surprised if you don't get a few jealous looks from the women in the dining room, as they all pale beside your radiant beauty." Chance grabbed Alex's hand and bent and kissed it.

Alex put her other hand to her mouth and giggled. At least that's what it sounded like to Winnie. It was a sound he wasn't sure he'd ever heard come out of her mouth before.

Chance's attention switched from Alex to something across the street. Winnie followed Chance's eyes. Two men emerged from a dark sedan, and were starting to cross the street. An MPD patrol car pulled up, blocking his view of the two men, and the cop in the passenger seat rolled down the window.

"Hey, Chance, how's the food tonight?" asked the cop.

Chance's attention shifted to the officer. "Only so-so Nick, as usual."

"Yeah, right." The cop glanced at his partner. "I took my wife here once, and she won't shut up about it." Turning back to Chance, he said, "Still the best meal I ever had."

The squad car radio squawked something Winnie couldn't understand, and the cop grabbed the handset and said something in code.

"What time is your guy's break tonight?" asked Chance.

The cop hung up the handset and leaned back out the window, ogling Alex, wanton lust plain as day on his face. Chance moved his body in a way to break the cop's view.

"Um, we're second shift, why?" asked the cop.

"Swing by for your break. I'll get you both dinner on me tonight."

"We'll take you up on that." The cop eyeballed Winnie. "Is there a prom going on here tonight?"

"Nah, these two work for me. I'm treating them to dinner."

"OK, well, great. We have to go make the city safe for you civilians, but we'll swing back for sure."

The cop car peeled out and sped off. Chance scanned the area. The two men who were crossing the street were nowhere to be seen. Chance's eyes kept scanning as a Yellow Cab pulled up.

"I think this might be my date." Chance opened the back door and extended his hand, as he'd done for Alex. "Mrs. White, please allow me."

A white-gloved hand emerged from the cab attached to a woman who had to be Mrs. White, but Winnie blinked twice to be sure. He'd never seen her out of her Country Kitchen uniform. Her full-length black dress was sheer above the chest, with sleeves tapering at the wrist. Her skirt's side slit went from ankle to mid-thigh, and her hat had a large brim. Her makeup was, for once, subtle. He knew nothing about makeup, but whatever she'd done made her look ten years younger. She was Jackie Onassis with red hair.

"Thank you, Mr. McQueen. I need to take care of the cab."

Yep, it was Mrs. White's voice.

"Vera, it's already taken care of. You're simply stunning this evening. I would say with the exception of your luscious hair, you're the spitting image of Jackie O."

Winnie was still too shocked to get annoyed at the theft of his own thought.

"Close your mouth, you'll catch flies. Alex, dear, you are a princess tonight. I feel like a fairy godmother."

Everyone responded at once.

Vera listened and waved her hand. "All right, all right, there's only so much an old woman can take. Winnie, you're gawking like you don't even know who I am. You forget Mr. White used to take me dancing all the time. I still know how to get dolled up, young man."

Winnie, who'd known and cared about Mrs. White the longest, felt like crying. He pushed the urge down and hugged her. She gave a surprised sound, but wrapped her slender arms around him.

Chance stepped back. Winnie felt another pair of arms around them. Alex. Part of his brain wondered what had gotten into her lately. Hugs were not something she was prone to. But the thought slipped away as he let himself fall into a safe place. A place he needed.

It took everything he had to avoid bawling, out of pain or out of joy—at the moment his soul was bouncing around both emotions like a pinball. He recalled as a child how his dad would toss him backward onto his parents' massive bed. Falling was scary and exhilarating at the same time. He would land safely, plunging deep into the soft down blanket. Fits of laughter would erupt from inside him. His dad would tickle him, but then as he caught his breath, he would always say in his little Muppet voice, "Again!"

Years later, after a hard day at school, his dad told him sometimes life was like falling onto concrete. Those were the bad days, and no matter how bloody you were, you picked yourself up and stood tall. But sometimes life was like falling onto cotton. And on those days, you lay in the rich softness and warmth of your feelings. Loving the world and all its splendor. Winnie was having one of those days.

CHAPTER FORTY-FOUR

ONLY THE GOOD DIE YOUNG

With her plan in place and the Carmelo crime family about to implode, it was time to get the hell out of Dodge. She wasn't sure if the tapes she had so carefully collected over the last two years would be enough, but she predicted the meeting between Uncle Vinnie and Frank would end in a hail of bullets.

She folded one last sweater into her suitcase and looked around her bedroom. All of her jewelry was packed. In between two sweaters, she carefully placed a picture of her sister in a pewter frame. She allowed herself a moment to look at Bethany, then closed and zipped up the suitcase. Her other suitcase contained a little over a half million dollars in cash, which Frank stupidly thought would be protected in a safe with a combination of one, two, three, four.

She sat on the edge of the bed between the two suitcases. Her chest expanded and contracted slowly—as if breathing alone could exorcise the taint that came from the role she'd adopted for her revenge. Like a snake shedding its skin, the first layer of Sloan Bartallatas fell away, bringing her closer to the person she used to be, Sloan Carter. Expensive therapy loomed on the horizon.

The second she stopped moving, Chance popped into her head. Dammit. She pushed him away and picked up one of the suitcases, carrying it down the stairs, out the front door, and into the trunk of her car. As much as she tried to focus on the task at hand, he kept invading her thoughts. Like the whisper of heroin or the shouts of cocaine. Right there in the back of her mind, his hands always reaching for her.

She reentered her bedroom with relief that it was for the last time ever. All her work, all of her sacrifices, were coming to fruition. She grabbed the suitcase with the money, surprised at how heavy it was. She'd read in a thriller that Grand Cayman was an excellent place to park ill-gotten gains. Bring on umbrella drinks and pool boys.

After putting the suitcase in the car, she returned to the front door, pulled out her keys, and stopped. She snorted at herself, took the house key off the ring, and threw it into the bushes.

An image appeared in her mind of lying in bed with Chance. His hand reached out and moved some hair from her face to behind her ear. Sunlight warm on her skin, the smell of musk hovering above the bed. Forward and backward, the scene played out in her mind. A low growl rattled in her throat and she opened the front door and walked to the end table in the foyer. Her hand hesitated over the phone.

"Dammit." She picked up the cordless phone and dialed the number she knew by heart. When she'd started her affair with Chance, it had been for two reasons. One, because she'd wanted him. And two, as a possible catalyst between Frank and Uncle Vinnie. When she'd met Frank, she surmised correctly that he'd never be made Don. Ambition was there, but the will and ability to think four moves ahead wasn't. She'd spent a year researching, enticing Frank, and putting a plan together. As a backup, because no plan survives contact with the enemy, if Frank didn't have the balls to take out Vinnie, his rage at finding out Chance was fucking his wife would be enough. If Frank killed Chance, Vinnie would have to move against Frank. As it turned out, power was more than enough motivation for Frank. Sleeping with Chance had been a bonus.

"Bella's, how may I help you?" said the offensively cheery feminine voice.

"Let me talk to Chance, please."

"Um, just a second, please."

She heard a muffled discussion.

"Um, he's busy right now. Can I take a message?"

"It's critically important I talk with him, so please get him. This is Sloan Bartallatas."

"Oh, Mrs. Bartallatas, yes, sorry, yes. He's out back. I think he's smoking. Can I tell him you called?"

"Tell him." She held the phone away from her ear and looked at it.

"Hello? Mrs. Bartallatas?"

"Just tell him I'm sorry." Sloan hung up the phone, closed her eyes, and let out her breath slowly. She'd tried, but it was out of her hands. She turned to leave and jumped as the phone rang. She grabbed it. "Hello?"

"Sloan."

"Frank? What happened?"

"It was a trap. He... for me."

He was cutting in and out. She moved the receiver from her ear and looked at it. As if that would tell her anything.

"There's a bad connection. I can barely hear you. Are you on a pay phone?"

"...waiting for me. Sloan? Sloan? Goddamn it. He knew, dammit. He's still alive."

"Where are you?"

"Get the... safe. One, two... four. I forgive you but I need that—"

She sneered and looked around the room.

"...airfield. Can you get to the airfield? Sloan? Sloan!"

She hung up, hands shaking, and slid down onto the armchair. She needed to think. Uncle Vinnie was still alive. Shit! The whole point of her plan, everything she'd worked toward. It was possible Mitchell Genovese would have enough to charge Vinnie. Or maybe get someone to flip, but it wasn't a guarantee. Her flight out of Chicago wasn't until six a.m.

Each time she'd gone to Uncle Vinnie's, they'd never frisked her. The outline of a plan formed in her mind. She would have to find a way around Giorgio. But maybe...

She went up to the bedroom and stopped in front of the full-length mirror. She ripped her blouse at the neckline. Next, she reached into her purse and grabbed a bottle of visine. She held it over her eye and squeezed the fake tears until a track of mascara ran down her face. She looked into the mirror. "Oh, my god, he was crazed. He ran into the house screaming. I've never seen him like this. He was like a wild animal. I was so scared."

Her lips moved into their natural smirk position. Men saw what they wanted to see, and what man doesn't like a damsel in distress? Especially one flashing a little boob. She went into the walk-in closet and spun the dial on the wall safe. One, two, three, four. What a fucking idiot. She reached in and pulled out a handgun. She looked at the shiny chrome and took a deep breath. It didn't matter what happened to her, as long as she got her one shot. Uncle Vinnie had to die.

CHAPTER FORTY-FIVE

STAYIN' ALIVE

"…So," he finished, "those are all the reasons I think it might be possible that Jed knew Vera's sons." He put the lighter on the table. Vera had excused herself to go to the bathroom, and Chance used this opportunity to bring Alex and Winnie up to speed.

"You're talking about the old man who lives in the alleyway?" asked Alex.

"Yes."

"You say his name is Jed?" said Winnie.

"Yes… have you met him? He's a sweet man. I've been kind of taking care of him for the last few years, and we've become friends."

"I know."

Chance raised an eyebrow.

"I know him too," said Alex. "I never knew his name. He wouldn't tell me."

"How do you know him, Alex?" asked Winnie.

"He saved… he helped me once."

Chance observed Alex. "Right. Jed is very helpful."

"He stopped something; I mean he stopped something bad—" Alex clenched her hands into fists.

Chance jumped in. "Well, I think Jed could have known her sons."

Winnie reached out and put his hand over Alex's.

She ignored it and glanced at Chance. "I think it's possible. But it'll be delicate. I think I should go out there first and talk to him a little bit. Sort of get him ready."

"I don't know, Alex. I don't want to spring it on them both. But he can be shy."

"Oh, he'll come out if I'm there," she said with conviction.

"Just wait a second," said Winnie. "Because this guy in the alley is a Vietnam vet, has a matching lighter, and mentions an Isaac, you want to bring Mrs. White outside to meet him? She's fragile, and sure as hell doesn't like talking about her sons' deaths. Plural... you get that, right? I don't know, I'm sorry, Mr. C., but I don't think this is a good idea."

Chance had never seen Winnie this assertive. Though this gratified him, he had other things to concentrate on. "Look, I understand the possibility is tenuous at best. But what if I'm right? Isn't the opportunity for her to finally know, to heal old wounds, worth the risk?"

"I agree with Chance. I think it's worth the risk," said Alex.

"Here's what I'm thinking: I'll roll back Mrs. White's expectations a little. Tell her he probably didn't know her sons, but if she still wants to meet him, I'll take her outside."

Winnie still didn't seem convinced.

In a soft tone, the way only a woman can speak to a lover, Alex gazed at Winnie. "Win, if there's even a chance he might know something, we have to take it. It isn't like she's never come across a Vietnam vet since then. Worst case, he doesn't know, and she's a little upset. Come on, Win, this could be something we do for her. Give her closure."

Winnie stared at Alex. The lines of worry abated. Chance recognized the love shared between them. He hoped they'd do something about it soon.

"OK," said Winnie. Alex reached out and grabbed Winnie's hand and hugged it to her chest. She leaned over and kissed him lightly on the lips. Winnie's wide eyes and slack jaw were almost comical to Chance. Like Winnie had never been kissed before.

Vera came back into the room.

"I really shouldn't, but is there any more of that wine left?" said Vera as she sat back down. "What? What did I miss? Winnie, you look positively starstruck. It's just me." Chance and Alex giggled. Winnie's eyes were still wide, and his cheeks had turned fire-engine red.

Alex stepped into the alley. "Hey, old man, you out here?" She glanced left and right. She lit a pre-rolled cigarette from her case.

"Little Cat shouldn't smoke. It's bad for the skin," said Jed, coming out from behind the dumpster.

"Hi, Jed."

He paused. "Well, beautiful Little Cat, are you on a date?"

"Yes, no, sort of, I guess. Chance took us to dinner tonight."

"Us?"

"Me and Winnie. And a special friend of ours. In fact, they're going to come out here in a minute so you two can meet." She flicked her cigarette repeatedly. She took a quick drag and walked closer to Jed.

"Why? I have plenty of friends."

"It's kind of a long story. I wanted to tell you again how thankful I am for what you did."

Jed scanned the area, wary of shadows, it seemed. He sniffed the air like something a dog would do. "Little Cat, I think you should go back inside now." Jed stepped closer to Alex.

The back door opened, and Chance walked out. Followed by Vera and Winnie. Jed froze.

"I promise I haven't gotten my hopes—" was all Vera got out. Her hands went to her mouth in a frozen, silent scream. Everything seemed to happen at once. Vera started to collapse, and Winnie caught her before she fell onto her knees. Jed visibly flinched, then turned and ran behind the dumpster.

Chance called out to him as two men appeared out of nowhere. Both wore suits, and they seemed out of place even before she registered that they'd taken guns from their coat pockets.

The shorter one headed in Jed's direction.

"Leave him. He don't count," said the taller one.

Alex's first thought was robbery, which didn't make any sense. They were dressed like businessmen. Her second thought was of rape—something that had almost happened right in this alleyway eight months before. She dropped her cigarette and stepped back toward Chance. Nothing registered, nothing in this moment made sense as she watched the taller man raise his gun towards Chance. Her breath froze as the shorter man raised his at her.

Geoff walked into the private dining room and saw no one there.

"Shit!" He passed through the main dining room on his way to the kitchen.

"Excuse me, waiter," a guest called with a raised water glass.

"One moment, madam," replied Geoff as he kept walking. He went through the double doors and saw Maggie loading up a tray.

"Mags, where's Chance?"

"He said he was going out back for a smoke. I'm going out there with Jed's dinner if you want me to tell him you're looking for him."

"Did he take the older woman with him?"

"I think so. They all came through here together. What's going on?"

"Look, I'll take this out to Jed, but can you do me a favor and water table six before they die of dehydration?"

"Sure."

Geoff shook his head as he grabbed the tray. "Dammit, Chance."

Geoff pushed open the back door with his hip, expecting a groveling Chance apologizing profusely to that woman.

The door swung open. The first thing Geoff saw was Winnie bending over about three feet in front of him. The second thing he felt more than saw: the vibration of a bullet passing close. He felt the sting of either bullet fragments or pieces of the brick building hitting him on the cheek.

Point four seconds later he was moving. His eyes took a snapshot of the scene. Two men, one tall and young, one short and older, both wearing suits, approximately fifteen feet in front and to the right. One had a gun pointed in his direction, but not at him. The second pointed in the direction of Alex or Chance. Both men were right-handed. Alex was fifteen feet to his left, Winnie directly in front, holding a woman in his arms. Chance was about twelve feet in front, slightly hunched over. Geoff sensed the kinetic energy in Chance waiting for release. In one motion, he pushed Winnie forward with his right arm and threw the tray at the tall man with his left, the dinner plate sliding back onto Geoff. It was a good throw, considering he was off-balance, and the tall man barely got his head out of the way, though his next shot was messed up.

Chance threw his body toward Alex. The gun pointed in their direction went off. Each tenth of a second lasted a lifetime. Geoff judged it was going to be close on the third shot. Short of a head or perfect heart shot hitting him, he'd make it to the man and take him out, but there was no way he could stop the second man from shooting at him. Adrenaline coursed through his body. He traveled eight feet before the third shot fired. A miss, and Geoff knew he'd made it. He leaped the last five feet at almost fifteen miles per hour. At that speed, he would cover the five feet in less than point six seconds. A lifetime in combat.

His aim was perfect as his left hand grabbed the hot barrel of the gun and the momentum of his leap broke the man's trigger finger. The key would be to land on top of the guy. Pull him over his own body as a shield, hoping to cause a second of hesitation in the shorter gunman, all the while getting the gun loose of a mangled finger. It was going to be close.

CHAPTER FORTY-SIX

THE FINAL COUNTDOWN

Chance knew what this was, and he could guess why. A million things flashed through his mind. This wasn't the first time a gun had loomed in front of him. The first time he had reacted too slow and lost Ellie.

They had him dead to rights. His only hope was they'd talk. Bad guys always seemed to want to talk first. Possibly fulfilling a terrible movie cliché. They were experienced; Chance could tell by the way they carried themselves, the smaller directly behind the bigger one so he wouldn't get in the field of fire. The man smirked, and hope glimmered within Chance. *The idiot was going to talk.* After all, you don't just smirk at someone and shoot them. You want them to know why you're smiling at them. Pros, but arrogant.

"You had to know this was coming, Chance," said the bigger man. He looked oddly familiar, but he couldn't place it.

"Is my uncle dead?" *Keep him talking. If he's talking, then nobody is dying.*

The man glance at this watch. "Should be by now. You don't remember me, do you?"

Chance wracked his brain. Understanding flashed in a microsecond. "You're Frank's kid."

"Yep," said Junior. "He sends his regards, and to say hi to Ellie when you see her."

Chance's eyebrows moved closer together. He had to think. Ellie was a distraction.

"Let the kids and the old woman go, and I'll go anywhere you want. I won't fuss."

"No, we're fine here in the alley. In the last twelve hours the only thing that's come out of this alley is a garbage truck. That was six hours ago. So, I want to know, was she worth it? I don't really know my stepmom, so I'm curious."

"To be honest, at the time I thought so, but I'm having second thoughts."

Junior chuckled. "I always thought she was the type that would get men killed. It's a shame, though. You do make a mean sauce."

"Why don't you put your guns away, we can go inside, and I'll cook up something that'll literally blow you away?" Chance was slowly sliding closer to Alex. Winnie was still trying to get a better grip on Vera, who appeared unconscious. If the worst happened, thankfully she wouldn't know it.

Junior glanced at the smaller man. "I'd love to take you up on that offer, but I'm afraid it's not possible."

"You know you're making a mistake, and I'll tell you why."

"Well, since I have the gun, shoot." Junior guffawed at his own joke.

The smaller one was all juiced up, craving the violence, about to erupt.

"You're working for the wrong team. If you think Frank could get the jump on my uncle, then you are overestimating your dad, and you most certainly don't know my uncle. He'd have seen Frank's play a mile away. Frank is probably dead right now. And since I know Chicago would never have signed off on this, you're working for somebody not high up enough to understand what a bad play this is."

"All right, smart guy. If that's the case, why are you standing out in an alley with no protection? Why aren't there ten of your uncle's guys out here with you?"

"Allocation of resources. And let me give you another reason why Frank's play didn't work."

"Yeah, keep talking, buddy. You have about thirty seconds, so use them however you want."

"Well, Frank didn't allocate his resources very well. You guys are the A-Team, right?" The smaller man gave the bigger man a "hell yeah" face.

"Right. I could tell how you carry yourself. The problem is, I'm nobody. I'm not in the family. I'm just a guy who owns a restaurant."

"So fucking what!" said the smaller guy.

"Well, Frank was blinded by his hatred and pride, and he sent his best shooters to kill a nobody. And what? He sent the B-Team to take out Giorgio and my uncle. Did he send that idiot Ralph?" The two men shared a look of concern. "I admit, Giorgio is a fat fuck, but the guy knows his shit. How do you think my uncle has lived so long? Not to mention there're at least three Capos that no matter what would be loyal to my uncle. And they came up the hard way. So, what, did Frank send the C, D, and E team against them?" Chance started to laugh—a calculated risk, but Chance was playing for time. Without moving his eyes, he adjusted them past the man with the gun.

"Come on, let's just do this," whined the smaller man.

"OK, smart guy. Say all that's true. How do you think it's going to help you right now?"

Chance knew he'd run out of time. Ellie entered his mind even as he frantically tried to figure out a way to save Alex and Winnie.

God, Ellie, or providence shined on him as the door swung open. He barely had time to register Geoff before Frank Jr. swung the gun at Geoff and fired. Chance marked the bullet hitting the wall. Geoff reacted faster than humanly possible, pushing Winnie with one hand and throwing something with the other. It almost hit the guy. Chance leapt toward Alex when he heard the second shot. He felt the third before he heard it and knocked into Alex, who screamed. He tried to brace his fall, but Alex took the brunt of his deadweight.

Jed smelled them first. A heavy mixture of Old Spice and Aqua Velva.

"Little Cat, I think you should go back inside now," said Jed, approaching Alex.

The back door opened, and Chance walked out. Followed by his mother! All dressed up and talking a mile a minute. She saw him and started to scream without sound. He didn't freeze. He reacted like a cat, darting behind the dumpster into the trees that lined the alleyway. Chance called out.

Their only hope was the men wouldn't start shooting right away. Jed went deeper into the trees. He turned south, and as quiet as a two-tour vet could be, made his way about twenty yards, until he was ten yards behind the two men. He slowly crept forward, knowing exactly where everyone was.

Chance was talking. Jed knew every branch and pine needle in this little spot of trees. Silently, he got closer and closer. Even if they glanced this way, they wouldn't notice him in the treeline. The gooks had taught him that the first week he was in-country.

Jed saw the back of the two men he'd been watching for most of the day. He hadn't known why they were here, but he'd guessed. It was the only reason he was sober right now, not having partaken of Chance's ample bar that he'd been left alone with.

He pulled out his KA-BAR Marines-issued fighting knife. It had a seven-inch blade, and was one of the most successful weapons ever produced in the history of U.S. warfare. He crept up another couple of feet. He coiled his body. Ready for what was about to happen.

"Come on, let's do this," whined the smaller man.

"OK, smart guy. Say all that's true. How do you think it's going to help you right now?"

The backdoor to the kitchen opened, and Jed heard the first shot. Jed identified Geoff and thanked God, even as he was moving. The taller man jerked his head and the second shot went wild. *Man, that swabby moves fast.* The smaller man aimed at Chance and Alex. Chance launched his body just as Jed threw his deadly knife at the smaller man's back. Two more shots rang out, as Jed's knife plunged into the smaller man above his kidney. Geoff landed on the taller man, and both went down. Geoff smashed his forearm into the man's neck, crushing his windpipe, and rolled his body over, expecting more gunfire. Geoff rolled out from under the dying man and kneeled in a modified Weaver shooting position, the pistol in his hand pointing at the smaller guy, who'd fallen to his knees. But Jed was already there. The shorter man was frantically trying to reach behind himself, trying to get to the knife. Jed obliged him and pulled the knife out of his back, and with a fluid motion cut his throat. *Only bad guys give their enemies time*, he thought.

The shooting stopped, and Winnie lifted his head. He was lying on top of Mrs. White, covering her body as best he could. He'd been violently pushed in the back, and luckily was able to brace Mrs. White as he fell. Chance had fallen on top of Alex, and Winnie's heart sunk into the pit of his stomach. Geoff was prone, gun in hand. A man Winnie assumed was Jed was coming toward him with a large, bloody knife. Winnie tried to get up, but his legs didn't seem to be working. He looked down and saw a dark spot around his crotch. Mortified he'd pissed his pants, he tried to get up again, concern for Alex overriding his embarrassment. He tried to move his leg, but nothing seemed to be happening. Chance rolled over, off Alex. She sat up, and relief washed through Winnie. She was OK. She was safe. If he could get up, he'd kiss her right then and there. He would kiss Chance. Hell, he would even kiss the old guy in the camo.

"Hey, kid, it's all right. Why don't you sit down for a minute, OK?" said Jed.

"Everybody OK?" called out Geoff.

Jed seemed to be checking on Mrs. White. Alex looked at Winnie, fear written all over her face.

"I need a medic over here," said Jed.

What, did he think he was still in 'Nam? thought Winnie.

"Geoff, you're shot," said Alex.

"It's just pasta sauce," he replied.

"But your face?"

Geoff put his hand to his cheek and came away with blood. "A ricochet. I'm fine."

He didn't look fine, Winnie thought. His bronze skin actually seemed pale.

Geoff headed over to Chance, still lying there.

"I think I've been shot," said Chance. "In the butt."

Geoff barked out a laugh.

Jed leaned over Winnie, who could see a dead leaf stuck to his beard. He straightened out Winnie's leg, and fire shot throughout his body. He felt dizzy.

"Little Cat, I could use you over here."

The old guy started taking off Winnie's tie. *Why is he undressing me?*

"Kid, can you hear me?"

Winnie thought he said yes, but wasn't sure. Alex bent over and he could see down her dress. She was crying, and Winnie felt guilty staring at her chest at a time like this.

"Winnie, oh my god, Winnie!" She was shouting at him again. She sure did yell at him a lot.

"Alex, you don't always have to yell at me."

"Winnie, don't talk."

"Winnie, this is going to hurt like a son of a bitch, but I have to stop the bleeding," said the old guy.

A bolt of lightning jumped through Winnie's body. More pain than he'd ever felt in his life. He thought he screamed, but wasn't sure. As fast as it came on, the pain was already subsiding.

"Alex..."

"Winnie, it's OK, it's going to be OK." Her mascara was smeared, and she looked a little scary.

"I'm cold, Alex."

"Stay awake, Winnie. Please, just stay with me."

"Alex." It seemed like somebody was turning out the streetlights. Darkness was closing in all around him.

"Alex... I love you." Before he could catch what she said, Winnie was blissfully gone.

"Winnie! Winnie!" screamed Alex.

"It's OK, Little Cat. He only passed out from the pain. See, I tied off the leg, so he isn't losing much blood. He should be... OK. Stay here and hold his hand. That's the best thing you can do for him." Jed got up and went over to his mother. She was breathing fine, and her pulse was strong. The back door opened, and several people came running out. A young woman ran over to Chance.

"I'm fine, Maggie. I just got shot in the butt is all," said Chance.

"Umm, Houston, we have a problem," said Geoff, falling to his knees. Jed knew it wasn't spaghetti sauce staining Geoff's white uniform. Geoff ripped open his shirt. Blood was leaking out of an entry wound in his stomach.

"Geoff! Oh my god, what the hell happened here?" Maggie rushed over to Geoff.

"I guess he didn't miss me after all." Geoff stumbled against Maggie. She couldn't support his weight and he collapsed onto his back.

A group of cooks stood outside of the doorway. "Amigos," Jed said, "take this woman inside and lay her on a couch in Chance's office. She'll be fine. Call the police and tell them to send three ambulances. I'm sure they're already on the way, but tell them to send three. Tell them three victims have gunshot wounds. You got that?"

"Si," said the dark short one. He said something in rapid-fire Spanish and four of the cooks lifted Jed's mother and carried her inside. Jed ran over to where Geoff was lying. He examined the wound and knew.

"You! You're Maggie, right?" asked Jed. She didn't respond, and he snapped his fingers in front of her face. "Maggie!"

"What, yes?" she replied finally.

"Grab that towel from your apron and push it onto the wound. Here, give me your apron."

He carried the apron over to Chance. "Don't take this the wrong way, brother." He applied the bistro apron to Chance's butt. "Give me your hand, OK, yeah, just hold there. You're bleeding a shit-ton, but you'll live. It's the million-dollar wound, as we used to say."

"What's happening with Geoff?"

Jed shook his head slowly. Chance started to get up, pain shooting across his face.

"Whoa, brother... you need to stay down."

"Fuck that, you just said I'd be fine." Chance pulled himself over to Geoff. Maggie was still holding the towel on the wound, but it was already soaked with blood. Chance grabbed Geoff's hand. "Hey, buddy... I'm not paying you to lay around."

"Yeah?" said Geoff. "Consider this my two weeks' notice." His face contorted in pain.

"No fucking way you can quit this job until I say you can."

Jed heard sirens in the distance. A crowd was forming at the end of the block. Some of the less-passive ones were starting to come closer. *Nobody was running, though*, noted Jed.

"Not too bad for a jarhead," Geoff said to Jed.

"Not bad for a squid." Jed knelt and grabbed Geoff's other hand. Maggie was quietly sobbing as blood gushed through her fingers.

"If we'd had a few like you, we'd have never lost that stupid war," said Jed.

"You did have a few like me."

"Yeah, we did. But maybe not quite your caliber."

Geoff smiled, but it turned into a grimace. Geoff let go of Jed's hand and grabbed Chance's.

"Hey, listen. I was never supposed to live this long. Don't let me sit up in heaven and watch you fuck up your life over this. No more bullshit, Chance. I love you, man, but get your shit together."

"Don't talk. The ambulance is almost here. Hold on. We're going to be drinking scotch in my office in no time."

Geoff coughed hard. Turning his head, he spit out a mouthful of blood. He looked up at Jed. "How's Winnie?"

"He should be OK. He caught one in the leg. I put on a tourniquet, so if the shock doesn't kill him, he should pull through." Jed glanced at Alex, talking into Winnie's ear.

"Go to him, Jed. You can't do anything for me. Maggie?"

Maggie just sobbed out loud. She kept trying to wipe up the blood, but it kept coming.

"Maggie, you tell Cassie Bear her Uncle Geoff will watch over her always. You tell her I love her, and she can talk to me anytime she wants in her prayers. Maggie?"

"I will," Maggie sobbed.

"Chance, this isn't your fault. There're just some bad people out there. Shit like this happens. This is a good death. I got to save people I love."

"Come on, man. It's going to be OK. Don't die on me, Geoff, please don't die on me."

"Chance, sing 'It Had to Be You.' Would ya? I always loved..." But his eyes were distant. Jed said a silent prayer. Multiple sirens were getting closer now. A police car and three ambulances pulled down the alley. They were finally here, but not even the best medics could save him.

CHAPTER FORTY-SEVEN

IT'S THE END OF THE WORLD AS WE KNOW IT (AND I FEEL FINE)

Winnie lay in a hospital bed, his leg wrapped in a massive bandage. He was bored out of his mind after two days there. The hospital TV had cable, something new for him, but his roommate only liked soap operas. He knew he was starting to go crazy when he felt anxious for Frisco Jones in General Hospital.

His roommate, some old Black guy with curly white hair and liver disease, was snoring away right now, so Winnie watched HBO on mute. But he needed the distraction of noise. Something to take his mind off what had happened. But all there was to do was mourn. Geoff was dead. Winnie still couldn't believe it. He hadn't known Geoff well, but Alex did, and he knew she was taking it hard. She was distant, and appeared shellshocked each time he'd seen her. He shifted and pain shot through his leg. He hit the button on his self-administered drugs and instantly felt better. This wasn't so bad.

He thankfully didn't remember his surgery the first night. He'd woken up alone. Not able to move and scared out of his mind, it had taken ten terrifying minutes before a nurse could calm him down enough to tell him what had happened, and that Alex was OK.

He remembered some things, seeing the guns, hearing the shots. Seeing Alex fall with Chance on top of her. The rest was blank. Alex had visited twice. The first time, she hugged him as tight as she could. But she didn't say anything. The second time, she talked a little, but not about anything important.

There was a hesitant knock on the door. Alex slowly walked into the room.

"Hey."

"Hey. I brought your drawing pads and pencils." She tentatively walked to his bedside, setting a plastic bag on the table across from his bed. She stepped back. She put her hands together behind her back and did a slight bob. Her eyes wandered around the room, looking everywhere except at him.

"How are you doing?" he asked. "You don't look like you got much sleep."

"Yeah, not much."

"Anything I can do?"

Her eyebrows raised. "Win, you're in a hospital bed with a gunshot wound. I should be the one to ask you that."

"This didn't just happen to me. We were both there."

Alex didn't respond. There was so much to say, but Winnie didn't know how to start. He'd been given another chance. Was it luck, or a god, or fate? The woman he loved was safe and standing before him. He knew what he needed to say. "So."

Alex watched him.

"Um, so let me get this straight. Jed, the homeless vet with the large knife, is actually Ishmael. One of Mrs. White's missing sons? How does that work?"

The relief on Alex's face was obvious. "Yeah, far out, right? Apparently in the war, Ishmael was somehow responsible for the death of his brother and friend. Or at least he blamed himself for it. I don't know, it's all crazy confusing. Jed is Ishmael, who took the name Jed, who was his friend. He came back to Milwaukee to be near his mom, but couldn't face her after what he'd done or something. Chance was right, he's not really all there in the head. But Mrs. White is over the moon. So, I guess it doesn't…"

Alex trailed off. She looked down at the floor. When she lifted her head, tears hung heavy in her eyes. She blinked and they cascaded down her face, dripping onto the cold tile floor. A short sob burst out of her as she brought her hand to her mouth. "It's all my fault. If I hadn't convinced you to take Mrs. White out back, none of this would have happened. Geoff would still be alive. You wouldn't be shot."

"Alex," he whispered, and leaned forward with both arms extended. She hesitated a moment and practically jumped into his embrace. Her tiny frame trembled.

"None of this is your fault. None of it. This had nothing to do with us. This is Chance and mob people and bad luck. We didn't cause any of this."

She crawled up onto the bed, still within his arms. His chest wet from her tears, he stroked her hair, the faint scent of strawberries teasing his nose, causing his stomach to grumble. Slowly the sobs faded, only to be replaced with a soft snoring as sleep overcame her grief.

"I love you," he whispered. He liked the way it sounded, so he said out loud again. He closed his eyes, living in this moment. He fought the fatigue, which started in his arms and legs. Valiantly trying to stay awake, he slipped away into a peace he'd never known before.

Chance lay on the world's most uncomfortable bed, waiting for Maggie to visit him. He acknowledged it could be the bullet wound, but no matter what position he was in, this bed sucked. A cop was in the room reading a paper. A humorless man who took his job way too seriously. Chance lay there, staring out the window, guilt and sorrow weighing on him like a wall of bricks had collapsed in an earthquake and he was buried alive.

Geoff... He kept picturing him in his head. Something had been ripped away, because of Chance. Because of his own selfish actions. A friend had died. Geoff's parting words were of little comfort. It wasn't a good death. It shouldn't have been any death. Frank might have ordered the hit, but it was Chance's choices that caused it.

Mitchell Genovese walked into the room, haggard, deep bags under his bloodshot eyes. He carried a manila file in one hand and a briefcase in the other. He glanced at the cop and tilted his head for the door.

The cop slowly folded up his paper, put it on the chair, and gave Chance a hard stare before walking out of the room.

"What, no flowers?" asked Chance.

"I know you've been asked this already, but I'm gonna ask you again, Chance. Do you have any knowledge directly or indirectly of the whereabouts of Frank Bartallatas?"

"As I've already explained, I don't. Frank and I were not friends. I don't know anything about his life."

"Besides doing his wife, you mean."

Mitchell set his briefcase on the small table stretching across Chance's lumpy hospital bed. He opened it, pulled out a small pad of ringed paper, and flipped several pages. "I have five bodies in a Chinese restaurant I need to be able to explain. I have parts of two other bodies in a boxcar in Chicago that I believe originated here and are a part of this shit. Two more bodies in the alley behind your restaurant. One civilian killed. A former Navy Seal who, incidentally, has more medals than most people have fillings. Two more civilians shot: a teenager, and you."

"You don't need to give me the play-by-play, Mitch. I was there." Chance pointed with his thumb toward his butt.

"Yeah, well, I have bosses that are breathing down my neck for an arrest. Mob violence is not something the good folks of the Midwest want to hear about. Nor is it something my bosses want to see in print. That's New York, maybe even Chicago, but not Milwaukee. This is the most famous thing to happen in Milwaukee since *Laverne and Shirley* got cancelled. They're bringing a ton of pressure on me, Chance. RICO all the way on this."

"Honestly, Mitch, I don't know anything. And that Navy Seal was my best friend."

"Frank's still out there. I'm pretty sure he's not done with you yet."

"Frank's stupid, but he's not stupid enough to stay in Milwaukee. Frank's in the wind. He's not coming back here."

"You killed his son. I don't think he's gonna let that slide."

"I didn't kill anybody."

"Somehow I don't think Frank will make that distinction," said Mitchell. Chance laid his head back on the pillow and looked out the window.

"All right." Mitchell dropped the pad back in his briefcase. "I'll give you a couple of days to think about it. But if there's so much as a whiff of something not right in your books, my bosses will go pretty hard on you."

"Do what you got to do. You probably know more about what's going on than I ever have."

Mitchell went to the window and peered out. "I'm sorry to have to be the one to tell you this, Chance, but your uncle is dead."

Chance took a long deep breath and let it out slowly, not hiding the relief he felt from his face. "Was it the cancer?"

Mitchell turned from the window, went to his briefcase, and pulled out a manila file. "No, actually, although we knew about that. We also know from Fat Giorgio that your uncle was trying hand over the family business to you, but that, and thank god for his corroborating evidence, you hadn't accepted. You see, your uncle wasn't nearly as sick as he pretended. He was setting you up to be the front man. A fall guy, if you will. He didn't know how, but he knew we were coming for him. We had an informant."

"What? He was setting… what?"

"Sloan Bartallatas had been secretly recording Frank, Uncle Vinnie, and the rest of the crew for a couple of years now. Her reasons are still sketchy, but we think her sister was sold to your uncle. Did you know Vinnie liked young girls? Like twelve or thirteen years young?"

Chance felt his stomach flip. He grabbed a handful of sheets into his fists and shook his head.

"I know we go back a long way. But if you were a part of this in any way, so help me god, I will fucking bury you."

"I didn't know, Mitch. I swear to god I didn't."

"That's what I told my boss. It's what I'd like to believe." Mitchell pointed at Chance. "We think Sloan was on her way out of town. But somehow, she found out Uncle Vinnie survived his meeting with Frank, and went there to take him out herself. Pretty fucking brave if you ask me. She shot your uncle and Fat Giorgio shot her. She's dead, Chance."

Chance closed his eyes. He could feel the tears leaking out down the side of his face. Tears for Sloan, tears for Geoff, and tears for Ellie. In some way or another he had a lot to answer for. He blinked, but Mitchell stayed blurry. As an undeserved kindness it seemed, Mitchell gave him a few minutes to compose himself.

With his uncle dead and Frank in the wind, Chance wondered if this didn't solve at least one problem. "So, what's gonna happen next?"

"I have over forty-five hours of recordings from Sloan on just about everybody that's left in the Carmelo crime family. We're gonna roll up every single one of these motherfuckers." Mitchell eyed Chance for a long moment. "I hope, for your sake, none of them even breathes your name."

Chance slowly shook his head. "They won't—"

"I'm gonna tell you something, and I want you to listen. You used to be somebody I looked up to. Somebody I respected. You were on the verge of something. Then Ellie died, and that's a horrible blow. For anybody. But you used it as excuse to climb into a bottle. Be the life of the party. You're not evil like Frank. But in some ways, you're just as complicit. You hung out on the edge of the wild side. And bad shit happened to some good people." Mitchell went to the window again. He let out a deep breath that sounded like the exhaustion on his face.

"It's hard to recognize what's going on around you when you have scotch eyes. So, no offence, buddy. But some of this…" Mitchell threw a manila file onto the bed, and black-and-white photos spilled out. "Some of this is on you."

The top photo was a picture of Sloan. Eyes closed, she looked like she was sleeping. Chance stared at the photo as his mind flashed from Sloan's face to Ellie choking on her own blood. His head was spinning, and he reached out for the rail on the side of the bed. He promptly threw up the green Jell-O he'd eaten earlier.

"I'll send a nurse in." Mitchell turned around and walked out. Chance turned onto his side and brought his knees up closer, not even caring about the pain.

He stared out the window for an hour, watching the few puffs of white pass from one side of his view to the other. He grabbed the phone and put a call in to Bernie, his former manager and now accountant, letting him know Mitchell would be around and to give him everything he asked for. Bernie reassured him everything would check out. Restaurants are a great cash business. Not that he'd done anything wrong. Chance also asked Bernie a few questions about transferring ownership, and a couple of other questions about the Hazelden Addiction Center. Bernie sounded surprised, but gave him the necessary information.

A while later, Maggie entered, holding Cassie's tiny hand. Cassie looked scared, clutching a stuffed gorilla in her other arm.

"Hey, sweet girl. It's OK, Miss Cass, I'm all right. You don't need to be scared. It's just a bee-sting on my bum." Cassie took a tentative step over to Chance. Then a second one. She held out the stuffed purple gorilla toward Chance. He reached out for it.

"What's this guy's name?"

Cassie gazed up at her mom. Maggie nodded, and Cassie smiled at Chance. "Geoffrey," she said.

The smile on Chance's face froze.

"It's what she wanted to name it."

"It's a perfect name, Miss Cass. I'll treasure Geoffrey always," he said, petting the gorilla.

"Cassie, why don't you go over there and color something for Uncle Chance, OK, honey?" Cassie dutifully went over to the table and from her small backpack took out crayons and paper. Her tongue stuck out as she concentrated.

Just like her mother, thought Chance.

"How are you doing?" Chance could tell she'd been crying. He held out his hand toward her. She hesitated a second, then grabbed it. A small sob came out of her.

"I was so scared, Charlie. Seeing you lying there. And Geoff..." Tears silently fell.

"I know, Maggie. I'm sorry. It's all my fault."

Maggie squeezed his hand tightly.

"If I had been faster. Clearer headed. I was drunk, Maggie. I was drunk. That's why my friend died."

"Charlie, you heard Geoff. He didn't blame you. He doesn't want this to haunt you forever. Like Ellie. You have to get over the blame you're putting on yourself. You won't honor Geoff by holding all this pain in."

Chance turned over to his side, facing her, still clutching her hand. "I have some things I need to discuss with you. I need to get out of town for a little while. I need to take some time to figure some things out. My culpability in this situation, what I'm doing with my life."

"You're leaving town?" Maggie's voice rose.

"I'm not running away. Not from my problems… not from you. I just don't think I can walk into the restaurant anymore. I love Bella's. But with what's happened, and also…" He let go of her hand, his head hanging limp, chin on his chest. "I think I need to go to a rehabilitation place." He looked up at her, making momentary eye contact. "You know, for alcohol."

She slowly nodded her head once and glanced over at Cassie. "So, you're going to close it down?"

Chance perceived the fear in her voice. "No. I'm going to sell it to you."

She frowned and shook her head. "I don't have any money. I can't buy a restaurant!"

"Maggie, listen. It will be on a land contract. What that means is we'll agree on a fair price for the restaurant. I'm not handing you anything here. Every month you'll make a payment toward the purchase price we agree on. Bella's is paid off. In the winter, she clears around $14,000 in profits a month. In the summer, it's more like $35,000. What I propose is, each month you pay half of the profits back to me against the purchase price. If there are no profits, which is extremely unlikely, you don't pay anything that month. In a few years you'll own Bella's free and clear. The money you'll make will more than take care of Cassie and you."

Despite the small measure of hope in her eyes, she was still shaking her head. "This doesn't make any sense. I don't know the first thing about owning a restaurant."

"Come on, you've been running the front for a year now. Chico can handle the kitchen, as long as you don't let him put cilantro in the sauce. Bernie can teach you the business side. Mags, you're smart. You understand the industry. You can take over in a heartbeat. I have complete faith in you, and I wouldn't offer it to you if I didn't."

She was still shaking her head, but he could detect her eyes swimming in the possibilities.

"Did I mention Bella's comes with a beautiful two-bedroom condo inside the Knickerbocker?" he asked.

"What? Your condo?"

"It's not my condo; Bella's owns it. I already have movers packing up my stuff. I don't think I can live there anymore. So, it'll belong to whoever owns Bella's. Just think about it, Maggie. You could move out of the... place you live in now. Cassie could go to St. Andrews. It's the best school in the city, and only three blocks away."

Cassie was humming over in the corner, but seemed intent on what she was doing. Maggie glanced at her. More tears started to flow. Chance hoped she was thinking about the possibilities for her and her daughter.

"I just don't know, Charlie. It's all so overwhelming." She paused as she peered down at him. "What about us?" she whispered.

"Maggie, you have to do what's right for you and Cassie. Maybe someday I'll fit in the picture, and maybe not. You were right in your letter. I am broken. I'm not able yet to have a healthy relationship. There's so much I need to work on before I can honestly give my all to someone. Someone as special and beautiful as you. Someone who deserves my full, honest and healthy attention."

Maggie reached back for Chance's hand. He took it and put it against his cheek, loving the warmth.

"Just talk to Bernie today. He's expecting a call. He's a bit of a toad, but you can trust him." He took a deep breath. "Maggie, let me do this for you. Let me salvage something from this horrible situation. Please. Just think about it."

She nodded at him. A frown on her beautiful face.

G.P.

CHAPTER FORTY-EIGHT

WHO WANTS TO LIVE FOREVER

The twenty-four-hour diner was only a quarter full, and Mrs. White was standing at the counter, her eyes a million miles away. The bar crowd was still an hour away, and she was smoking her fourth Lucky Strike in a row. Occasionally she would glance at Chance and give him a smile. It had been a warm reunion, but after a couple minutes of catching up, they realized they didn't really know each other. Awkward, but not uncomfortable. Jed, or rather Ishmael, was doing well. He'd left the psychiatric hospital and was living with Vera. And he wasn't gonna be charged for the death of Mickey Russo. At least something good had come out of the tragedy.

Chance had only arrived back in town the day before, after being gone for a month, and he was anxious to conclude his business and leave again. His meeting with Maggie had been tense. Too much had happened. Not enough time had passed, with too many feelings yet to be resolved.

His counselor had strenuously warned him about beginning any romantic relationship freshly sober. A warning Chance had taken to heart.

Vera perked up at the sound of the bell on the door and rushed to embrace Winnie. They spoke for a couple of seconds, then Vera pointed over to Chance. Winnie turned and a smile crept over his face. He was the same, albeit now with a cane. Somehow, he appeared taller.

Chance got out of the booth and engulfed the young man in a bear hug. "'O Captain, my Captain,'" he said.

Winnie stepped back and grinned. "I thought that was my line."

"No, I think you've earned it. Sit, sit. How's the knee?"

"Getting better. Not quite ready to do the electric slide, but getting there."

Vera approached the table with a pot of coffee. "I swear, Winnie, when you came in, I thought you looked taller. Is it possible you're still growing?"

"I don't think so, Mrs. White. Maybe it's just my third leg."

She poured Winnie coffee and refilled Chance's. "You boys must have a lot to talk about, so I'll leave you to it. But it warms my heart to see you both."

"Thanks, Mrs. White."

"Thanks, Vera."

Vera's eyes were sparkling as she turned and walked back behind the counter.

A middle-aged man one booth over lit a cigarette. Chance's hand went to his empty pocket. For a second he considered asking the man if he could bum a smoke. The man in a *Rather Be Fishing* hat and camouflage coat looked away as soon as Chance caught his eye.

"She is a sweet lady," said Chance.

"The best," replied Winnie.

Now that he had a second, Chance just studied the young man. Definitely something different about him, but he couldn't quite nail it down.

"You're drinking your coffee black now?" Chance asked.

"Yeah, the place I go to for physical therapy doesn't have any creamer, so I just ended up switching."

They sat in silence for a minute. Made eye contact and both started laughing.

"There's something different about you, Winnie. I can't put my finger on it, though."

Winnie shook his head. "I don't feel different, besides the obvious. But then sometimes I don't feel the same either." Winnie stared at Chance. "You're different, too. I don't know, cleaner? No... sorry, not cleaner, I mean you were never dirty."

"I think I understand what you're getting at, Win. It's amazing what being sober does for your body and mind. I'm sharper than I was, that's for sure. Like to think more handsome, too."

They both chuckled.

"So, are you back in town to stay?" asked Winnie.

"No, I don't think so. Just have some loose ends to tie up. In a way, you're one of my loose ends."

Winnie took a sip of his coffee. "If this is one of those 'amends' things, Chance, I'm fine. You don't have to say sorry again."

"Huh. You are different. I don't think you've ever called me Chance before." He grinned and reached his hand into his jacket pocket. "Ugh. I keep forgetting I quit smoking. Gotta figure out something to do instead, like chew on straws or something." His eyes went back to the man in the camo jacket. He caught his eyes for a moment and the man immediately looked away, grabbing his pack of cigarettes and putting them in his jacket pocket. *Relax, buddy. I won't ask for a smoke,* thought Chance.

"Good for you. Seems like things have changed for the better."

"It's a start. As they say, one day at a time."

Winnie nodded.

"In a way, the reason I asked you here tonight was for amends. But not to apologize again. While I was in, Alex wrote me a couple of very nice letters. In one, she mentioned you guys were still planning on going to San Diego."

Winnie shrugged. "Yeah, I'm not sure. Hunter had to sell his car. Apparently, however he was making his," Winnie indicated air quotes with his hands, "'other income,' it stopped. So right now, it's looking like we might take a Greyhound. But I'm not sure my leg can take that kind of trip."

"That's why I wanted to see you." Chance reached into his other jacket pocket and pulled out a set of keys. He put them on the table and slid them across to Winnie. Then he reached into the inside pocket of his jacket and pulled out a folded piece of paper. Put it on the table and slid it across.

"What's this?"

"Those, my friend, are the keys and title to Gracie. They're a congratulations-on-getting-into-college gift."

"I can't take this. This is too much—it's your car."

"You can and will take it. If you're going to visit Alex in Chicago on weekends, you're going to need a car. Thankfully your colleges are close. I do have one favor to ask you, though."

Winnie had reached out and picked up the keys, his eyes still wide, his mouth still making an O. "What do you need, Chance?"

"Take good care of her."

"Gracie?"

"Alex. She's one in a million. The other thing I need is a ride. When you guys head out, can you stop in Madison? I'm twenty years late for a gig, but I think they'll still let me sit in and play."

. . .

The man in the camouflage jacket stood next to a payphone outside of the Country Kitchen. He watched as the taillights of a black Lincoln Continental pulled away. He picked up the receiver, dropped in a quarter, and dialed a number with an 816-area code, from memory.

"Please deposit two-dollars and fifty cents," replied the automated voice.

He dropped in ten quarters and waited.

"Ya," replied an accented voice.

"The pepperoni cannoli is leaving for Madison with a group of kids."

"When?"

"Couple days, it looks like. But he gave one of them his car, and they are pushing on to San Diego. Sounds like he's staying in Madison."

"OK, hold on," said the voice. Ray heard muffled talking in the background. A new voice came on the line.

"Yeah, OK, we need that delivery to leave Wisconsin. Babysit the kids. Will send somebody to coordinate Madison."

"Babysit? I can't just leave. Nobody is handling the drivers here. We're missing deliveries," whined Ray.

"I don't give a fuck about that. That route is dead. Stay with the kids. They're the ticket to making sure our special delivery leaves Madison. Got it? Don't fuck this up, and don't lose those kids. They're the only thing that will keep you from getting fired."

"OK, OK. I got it."

"Call from the road at each stop." A buzzing indicated the other person had hung up.

Ray stood there a moment, lifted the hat, and ran his hand over his thinning hair. He turned and half-heartedly kicked the brick wall. "Fuck you, Frank. I never liked Junior anyway." He quickly looked around, like somebody was just waiting for him. He put his hands in his pockets and walked to his car.

CHAPTER FORTY-NINE

IN YOUR EYES

Alex's father was sitting at the kitchen table. "Vhat time do you think you and the Pooh bear are going to leave?"

"Early, Papa. Before you get up."

"Pooh bear can make the trip OK?"

"He's doing well, Papa."

"But he vill have a cane for the rest of his life?"

"Yeah."

"Sad."

"He isn't the same. Before he was always so quiet and reserved. Now he's still quiet, but there's something underneath. A fierceness, maybe."

"Sasha, he's been through trauma. Something like that will change a person. You are not same either."

Alex looked away, heat rushing to her cheeks, hoping her father hadn't guessed what was different now.

"So, tell me about dis trip. You're all going to ride across country to see a bunch of people dressed up like *Star Trek*?"

"Yes, Papa. They're called Trekkies. Chance gave Winnie his massive car. It's like a tank, so we'll be safe."

"Pooh bear, Hunter, Prez, and you. So, how long will you be gone?"

"We're planning on three weeks. Don't worry, I'll be back in plenty of time for school."

"The Pooh bear can spend that much time in car?"

"Papa, it isn't a car, it's a whale!"

"It seems nice of your boss to give Vinnie dis car."

"I think he feels responsible for Winnie. I think Chance just wants to make amends."

Her papa pulled on an imaginary goatee on his chin.

"Vell, all right. I'm excited for you. It's a beautiful country to drive across and see."

"Will you talk to Mama for me? You understand how she is. She thinks the worst of everything."

"I vill talk to her, Sasha, don't vorry. I've got your mama wrapped around little finger. You can go. Just call us from the road, OK? Every day, collect. Just let us know you're safe."

"I will, Papa." She got up and hugged him. She went up to her room and started to pack. She put the suitcase on the bed next to Monkey. She stared at the backpack for a moment.

"I think, Monkey, that it's time for—" she paused as she realized she was talking out loud to her backpack. She brought him up and hugged him tight. She opened her closet door and gently placed him in the back.

Hanging in her closet was the pink dress, wrapped from the drycleaners. She took it out of the plastic and sat down on her bed. Laying it out next to her, her fingers traced some of the bloodstains. The paralyzing terror, leftover from that night, was still there, the sensation of it like arms tightening around her chest. She closed her eyes and practiced her breathing exercises Valerie had taught her. In to the count of four, out to the count of four.

After a couple of minutes, she felt better and went over to her vanity desk. She opened the middle drawer and pulled out a piece of paper wrapped with a red ribbon. The lingering scent of Polo brushed her nose. Her cheeks warmed. Unwrapping it, she read the touching words again. Her bashful lips moved upwards, and she held the paper to her chest. She thought of something Winnie's dad once said. Sometimes, life was like falling onto concrete. With the events of the past year, she knew for a fact this was true. But sometimes, everything comes together, the stars in the heavens align, and in a rare perfect moment, like the smell of Winnie's beautiful words, life truly was falling onto cotton.

The End

WINNIE'S MIX TAPE
FOR ALEX

SIDE A – CIGARETTES AND 24-HOUR DINERS

Take on Me – a-ha
Cruel Summer – Bananarama
West End Girls – Pet Shop Boys
Mad World – Tears for Fears
Blister in the Sun – Violent Femmes
Let's Dance – David Bowie
99 Luftballons – Nena
Mr. Roboto – Styx

SIDE B – HEART IN MY HANDS

You're My Best Friend – Queen
Need You Tonight – INXS
In Your Eyes – Peter Gabriel
Eternal Flame – The Bangles
Broken Wings – Mr. Mister
Time After Time – Cyndi Lauper
All I Need – Jack Wagner

ALEX'S MIX TAPE

SIDE A - DANCE MONKEY DANCE

How Soon is Now - The Smiths
Cuts You Up - Peter Murphy
So Alive - Love and Rockets
Don't Change - INXS
Under the Milky Way - The Church
Just like Honey - Jesus and Mary Chain
Bizarre Love Triangle - New Order
Love Will Tear Us Apart - Joy Division

SIDE B - MONKEY SAD

This Woman's Work - Kate Bush
Reflections of my Life - Marmalade
True Colors - Cyndi Lauper
Here Comes the Rain Again - Eurhythmics
Somebody - Depeche Mode
Sorry Seems to Be the Hardest Word - Elton John

MUSIC CREDITS & ARTISTS

CHAPTER 1: YOU CAN'T ALWAYS GET WHAT YOU WANT
THE ROLLING STONES – CREDIT JAGGER/RICHARDS

CHAPTER 2: NIGHTS ON BROADWAY
THE BEE GEES – CREDIT ROBIN, BARRY, MAURICE GIBB

CHAPTER 3: FORTUNATE SON
CREEDENCE CLEARWATER REVIVAL – CREDIT JOHN FOGERTY

CHAPTER 4: YOU'VE GOT A FRIEND
JAMES TAYLOR - CREDIT CAROLE KING

CHAPTER 5: OLD AND WISE
ALAN PARSONS PROJECT - CREDIT ALAN PARSONS, ERIC WOOLFSON

CHAPTER 6: ABOUT A GIRL
NIRVANA - CREDIT KURT COBAIN

CHAPTER 7: GOD BLESS THE U.S.A.
LEE GREENWOOD -CREDIT LEE GREENWOOD

CHAPTER 8: RUN TO YOU
BRYAN ADAMS – CREDIT BRYAN ADAMS, JIM VALLANCE

CHAPTER 9: TURNING JAPANESE
THE VAPORS – CREDIT DAVID FENTON

CHAPTER 10: GIRL YOU KNOW IT'S TRUE
*MILLI VANILLI – CREDIT BILL PETTAWAY, JR. SEAN SPENCER,
KEVIN LYLES, RODNEY HOLLOMAN, KY ADEYEMO

CHAPTER 11: YOU SHOOK ME ALL NIGHT LONG

    AC/DC CREDIT* ANGUS YOUNG, MALCOLM YOUNG, BRIAN JOHNSON

CHAPTER 12: GANGSTA'S PARADISE

    COOLIO - CREDIT ARTIS IVEY, JR, LARRY SANDERS, DOUG RASHEED, STEVIE WONDER

CHAPTER 13: I FOUGHT THE LAW

    THE BOBBY FULLER FOUR - CREDIT SONNY CURTIS

CHAPTER 14: WHEN DOVES CRY

    PRINCE - CREDIT PRINCE

CHAPTER 15: FAITHFULLY

    JOURNEY - CREDITS JONATHAN CAIN

CHAPTER 16: HOLDING OUT FOR A HERO

    BONNIE TYLER - CREDIT JIM STEINMAN, DEAN PITCHFORD

CHAPTER 17: TAKE THE MONEY AND RUN

    STEVE MILLER BAND - CREDIT STEVE MILLER

CHAPTER 18: SMOOTH OPERATOR

    SADE - CREDIT SADE ADU, RAY ST. JOHN

CHAPTER 19: BRIDGE OVER TROUBLED WATER

    SIMON & GARFUNKEL - CREDIT PAUL SIMON

CHAPTER 20: BABA O'RILEY

    THE WHO - CREDIT PETE TOWNSHEND

CHAPTER 21: COWARD OF THE COUNTY

    KENNY RODGERS - CREDIT ROGER BOWLING, BILLY ED WHEELER

CHAPTER 22: I WANNA BE SEDATED

    RAMONES - CREDIT DEE DEE RAMONE, JOEY RAMONE, JOHNNY RAMONE

CHAPTER 23: I WANT YOU TO WANT ME
CHEAP TRICK – CREDIT RICK NIELSEN

CHAPTER TWENTY-FOUR: SHOULD I STAY OR SHOULD I GO
THE CLASH – CREDIT TOPPER HEADON, MICK JONES PAUL SIMONON, JOE STRUMMER

CHAPTER 25: LIMELIGHT
RUSH – CREDIT GEDDY LEE, ALEX LIFESON, NEIL PEART

CHAPTER26: PIANO MAN
BILLY JOEL – CREDIT BILLY JOEL

CHAPTER 27: PARENTS JUST DON'T UNDERSTAND
DJ JAZZY JEFF & THE FRESH PRINCE – CREDIT HARRIS, SMITH, TOWNES

CHAPTER TWENTY-EIGHT: CAN'T FIGHT THIS FEELING
REO SPEEDWAGON – CREDIT KEVIN CRONIN

CHAPTER 29: THE WAY WE WERE
BARBRA STREISAND – CREDIT ALAN BERGMAN, MARILYN BERGMAN, MARVIN HAMLISCH

CHAPTER 30: SHE'S GONE – STEELHEART
CREDIT MILJENKO MATIJEVIC

CHAPTER 31: BREAKING UP (IS HARD TO DO)
NEIL SEDAKA - CREDIT NEIL SEDAKA, HOWARD GREENFIELD

CHAPTER 32: SHE'S ACTING SINGLE (I'M DRINKING DOUBLES)
GARY STEWART – CREDIT WAYNE CARSON

CHAPTER 33: DEATH ON TWO LEGS
QUEEN – CREDIT FREDDIE MERCURY

CHAPTER 34: I WON'T BACK DOWN
TOM PETTY – CREDIT JEFF LYNNE, TOM PETTY, MIKE CAMPBELL

CHAPTER 35: KISS THE GIRL
SAMUEL WRIGHT – CREDIT ALAN MENKEN, HOWARD ASHMAN

CHAPTER 36: LET IT BE
THE BEATLES – CREDIT LENNON/MCCARTNEY

CHAPTER 37: YOU'RE MY BEST FRIEND
QUEEN – CREDIT JOHN DEACON

CHAPTER 38: ONCE IN A LIFETIME
TALKING HEADS – CREDIT DAVID BYRNE, BRIAN ENO, CHRIS FRANTZ, JERRY HARRISON, TINA WEYMOUTH

CHAPTER 39: DAYBREAK
BARRY MANILOW – CREDIT BARRY MANILOW, ADRIENNE ANDERSON

CHAPTER 40: MAYBE I'M AMAZED
PAUL MCCARTNEY – CREDIT PAUL MCCARTNEY

CHAPTER 41: PSYCHO KILLER
TALKING HEADS – CREDIT DAVID BYRNE, CHRIS FRANTZ, TINA WEYMOUTH

CHAPTER 42: IN THE AIR TONIGHT
PHIL COLLINS – CREDIT PHIL COLLINS

CHAPTER 43: BAD MOON RISING
CREEDENCE CLEARWATER REVIVAL – CREDIT JOHN FOGERTY

CHAPTER 44: ONLY THE GOOD DIE YOUNG
BILLY JOEL – CREDIT BILLY JOEL

CHAPTER 45: STAYIN' ALIVE
BEE GEES – CREDIT BARRY GIBB, ROBIN GIBB, MAURICE GIBB

CHAPTER 46: FINAL COUNTDOWN – EUROPE – JOEY TEMPEST

CHAPTER 47: IT'S THE END OF THE WORLD AS WE KNOW IT (AND I FEEL FINE)
R.E.M. – CREDIT BILL BERRY, PETER BUCK, MIKE MILLS, MICHAEL STIPE

CHAPTER FORTY-EIGHT: WHO WANTS TO LIVE FOREVER
QUEEN – CREDIT BRIAN MAY

CHAPTER FORTY-NINE: IN YOUR EYES
PETER GABRIEL – CREDIT PETER GABRIEL

OTHER SONGS

DON'T YOU FORGET ABOUT ME
SIMPLE MINDS – CREDIT KEITH FORSEY, STEVE SCHIFF

SATURDAY NIGHT'S ALL RIGHT (FOR FIGHTING)
ELTON JOHN – CREDIT ELTON JOHN, BERNIE TAUPIN

RETURN TO ME
DEAN MARTIN – CREDIT CARMEN LOMBARDO, DANNY DI MINNO

IT HAD TO BE YOU
HARRY CONNICK JR. – CREDIT GUS KAHN

FLY ME TO THE MOON
FRANK SINATRA – CREDIT BART HOWARD

BROWN EYED GIRL
VAN MORRISON – CREDIT VAN MORRISON

LOVE SHACK
THE B-52'S – CREDIT KATE PIERSON, FRED SCHNEIDER, KEITH STRICKLAND, CINDY WILSON

THE AIR THAT I BREATHE
THE HOLLIES - ALBERT HAMMOND, MIKE HAZLEWOOD

BETH

KISS – CREDIT PETER CRISS, STAN PENRIDGE, BOB EZRIN

GLORY OF LOVE

PETER CETERA – CREDITS PETER CETERA, DAVID FOSTER, DIANE NINI

ADAGIO FOR STRINGS

SAMUEL BARBER – TRANSCRIBED BY NEO SCOTT

Still here? Thank you for reading this novel. Seriously I am sending you an elbow bump or faux-hug. The only way a new author like me, with no platform or literary contacts, can make it, is by readers like you leaving honest reviews on the site where you purchased this book. Please consider taking the time to leave your thoughts. Or just call me. My number is (555) 867-5309.

Barnes & Noble: shorturl.at/nqA59
Amazon: shorturl.at/eovHP
Goodreads: shorturl.at/ciNUW

To listen to Winnie or Alex's mixtape, or for other great interactive activities, please visit my website at **www.matthewEwheeler.com**

For updates on the sequel or for more insider content please sign up for my mailing list at **matthewewheeler.com/joinus/**

MATTHEW & MOM 1993

ABOUT THE AUTHOR

 **Matthew E. Wheeler** grew up in Wisconsin, where the winters can last a lifetime—and epic novels and movies of the 1970s and 1980s became his escape. After working for over twenty years in the restaurant and bar industry, Matthew turned to writing (with detours through rehab, marriage, and fatherhood along the way). He lives just outside of Seattle with his family, and is a member of the Pacific Northwest Writers Association. To find out all you ever wanted to know about Matthew and listen to mixtapes from *Falling onto Cotton*, please visit matthewewheeler.com.

END CREDITS

Music: "Reflections of My Life" – Marmalade

STARRING

Charles "Chance" McQueen

Winston "Winnie" Morris

Alexandra "Alex" Kopoff

Frank Bartallatas

Sloan Bartallatas

Geoffrey Anders

Ishmael "Jed" White

Vera White

Vincent Carmelo

Isabella Joy Antonia

George Washington Lincoln

Richard "Hunter" Lee

Maggie Edwards

Casandra "Cassie" Edwards

Giorgio "Fat" Vasari

Stella Rousseau

The Honorable John Rousseau

Mitchell Genovese

Frankie "Jr." Bartallatas

Tom Murray

Anthony D'Amico
Katiana Kopoff
Andre Kopoff
John Carbone
Gary Locke
Chico Hernandez
Jose Zapatero
Miguel Guerrero
Leah Luong
Tito Alvarez
Bob Dillard
Mickey Russo
Bernie Berkowitz
Bartender as Himself

Written By
Matthew E. Wheeler

Editors
Steve "Birdman" Kaufman
Jennifer Munro
Katie Zaborsky
James Osborne
Dominic Wakeford

Original Cover Design
Keith Negley

Cover/Interior/Formatting
Sarah Beaudin

Website Design
Deborah McReynolds

Marketing
Elizabeth Psaltis

Audiobook
Linda Jones

To the beautiful city of Milwaukee, WI, and its wonderful citizens, I apologize for changing the geography to suit my needs. Also, I'm sorry I was mostly drunk when I lived there.

National Sexual Abuse Hotline
1-800-656-HOPE

National Domestic Violence Hotline
1-800-799-7233

STILL HERE? IT'S OVER... GO HOME... GO."

—FERRIS BUELLER

ACKNOWLEDGMENTS

When I was turning forty, I had worked for over twenty years in the restaurant and bar industry. Anyone that has done that type of work knows the many pains it puts you through, both physically and mentally. I was an alcoholic, never-married, middle management slob, with hundreds of nights I couldn't remember and not much in the way of prospects. I decided right then and there to change that. I quit my career to write a novel. Because authors and alcohol just don't mix. Cough-cough.

I knew nothing about how to go about this. But I'd read thousands of books so really, how hard could it be? It took me a year to write 170,000 words of crap. It took me another five years to figure out how to turn that crap into a real novel.

It was a turbulent five years. I met the woman of my dreams, hit rock bottom, went to rehab, got married, lost my mother, and became a father. Through it all, this novel was with me. So, in a way, you were with me also. For holding and reading my heart of hearts, I thank you. Without you, Chance, Winnie, and Alex would have stayed my imaginary friends.

Everyone listed above worked on my behalf to make this book better than I ever could alone. Thank you.
To my friend and early reader Emmanuel Fonte, your encouragement made all the difference.
Sheila A. Brown and Jeannie Holt for your early support.
Mitchell, Marieke, Cassie for sharing Christmas.

To the PNWA, the most excellent writer's organization a novice writer could join—thank you Pam, Jennifer, Maria and Adam.

To my writer's group that includes two of the best writers I know: Jackie Kang and Heidi Jenkins, thank you for your critiques and support.

To Dave Chesson, founder of Kindlepreneur and Publisher Rocket. If you found this book on Amazon, you probably have him to thank. He is a classy guy and a great teacher.

To Ricardo Fayet and his entire team at Reedsy were instrumental in bringing this book to light.

To Rust Strong and Grey Mirick, both of whom are better beta readers than I am. Lady Diane M. for your kindness.

To the fantastic writer, speaker, and teacher, Kim Hornsby—a treasure of the Pacific Northwest.

To Al Balda for giving me the talk.

To Marcel Beauclair and Dennis DeVere, you know why.

To my extended family: Negley, Kaufman, Roberts, McReynolds, Collins, and Barnett.
"Smiles are free, don't save them." —Emily Willegal

To all the people that ha
or negative. You shaped
To all my exes, please ch
Thank you, I'm sorry, or

To the underpaid/overw
industry.

To Jack Wagner for not su
and every woman wanted

To all the artists that ma
book I ever consumed: Ro

To Rory, who is by far the
grow up too soon for my lik
with you is the best Disney
amazing things in your life,
and laughter to everyone yo
and mom drools.

To Deb, my partner, friend, b
I love with my whole heart, w
passionate, solitary man. You
you, there is no me.

"YOU'RE